Puck Boy

HANNAH GRAY

playlist

Listen to the music that inspired *Puck Boy* on Spotify.

"Handle on You" by Parker McCollum

"Never Leave" by Bailey Zimmerman

"Times Like These" by Five Finger Death Punch

"Praying" by Kesha

"Going, Going, Gone" by Luke Combs

"Heartless" by Diplo, featuring Morgan Wallen

"HandClap" by Fitz and the Tantrums

"Thought You Should Know" by Morgan Wallen

"Nonsense" by Sabrina Carpenter

"One Thing at a Time" by Morgan Wallen

prologue

ADDISON

I looked in the mirror at my tear-streaked face. No matter how many times I wiped my eyes, the tears just kept coming. Like a river after a rainstorm, rushing furiously with no sign of slowing. In just a few minutes, I was going to break my parents' hearts.

My heart ached, just like it had ever since I had peed on that stick. Since I had seen those two faint, life-changing lines. As a kid in high school, those lines were not my friends. Those lines ... well, they were going to change the course of my life—forever. And those same godforsaken, eye-opening damn lines were about to rip my parents' hearts into pieces. Since I'd been old enough to understand how reproduction worked, they had drilled safe sex into my head. At least, I'd thought they had. But life had gotten busy between school and work. And who actually knew missing those few pills would lead to this?

I couldn't stop all the questions in my head from brewing. Will I ever reach my goals? What dreams am I allowed to have now? How the hell am I supposed to raise a kid when I am a kid?

And then there was that perfect picture I'd had in my head for so many years. One that involved me as a wife, madly in love with my husband when we brought children into this world. I'd probably drive a minivan, but it would be a cool one. And I'd be settled. I'd be prepared. But then life laughed in my face, changing that plan on a dime. And I was suddenly alone. And the reality was, that perfect picture I had painted ... wasn't my story anymore. I didn't know what was.

With a last-ditch effort to wipe my eyes, I let out a long sigh and straightened my back, sitting up taller.

"It's going to be okay," I whispered to myself as my lip trembled. "They love me. They will always love me. Even if they act like they don't after this. Whatever they say, they won't mean it."

Resting a hand over my stomach, I looked down. "I don't feel connected with you yet. In fact, I resent your tiny existence right now. I hope you understand. I hope, one day, you'll forgive me for having these thoughts. It's not you, baby. It's me. I'm scared. I'm not ready for this." More tears fell. "I'm not ready for you."

I remember that feeling of helplessness. And defeat. Like my entire life was ending before it barely even began. I was angry with myself. I was angry with the boy who had put me in this position. But mostly … I was angry with the tiny bean sprouting in my uterus. Even if I was aware it wasn't their fault.

Thinking back to that moment, a moment where all seemed lost, I cringe. Because now, I know my life wasn't ending.

It was beginning.

And even though I thought I'd never get the happily ever after I wanted, I was wrong. Because what I end up getting at the end of this story means much, much more.

CAM

"What'd you say your name was, sweetheart?" I mumble, peeling the black shirt over her head, not missing how her arms wrap around her body in an attempt to cover herself.

Golden-blonde curls fall down her back, making me eager to give them a tug. This chick is gorgeous, and her body is rocking.

"Not that it matters," she says, breathing the words out before returning her lips to mine, "but it's Addison."

"Addison—that's pretty," I say, thinking out loud. "I know a town named Addison. Are you named after a town?"

"No." She attempts to pull my mouth to hers again before she unbuttons her jeans.

"This town is about an hour from where I grew up in Alabama. Small town. Two stores. One restaurant. But it has the best fried chicken—"

"Less talking. More ... you know," she growls.

"More what, Addison? More fucking?" I pull away, looking down at her. "That what you mean by *you know*, sweetheart?"

"Yes," she says boldly. "My friend just told me you're the campus playboy. Playboys aren't supposed to be Chatty Cathys."

I frown at her choice of words. Nobody has ever complained if I try to talk to them before fucking their brain out.

This is weird. And sort of hot.

"What does that have to do with anything?" I ask. "Playboys don't talk?"

"You aren't supposed to want to talk this much!" She sounds frustrated. "Or ask me questions! That's why I went out on a limb here by coming to your room. And also the reason I didn't tell you to piss off when you came on to me downstairs."

"Whoa, whoa, whoa." I rear my head back. "Make no mistake. I know what I'm doing in bed. I'll make your toes sore from curling and your voice hoarse from screaming my name. And, hell yes, I'm *experienced*. But look here, babe. If you want a ride on my dick, you can at least talk to me before I take you on a trip." I feign being hurt. "I'm more than a pretty face and a nice cock, you know."

Rolling her eyes at me, she grabs her shirt and pulls it back on over her head. "This was a mistake."

"Wh-what are you doing?" I run my hand up the back of my neck. "Why are you putting your clothes back on? Normally, it's the opposite. Is this some kinky game? Reverse psychology? If so, I could probably be into it. Just as long as, in the end, we're both naked."

Sliding out of bed, she walks toward the door before turning around. "Look, I don't do this. Ever. I don't look for hookups because, typically, I don't have time. My life is busy. *I'm* busy. So, while I'm sure you're a nice guy with big feelings and lots to talk about, that isn't what I'm looking for. I came here tonight, looking for an orgasm. One to blow my mind enough to get me through this school year." She puts a hand on her sexy, curvy hip. "Hot, dirty sex with someone who wouldn't ask for my number. Not whatever the hell you're making this."

"Who said I was going to ask for your number?" I say cockily. "Sounds like wishful thinking on your end, babe."

"Oh my gawd. And you're much more annoying than I anticipated." She runs her hand through her curls, pushing them from her face before turning away from me. "Enjoy your night, *Cathy*."

I jump up quickly, taking a few long strides toward her. And as she reaches for the doorknob, I stop her by slapping my hand on the door.

Spinning slowly, she turns, pressing her back to the door. "What are you doing?"

"Addison?" I say sharply.

"Yeah?"

Removing my hand from the door briefly, I peel my shirt over my head. "If you're looking to get fucked thoroughly, I promise, you're in the right place." My hand grips the back of her neck lightly as I drag her mouth toward

4

mine. "Game on, baby. I'll have you seeing stars. I just hope you're ready. This ride could get rough."

Kissing her hard, I lift her up, and she wraps her legs around my waist.

I walk us to the bed before tossing her down and tearing her jeans and black panties from her body. She's got curves—delicious ones at that—making the fabric cling to her thighs.

Once I finally get her jeans completely off her body, I kiss her inner thigh and glance at her. "You don't want a nice guy, Addison? Good. Because there isn't one in this room."

Reaching for her shirt, I rip it in half, leaving it in shreds.

Her mouth hangs open. "What the hell? That was a brand-new shirt."

"And now, it's a scrap on the floor," I coo before unbuttoning my jeans and letting them fall to the floor.

She puts her arms over her stomach, as if trying to shield my eyes from her flesh, but I shove them down.

"Don't cover up this fucking work of art," I growl. "Let me look at every inch of you while you fuck me with your hand."

Reluctantly, she listens, though I can tell she isn't comfortable in her own skin by the sheer look of panic on her face.

As I peel my boxers off, I don't miss her eyes widening as she watches my cock spring free. The worry seems to melt away as she squirms beneath me in pure desperation.

"Careful what you wish for, babe." I pump myself a few times. "Because now, you can have it all. Every fucking inch."

When she swallows, I watch her chest rise and fall. She's nervous now. Suddenly second-guessing her decision in persuading me into a one-night stand.

"Talking doesn't sound too bad right about now, does it?" I wink, calling her bluff.

She glares at me before reaching forward and pushing my hand away from my cock. "No talking unless it's dirty."

Wrapping her fingers around my length, she slides her hand back and forth, licking her lips.

Reaching behind her, I unclasp her bra and let it fall. Her breasts make me that much harder as I watch her nipples harden as she continues to stroke me.

Running my hand down her thigh, I don't stop until I reach between her legs. Slipping a finger and then two inside, I groan, "So fucking tight."

The sight of her beneath me, legs open, hand wrapped around me as she jerks me off, is too much. And I fuck her with my fingers a little longer until I can't take it anymore. Stepping back, I grab a condom from my desk and tear it open before sliding it over myself.

I crawl over her, kissing her breast and up to her neck before the head of my cock nudges inside of her slowly.

Little by little, I feed her what she came looking for at this party. Her nails claw into my back, letting me know it's a tight fucking fit. But as I move in and out of her, her hisses turn to moans, and those claws retract the smallest bit.

"Oh my … God," she whimpers. "Oh … my … God."

"That's right, you dirty fucking girl. This is what you wanted, isn't it?"

She doesn't answer, so I stop fucking her and grab her wrists, slamming them against the bed. "Say it, darlin'. You wanted me for my cock, didn't you, Addison? You wanted to ride my dick. You came to this party, looking for this."

"Yes," she whines. "Yes, I did."

I start moving again. The sounds of my balls slapping against her plump ass and her sweet, soft moans fill my bedroom, drowning out the party downstairs. When her hand reaches around, cupping my nuts, I almost fucking lose it.

Quickly pulling out before I come undone and embarrass myself, I roll onto my back and tug her on top of me. "Show me what you came here for, filthy girl. Use me to get what you need." I grip her waist, pushing her body up so I can see all of her perfectly. "You need to come so good that it gets you through the entire fucking school year, huh? Still a long way to go. Guess you'd better ride me hard."

My dick continues to give this goddess on top of me a standing ovation. I might act like a dog, but I sure as hell don't like bones. She's got curves in all the right places. Her body is soft, not bony and rigid.

Gripping her hips, I guide her onto my aching cock, filling every ounce of her as a hiss escapes her lips.

When she starts moving and those tits start to bounce … *fuck*, I'm a goner.

She rides me like this fucking night depends on it. Like she's been chasing this high for a long time and she won't stop now till she gets exactly what she needs. Her hands grip my thighs as she tosses her head back, leaning back slightly. She doesn't care if I'm close or not. She's greedy. And it's really fucking hot.

I feel her begin to squeeze around me as her eyes close and a moan rips through her throat. Her movements start to slow, and eventually, she shudders.

I grip her waist, rocking her back and forth on my length while I pour myself into the condom, seeing fucking stars.

When her eyes finally flutter open, she looks down at herself briefly before scurrying off of me.

After yanking her panties and jeans on, she quickly slides her bra over her arms and fastens it. Snatching her torn shirt off the ground, she scowls at the scraps of fabric before marching over to my dresser.

Sliding her bra on, she pulls the top drawer open, rifling through my shit before pulling a shirt out. Lifting it up, she looks at me. "A shirt for a shirt. Hope you aren't too attached to this."

Standing, I peel the condom off and throw it in the garbage and shrug. "Fair is fair, I suppose."

After she pulls the shirt over her body, she frowns as she notices it goes halfway to her knees.

Taking her elastic from her wrist, she ties it up just above her waist. "There. Good as new."

Her cheeks are still flushed, and her blonde curls fall in every direction possible. "Well, thanks. For the ... service? Never mind. That makes you sound like a gigolo." She frowns. "Either way, it was greatly appreciated, but now ... I'm going to go home."

I stare at this creature in complete awe. She can't get away from me fast enough. And it's sort of fascinating.

What even is this shit?

I sleep around, sure. But I'd never kick a girl out of my bed. In fact, I have no problem if they hang around for a while after. I mean, hell, that usually leads to round two. And round two is almost always more fun because by then, we're more acquainted with each other's body.

"It was truly a pleasure, Addison. Can I call you Addy?" I grin, folding my hands behind my head. "And maybe next time you're looking for a dirty orgasm, you'll remember where to find me?"

She laughs, reaching for the door. "Not a chance in hell, playboy." Holding up her hand, she waves. "You enjoy the rest of your night."

And then she leaves, closing the door behind her. Leaving me wondering what the hell just happened.

And wishing it could happen again.

ADDISON

"Wowzer. You look like you've been taken to town ... hard." Tessa grins from ear to ear. "I'm so jealous. What was it like? Did I set you up, or *did I set you up*? Looks like Georgia isn't too bad so far, is it?"

Tessa is my best friend. She also made it her mission weeks ago to get me laid. Though I have no idea why. Aside from her claiming I've been too tense lately. So, when an attractive man made his way over to us, flirting like crazy, she whispered that I should go for it. My first instinct was to tell the guy to piss off, but my desperation to have sex for the first time in years overtook it.

"He talked far too much at first," I say, smoothing my hair down. "But, yeah, you did good. And that Southern accent certainly didn't hurt when he was talking too much." I laugh. "So, you claimed he's the campus playboy, but who even was that guy, and how did you know he'd be a good … ride, shall we say?"

"That was Cam Hardy," she says, and I stop walking. "The entire Brooks University campus knows he's got mad skills below the belt." She giggles. "And above."

I throw my arm out, stopping her too. "That was Cam Hardy? As in *star player of the Wolves hockey team* Cam Hardy?" My mouth hangs open. "For real?"

She shrugs lightly, still beaming. "For realsies."

"And why did you choose him?" I narrow my eyes. "You know jocks aren't my thing … well, anymore."

"Because I knew he'd be a good man for the job. From what I've heard, he's never been in an actual relationship. And even though he sleeps around, the women he's with always claim he takes care of them, if you know what I mean. Oh, and they say he's nice. By the glow in your cheeks—damn, girl—those rumors must be true." She winks. "And besides school, you don't leave home. A guy who moves on before your body stops tingling from him rocking your world? He's perfect."

"I'm not *always* home. I mean, I'm out tonight, aren't I?"

"Yeah, only because your mother forced you to hang out with me." She shakes her head. "Thank the Lord she did. You needed this."

"Yeah, yeah," I mutter and start walking toward the sidewalk. "Come on. I'm ready to go home."

Even as I walk, my legs are still shaky from sex with who could be the world's hottest dude from Alabama. The picture of him in his bed as I was leaving creeps into my mind. His messy brown hair and boyish grin flash through my brain once more. And I can't help but smile because Tessa is right. I did need this.

CAM

"Dude is such a hard-ass," Brody groans, glancing at me. "I miss Coach."

"Same," Link agrees.

"He *is* our coach now," I remind them.

"Well, we miss our real coach." Brody rolls his eyes. "You know what we meant, Hardy."

"The coach who showed up drunk to practice half the time, you mean? The same guy who was forced to resign because he was cheating on his wife with students?" I shake my head. "Yeah, what's not to miss?"

"At least he was fucking pleasant," Brody says, jerking his thumb toward the dude who took our old coach's place. "This guy is a dick. He acts like he has a stick the size of Texas shoved up his ass."

"He was probably pleasant because he was getting blowies under his desk," I point out. "I'd be fucking pleasant too if I was old as fuck and went to work and got blow jobs from hot young women."

As if on cue, our new coach continues to look at his clipboard as he speaks. "You all were an embarrassment at our opening game. A damn disgrace. Makes me second-guess taking this job to begin with."

"Yeah, you're right," I mutter to the boys. Agreeing with them because we won the game he's saying embarrassed him. "He *is* a dick. Maybe he needs a good blow job too." I try to fight my grin. "Hell, Link, why don't you volunteer that pretty mouth of yours?"

"Fuck off," Link grumbles.

"You boys have something you'd like to share with the team?" Coach's eyes look up at the three of us as he pulls his reading glasses off. "I'd love to hear what three brains like yours have to bring to the table."

"No, Coach," Link mutters.

"Nope, me neither," Brody says, shifting around nervously. "Nothing at all."

"Ah." Coach smirks, his eyes finding mine. "So, it was Mr. Cam Hardy who had something he needed to say, was it?" He doesn't hide his glare. "Go on, Mr. Hardy. I can't wait to hear this."

"No, sir, not me." I look around awkwardly. "Only thing I bring to the table is myself."

"Truth," Brody agrees. "I can testify to that."

The new coach has hated me since he arrived here a few weeks ago. He isn't exactly nice to any of the guys. But me? My very fucking presence seems to bother him.

"Good job, Hardy. Your sense of humor has earned all of you a prize." Angry, dark eyes burrow into my own. "Suicides. *Now*. For the entire team."

As we all skate toward the line, my teammates sulk, shooting me glares.

"How many?" Link says, keeping his voice low.

"As many as I say," Coach growls. "As many as it takes to sweat the smart-ass right out of Cam Hardy."

"Yes, sir," we all yell before skating toward the line.

"Good job, asshole." Trevor, another teammate, pouts. "I fucking hate suicides."

"You'll be all right. You were slow as fuck at the game," I point out. "What doesn't kill ya makes you stronger, Trev. Remember that. I'm basically doing you a favor. No thanks needed."

"Fuck that." He shakes his head. "Last time he made us do these, I puked all over the ice."

"Yeah, I remember." I grimace. "You had eaten a lot that day, my friend. Fucking nasty."

Barren LaConte was offered this position here at Brooks University to coach the Wolves after our prior coach was fired. He came all the way to Georgia from New England. I've heard nothing but good things about him, and it's clear the man knows his shit when it comes to the game. But still, he's an asshole.

As he tells us to start our suicides, I don't miss his scowl at me in particular. Dude has it out for me, and I have no idea why. Someday soon,

Coach LaConte will learn to respect me as a player. One day, every practice won't be a living hell.

I fucking hope so anyway.

But for now, he does hate me. And truthfully, I'm not all that fond of him either.

ADDISON

I yawn, pulling into the campus parking lot at nearly six at night. These late classes are taxing after an already-long day. And yet they are necessary if I want to graduate and become a registered nurse a little early. Transferring to a new college my junior year hasn't exactly made this goal easy, but I have faith I can do it.

When I had Isla, I had so many incredible women surrounding me in the hospital. And I knew right then that I wanted to become an RN. Eventually, I'd like to possibly go on to become a midwife. But only when Isla is a bit older. The training and schooling for midwifery are intense. And right now, I don't want to be away from her that much.

Taking a swig from the giant iced coffee in my hand, I try to suck it down as fast as I can while I still have a few minutes before I need to walk inside. I'm running on four hours of sleep. And as I look in the rearview mirror at myself, I see I'm starting to look exactly how I feel. *Like ass.*

I see some guys walking out of the arena in the next parking lot over, and there's no denying one of them is none other than Cam Hardy. His walk is noteworthy. The way he carries himself is hard to miss.

In an extremely rare occurrence, I went out to a party a few weekends ago, and somehow, Tessa convinced me I needed a palate cleanser. Which sounds … so gross. Nonetheless, insert Cam Hardy, and, voilà, my palate was officially cleansed. And while I'm not going to say it was my brightest moment, he was hot. His filthy words and the way he gripped the back of my neck—it was exactly what I needed. And something tells me he got what he wanted. So, I call that a win-win.

I can't think about the way his Southern accent drawled as he said those dirty things. If I did, I'd be staring at him, panting like a damn dog in heat.

But it was hot and casual. And our relationship ended exactly after he delivered an earth-shattering orgasm. Which was perfect because I don't date anyone. So, going into that hookup with a clear vision of how cut and dry it would be wasn't hard. Besides, even if I were in the position to date, Cam Hardy would be the last on my list as far as boyfriend-material dudes go.

Even if he is fun to look at.

I know if he spotted me right now, I'd be safe. Given the number of women who flock to him and his entire group or the rate at which he changes who's in bed with him … he'd never recognize me. That was a few weeks ago. He's probably had at least half a dozen hookups since that night.

Me? I've had a big. Fat. Zero. Just as I had for years prior to that one deliciously hot night.

As I watch him grin while he talks to his friends, a shiver runs up my spine as his deep voice echoes in my mind, saying all the dirty things he said that night in that sticky, slow accent. How I'll ever stop imagining that hookup is beyond me. He certainly set the bar high for any future sex I could potentially have with other men.

Once they are gone, I push my car door open and grab my messenger bag before closing the door behind me. I'd much rather be at home right now than here. *Likely in sweatpants without a bra on.* But here is where I need to be, unfortunately.

This year isn't going to be easy. I'll be starting my clinicals soon, and the real work at becoming an RN will begin. When I moved here from New Hampshire a few months ago, I had one goal in mind. Get this crap done as quickly as humanly possible. I don't want to be a college kid. I just want to start the next phase of my life.

Dragging my feet, I walk into the classroom and head to my desk.

Let's get this night over with.

CAM

After practice, I run to the coffee shop before heading to the library to pick up Layla. We don't get to hang out nearly as much as we used to now that she's going steady with her man and all.

As I pull up to the curb, she walks outside and heads toward my truck.

Pulling the door open, she grins. "Howdy, friend," she says, trying to talk in a Southern accent like my own.

"Your drawl needs some work, girl." I laugh. "Got you this. Maybe it'll make you realize that, deep down, you're madly in love with me, and then we can just go on and live happily ever after." I pass Layla an iced coffee as she gets situated in the passenger seat. "I would have gotten you one to give Henley, too, but she's too bitchy to deserve that."

Until I met Layla, I'd never even tried an iced coffee. I'm not addicted to them the way she is, but I do enjoy them from time to time. And whenever we hang out, I always try to surprise her with one. She's one of the good ones in this world. A true gem.

Her best friend, Henley, doesn't hate me nearly as much as she used to, but even when she did, Layla stood by my side. I'm not everyone's cup of tea. I've been known to ruffle feathers and step on toes. Layla might tell me to cut the shit when I'm in the wrong, but she's never walked away from our friendship.

"First off, all the coffee in the world isn't going to make me want your balls, Cam-Cam." She pats my shoulder. "Second of all, call Henley a bitch again, and I'm going to stab you right in the dick."

"A soft stab or a stab where I'll actually bleed?" I tilt my head to the side. "I mean, hell, at least you'd be touching it."

"You're nasty," she says before taking a sip from the shit she thinks of as crack. "Oh my good, loving Lord, that is good. You did good, Cammy. You did good."

Layla knows I'm kidding with her. She's in a relationship now, and I respect the hell out of her man. She and I did attempt to make out once before she was tied down, just to see if any sparks flew. Ended up feeling like I was kissing someone who was my sister. It was fucking weird. Hot as she is, she and I have zero romance flowing between us. Her friend Henley, however, I could have gotten on board with that. But she had some weird childhood love she never got over. And besides, she couldn't really stand me from the get-go. So, you see, that ship sailed before I even got a chance to climb on board.

"What have you been up to anyway, my dude?" She wiggles her eyebrows. "Any new looove interests I should know about?"

"I feel like you know the answer to that, babe." I pull away from the curb, heading toward her apartment. "But I will tell you that I hooked up with this chick a few weeks ago. She was really fucking hot. Didn't want me to talk during sex though unless it was dirty. Her words, not mine." I sigh. "Basically, she used my dick, and away she went."

She turns toward me, looking amused. "And how did that make you feel?"

I think for a second.

"Well, I don't really know." I scratch my chin. "Is that all I am to girls? A ride at the world's finest theme park?"

"Oh, honey, no." She shakes her head. "No ... I'd say a county fair at best."

13

"Dick," I mutter. "I'm so not a ride at a county fair. I'm a motherfucking Disney or Universal ride. The ones that make your head spin and your heart pound and you think about them for years—no, a lifetime."

"I was thinking more like the Tilt-A-Whirl or Thunderbolt. Possibly the Scrambler." She shrugs. "But, hey, whatever helps ya sleep at night, my friend."

"Those rides are rusty and rickety." I scowl. "I'm fucking smooth and robust."

"Robust, eh?" She pulls her lips to the side. "Odd word choice. Reminds me of a salad dressing of some sort. Or maybe a beer. But okay. Your dick is robust and smooth."

"Not my dick." I frown. "The entire experience of sex with me. Follow along, would you? It's a whole fucking vibe."

"My bad. Did you find this girl fascinating?"

"Sort of," I tell her, thinking back to that night. "She wasn't a girl. She was a woman."

"Ooh, a woman." She nods. "Do explain how you differentiate between the two."

"She knew what she wanted. And what she didn't want. For once in my life, she wanted to leave before I was ready for her to go. I would have liked to get to know her a bit better." I sulk. "Instead, she got her orgasm and ran for the door. I actually feel like I annoyed her." I sigh. "I've never felt that way with a chick."

Layla is quiet for a moment, but I know the wheels are turning.

"Maybe you didn't deliver?" She scrunches her nose. "Maybe she wasn't, you know … satisfied."

"Oh, she was satisfied," I say cockily. "Trust me on that."

"Well then, maybe she just didn't want anything more than sex." She looks out the window. "Perhaps relationships aren't her thing."

My lip twitches. "You mean, like you?"

She feigns being hurt. "Me? I am in a relationship. One where we don't sleep with other people and we text each other good night and good morning. We even send each other corny memes." She nods her head, smiling. "I'm adulting and shit. A grown-ass lady I am."

"Yeah," I say, giving her a pointed look, "but at one time, not all that long ago, you weren't ready for any of that. You were a *hump 'em and dump 'em* sort of girl."

"*Woman*," she corrects me. "I was still a woman. And, yes, I know that. So, maybe she could change? If you wanted that?" She narrows her eyes. "Do you even want that, Cam? I mean, it sort of seems like you're hung up on this girl—no, *woman*, friend."

"I barely know her! I mean, fuck, I'm not saying let's send out wedding invites or name our first fucking kid. I'm just venting."

As we pull in front of her apartment, she raises an eyebrow. "Have you been with anyone else since her?"

"No," I say. "Why? What does that matter? I've been busy."

"Have you ... you know ..." She widens her eyes, looking at my crotch area.

"What?" I look down, confused.

"Like ... imagined her. And you. Together. Perhaps while showering."

"Uh ... how many times?" I deadpan. Hell, I've revisited the memory of tearing her shirt from her hot-as-sin tits countless times.

Pushing the door open, she points at me and clicks her tongue on the roof of her mouth. "You, my friend, have been shot with one of Cupid's mind-altering arrows." Reaching over, she pats my shoulder. "Good luck. And remember, Dane tamed me. That makes *anything* possible."

As she walks into her apartment, I drag a hand over my face. I've been with a lot of women. What makes this Addison chick any different from any of them?

Well, I've replayed fucking her at least ten times ... that's one thing that's different.

3

ADDISON

"I really wish you would try to talk to the cross-country coach, baby." My mom pours a cup of coffee for herself. Filling a second cup, she slides it across the counter. "You miss it."

"Yeah, right. I'd be the laughingstock. I haven't run cross-country since junior year of high school. There're some real heavy hitters here." I pour some milk and a pound of sugar into the coffee cup before holding it to my lips. "I'm not the runner I once was. Besides, where would I ever find the time?"

"We would make it work," she says confidently. "Running makes you happy. It's your escape."

"I don't need to escape. I just need to graduate college so I can start making money." I sigh. "And maybe take a nap."

"Mommy," Isla says, tugging on my sweatpants, "I wub you."

Pulling her up onto my lap, I kiss her cheeks. "I love you too, Isla bug."

She's the most adorable little turd I ever did see. She's dramatic and sometimes a little cranky, but I wouldn't change her for the world.

"I want a *Fwozen* birfday." She nods her head, blonde curls falling in her face.

She got my hair, and even though it's taken me a long time to really appreciate my hair, I'm happy I passed it onto her. One day, she'll learn to love it.

"Girlfriend, your *birthday* is months away." I put my forehead to hers. "What if *Bubble Guppies* or Minnie Mouse pulls ahead in the lead again?" I scrunch my nose, glancing at my mom. "Or the dreaded *Peppa Pig*."

"Yes … she certainly loves Peppa." Mom sighs. "I'm surprised she didn't pick *Moana*."

"Ooh, Mommy, I also wuv *Bluey*!" Isla yells, clapping her hands. "But I'm havin' a *Moana* birfday. And … and I'm gonna have a bounce house too!"

"Well, that escalated quickly." I blow out a breath and put my nose to hers. "Let's first get through Halloween, Thanksgiving, Christmas, and the other five thousand holidays, and then we'll talk about your birthday, okay, babe?"

She stares at me, completely unconvinced. Even at three years old, she can have a full conversation with me better than most grown-ass adults. Heck, she's my best friend.

"Let's go on a run, Mommy." She wraps her hands around my neck. "You push me fast in my stroller, and I can take my snacks." Releasing me, she points to the floor. "And Teddy. He wants to come too."

My eyes dart down to Teddy, the gray teddy bear on the floor. She's had him since she was born. He goes where she goes. For a while, I worried what would happen if she ever lost him. So, to be safe, I ordered two extras on eBay.

When it comes to the dating world, this right here is why I don't pursue anyone. It's why I basically told Cam Hardy to shut his mouth and get to the sex part of it. I can't get emotionally attached to anyone. I have baggage. It's beautiful, hilarious, and adorable. But it's baggage nonetheless. And most college kids don't want to hear me talk about my toddler. And since she's the bomb and the only thing I really want to talk about, that makes it easy to isolate myself from most people aside from my family. Oh, and Tessa. She and I have been best friends since we were in nursery school. And when I got pregnant in high school, she was one of the few friends I had who didn't look at me differently.

Even when I told her I was transferring to Brooks University, she wanted to transfer too. In a way, I think she always wanted to live across the country, so maybe this was her chance. She got an apartment just off campus and offered to let us live with her, but my parents moved close to campus, too, and living with them made the most sense. My mom works from home and is a huge help with Isla. In fact, I couldn't do this college thing if it wasn't for my parents' support.

It's no secret it's no parent's dream to have their teenage daughter tell them she's pregnant. They were disappointed. No denying that. A big part of them felt like I'd thrown my entire life away, being so reckless. And angry. Oh, were they angry.

But above all that disappointment and anger was love. And when Isla's father didn't step up to the plate, they did. And since the day I told them I was pregnant, their support has never wavered.

Setting her down on her feet, I nod. "Yes, my lady. Let me go get your chariot and take my princess for a royal run."

As she runs off, her little feet pitter-pattering on the hardwood floor, my heart squeezes in my chest. No matter how exhausted I am, that little turd makes my whole world go round. Without her, I'd be lost. I'll never understand why her father didn't want to be in her life, but it's his loss. She's amazing. No, she isn't just amazing. She's out of this world. And even though she's half of him and she might question one day what was wrong with her to make him leave the way he did, I'll love her enough for the both of us. And the thing is, it isn't hard to do. Because I'm her mom. And I made that perfect, wild angel baby. In fact, loving her is the easiest thing I have ever done.

As we trudge toward her room to get dressed, I hear my mom call behind me, "Think about it at least. The cross-country thing. You deserve to have something for you, Addy."

"I thought about it, and kindly, the answer is no. And I do have something for me. Her name starts with an *I*. She wakes up at the asscrack of dawn and makes me watch way more Disney movies than I'd like to watch," I call back. "Thanks for the coffee!"

"I know how you get without it," she says. "Like an angry bear. I'm not setting myself up to deal with that all morning."

Isla comes from around the corner, carrying her shoes, and growls, pretending to be a bear, "Mommy bear."

I smile, watching her ridiculously cute expressions as she barrels toward me.

One day, there will be endless time for running and relationships that go further than a quick one-night stand. But right now isn't that time. Right now, I only have time for Isla and working toward the future she deserves.

Hours later, Isla snores softly next to me while I finish an assignment for a class that starts in a bit.

Shutting my laptop, I carefully prop a pillow next to her so that she won't roll off the bed.

I pull my hair up into a messy ponytail of ringlets. There's just enough humidity in the air today to make my hair do wacky things. Having naturally curly hair is challenging at times, to put it mildly.

Checking on my sweet girl one last time, I press a kiss to her forehead before tiptoeing out of my bedroom.

My mother sits at the bar, working on her laptop.

"You off to school, babe?" she says, pulling her glasses off.

I nod. "I am. Isla is napping in my bed. She's been out for close to an hour."

She stands, giving me a smile. "I'll go lie down with her. Heck, I'll probably doze off too."

I sigh, feeling jealousy rise through my body. I'd love to curl up with her for the whole day even though I know it isn't an option.

Toeing my sandals on, I grab my bag. "Thank you, Mama. I'll be home in a few hours."

"Oh, your daddy left this here." She grabs his cell phone on the counter before holding it out to me. "Can you drop it off to him? I know it's a short drive home after practice, but I like him to have his phone."

I narrow my eyes slightly. "Is he in the middle of practice?"

I don't think Cam Hardy would even recognize me. But I also don't want to find out for sure in case I'm wrong.

"He'll be finished by the time you get there. He will likely be in his office, getting ready to head home." She snorts. "Heck, knowing him, he'll be searching for the phone, thinking he left it there."

Taking it from her, I head toward the door. "Okay then, no problem. Give my baby a kiss when she wakes up." I sigh. "I really, *really* don't want to leave her."

As I watch her walk toward my bedroom, I feel a pang of guilt. Isla will wake up, and my mom will be next to her. She'll fix her snack. And together, they will make dinner. I'm missing so many moments. Crucial time I'll never get back.

I just have to keep reminding myself that I'm doing it for her future. For *our* future. One day, it'll all be worth it. I hope so anyway.

CAM

"O'Brien, are you a ballerina or a fucking defenseman?" Coach calls to Brody. "What in the hell are you doing out there? You're making even the ice look bad. That's how terrible you are. Hell, this whole arena looks like crap. Starting to smell too."

"Sorry, Coach," he mumbles before skating toward me. *Such a dick*, he mouths.

I tap my stick against his and tilt my chin in Link's direction. Keeping my voice low, I whisper, "Still not willing to take one for the team? A good blowie could take care of that tension. Hell, fucker would probably even smile the rest of the day."

Pretending to scratch his cheek with his glove, he holds his middle finger up.

"Let's run it again, boys."

Practice was due to be over a while ago, but because we can't do a fucking thing to the Coach's standards, here we are, still hard at it.

In his college days, Coach LaConte led his team to three Frozen Fours in college. Winning two of them and leaving the third on a stretcher with a nasty knee injury. Since then, he's coached some high school and college football, but he's yet to bring a team to the Frozen Four. After a tough loss last year, cutting our season short before the championships, we're ready to be one of the four who gets to fight for the title of champions. I just hope he's the coach to help take us there.

He still doesn't seem to like me much. And honestly, I don't get it. I'm a fun guy. A nice dude. I work my ass off on this ice, and I'm also the captain of our team. As a sophomore, it's a lot of pressure for me. But I'll take the challenge because hockey is my life. It's also my goal in life to make it to the pros.

We run through more plays, and finally, he stops telling us we suck. He doesn't say we're doing good either, but it's still a step up from him screaming at us every two minutes.

When he finally tells us practice is over, I'm sweaty and so tired that the thought of walking to the locker room sounds unbearable.

Heading off the ice, I muster every last bit of energy I have.

"Who is *that*?" Brody elbows me as I hear the rest of our team whispering about the same thing.

"That would be the coach's daughter, moron," Coach McIntire, the offensive coach, grunts as he walks by us. "He already can't stand you fools. Best not let him catch you staring at Addison."

With the mention of the name Addison, I turn my head. And when I do, I see a familiar head of blonde curls as she talks to Coach. And for once, the fucker *actually* smiles as she chats away. That is, until he catches us all staring at her.

"I tried to warn you." Coach McIntire shakes his head. "You dumbasses didn't want to listen."

Shooting us a glare, Coach points to the locker room door. "Get your asses out of here. And try not to suck as bad at practice tomorrow morning."

Addison's eyes find mine, and she looks like a deer in headlights. I smirk, letting her know I remember exactly who she is. But when Coach starts to turn around again, I figure it's time to get the fuck out of here. If that is his daughter, I don't imagine he'd be very happy if he knew about what I did to her precious body.

I already couldn't get that girl off my mind. Now, I find out she's the coach's daughter. My coach, who already hates my guts.

Looks like we'll be seeing each other more than I thought. And my life just got a little more complicated because ignoring her presence ... won't be easy to do.

ADDISON

Goddamn it, Mom.

She said Dad would be done with practice by the time I got there. Only too bad for me because he wasn't. And unless I was being paranoid, Cam Hardy totally recognized me. His green eyes pierced into mine as he smirked, realizing who I was. Almost as if he was remembering that night.

That hot, dirty, stupid night.

I know I haven't forgotten it—that's for damn sure.

So, after quickly giving my dad his phone, I told him I needed to hurry to class. I wanted to get out of there before Cam got done changing, just in case he tried to talk to me. Dad would lose his cool if he saw that.

My father would flip his shit if he knew that I already knew Cam Hardy. As in *know,* know him.

Dad is a hard-ass. He's strict and, frankly, a bit of a jerk at times to his team. He only wants the best for them, but sometimes, it comes off a tad harsh.

For as long as I can remember, he's felt this need to protect me from his players as well as all jocks. He tries his best to keep me away from them, though it hasn't worked. He claims so many of them don't respect women the way they should. My whole life, I've been forbidden to even look at any man on his team.

But there was that one time I didn't listen. And now, I have Isla Rose.

In that situation, my dad was right. Isla's dad is the equivalent of a flaming pile of dog shit. But had I listened to my father and not given Nick a chance, I wouldn't be the mom to the world's coolest kid. So, in a way, my biggest mistake ended up being my greatest blessing.

That being said, I don't want any more children for a long, long, *long* time. Which is why I had a seven-year IUD put in after having Isla. It's also why I went back for three extra checks at my gynecologist's office to make sure it had been placed correctly and would not result in a pregnancy. I wouldn't change being a mom for the world. But I know I'm not ready for another baby.

Thoughts continue to run through my brain. I wonder if he really does remember me. Or if he's thought about that night at all.

I shake my head at myself. *Of course he hasn't thought about that night.* I mean, even if he really did recognize me, it's not like he's going to chase me down and want round two. Not like that would be a bad thing as long as it was quick and easy. And feelingless. What could one more measly, mind-blowing, toe-curling, tummy-swirling orgasm hurt?

Ah, other than the fact that I suppose, more often than not, one turns to two, which turns to three, which turns to ten, and before you know it, you're humping like freaking rabbits, needing each other to breathe.

No. Pass. All set.

I'm sure we will be running into each other. There's no doubt about that. Hell, since I was a kid, I've always attended my dad's games. My mom and I sit in our designated seats, and I eat mountains of popcorn and sneak some of her soda.

But even if we do see each other at games, the good thing about a guy like Cam Hardy is, he'll never be desperate enough to seek me out for another hookup. Which is perfect because I don't have time for any men in my life. Even if all he is, is a fuckboy.

4

CAM

"So, let me get this straight," Layla says, picking up the massive burger she just ordered. "Last night at practice, you found out that the chick you had banged and are obsessed with is the coach's daughter? Like, your new coach, who hates you?"

"I am *not* obsessed with her, asshole," I grunt, taking a sip of my Coke. "She's hot. She was pushy and cold. I found her, like, charming or some shit. But I am sure as fuck not obsessed. This guy doesn't get obsessed. My talent is not falling for women."

The corner of her mouth turns up. "You sure about that?"

"Do I look like the type of dude who doodles hearts and shit on my notebook?" I toss a fry at her. "Fuck no. Never will be either. But do I wish I could get naked and roll around with her again?" I nod. "Of course I do. That doesn't mean I'm stalking her or some shit, Lay-Lay."

She wipes her mouth. "She must be your karma." Her eyes widen. "The question is ... is she good karma or bad karma?"

"Hell if I know." I sigh, leaning back in my chair. "But if her daddy finds out what we did, then she definitely ain't going to be good karma. Because he'll probably murder me."

"Would you hang out with her again?" She raises an eyebrow curiously. "Knowing he could find out and would be pissed? Making him hate you more than you already claim he does."

"Fuck yes," I say quickly. "Like I said … she's hot. And even though he'd make my life on the team hell—more than he already does—I'm thinking with my dick on this one. And my dick wants another go with her."

"Typical male," she mutters. "Always using the penis before the brain."

The door to the restaurant pushes open, and Brody and Link stroll in.

As they pile into our booth, Link shoots me a glare. "Oh yeah, I see how it is. Don't worry; we didn't want to join."

"For real, asshole. Some friend you are." Brody shakes his head.

"Y'all weren't even home when I left." I hold my hands up. "What am I supposed to do, just assume you're hungry when I am?"

"I'm always hungry. You ought to know that by now, ya dick," Brody says.

"Wow, you two are acting like little bitches." Layla laughs. "Here I always thought, females were the more annoying species. I might have just been proven wrong."

Link, Brody, and I met our freshman year here at Brooks and instantly became brothers. Brody is one of the best defensemen I've ever gotten to play with. Not only is he slightly insane, but he's also built like a brick house. One that not many hockey players want a piece of. And Link is Brooks's winger. He's stupid talented and crazy fast, like me. The three of us moved into an apartment off campus this year. Last year, as freshmen, we had to stay in a dorm. It wasn't terrible, but I'm definitely enjoying the hell out of the new place more. And a few other teammates—Hunter Thompson, Cade Huff, and Watson Gentry—moved into the apartment right next to ours.

The waitress comes over and takes their orders. Thank God, too, because I didn't want to listen to them whine any longer.

"Halloween is next week," Link says, smirking. "Please tell me we can throw a party so that we can see all the sexy costumes."

"Nah," I say, shaking my head. "Last party, our place got wrecked. Let Hunter and the boys have it at their place. He fucking lives for that shit. Then, they can clean up the mess."

Pulling his phone out, Brody nods toward Link and me. "Good thinking. I'll message him."

"Did you guys see the email earlier from Coach about this trunk-or-treat shit? He wants us to help at it. Isn't that Halloween night?" Link says, seemingly annoyed. "I fucking hate kids."

I pull my phone out and open the email. "Shit. That sucks dick. I don't want to do that shit."

Brody pouts. "Well, good-bye to the party then. We'll be too busy babysitting or whatever the fuck this is."

"Says it's at four in the afternoon till six thirty. Party won't get started till much, much later," Link assures him. "Won't fuck up the party plan."

"What the fuck even is a trunk-or-treat?" I look at Layla. "You must have heard of this nonsense. Is it when you bring a big trunk full of candy?"

"I know the swim team is participating in it. That's all I know." She scowls. "Why would I know what it is? Do I look like I have kids?" She holds her phone up. "Let's find out."

Skimming over whatever the hell pops up on Google, she sighs. "Basically, you deck out the trunk of your car—or in all of your cases, the bed of your truck—with some theme, and you hand out candy."

"I'm sure as hell not bringing my truck," Link scoffs. "Those little bastards might scratch the paint or leave their fingerprints on it. I just waxed it last weekend."

"Coach said he wanted as many volunteers as possible," Brody groans. "I'll do it. But only if Cam does too."

"Fuck you bringing me into this for?" I sneer.

"He already hates you, Cam. And he isn't any of our biggest fans," Link says, dragging a hand over his face. "We have to do this, or he'll be an even bigger dick than he is now."

"Fuck," I mutter.

"Come on. It'll be fun." Layla nudges me. "I'll help you. I know Henley is taking point on this, and from what I gathered at swim practice this morning, there's already a ton of girls helping with it. I'll make sure she parks next to you so I can help you too."

"What the fuck is this theme shit we're supposed to do?" I scratch my head. "Like a movie or some shit?"

"It can be anything," she says. "Henley mentioned something about the swim team doing *The Little Mermaid* theme. I thought she meant they were just going in costumes. Now, I know it's a whole trunk and everything."

"Swimmers and mermaids. How original," I deadpan before rubbing the top of her red hair. "Seriously, why wouldn't you be Ariel though? You already look like her with your fire hair."

"Rude," she mutters. "PSA: redheads don't want to be called fire hair."

"Sorry." I shrug before turning toward Brody. "If the swim team is doing a mermaid theme, that means you should do *Frozen*. You can be the blonde chick, and Link can be the brunette."

"Dude, I know what *Frozen* is because I have a niece. Why the fuck do you know about it?" Link says, narrowing his eyes.

"I have a sister. Asshole."

"Yeah, a really fucking hot one, who I doubt watches *Frozen*." Link shakes his head. "Who also races cars and looks like a sexy, dirty angel."

"Hey, brother, you want to eat that burger they are about to bring out to you?" I ask him.

"Yeah. Why?"

"Mention my sister and the word *sexy* or *dirty* in the same sentence again, and you'll have no teeth to enjoy it with." I hold my gaze on his. "In fact, you'll be eating your teeth for dinner instead when I ram them down your throat."

"My bad," he says nonchalantly.

"Damn right it was your bad," I agree.

My sister, Mila, is the golden child. She followed in our dad's footsteps, dominating the world of drag racing. I did it for fun, but never took it as seriously as she did. It was hard to when hockey became my life at age seven.

Drag racing might be a part of my bloodline, but at times, I curse it. It became a lot grimmer to me when my father was racing his best friend, and my dad's car caught on fire, making him hit a wall, taking his best friend, Dusty, out in the process. That day changed my entire life. For a while, I even lost my best friend, Beau Bishop. He couldn't stand to be around any of my family for years.

That's not to say I'm not proud of my sister for chasing her dream of racing. I am. She's paving the way for future female drivers in a male-dominated sport. And she's done it while also being a full-time college student. Attending college in hopes of one day owning and operating her own shop, building race car engines. She's a badass. And way fucking cooler than I ever thought of being. But I still worry about her. I can't help it.

Dane Wade strolls through the door, and Layla's entire face lights up as she pushes Link out of the way to get to him.

"Dane!" she squeals, leaping into his arms. "How are you even here right now?"

"Had an early morning practice," he says, kissing her. "Now, I'm here."

She grips his face. "You're too freaking adorable right now. Rolling up in here to surprise me."

"Missed my girl." He grins before his eyes find mine. He looks amused. "What's up, Hardy? Keeping your grubby hands off my girl and to yourself, I hope."

"Keeping 'em off your girl. But sure as hell ain't keeping them to myself." I tip my chin up. "That shit gets boring."

He chuckles before setting her down onto her feet. "Hey, as long as they aren't on this girl, do whatever the fuck you want with 'em, brother."

Not long ago, he hated me. So did his twin brother, Weston. Now, we're all good. Weston's girl, Henley, still likes to pretend to be disgusted by me, but I know she really isn't. She's just a tough chick.

I look at my phone and take some money out, tossing it on the table. "Look, y'all, I gotta run. That'll cover my bill and tip."

Brody stands, letting me slide out of the booth.

"Where you off to, playboy?" Layla coos, unable to take her hands off Dane. "Going to see a secret little lady, are you?" She attempts to wink but fails.

"You trying to wink, Lay-Lay?" I shake my head. "Because you're closing both eyes."

"She can't wink for shit." Dane grins and kisses her forehead. When she scowls and swats his stomach, he laughs. "It's adorable, babe."

"Catch ya later." I hold my hand up as I push the door open. "Y'all stay out of trouble."

"No promises!" Layla calls behind me.

I don't want what she and Dane have. At least, I don't think I do. But it's only a matter of time before Layla moves down to Florida East University to be with him full-time and I'm going to lose her. And even though I have Link and Brody and my other teammates, Layla is basically my shrink. She's like a girl version of me. We need each other.

As I head to the truck, I pull my phone out to return my dad's call.

"What's up, old man?" I grin against the phone. "Sorry. I was getting dinner, and it was loud as hell. Figured I'd call ya back in the truck."

"Who are you callin' old?" my dad grunts. "I'm fresh as a fucking daisy."

"Sure you are."

"Yeah, yeah," he says. "What's new with you, boy? How's hockey and school?" There's a short pause, but I can predict what's going to come next. "Any girlfriend yet?"

"Hockey is fine. School is … well, it's school. You know I've never been big on the whole learning shit."

"And a girl? Don't leave me hangin'." He sounds hopeful.

My dad and my mom got together when they were young. He hates the fact that I don't really date anyone long-term. I've always said I'll never get married and that I don't want kids. Truthfully, I don't think I'd be a good husband or dad. Shit scares the piss out of me.

"Nah, not really." I open my truck door and climb in. Pulling my ball cap off, I toss it onto the dashboard. "Ain't really got time for that anyway."

"There's always time for that," he says, keeping his voice low. "You talk to Mi lately?"

He always calls my sister, Mila, Mi. I suppose I do, too, most of the time. Since my dad used to be big into drag racing and Mila followed in his footsteps, she's definitely a daddy's girl. They're like two peas in a pod.

"Yeah, a few times," I tell him. "Seems to be liking Florida East."

"Course she is." I can hear his grin. "Finally got all she ever wanted."

"I guess so," I mutter. "You get your candy for Halloween yet?" I chuckle. "I know you live for that shit."

"You know I did," he answers quickly. "Your mom was tryin' to cheap out on the candy this year. Said we wouldn't have as many kids trick-or-treating."

"So, naturally, you went and bought more." I grin. I know my dad, Jaxon Hardy, all too well.

"Hell yes, I did. I reckon we'll have over one hundred this year."

Even though the town I grew up in, where my parents still live, is small, they always get a shit ton of trick-or-treaters. Mom and Dad would leave a huge box on the front step when they took me and Mila house to house, and when we got back, it'd be damn near empty. Now, my dad keeps a notebook and a pen. And he keeps track of every one of those little bastards who rings the doorbell to know exactly how many trick-or-treaters have come to our house. He even gets bags of chips and full-sized candy bars for the kids who are his favorites.

"Coach is making us do some trunk-or-treat shit, where kids walk around trick-or-treating from the backs of people's vehicles." I tip my head back against the headrest. "As much as I don't want to do it, I have to. Layla's gonna help me with it. You know I ain't got a clue about what I'm doing when it comes to kids. Or Halloween shit for that matter."

"Shame you didn't lock that girl down before Wade did," he jokes. "She's a riot. And a damn good girl from what I've seen."

"She's something all right." I smile. "I've gotta hit the gym for a late-night session. Tell Mom I said hello."

"I will. Then, she'll probably start cryin' about how she misses her kids." He sighs. "Damn woman is an emotional wreck these days."

"I bet." I laugh.

"Nice talkin' with you, Cam. Check in with your mama this week, please. I'm hoping Mi will too. She misses y'all. Have a good night. Be safe."

"I will. Bye, Dad."

Ending the call, I start my truck and pull out of the parking lot. The last thing I want to do right now is work out. I'm already dead tired. But off I go.

ADDISON

I eye the chocolate chip cookies my mom made earlier as they sit in the kitchen, taunting me. She's a hell of a baker, which is great to have treats around, but not so good for my waistline.

Since having Isla, my body has changed. My hips are wider, and my butt is fuller. And I notice that everything I eat goes to my waistline.

You don't need one. You don't need one. You don't need one.

"Screw it. I do need one. Heck, I *deserve* one, damn it," I murmur and grab a cookie before taking a huge-ass bite. "So worth it," I practically moan.

I look down at myself in my loose sweatpants and ratty T-shirt in a house that is far too quiet. My parents insisted on taking Isla to a movie. I basically begged to go with them, but they told me no. They used some lame excuse that when I'm around, it takes away from their time with Isla because she's up my ass the entire time. I suppose they have a point, but I don't want to hang out alone. I want to be with my daughter. And Tessa is working tonight, leaving me with a heaping pile of cookies and *Keeping Up with the Kardashians*.

I head to my bedroom, but not before grabbing a second cookie and devouring it embarrassingly fast. I'm just settling in, picking the remote up, when I groan at myself. "Seriously, get off your ass and go get your mojo back."

Leaping up, I trade my sweatpants and T-shirt for some workout gear. I have hours before Isla will return home to me, so I might as well try to somehow better myself. Working out and running have always helped me keep my mental health in check. I can't snooze on that now. Besides, it's getting late, so the gym is probably dead by now. Just how I like it.

I walk into the gym, and just as I suspected, it's eerily quiet. Technically, I shouldn't be in this gym because it's for athletes. But I'm the coach's daughter, damn it. And the regular gym for plain ol' students like me closed an hour ago. So, right now, I'm reaping the benefits of my father's career. Even if he doesn't know it.

Popping my AirPods in, I head for the treadmill. Adjusting the speed to a comfortable yet challenging pace, I dig in, instantly enjoying the spike of my heartbeat and the sheer layer of sweat that starts to build, letting me know I'm working.

Halsey's haunting voice screams in my ears as I try to keep my breathing steady. I certainly don't have the endurance I used to, making getting winded incredibly easy to do. But even so, once a runner, always a runner. And this is sort of my happy zone.

A flash of blue has me turning my head, and when I do, I'm so startled that I lose my balance and start to fall off the piece of equipment. Even as I try my hardest to regain my footing and grab the railing of the treadmill to steady myself, it's no use.

31

I never said grace was my strong suit.

Once I know my ass is going down, I prepare myself to fall into a pile on the hard ground by squeezing my eyes shut and holding my arms out to catch me.

Should have stayed home and eaten the damn cookies.

Instead of the cold, hard floor though ... I'm embraced by warm, huge arms.

Cracking my eyes open, I peek up at lips as they move. But even in the midst of the chaos, my AirPods never fell out.

Reaching for them, I peel them out.

"Um ... what are you doing?" I look up at Cam Hardy. A *shirtless* Cam Hardy. "Why are you holding on to me like I'm a damn stuffed animal you just won at a county fair?"

His lips twitch. "It was that or let you fall on your ass." He shrugs. "Figured you'd go for this."

He smells so good. And forbidden. But good nonetheless. Like sex. And man. And woods. And musk.

And did I mention sex?

"Thanks. I, uh ..." I say, starting to scurry from his hold. "I'm going to get back to it. So, if you could try not to scare me half to death again, that would be great."

"Sorry. I just came from the locker room. I was going to use the treadmill next to you—that's all, darlin'." He drawls the words, and I swear my thighs clench from his Southern accent as I watch him lean forward and turn the treadmill off.

As I stand, I brush myself off. "Okay, well ..." I wave at the treadmill next to mine. "As you were. Live your life."

His eyes continue to watch me, an amused look resting on his way-too-perfect face. Nobody can look that good and not have some serious flaws or skeletons in the closet. There's just no freaking way.

Tearing my attention from him, I pop my earbuds back in and turn the treadmill back on. I am painfully aware of Cam's presence next to me the entire time. I'm also aware of the fact that he just witnessed me basically fall on my ass, and he likely thinks I'm a nutjob.

From the corner of my eye, I see as he runs for a while before moving on to various other equipment, eventually lifting weights. I try to ignore him and just run for as long as I can. Run until my legs physically can't take it anymore.

One thing that's blatantly obvious ... Cam Hardy isn't a guy who's easy to ignore.

32

PUCK BOY

CAM

Fuck, that girl is distracting.

I need to get a good workout in. I would never have come here tonight if I had known she'd be here. Especially if I had known she'd be the *only* other person here.

The dirty thoughts won't leave my brain. They are constantly filtering through. And every one of those filthy thoughts is sticking inside my head, eating me alive.

She can run—that's a given. I'm not sure if she's on the track or cross-country team, but if not, she should be. After running, she does some light weightlifting for a bit before chugging her water. Hard as I try, I can't keep my eyes from wandering her way. She's thick in all the right places. Curvy and scrumdiddlyumptious.

Once I'm finished with my workout, I take my earbuds out and grab a towel. I probably didn't hit the gym as hard as I should have. It was basically impossible with that angel just a few feet away. I make a mental note to double up tomorrow.

"So, Coach's daughter, huh?" I ask her.

She breathes out the smallest laugh. "Yep. Hopefully, my dad's not being too hard on you all."

"He's ... well, he's not exactly easy." I shrug. "But he's not terrible either," I lie. *Fucker is terrible.*

"Hmm, I call bullshit." She smirks, and her eyes dance with amusement as she heads toward the locker room. "Have a good night, *Cam Hardy.*"

I walk behind her to the locker room door right next to the one she's heading to. "You too, Addison LaConte." I wink as she looks back at me. "You know, I meant what I said at that party that night. If you ever want round two, I'm game."

She looks stunned. "I'm actually shocked you remember a hookup from yesterday, let alone weeks ago."

"Well, let's see ... you called me a Chatty Cathy. That was a first." I narrow my eyes. "So, tell me, am I allowed to talk tonight?"

"You *are* talking. Once again proving my point that you are a Chatty Cathy."

"Who even was this Cathy person, and why was she always talking? And who the hell is Nancy, and what made that bitch so negative?" I keep my face straight. "And for the love of fuck, why is Luke always warm?"

"You're an idiot." She shakes her head, looking down as she smiles.

"Maybe." I shrug. "But I still made you smile. So, maybe you like idiots."

"Maybe I don't." She takes a step backward so that her ass presses on the locker room door, cracking it open the smallest bit.

33

Before she can leave, I stop her. "Hey, why did you seem surprised that I remembered things from our hookup?"

"Honestly? As much as you get around, I figured you probably didn't even remember our … encounter."

"Encounter?" I laugh. "Is that what we're callin' it?"

"What would you call it?" she says.

Her body glistens with sweat, and, fuck, I'd love to help her wash it off.

I walk closer to her, dipping my head down slightly. "I'd like to say it was me fucking you, but, babe, I think you fucked me even harder when you climbed aboard." I watch her drag in a breath. "So, I'd call it, you wanting my dick, so I gave it to you. You got what you needed. And I sure as hell did too." I lean closer, putting my hand on the door next to her head. "But now, Addison, I'm bettin' you need it again. And I know I do."

"No," she says quickly, shaking her head. "I-I don't."

"And why is that?"

"Because I don't. That was a onetime thing. I don't sleep around."

"I wouldn't judge you if you did." I shrug. "But I'd be jealous of the other lucky bastards."

"No, I mean, I don't do that … ever."

"Yeah, but … I've already been inside of you, *Addy*. So, what would the harm be in one more time?" Brushing a strand of hair from her face, I tip her chin upward with my fingers. "You know it sounds fun. You know it sounds *good*."

"This is crazy." She looks unsure before licking her lips. "Where?"

Jerking my head toward the guys' locker room, I slide a hand to her waist. "In there, beautiful."

"What if someone comes in?" Wide eyes look at me, panicked.

"There's a lock. Besides, no one is coming in this late."

Taking her wrist in my hand, I pull her toward me as I lead us into the locker room. I didn't come here tonight, expecting round two with the hottest chick I've ever been with. But fuck it. This night just got a whole lot better.

Walking over to the shower, I turn it on before going back to her.

Pulling her tank top over her head, I capture her lips with mine. I brush my hand past her cheek and to the back of her head, gripping her hair as I kiss her hard.

When I step back slightly, her hands fly to her stomach.

"I told you last time, don't fucking hide this beautiful body," I growl against her skin as I pull her arms down. "I want to see every inch of it."

"Cam," she whines, "can't we turn the lights off? It's so bright in here."

"Hell no, we can't. I want to watch while I fuck you against that shower wall. You aren't hiding from me."

Reaching for her sports bra, I unzip it in the front and push it from her arms. Thankful as hell for the invention of this type of bra. They are hot as hell to take off.

Her tits are bigger than average, and blood rushes to my cock as I cup them in my hands.

"You are fucking perfect," I mutter, taking her in.

"None of that nicey-nice crap. It won't work on me," she says before pausing. "I mean, not more than just a hookup anyway. And the nicey-nice isn't what got us in this situation."

"You want me to be a dick to you?" I kiss her neck, running my tongue against her flesh. "Tell you this means nothing to me?" Sliding my hands down her hips, I peel her shorts and panties off her body, tossing them to the side.

"Yes," she pants, pulling my sweatpants and briefs down. "That's what I want."

As my hard dick springs free, I pump myself a few times before leaning down and reaching in my duffel bag to find my wallet. Grabbing a condom, I tear it open and roll it down my length.

Backing her up against the shower wall, I press my forehead to hers. Lacing my hands in hers, I push them roughly against the tiles. "You mean nothing, Addison. Not a fucking thing. But I'm still going to bury my cock inside of you. I'll still make you cry out my name. And you'll still go to bed tonight, thinking about me fucking you the way I'm about to, sore and all."

Sliding my hand down her stomach and between her legs, I fuck her with my fingers for a few minutes, listening to her pant against me as the water falls down her hot body.

Gripping her ass, I lift her up and press her back to the wall. My cock nudges inside of her, going deeper and deeper as I begin to thrust in and out.

She grinds against me, clawing up my back.

"You're so tight, taking me inch by inch like a good girl," I mutter. "I know you missed my cock."

"No," she moans.

"Oh, you did." I dig my fingertips into the flesh of her asscheeks. "This fuck can mean nothing to you, but you're sure as hell going to miss my dick when it leaves your body." I smirk. "I promise you that."

I continue to fuck her for a few minutes, both of us dripping from the water as her tits thrust against my chest.

She looks so hot this way. Her hair soaked, pushed away from her face, water dripping from her plump pink lips as I fuck her against the wall, digging my fingers into her flesh. Her head tips back, and her nipples harden. I feel her body start to melt against mine as she comes undone. I'm close, but I'm not ready for this night to be over.

Her nails scrape into my shoulders as she rides her orgasm out. "Cam," she moans. "Oh … my God."

"That's right, darlin'. Say my name."

"Cam … ah … oh God." She continues to claw at me as her movements begin to slow.

Once she stills, she looks at me. "You didn't … uh … go?"

I grin at how red her cheeks are getting. "No, but not because I wasn't turned on. Because I fucking could have lost it ten times. But there's so much more I want to do with this perfect body."

"It's just sex," she answers quickly. "That's all."

"That's good, gorgeous. Because sex is my middle name," I say. "Besides, that release you just had? It's healthy. And you need another. And I'm a giver, not a taker. So, let me give you another one."

Her eyes burn into mine before she slides out of my hold and pushes me against the wall. Sinking to her knees, she peels the condom from my body. The water sprays over us as she stares up at me, blue eyes burning with craving.

Slowly, she does the unthinkable and nudges her head closer to my thighs. I wasn't expecting her to suck my dick tonight. But, hell, I just got harder at the thought alone.

I push her wet hair away from her face as she leans her head closer before running her tongue up the length of me. And when she gets to the head of my cock, she looks up at me as her tongue laps me.

"Fuck," I hiss, taking my hand from her hair and steadying myself against the tiles.

Parting her pretty lips further, she takes my cock into her mouth.

Watching her take me with her mouth is the hottest thing I've ever seen, and I have no doubt I'll never come back from this right here.

She moans against me, clearly getting more turned on just from blowing me. She takes me deeper and deeper before dragging her lips back down the length and then going in deep again.

"Fuck, Addison," I say, returning my hand to her hair and fisting it in my fingers. "Goddamn, you're going to make me come in your mouth."

She continues to work me over, so I force her head upward.

"If you don't want to taste me, you'd better stop right now."

Her eyes darken. And instead of slowing, she picks up the pace.

Knowing she's going to take me to the end makes me fucking lose it. Everything starts to tingle as I throw my head back against the wet tiles. And she takes what I give her as my hips involuntarily rock against her face.

I damn near black out for a second, my head spinning.

As she stands before walking to the sink, I drag a hand through my hair. "Goddamn, girl. You tryin' to kill me?"

She smirks in the fogged-up mirror at me, clearing it with her hand. "Maybe. Look, I need to go get my clothes and towel. So, it's been ... fun." She smiles.

"What, no dessert for me?" I keep my gaze on her. "Here I thought, I was going to get that something sweet my tongue's been craving."

Her eyes widen as she stares at me.

"Come here," I say sternly. "Come sit on my face like a good girl."

"Cam," she whispers, "I don't think—"

"Don't make me ask twice," I growl. "Eating you like a fucking cupcake doesn't mean we're going to name our babies." I stand in the spray of the shower. "But, hey, your loss if you don't want me to taste your—"

Before I realize she's left the sink, she's standing in front of me. Eyes wide and cheeks flushed.

Kneeling down before her, I slip a finger and then two inside of her. Slowly moving them in and out of her heat as her hips begin to buck.

"Climb up here, beautiful." I pull my hand away, gazing up at her. "Sit right on my face."

Nervously, she straddles my face, landing her sweet spot right on my mouth.

I dip my tongue inside of her, and she whimpers as I grip her ass and push her down.

As my tongue gets deeper, she starts to grind herself down on my face more.

Her palms press against the cold, wet tiles as I eat her like she's fucking apple pie, enjoying every moment of it too.

"Cam," she cries. "Oh fuck," she hisses as she greedily grinds on my mouth.

She comes undone on my tongue, and I grip her waist, pressing her down onto me roughly until I know I've gotten every bit of orgasm out of her.

As she steps down, her legs shake.

"Wow," she whispers. "That ... yeah."

"You're just as sweet as I figured you'd be."

Turning the shower off, I grab her and myself a spare towel from the facility's stash.

Wrapping it around her, I look down at her. "Thanks."

"For what?" she says, confused.

"For making this night way less boring." I brush my thumb against her chin. "Offer still stands. Any night you need to use me again ... I'm here for it."

"I didn't use you," she says, appalled, snatching her clothes from the floor.

"Fine, we used each other." I wink. "And it's all good. That's all sex really is, isn't it? Two bodies looking for a feeling? Chasing a high?"

37

"I suppose so." She shrugs her shoulders before discarding the towel and throwing her clothes on. "Look, can we keep this between us? This can't get back to my father."

"Secret's safe with me."

"I'm going to go now. Night, Cam."

"Use me again, Addy. I'd be honored to be your living, breathing dildo."

She swats at me. "You're gross."

"Maybe," I say. "But do it anyway. When you need to be fucked properly, come to me. We have hot sex. I don't have time for much more than that, and you hate my guts unless I'm balls deep inside of you. So, this should be the perfect arrangement. What do you say?"

Her eyes hold mine. "My dad would murder you."

Ah, yes. Her dad ...

"That's why your daddy ain't gonna find out." I laugh. "Besides, he hates me anyway."

"He's always hardest on the ones he sees the most potential in." She shrugs. "Maybe that's you."

"Maybe," I drawl slowly.

"Anyway, look here, playboy. I can't be your booty call. I'm busy. I don't have time to drop everything and be a hole to stick your penis inside of."

I try to keep a straight face because, damn, this girl is feisty.

"So, what are you saying?" I brush her hair away from her eyes.

"No arrangements. If we see each other and we're both bored, then sure. But I'm not looking to have someone texting and calling me, blowing up my phone for attention."

"So, if I see you at the grocery store, I can sneak you into the restroom and fuck you in there?"

"Maybe. Maybe not." She steps around me, heading toward the door. "Maybe we'll see each other again. Maybe we won't."

I turn around as she stands in the doorway, looking over her shoulder.

"Your dad's my coach, babe. You'll be seeing me."

"Yes, but will I be seeing your penis?" She shrugs. "That's the million-dollar question. I guess we will have to stay tuned to find out."

With a devilish grin, she leaves.

And it's then I realize that I really, *really* can't wait to see that girl again. Even if she only likes me for my penis.

ADDISON

I get back to my house a few minutes before my parents pull in with Isla. And as I open the door, I see Dad carrying her over his shoulder as she sleeps softly against her papa.

"She's out cold," I whisper, propping the door open so he can walk through, my mom close behind.

I follow him to her room, and he sets her down in her bed.

"How was the movie?"

"It was a Disney movie. They are all the same," my dad grunts.

"I beg to differ, but whatever you say, Daddio. Was she good?" I say, pulling the blanket over her and brushing her hair from her forehead.

"Of course she was." He looks down at her, proud as can be. "She's always good."

"I wouldn't go that far. Do you not remember last week, when she dumped out nail polish all over the bathroom floor?"

He shrugs. "She was trying to make different colors. She didn't like any of the ones you had."

I chuckle and kiss her good night. As I follow my father out into the kitchen, I see my mom getting a glass of water.

"So, chickee, what did you do with your night off?" Mom smiles. "Hopefully something fun."

"I went to the gym after inhaling two of your cookies," I deadpan. "That's all. Nothing too fun going on here." I swear a small cough escapes me as I try to lie.

They aren't on my trail, not in the least. And yet my guilty conscience is making me act like a paranoid weirdo.

"Which gym?" Dad asks. "The main one on campus closes fairly early, I thought."

"Yeah, it does. That's why I went to the one for athletes."

"How did you get into that one?" he fires back.

"Took your key card." I shrug. "Figured I might as well act like the coach's daughter, right?"

He watches me for a moment. "Just be careful in there, Addy. The jocks around any college campus are horndogs. You don't need to be getting mixed up with that again."

"I know, Dad. I wouldn't dream of it," I lie.

They should have let me go to the movies with them. Then, I wouldn't have seen Cam Hardy tonight. He wouldn't have done dirty things to me in the damn locker room. And I wouldn't still be thinking about those things right now.

Let's be honest. I'll be thinking about it for days—maybe weeks. I'd never had anyone go down ... *there* with their mouth before. It was really,

really hot. And somehow felt dirty and forbidden. Still, it shouldn't have happened, and I can't let it happen again. Even if he did proposition me with an offer that was almost too good to refuse. He claimed he doesn't have time for anything more than sex either or that I could essentially use him for a release. But I'm no dummy. Eventually, one of us would catch feelings, and that would leave the other to have to hurt them. He doesn't seem like the type who gets attached, but he sure seems like he'd be easy enough to get attached to. I have to protect my heart on this one. But above everything, I need to protect Isla.

"What's so bad about jocks anyway?" my mom teases him. "Seeing's I met you in college and you were one of those guys you always warn Addy about. I think taking a chance on you ended up okay for me, grump."

He waves her off. "Boys are different nowadays. They just see one thing when it comes to females." He looks angry. "I won't have any of the players here around Addison."

"Uh-huh. Is that so?" Mom taunts, raising an eyebrow. "I don't remember you being quite as pure as you seem to recall. But okay. Whatever you say, hon."

When my dad opens his mouth to answer, I cut him off. "I'm headed to bed. Thanks for taking my girl to the movies. *Even* if you didn't let me go. Assholes."

"Sorry, babe. But most grandparents get sleepovers and time with their grandkids without the parent hovering over them the entire time. You live here. You're *always* around."

"I go to college," I say, shaking my head. "You have her to yourself a ton."

"And half the time, she's asleep because you set your classes up that way." Mom laughs. "You don't like missing any moments. You hog her."

"Do not," I say, giving them both a smile. "Night-night. Love you."

"Love you," they both call back.

As I slink toward my room, I know I'm going to go to sleep tonight with visions of Cam Hardy clouding my brain. Which is a problem because he isn't a guy that should be consuming my thoughts. No man is. Especially one my dad forbids me to so much as look at.

I already knew my dad would be against him. But I had no idea just how much.

5

CAM

"I have to say, I'm impressed." Layla looks at the bed of my truck, which is all decked out. "I barely even helped, and you did all this basically on your own. There might be hope for you yet, Cam-Cam."

"For real." Link's eyes narrow as he looks at my truck. "Who knew you were so fucking crafty, Hardy?"

"The hell y'all think I was going to show up with? Nothing?" I look at the small area around my truck, admiring my handiwork. "My dad lives for Halloween. Couldn't let him down by not showin' up with a ballin' trunk and a shit ton of candy."

"Dude, you're annoying," Brody whines. "Nobody even knows what mine is."

I eye over his truck, frowning. "Yeah, dude. I gotta be honest. I don't get it. It's just really, really fucking creepy."

He walks to the front of his truck and grabs a mask. Pulling it on, he holds his arms out. "You think that's creepy? What about this?"

"Christ almighty, Brody." Layla points to the bed of the truck. "This is a trunk-or-treat for kids. Not grown-ass adults. Why would you do a *Saw*-themed trunk? You're going to terrify the kids."

"For real," I agree with Layla. "Even I knew not to do something that intense, and I don't even really like kids."

"I told you it was too much," Link grunts. "Some kid will probably shit their pants, and Coach will have our asses."

"How was I supposed to know? It's Halloween. I thought we were supposed to do some creepy shit." Brody points to my truck. "Then, Hardy went and did this shit. Are you trying to kiss Coach's ass, man? What even are you supposed to be?"

"It's Disney's *Moana*, and I'm Maui." I smile proudly, showing off my costume. "And apparently, kids eat this shit up. I hope there's a fucking award for best setup. I'll so get it if there is."

"I feel like *Frozen* is more popular, but whatever," Henley grumbles, appearing out of nowhere. "Whatever floats your boat."

"Always so uplifting and positive you are," I mutter. "Ray of fucking sunshine basically."

She pretends to turn a jack-in-the-box on her hand, and her middle finger pops up. "Whoops." She shrugs. "How rude of me. My bad."

"You two, enough," Layla hisses. "You're giving me a headache."

As Henley turns away, I look around at the other people who came out to help with this event. A big part of me is just hoping to see Addison's familiar face in the crowd even if I don't really know why. The chances she'd be here are slim though unless she got roped into helping too.

It's been a week now, and I haven't seen Addison anywhere. She hasn't stopped into practice to see her old man, and I haven't seen her at the gym or on campus. There's something about that girl. She's different from the rest. She gives zero shits about how it comes across that she's only using me for sex. I dig it. But now, I want more sex. A week is too damn long.

I want to know her story. I'm curious to learn more about her. But she's cold and closed off, never giving me much of herself besides the best sex I've ever had. Still, I want to know more. And lucky for me, I'm pretty persuasive when I want to be.

"Okay, everyone," the event coordinator says. "The trick-or-treaters are going to start getting sent through." Glancing at Brody, she points at his face. "Lose the mask, dipshit. The majority of the kids are under eight years old. Are you trying to scar them for life?"

Peeling the mask off, he looks at Link. "This day sucks."

He shrugs. "Don't be a bitch. We've got candy to pass out."

Within minutes, the floodgates open, and kid after kid comes to our stations, and the event is going by in a blur. Hell, I've never seen so many kids in my life. Most of them are respectful. A few are dicks. One tells me *Moana* is lame. I want to tell him to piss off, but I assume that isn't appropriate.

The line of kids begins to slow when, suddenly, the cutest girl with curly hair, dressed as a princess, walks up to my candy bucket.

"Trick-or-tweat." She smiles, and her eyes widen.

Kids aren't really my thing, but this little girl looks like a damn angel.

"Maui! Wow. I wuv *Moana.*" She sighs. "Not as much as *Frozen* though."

Layla chuckles. "Why, hello there, Queen Elsa. You are the cutest thing I have ever seen."

"Queens are not cute. They are boo-tiful," she corrects Layla. "Don't get it twisted."

"Isla, you can't run off like that!" I hear a familiar voice call. "There are strangers here!"

As the familiar voice grabs the little girl's hand, her eyes connect with mine and widen when she takes me in.

"Addison?" I say, looking from the girl to her. Most likely looking like I've seen a ghost.

"She is *not* Addison. Her name is Pwincess Anna," the girl scolds me. "I'm Elsa, her older sister."

I look at her again, confusion written all over my face. "What, are you babysitting or something?" I smile. "I'm digging the costume."

She's dressed as a princess, and, hell, she looks beautiful even if she is on babysitting duty.

She opens her mouth to answer, but before she can speak, Coach walks next to her. "Well, well, well. Not bad, Hardy." He jerks his chin toward Brody. "Way better than that shit."

I try to laugh, still confused as to why Addison and her dad are with this little girl. That is, until the little girl grabs Coach's hand.

"Papa, come on! Mommy said there's still lots more! She said there's even a *PAW Patrol* one!"

He smiles down at her. "Okay, babe. Okay. Let's go."

"Mommy!" The sweet girl bounces up and down, gripping Addison's hand. "Let's go!"

She nods, her eyes looking anywhere but at me. "Okay, love."

Gazing at me, Coach gives me a short nod, and I swear I almost see a smile. "See you at practice."

"Yes, sir," I say, fighting the urge to look at Addison.

As they start to walk away, she looks back slightly, finally connecting her eyes with mine. Her lips turn up the smallest bit, and then she's gone.

It hits me hard that the girl I can't get off my mind has a kid.

And I had no fucking idea.

ADDISON

Well … I suppose the cat is out of the bag that I've pushed a child out of my vagina. Now that Cam knows this, I certainly won't have to worry about any future hookups. I'm okay with that too. After all, even strictly sex relationships become messy. Because one person inevitably falls for the other.

I'm not ashamed of having a daughter. Not one bit. Isla is the thing I'm most proud of in my life. She makes me a better person and, quite frankly, brought me to life. The reason I never mentioned her to Cam is simple. He isn't actually in my life. Not really anyway. We've hooked up—twice—and that was it. There's no emotional connection, and he isn't going to be in my daughter's life, so I didn't feel the need to spill my story to him. Besides, Isla is sacred. I don't need anyone casting their judgment on the fact that I had her so young.

It's just as well that he knows sooner rather than later. I know it'll shut off any interest he potentially had in seeing me again. I'm sure college dudes don't exactly love the idea of being with a woman who has a child. I could tell after the last hookup that he wanted to do it again, and while sex is fun, he seemed more interested in me than I was him. That's complicated. I don't need complicated.

I kneel down next to Isla once we're done going through the line of trunks. "How was your Halloween, baby?"

She grips my cheeks, putting her nose to mine. "It … was … PERFECT!" she squeals, assaulting my ears.

I cringe, my ears still ringing. "Good, sweetie. I'm so glad!" I look at Dad. "I can't believe you made your team do trunks for this. You never mentioned that you did."

"Honestly, I didn't think they would." He sounds surprised. "I sure as hell didn't think puck boy, Cam Hardy, would show up. Especially with a damn *Moana* theme, dressed as Maui." He chuckles. "I think I've seen it all."

"Did you just say puck boy, Dad?" I scrunch my nose up.

"Yeah, like F-U-C-K-boy," he says, spelling it out so that Isla doesn't know what he's saying. "But puck boy. I've heard that's what the guys who sleep around are called. Well, with an *F*. But since he's a hockey player …" He waves his hand. "You get it."

"Sure do. Loud and clear." I nod, pushing myself back up to stand. "You and Mom have a Halloween party tonight, don't you?"

"Yes," he grumbles.

I tilt my head, looking at him curiously. "Are you, like … dressing up? As in a costume?"

"Yeah! Yeah!" Isla giggles. "Papa is going to be a cowboy!"

His cheeks turn red, and he drags a hand down his face. "Isla ... that was our secret."

"Dad," I say, widening my eyes, "what's your costume? Are you really going as a cowboy?"

He sighs, his cheeks darkening more. "Apparently, I have to be Rip. You know ... from *Yellowstone*. And your mother is—"

"Beth? Beth Dutton?" I cover my mouth with my hand, fighting back laughter. "Oh gawd. No. Just ... no, Dad."

"Trust me, I don't want to! But she didn't leave me much of a choice. I'd rather stay home and watch game tape to prep for our next game. Never mind this *having to dress up as a damn cowboy* bullshit."

"Welp, I guess after all Mom's done for her family, this is just a small price for you to pay. Even if I am totally cringing right now and praying nobody I know sees you." I pat his back, trying to straighten my face out. "I'll just be home with all my friends." I look down at Isla. "Wild Halloween night."

As we walk around the commons, letting Isla do each and every single activity Brooks University has out for this event, I look over my shoulder to see Cam talking to some guys as he leans lazily against his truck. His costume is off now, and even though he's in a conversation with them, his eyes are solely on me.

He's beautiful to look at. But I suppose I won't be looking at him much anymore.

All good things must come to an end. No matter how good they might feel.

CAM

Addison, Coach, and the tiny person between them walk away. Just minutes ago, I watched her in awe as she knelt down, and then her daughter pressed her nose to Addison's. The little girl has the same curly blonde hair as her mama. I've never been with someone who had a child. At least, I don't think I have. Normally, that would be a turn-off for me. But today, I found myself watching them interact. Reaching for her mom's hand, the little girl would look up at her and giggle.

It's weird. I've never even liked kids all that much. They tend to be annoying and talk too much to even be considered cute. They have boogers in their nose and food all over their shirt. Gross. But that little girl? She is cute. And her mother? Easily the most beautiful woman I've ever laid eyes on.

I should be turned off right now.

Only I'm not.

It all makes sense now—why Addison told me she was too busy for anything. Or the reason why she wanted strictly sex, no feelings. She not only has to protect herself, but that tiny person she clearly adores as well.

The smile she gave me as she walked away almost seemed like a parting one. Like, *It was nice knowing you. See you never.* She probably assumed that would be the end of our days hooking up and was fine with it. Well, fuck that. I'm not done with her yet.

"You fuckers ready to head out?" Link throws his arm around my shoulders. "I'm over this shit for the day. I need a drink."

"Word. All everyone has done this entire time is shit all over my costume," Brody says, nodding as he heads toward the truck. "Let's roll."

"Y'all sure are fierce for this party." I grin as Link releases me.

"Hell yes, we are. It's Halloween. Hellooo, slutty costumes," Brody says before opening his door. "See you at home."

As we all load up and take off, I realize how much I actually don't give a fuck about going to this party tonight. I'd rather sit at home, truthfully. But let's be honest. I don't have much of a choice but to go. Because if I don't, all of my teammates will be pissed. They expect me to be there, and even if it isn't what I want to do, I have to. So, in a few minutes, when I pull up in front of our apartment and walk next door to the party, I'll put on a happy, carefree face. The Cam my friends and teammates know isn't the type to miss a party.

And he sure as hell isn't the type to be thinking about some chick who has a kid.

The music blares in the house. I normally love the smell of weed and liquor in the air, but not right now. Tonight, it's just giving me a damn headache. The sounds and smells I normally live for on the weekends are now aggravating the hell out of me, and honestly, I don't know why.

As soon as I sit on the couch, a girl dressed in a slutty nurse costume sits down on my lap. Once she's there a few minutes, she giggles as my teammates and I joke around, pretending she actually gives a shit what we're talking about even though I'm sure it's boring as hell for her.

She's drunk as she slowly lifts a finger, running it along my jawline before kissing my neck. I'm uncomfortable as fuck, and I'd give anything not to be on this couch right now. But the last thing I want to do is hurt her feelings. She's beautiful. She doesn't need me rejecting her and making her think otherwise.

"Let's get out of here," she says, lacing her fingers around my neck. "I've heard good things about you."

The old me would be ready to jump on this train before it even opened its doors to let passengers in. I'd be all over this offer before she could get her tits out of her bra. But right now, I just want to get the fuck out of here. Right now, the very thought of it makes my stomach turn.

I give her my best carefree grin. "I'm so sorry, beautiful, but as tempting as that sounds, I've actually gotta run." Giving her leg a gentle pat, I lift her off of me before setting her on the other side of the couch and standing up. "Have a good night. Be safe."

She looks at me, confused, but slowly nods, smiling the smallest bit. "Thanks. You too."

"Where are you going, dude?" Link calls out as I start toward the kitchen.

"Headed out. I'm too tired for this shit," I lie.

"Should we get you a walker, old man?" Brody smirks. "Some Velcro sneakers?"

I shrug. "Maybe. But I bet I'll feel better than either of you for our early workout tomorrow morning, huh?"

Both of their smiles disappear, and they groan.

"Y'all have a good night." I hold my hand up. "Don't do anything I wouldn't do."

"Lucky for us, that list is pretty damn short." Brody grins. "Have a good night, brother."

As I walk toward the kitchen, I see a girl dressed as Dorothy that I recognize right away. She was with Addison the night we hooked up the first time. And whether she likes it or not, I want to prod her for more information about the chick who's been invading far too many of my thoughts lately.

"Hey, you were the chick with Addison at that party a while back, weren't you?" I ask her. "Is she here?"

"Well, interestingly enough, I actually have a name. It's Tessa," she says bluntly, taking a sip of her drink. "And, no, she's at home."

"With her daughter?" I say, holding her gaze.

"You know about Isla?" Her eyebrows pull together. "She told you?"

"Isla," I say softly. "Yeah, I saw her today, trick-or-treating with her. Sort of put two and two together."

"I see." She nods.

"You know, Tessa, I'd love to go visit her." I turn on every ounce of charm I have. "If only I knew where she lived."

"Ew, stalkerish." She scowls. "That's plain creepy."

"She hasn't left me much of a choice, *Tessa*." I lean against the archway. "She's a tough nut to crack."

She stares at me a moment. "Does Cam Hardy, the infamous fuckboy of Brooks University, have a crush?" She rears her head back. "Are you into my friend?"

"Why am I *the* fuckboy of Brooks? Am I the only dude here who has a penis and uses it? I think not. Look around, Tess—can I call you Tess now that we're friends? Anyway, a lot of these dudes in here are thinking with the wrong head tonight. Why am I the only one on campus who gets the shitty rep?"

"I asked you a question. Are you into my friend?"

"Maybe," I say, shrugging. "So what if I am?"

"So, that means I chose wrong." She sighs. "She isn't interested, Cam. Give it up now."

"How about we let her make that choice on her own?" I wink. "I'm pretty damn irresistible, really. If I could go see her tonight, that'd be a good start, don't you think?"

"Dude, she lives with her parents, and I'm not about to give you their address." She takes another sip from her drink. "Besides, her dad would probably hang you from your nutsack and make you beg for your mama if you showed up there."

"Very true." I cringe before realizing she just gave me all the information I needed. "It was awfully nice, talking to you, Tessa. Put in a good word for me with your friend, would ya?"

"It won't matter." She rolls her eyes. "Nobody tells Addison how to think or what to do. *Nobody*."

"Guess I'll have to do all the work by myself then, huh?" I turn and walk away, making my way toward the front door.

I already know where Coach lives. We drove by his house the other day, and Brody pointed it out. Now, I just have to hope he isn't home.

ADDISON

I peek in on Isla, who snores softly, still in her Elsa costume from trick-or-treating. When she asked to sleep in it, just for tonight, I couldn't say no. In motherhood, I've learned to pick and choose my battles. What is sleeping in a dirty, cupcake-stained dress going to hurt? Not nearly as much as all the candy she had today will.

I close the door halfway and head toward the living room. After the trunk-or-treat, we went to a few houses around the neighborhood and then came back home and watched a movie and ate popcorn and way too much junk food. She was asleep before I even got four pages into the book she had picked for me to read.

A knock at the door has the hair on the back of my neck standing up. Mom and Dad won't be home till much later. And I'm not expecting company. Plus, it's Halloween. It's probably a serial killer with a knife and a mask.

Grabbing the broom, I walk slowly toward the door, looking through the side window.

"What the hell?" I mutter before flinging the door open. "What in the world are you doing here, Cam?"

His eyes move to the broom in my hand, and he chuckles. "What were you going to do, sweep me to death if I was a psycho killer?"

"No," I say, popping a hip out. "I'd smack you in the balls and then bash you in the head."

"Jesus, Addison," he mutters.

"Yeah. Anyway, why are you here? Please say you're looking for my father."

I wait for his answer. Hoping like hell that he'll confirm he just came by to see my dad.

"Nope, looking for you," he says confidently. "So … you have a daughter?"

He doesn't say it in any type of way. He's not disgusted or surprised. He's just … asking.

"Yep, I do. Why do you care?"

"Well, I really don't know." He swallows. "How old is she?"

"Three."

"You had her—"

"When I was in high school. Seventeen years old, to be exact," I say, cutting him off. "Here to judge?"

"What? No. Fuck no, I'm not."

"You shouldn't be here at all. You need to leave," I say, starting to close the door.

Slapping his hand on the glass, he pushes it open. "Why is that, beautiful? I mean, hell, not long ago, you basically hunted me down, and I gave you what you needed." His chest rises and falls as he glares down at me. "You were hungry for something besides food. And I was your prey. Now, you're telling me to leave?"

I roll my eyes. "Pfft, please. You aren't exactly a helpless little rodent." I shake my head. "And from what I remember, you wanted it too."

"Fuck yeah, I did," he says bluntly. "I still do."

His words take me aback for a moment before I gather myself up, pushing the thoughts of him ravishing me against this door out of my dirty, corrupted brain.

"Why are you here, Cam?"

"Because I wanted to see you," he utters. "And I think you wanted to see me too."

"No." I shake my head. "What we did was fun." I squirm, thinking back to how hot it was before forcing myself to snap back to reality. "But it can't keep happening. And now, you showing up here? That's nothing I want, Cam." I sigh. "I'm sure under all of the hookups, partying, and one-night stands, you're a nice guy. But I have a little person who depends on me. And taking care of her is my top priority. You, unfortunately, don't fit into that."

I give him a small, apologetic smile and start to shut the door, but before I can, his mouth is on mine as he makes his way inside and pushes me against the entryway wall, cupping my cheek with one hand and moving the other to my neck softly.

He kisses me hard before finally pulling back, leaving me breathless.

"So, you're saying you don't think about my dick inside of you, Addison?" he murmurs, his lips hovering over mine. "You don't replay my face buried between your thighs in that pretty brain of yours over and over again? Remembering how you came on my tongue?"

"I-I ..." I stutter, not knowing what to say. *Of course I have. How could I not?*

"That's what I thought," he says smugly, reading my mind before brushing his thumb on my lips. "I know I've thought about these lips wrapped around my cock since the moment you got off of your knees and stopped sucking my dick."

I swallow. And clench my thighs. And suck in the deepest, shakiest breath. And almost faint ...

Dear Lord.

"Cam," I whisper, "my dad is your coach. I have a daughter. This is a disaster waiting to happen. And frankly, a waste of both of our time."

"But think of how much fun it would be." He tilts my chin upward.

"I don't have time in my life for fun. I've told you that." I plead, "Why can't you just leave it alone?"

"We'll work around when you do have time. I can give you what you need."

I stare up at him for a moment. The most beautiful man is asking—begging—for me to use him.

"So, you're saying, no feelings? No dates?" My eyes widen. "Basically ... fuck buddies?"

"I guess if you want me to treat you like a meaningless fuck, Addison, that's what I'm going to do." He looks at me, his eyes darkening. "I'd be honored to be your fuck buddy."

I chew my lip. I don't have much time, but there is always an hour here or there when my mom insists on taking Isla somewhere. Or between classes when I'm already on campus.

The gnawing feeling of guilt consumes me, making its way throughout every crevice of my body. I hear that little voice in my head, telling me I'm a mom, that I'm not allowed time to myself.

I push it all aside. Yes, I *am* a mom. And a damn good one at that. But my mom is right; it's okay to have time for things I enjoy.

Though I'm not sure using someone for sex was what she had in mind. But, hey, whatever eases my tension, right?

"My terms?" I ask, raising an eyebrow.

"To a point." He smirks. "But when it comes time for me to fuck this hot body of yours, I'm calling the shots on what I want to do with you." He leans in until his lips are at my ear. "When I say sit on my face, you'd better sit on my face. And when I say climb on, you'd better be ready to ride."

My cheeks heat. "Okay," I mutter, chewing my lip.

His fingertips dig into my hip as he runs his hand up my side before raking it through my hair. "I'm going to go now, beautiful. Even though it's fucking killing me to. But I have to. You know, just in case your daddy shows up. I'd like to live to see tomorrow." He kisses me hard. Leaving me wanting more.

"I'll see you soon. Best be ready." He steps back, turning away. "Happy Halloween, Addison."

I watch him walk down the porch and to his truck. Closing the door, I lean my head against it, squeezing my eyes shut.

What did I just agree to?

And how am I going to keep it from my family?

CAM

The scorching hot water sprays down my body, giving my aching muscles the smallest bit of relief, though it's short-lived when I turn the spray off and step out of the shower.

After another grueling practice, I'm ready to go the hell to sleep.

We have a game in two days, and even though it's a team we should easily beat, crazier things have happened than an upset. So, we won't take it lightly. And Coach, well, he sure as shit isn't going to either.

We won our first game of the season, but barely. Coach called us an embarrassment, although I, myself, didn't think we played all that bad. Game number two and three, we wiped the floor with the other team, and he still didn't give us credit. Now, we're onto game four, and I think every one of us feels like we have something to prove. We want him to see us as the players we all know we are. If he refuses to believe in his own team, all we can do is show him he's got it wrong.

Over a week ago, I showed up at the coach's house to see Addison, and I haven't laid eyes on her since then. I left there, thinking we had come up with an agreement. That we had a weird little "deal" worked out. And even though the deal basically means it's just physical, I don't think I'm allowed to hunt her down for sex whenever I want to. She was pretty clear on the fact that it had to be the right time and place. A time when she had a few minutes to spare. And I get it; she's a mom. I respect her reasoning for wanting things this way. She doesn't want to ditch her daughter for a dude.

I keep wondering if she'll come to the game this weekend. If she was at the last few, I never saw her. Then again, maybe she has special seats. Box seats, I bet. I never gave it a thought to look … until now.

I make a mental note to try to check at the next game.

I pull my jeans on before tugging my shirt over my head.

"Yo, Cam," Brody says from his locker. "Bunch of us are going to shoot some pool after this. You game? Or are you too scared to be beat like a little bitch again?"

"Fuck off." I shake my head. "And that depends. Is the kitchen open?" I pull my sneakers on.

"You fucking know it is." Link throws his hoodie over his shoulder. "They always keep the grills going for us."

"Good." I stand up, heading toward the exit. "I could eat the ass right off a rhinoceros."

"I'm getting onion rings with my burger," Brody says proudly. "We earned these calories, boys."

"Hell yeah, we did, brother," Link agrees, walking behind me. "I'm getting mozzarella sticks."

"Y'all sound like little bitches." I laugh. "Like you're some chicks who just left a cycle class or some shit."

"I don't even care really." Brody shrugs. "But I am hungry, so let's hurry the fuck up."

After playing a round of pool, none of us misses the waitress heading to our table with the food we ordered. And even though we look like cavemen, we chase her over to the booth and slide in.

Devouring it, we hardly talk until every one of our plates is empty.

"That hit the spot." Brody sits back in the booth. "Wheel me home, fellas. I'm ready for fucking bed."

"Practice with Satan has been brutal." Link shakes his head. "Hell, I think he might be trying to kill us."

"Least his daughter's hot though." Brody grins, half-closing his eyes. "Really, *really* hot."

My jaw tightens at the mention of Addison. These guys have no idea I've been hooking up with her. And that's not because I'm ashamed to tell them because I'd be proud as hell about that. She's a catch by anyone's standards.

I'm keeping it on the down-low because I don't know if she wants anyone to know, and I want to respect her wishes on that. Besides, her daddy can't know. So, the fewer who are in on the secret, the less chance of him finding out.

"Dude, yeah, but did you see she had a kid with her at that trick-or-treating bullshit we had to do?" Link widens his eyes. "No fucking thanks. Hard. Pass."

"Trunk-or-treat," Brody corrects him. "And maybe it's her sister? Or perhaps she was babysitting?"

"Nah, dude. I could just tell." Link moves his head up and down. "Same wild hair. Same eyes. Plus, it was plain as day with the way they acted together."

"Who cares?" I shrug. "She's got a kid. She's an adult. Shit happens."

They both stare at me in shock before Link's face twists in disgust.

"Dude, it's a kid though. Like, good for her, but, no, I'm not trying to be anyone's daddy. I would suck at being a father to my own fucking kids if I had any. Let alone someone else's. No doubt, she's hot as hell. But seeing her with a kid, well, it erases her right from my picture."

"What picture?" I frown.

He taps his head with his finger. "The one up here. In my brain. Had me and her in it. Butt naked. Some whipped cream ..." He sighs. "But now, that ain't gonna happen. Because, you know, she—"

"Has a kid," Brody interrupts him. "Yeah, we get it." He smirks. "I don't know ... I kind of love me a hot MILF. And she's definitely one of those. There's just something sexy about a mom." He sighs. "But I'm not about to go there with her. Coach would cut my dick off and probably nail it to my locker."

My fists are curled before I even realize it. But I can't show them I'm irritated that they are talking about my ... *Addison* that way.

"Fuck yeah, he would." I blow out a breath, trying to steady myself. "You don't need any distractions anyway."

"Damn right I don't," he agrees with me. "Not even ones who look like an angel with a Playboy Bunny body." He blows out a breath. "That ass though ... damn."

I swallow hard. Trying to calm myself down. Reminding myself that he doesn't know I'm sleeping with her. If he did, he wouldn't be running his mouth this way. What do I expect my friends to say? She *is* drop-dead gorgeous. And her ass? Fucking hell, it's out of this world. Of course they noticed it too.

I just really wish they hadn't.

"Speaking of naked women ..." Link tips his chin up toward me. "You've been on your best behavior lately."

"How so?" I ask. Pretending not to know what he means.

"I haven't seen you with a female in weeks. What gives, man? You're usually charming the pants off females nightly."

"Just tired of the same old shit, I suppose." I mess with the straw wrapper in front of me, folding it down. "Gets old."

It does get old, plastering on the magical charm that Brooks University always expects from me. For as long as I can remember, it's been second nature. It's always been who I was as a person. I liked being the life of the party. Now, I don't know. I find myself exhausted with the act.

That's why strictly sleeping with Addison would be the best-case scenario. She doesn't have much time. I don't have much time. Win-win. Besides, sex with her is top-notch.

When I finally pull myself from my thoughts, I find Link staring at me with his mouth hanging open. He reaches across the table and taps his hand against my head, but I shove him away.

"You got a fever, man?" He sounds surprised. "I know you didn't just say that."

"I gotta give it to my boy. He's right," Brody agrees. "You're normally like the campus gigolo. Except ... you don't get paid."

"Dude, I don't fuck girls *that* much," I growl. "No more than any other athlete at this school. Especially no more than you fuckers."

"Maybe so, but you flirt. You buy girls drinks. You make your presence known to every female in a fucking room." Link shakes his head. "It's your ... your ..." He scratches his chin, thinking.

"Swagger." Brody nods. "Your swagger has been off lately. Way off. Still got way more than Link though."

"Piss off." Link scowls. "I have plenty of swagger."

"Whatever," I mutter, sitting back in my seat. "I'm the same me I've always been. Just focused on hockey. Just like y'all ought to be."

I know I've been different lately, and honestly, I don't know why. Maybe it's because I'm getting older. Maybe it's because I have been devoting every ounce of energy to hockey.

Or maybe it's because a certain woman has taken up residence in my fucking brain.

I'm not used to this shit. It's like it's sending my mind into a weird tizzy of unfamiliarity.

"No, like, right there." Link points at me before looking at Brody. "In the time I've known you, you've never copped an attitude. You've never been this grouchy and shit. You just never give a fuck ... about, well, anything."

"I give a fuck," I argue. "I give a lot of fucks."

"You care about the game, yeah." Brody nods toward Link. "But aside from that, you're usually the dude who doesn't get wound up over shit. You're happy-go-lucky."

"Y'all are annoying the piss out of me right now." I shake my head. "For real."

"Sorry." Link shrugs.

"I'm not." Brody sits back, narrowing his eyes. "We're telling it like it is."

"Whatever you say." I sigh. "I have to head back to campus," I say, jerking my head toward the door. "Afternoon class."

They both nod their chins to say good-bye. And as I slide out of the booth, an unsettling feeling grows in my stomach.

I don't think I've changed that much. I hope not anyway. But if I have, what caused it?

And how do I make it stop?

ADDISON

There's a bit of a chill in the air as I stroll along the sidewalk, a coffee in one hand and a half-eaten doughnut in the other. I ran out of the house ten minutes behind schedule and needed a quick fix along the way. As sweet as my angel baby Isla is, she can be a monster some days. Today happened to be one of those days. Since early this morning, everything was making her mad. She wanted to pick her own outfit out, and we didn't have the cereal she wanted for breakfast. Then, she stubbed her toe in the kitchen. It. Was. A lot.

"I feel like I haven't seen you in a thousand years," Tessa whines, taking a sip of her coffee. "What's new, mama?"

We continue to walk through the park at the center of campus. Both wasting time till our next class begins.

"Not much." I smile. "Isla started ballet, and it's freaking adorable. She has this little leotard, and don't even get me started on the tiny ballet slippers." I sigh. "Melts my heart into a puddle."

"She's pretty perfect, isn't she?" Tessa says.

"She's the best."

"How's she liking it in Georgia?" She looks at me, raising her eyebrows. "And how are *you* liking it here?"

"I think she likes it. Most days anyway. Today, she's just … a three-nager." I exhale. "But aside from the occasional rough days, she seems to be settling in. She misses my grandparents, aunts, uncles, and cousins. As do I. But overall, there are more opportunities in this area for kids. And besides, once she's old enough to understand things better, I won't have to worry about her running into Nick here." I cringe. "That would be awful—if she ever knew that was her dad but that he chose to stay away."

"He's a coward," she says flatly. "Always has been. Always will be. You're more than enough parent for her, Addy. I promise."

She reaches for my hand and gives it a quick squeeze, knowing anything more than that will make me uncomfortable. Aside from Isla, I'm not a touchy-feely person.

Releasing my hand, she stands taller. "She is loved. She is cared for. That's what matters."

I take in a long breath and let it out. "Thanks, Tess. Sometimes, I have a hard time, remembering that. Some days, all I can think about is how much it'll hurt her to not have both parents when she gets older. What if she feels like it's her fault he didn't stay? I wish I could guard her from that pain forever. But she's three, and already, she has asked countless times why she doesn't have a dad like the other kids she sees. She's still young enough to not really comprehend everything, but I know when she looks around, she puts the pieces together."

I swallow a lump as I remember her ballet class. I saw her sweet blue eyes dance around the room as a few dads helped their daughters put their shoes on. One lifted his daughter up, swirling her around. She watched in wonder. And for probably the thousandth time, I felt like I often do. That I'm not enough. That I'll never be enough. But I pulled myself together and swooped her up, pecking her cheek and distracting her by making her giggle.

"So, Nick still has never reached out to try to be in her life?" She looks angry. "Or his family?"

"Please," I say, breathing out a bitter laugh. "You know the Pelletiers only care about their reputation. You think they want to risk the world finding out that their perfect son knocked someone up while in high school? Or that said girl wasn't quite up to par with what they expected of him?" I shake my head. "They'll never acknowledge Isla's existence. But you know what? That's their loss. She's amazing. She's smart and funny." I suck down the last bit of my coffee before tossing the empty cup into a trash can. "As for Nick, no. Still nothing. The day I told him I was pregnant and he told me it wasn't his baby was the most we've communicated about Isla."

I think back to when I called him from the hospital after she was born to give him one last chance, only to find out he had blocked my number. And when that wasn't clear enough for my stupid brain, one night, I left Isla with my mom and dad, and I drove to his house. I wanted him and his family to be sure that this was what they wanted. Before too much damage was done between us and we couldn't ever make it all work. It was clearly a mistake, showing up there. Nick told me he wanted nothing to do with me or *my* child, and he refused to be listed as the father on her birth certificate. From that moment forward, I knew he would never be in her life.

"Asshole." Tessa stops walking and stares at me. "All of them. My memory is fuzzy on exactly how it all went down, but didn't they try to drive you out of town right after you had her?"

I nod. "Oh, yeah, in true Pelletier fashion, they offered us money to leave town and never look back. They didn't want Isla growing up in a town where Nick's father was the mayor." I shrug. "Obviously, we would never take a cent of their dirty money. And honestly, Tess, we had no intentions of leaving either. But after about half a dozen times of seeing them walk by me in town when I was pushing their own damn blood in a stroller, I was ready to get the hell away from that place. And then Dad got the job offer here, and I guess it ended up working out."

I smile at the memory. It seemed like a sign from somewhere up above that it was time to move on. Not just for myself, but for my daughter too.

"It did." She blows out a breath like she's preparing to tell me something before she starts walking again. "But now, she's three, and you've never dated anyone since that scumbag. Aside from that one hookup with Cam Hardy, your love life is about as boring as my math class." She elbows me and grins. "But I will say, I'm glad Cam cleaned out whatever cobwebs were growing inside of your vajayjay."

I swat her. "I don't have cobwebs, asshole."

She looks nervous suddenly. "So, I sort of forgot to tell you. Halloween night, he was at the same party I was at. Anyway … he asked about you."

"What do you mean, he asked about me?"

"Well, for starters, he knows you have a daughter. And the craziest part? He didn't even seem weirded out about it. Not that he should be. It's just … you know how college boys are about that sort of thing."

"Really?" I whisper before looking around, making sure nobody is close. "If I tell you something, will you not look at me like I'm a dirty, filthy, horny slutbag?"

"No promises." She shrugs. "But do tell, sis."

I feel my cheeks start to burn. "I sort of slept with him … again."

"What?!" She puts her hands on my shoulders. "When? Where?"

I cringe, looking down at the ground. "A locker room at the workout center." I chew my lip. "Like I said, don't judge me. It just sort of happened."

She jumps up and down with excitement. "Addison LaConte. You naughty, filthy girl! Oh my gawwwd." Her expression grows serious, and she taps her chin. "I actually sort of love this. Like … I'm totally here for it." She raises an eyebrow. "Are you going to do it again? I would if I were you. He's delicious."

"No. Yes. Grrr … maybe." I throw my hand through my hair. "Ugh. I don't know. He wants to. I mean, heck, he basically offered to let me use his body as an escape. But I don't know, Tess. That isn't really my thing. And besides, I don't have time for things like, well, sex."

"I get the time thing, Addy. Really, I do. But you're the best mom I know. You can make time for something that doesn't have to do with Isla, you know?"

"But you don't get it. I don't *want* to take time away from Isla. She already has a dad who doesn't want her. I can't be a half-assed parent. That just isn't fair to her."

"Do you like spending time with him?" she says curiously.

"I like having *sex* with him," I correct her. "That's fun."

"That good, huh?" She raises her eyebrows.

"That good." I sigh. "Should probably be illegal."

"So, if you had half an hour to spare and he happened to be walking by, you'd diddle him again?"

I snort at her word *diddle*. Something we used to say in high school.

"I think I would," I say honestly. "As long as it stayed strictly physical and I felt in control, I feel like it'd be fine. Oh, and as long as it wasn't cutting into my time with Isla."

"Good answer," she whispers. "Because guess what. He's walking toward us right now, and you have some time to kill before your next class."

I turn, and my eyes follow hers just as he struts toward us, looking down at his phone.

"Shh," I warn her. "Don't you dare yell anything out. Maybe he won't notice us."

The second the words leave my lips, he looks up. Seeming puzzled for a brief second before he waves and his boyish grin takes over.

"Addison," he says before turning toward Tessa. "Addison's friend."

"Tessa," she says quickly. "And I was just leaving. Busy. Super, super busy." She looks at me, an amused look on her face. "But you two should talk. Maybe get coffee. Maybe go somewhere alone. So many options. You know, since Addison has time to kill before her next class. Isn't that right, Addy?"

As she waves and walks away, I narrow my eyes at her. Doing my best not to mutter *little bitch* under my breath.

When I turn my attention back to Cam, a devilish smirk creeps onto his lips.

"Long time no see, beautiful." He stuffs one hand in his pocket. "Even went to the gym late every night this week, hoping for another round in the locker room. Next time, I figured I could bend you over the bench."

The filthy words roll from his lips so easily. Like it's absolutely no big deal that he's speaking to me this way in the light of day.

"I don't use that gym." I shrug. "I'm not a hotshot athlete, so I use the plain, average, far less extravagant one."

"But you were using it the other day." He tilts his head to the side. "Were you an athlete for the night? Sure seemed like it with the way your legs wrapped—"

"The other one was closed," I quip back, cutting him off. "Leaving me no choice but to use my dad's key card to get in while my parents had Isla."

"I like the name Isla," he says, his lips turning up. "Cute kid."

A cough comes out of nowhere, and I change the subject. Not because I don't want to talk about my daughter—I always want to do that—but because I don't know what his angle is. I don't understand his intentions.

"And besides, my dad told me I should avoid your gym. Evidently, too many jocks around."

"Is that right?" He smirks. "Does daddy know his daughter likes to get taken against the shower wall?" He leans a little closer. "Or go down on her knees on the cold, wet floor and—"

"Shut up." I shoot him a warning glare. "Shut. Up."

"Put something in my mouth to make me." His eyes darken. "I dare you."

My body heats. The truth is, when I went so long without sex, it was easier to not think about it. Now, after sex with Cam … I think about it. *A lot.*

"Come on, sweet thing. You know you want to. *I* know you want to."

I shift on my feet uncomfortably. "I don't really have much time. Class starts in a half hour. By the time I walk there … that'll leave me, like, fifteen minutes."

"Girl, all I need is five," he says. Nodding toward the parking lot, he clasps my wrist softly. "I know you've been thinking about me. Just like I've been thinking about you."

I glare at him. "You'd better mean you've been thinking of sex with me, puck boy. We had a deal."

His lip twitches with amusement. "Truthfully, what I've thought of most is when you rode my face, babe." He takes another step closer. "You tasted like cake. And, hell, don't I have a sweet tooth."

When I don't answer, his gaze holds mine. "Come on. You're cutting into my five minutes."

As he starts to walk backward away from me, a knowing grin on his lips, I suck in a breath. Before I know it, my damn legs are carrying me, and I'm following him like a lost puppy dog or something.

Sex with Cam Hardy is apparently like doing crack. Damn irresponsible but oh-so addictive and almost impossible to turn down once you've tried it.

CAM

After driving a short distance down the street and turning left, I reach an open lot at the end of a long road. A construction site at Brooks University. One day, they are adding another set of dorms among other things out here. I've driven around it when I was bored and wanted to explore. Nobody is ever around.

"What is this place?" she asks, gazing out the window. "Doesn't seem all that hidden either."

"Future plan to add on to Brooks," I say, backing in along the tree line. "Nobody's ever out here."

"Wow." She breathes out a laugh. "You really are the campus puck boy. This your usual hookup spot?"

"No, ma'am." I shrug. "Usually, I just fuck 'em in my bed or theirs." I wink. "Looks like you're special."

"No, I'm not," she snaps. "Don't say that sort of stuff. This is sex. A hookup. That's it."

"Christ, would you calm down? I haven't picked out the ring … yet," I joke, watching her face pale. "So, anyway, how's your week been going? Ain't seen you around."

Her blonde curls are pulled into a ponytail, showing off her pretty face. She doesn't wear much, if any, makeup, and for that, I'm thankful. She's hot as hell naturally.

She gives me a look, like I'm being annoying. "Why are you asking about my week? Are we having sex, or are we not? Should I get a teapot and some cups, and we can have a freaking tea party, too, while we're at it?"

"Look here, woman. My mom and daddy didn't raise me to be a dickhead. I'm not just going to pull my pants down, slam my cock inside of you, and not at least check in on you first." I narrow my eyes. "Guess you have to deal with my being a perfect gentleman sometimes if you want me to make you come."

Tossing her head back, she pinches the bridge of her nose. "Fine. I'll entertain you. It was good." Looking at me, she peels down her leggings. "And now, you really are down to five minutes, so hopefully, you weren't bluffing that you only need that much time."

Unbuttoning my own jeans, I smirk. "Pfft … I could get the job done in one minute. Trust me, babe, this will be the best quickie you've had in your life. You'll be walking into your class with a fucking smile on your face the size of Texas." Reclining my seat, I jerk my chin at her. "Now, come on over here and sit on my cock like a good girl."

Her chest rises as she sucks in a breath, watching me palm myself and pump a few times as I lock my eyes with hers.

Pulling her leggings the rest of the way off, she's eager to climb over the console.

When she straddles me, my dick hardens as her ass rests against my legs. I bring her face to mine, and my mouth is on hers, attacking her lips.

"You're so fucking hot when you're turned on," I groan, sliding my hands to her thighs before one sneaks between her legs. "And always so wet for me."

Pumping my fingers in and out, I move my lips to her neck. Her body presses against me more as I run my tongue along her flesh, tasting her.

In an instant, she pulls back, putting her palm to her mouth, and her tongue pokes out and laps it, getting it nice and wet just in time for her to reach down and take my dick into her hand.

"Fuck," I hiss as she begins to pump me slowly, tightening her hold as her hand starts to work faster. "I need to be inside of you—right now."

"Condom," she breathes out.

Reaching across the console, I pop the glove box open and grab a small foil packet. Before I can open it myself, she rips it from my hand, tearing it open with her teeth before sliding it over my length.

Moving a hand to each side of her waist, I lift her up just enough to let her sink back down onto my aching cock.

"Cam," she whines, a small hiss escaping her lips.

"Almost all in, baby," I say, running my tongue up her neck and down her throat. "You take me so good."

Once the shock of me stretching her to her limits wears off, she begins to ride me. She's not shy about taking what she needs, and maybe that's what I find so endearing about her. She doesn't skate around what she's looking for. She's mature. Something I guess I'm not used to.

Moving one hand under her shirt, I cup her tits in my hand, one at a time. "Fuck, you're perfect."

Her eyes stay on mine while she fucks me, her hips rocking back and forth as she grinds herself hungrily, completely consumed and greedy with chasing down a high I plan to bring her to shortly.

I tangle my lips with hers again, dragging my fingertips up her back. Her hands reach around, gripping my thighs as she thrusts her chest upward while she moans. Her body is so gorgeous, and I could get lost right in this moment. But she'd never let me. When she whimpers even louder than I've ever heard her before … I fucking lose it. Unable to stop the tingle that starts in my balls, washing over my body.

"Come with me, Addison." I tremble. "Let me feel you come on my dick."

Reaching forward again, she digs her fingernails into the flesh of my shoulders as her back arches and her chest shoves against me. I feel her squeeze around me as she loses all control.

"Cam," she whimpers, eyebrows pulling together.

Slowly, her forehead moves to mine, and she shudders against me. As our orgasms end, she doesn't immediately scurry away, like usual. Breathless, she drops her head to my chest and rests for a few minutes. Both of us continue to pant, trying to catch our breath.

I strum my nails along the skin of her back, wishing she'd stay right here a bit longer. She smells like some kind of flower, and I drag in a long breath, inhaling her.

"Guess it's time for me to go," she says, pulling back and making my heart sink. "Thanks for the quickie."

"Hey, anytime." I wink, pretending I'm not disappointed that she can't wait to get away from me ... again. "Told you it would be the best quickie you've ever had."

"Was it though?" She taps her chin, narrowing her eyes. "Maybe I've had better."

"Have you now?" I tilt my head to the side. "If that's the case, guess I'd better up my game. Next time, sweetheart, you won't be able to walk the next day."

Her eyes widen slightly, and her cheeks grow pinker. But just as I suspected, she comes back with a smart-ass comment.

"Who says there will be a next time?" she says, trying to fight the grin from coming onto her face. "That's very presumptuous of you, puck boy."

"I'm confident enough in my manhood to know you'll want more of this," I joke. "And what the fuck is this *puck boy* bullshit? Why are you calling me that?"

She blows out a laugh. "Well, my dad sort of calls his hockey players it. He replaces the *F* with a *P*. For puck boy. Guess I kinda like the way it sounds."

"Who says I'm a puck boy?" I narrow my eyes. "Maybe you took my virginity, woman."

She bursts out laughing this time before she seems to suddenly realize she's still on my lap. Climbing back to the passenger side and pulling her leggings up, she grins. "That's a good one."

"But for real," I say, unable to help myself. "Why do you assume I'm a fuckboy? I mean, I get it. Word gets around campus. But I'm not *that* bad. And I respect the hell out of women. And as much as it might seem I use them ... they use me right back."

She seems surprised. Reaching over, she touches my hand. "I'm sorry, Cam. I didn't mean anything by it. You're just sort of the *it* guy on campus. The ladies all drop their panties when you walk by. I can't go into a class without someone gushing about you." She sighs. "I'm sorry I stereotyped you though. That wasn't cool of me."

I get what she's saying. I'm a sophomore here at Brooks, and it's obvious that, last year, I fucked my way through campus. So many of the hookups, I was drunk. Still, I liked living that lifestyle. Even in high school, chasing women and playing hockey were my two favorite things. Oh, and partying.

"For a long time, I guess I probably was Brooks's own fuckboy and entertainment. But truthfully, Addison? I'm just over it." I shake my head. "Gets old, being on all the time. Being everyone's entertainment with my dumbass jokes and carefree demeanor. Always acting like nothing matters." I pause. Clearing my throat, I look at her and run my hand over my face. "What the fuck am I saying? Sorry. I'm not a weirdo, I swear."

"I get it though," she barely whispers. "I'm sure it does get old, always having to be the life of the party and someone's good time."

When I don't answer, her eyebrows pull together. "Cam, you know this thing between us is strictly platonic, right?" She looks embarrassed. "I know I shouldn't assume someone like you would even be interested in *that* way in a girl like me. But just in case, I want to make sure my intentions are clear and that I don't give you the wrong idea. You said you're over just sleeping around. And I just want to make sure I'm not a factor in that decision." She wrings her hands together. "I can't give you or anyone else anything more than this right here at this point in my life."

She's so fucking scared I might fall for her. I don't get it. That's what most girls dream of. Addison though? It's her worst nightmare.

"You're a kick-ass chick. And if I'm being honest, I really, *really* like fucking you, Addison," I say bluntly and watch her cheeks turn crimson red. "I'm not trying to marry you or be your Prince Charming. That ain't me." I pause. "But I like what we have going on here. Even if it isn't actually anything."

She looks relieved. "Same. My life is too complicated to add in feelings."

As I button my pants back up, I smile. "For whatever it's worth, I think it's pretty badass that you're a mom."

Her face changes to something unrecognizable. "Thank you, Cam. That means a lot. Isla is my entire world. Being a young mom isn't easy. But it's everything, and I wouldn't have it any other way."

I smile at the genuine tone of her voice as she speaks about her daughter. It's clear she's a damn good mother. Somehow, that makes me like her even more.

"Let's get you to class." I put the truck in drive. "Thanks for the quickie, babe."

She gives me a lopsided smile. "Oh, you're so welcome."

I've never even liked kids that much. Now, suddenly, I find myself in awe of the fact that Addison has someone she loves and cares about that much.

I can't imagine what that would feel like. And honestly, I've never even thought about it … until now.

ADDISON

The cold air of the arena hits the tip of my nose as I sit, looking down at the ice below. I've always loved the sensation of the frigid air nipping at my skin, and now that we live here, in Georgia, which is typically warm, it's somehow more comforting to feel than ever. When I'm in the arena at Brooks, it's sort of like being back home in New England.

I sigh, remembering the fact that we won't have a white Christmas. And that fall came and went here and was so incredibly different than fall in New Hampshire. Where every October, my parents and I would drive through the White Mountains just to see the foliage. The endless waves of orange, red, and yellow as far as the eye could see somehow always took my breath away, no matter how many times we took that same drive. We'd drive up Mount Washington, where it was always really freaking cold at the top. I like Georgia and all, but it isn't home. Not really anyway.

My eyes dart to number nineteen as Cam floats across the ice with ease, making it look like he could do it in his sleep. Something about seeing him down there tonight is much sexier now that I've seen him without his clothes on. It's like the best of both worlds—a hockey uniform and naked.

He's a force in the arena. It's no wonder why he said my father seemed to hate him. My dad has a history of being the hardest on the most talented players. I think, in his head, he believes it will make them better, stronger players. He might seem like a jerk to the team, but deep down, his team is his pride and joy. Well, besides his family, of course.

"Want some, Mommy?" Isla says from her chair. "It's reawy, reawy good."

I glance over at her mix of popcorn, a blue slushy, and Dippin' Dots. I cringe at the amount of sugar this kid is inhaling tonight. But everyone here loves Coach LaConte's grandgirl, so they can't help but spoil her. Even if I want to tell them to cool their jets.

"I'm okay for now, but it sure looks delicious, baby. What a good girl you are to share."

"Welcome, Mommy." She smiles proudly before her eyes float to my dad. "Papa looks mad."

I lean forward to look at him. "That's just his face during a game, love. He's not really mad."

"What if they don't win, Mommy? Will Papa be mad then?"

"Probably," I say, looking at the scoreboard. "But right now, they are up by two whole points."

"Well, if they don't win," she says, "I'm going to give Papa ice cream. Ice cream always makes me feel better."

"Me too, babe. Me too."

I turn my attention back to the game as a person on the opposing team slams Cam into the Plexiglas.

"Ouch." I sit forward in my seat. "That's gotta hurt."

"He is a big boy, Mommy. Him is fine," Isla says through her mouthful of whatever concoction she's mixed.

She's right, too, because not long after, Cam returns the favor and gives him a nice body check, no doubt shit-talking in the guy's face while he's at it.

When the dude slams into him again, I throw my hand up. "Seriously, ref. You gonna call that?" I mutter angrily. Not because I care about Cam, but because this guy is openly beating the shit out of our guys.

Hockey is a rough sport—everyone knows that—but there comes a point where it's too much. This is that time.

Despite the other team's efforts, Cam is just too damn fast. Breaking away from the defense line, he skates toward the attack zone, where Link passes to him, and he connects with the puck, sending it straight toward the goal. The goalie fumbles around, trying to stop it but miserably fails.

And the light flashes, indicating a goal made. The song "HandClap" by Fitz and the Tantrums begins to blare through the arena just as Cam looks my way. And even though he's down on the ice … I swear he winks before giving me a boyish grin.

Looking away, I play with Isla's hair, needing to break eye contact before his gaze melts my entire face off and I turn into a puddle.

Even after looking away from him, I still can't freaking breathe.

I focus on the game, all but Cam Hardy anyway. And I stuff popcorn and candy in my mouth to dull whatever this feeling is in the pit of my stomach when I think about him looking up at me and winking. My entire life, I've been a nervous eater. This junk food my daughter has seemingly stockpiled will get me through this game—I hope.

The last half of the third period goes by incredibly fast. Both teams have been playing rough. The away team is desperate and frustrated, making them lose control of their actions. And Brooks is simply fed up with the roughhousing and ready to fight back.

Elbowing, holding, and roughing land players from both teams in the sin bin. Even the crowd is getting rowdy and restless, yelling out cruder things than normal. And even though we're now winning three to one, my dad's face is still beet red just from the sheer intensity. And when it's finally over, I'm not surprised when Isla thinks we've lost simply by how angry her papa looks as he smacks on his gum, glaring out onto the ice.

CAM

I sit on this uncomfortable bench, thankful as fuck that I was a good boy tonight and behaved for the most part out there. Unlike Brody and a few of the other guys, who lost their shit and ended up in the penalty box multiple times. I can't complain though. Brody was just protecting his team. Well, for the most part. A few times, he slammed dudes definitely for himself.

Coach is mad. Even though we won, he's pissed off because of their actions. But he can't yell at me. Hell no. I scored two goals, and I behaved like a fucking king—if kings behave, that is.

Once my eyes found Addison, I had to look up there every chance I got. Next to her sat a pile of blonde curls with a bucket of popcorn bigger than she was. I wonder where the father of her daughter is. I can't stop thinking about the fact that he might be someone I know. Maybe he's even here, at Brooks. Who really knows?

Once Coach gets done lecturing us, never actually congratulating us on our win, I head for the showers. I'm sweating. I smell. And I'm fucking tired.

"I dare say you ate your Wheaties today, brother." Brody grins. "Also, how the fuck do you stay that calm when you're getting the piss beaten out of you?"

"Because we aren't cavemen, like you," Link says, shaking his head. "How much do you enjoy getting into fights? On a scale of one to ten."

"Twenty," Brody deadpans before nodding toward another defenseman, who also has a few screws loose. "Somebody's got to do it, right, brother?"

I laugh lightly. "And that's why y'all got yelled at by Coach. You need to put on some Bob Marley and chill the fuck out. It ain't all about fightin'."

"Noted, ol' boy. Next game, when you've got giants on your ass, trying to flatten you, I'll just *chill out.*"

I point to him. "Yeah, forget what I said. Be as crazy as you want. I don't want to get murdered out there." I shrug. "But what goes on inside your brain? You're the most easygoing motherfucker I know off the ice. But the second we get into the rink?" I give him a stunned look. "You're a whole other animal."

"Some of us are lovers; some are fighters. And I sure as hell ain't no lover," he says nonchalantly. "I could use a joint right about now."

"Fuck that. I just want a fucking pot brownie." Link widens his eyes. "That's what I need."

"Neither of you needs weed, dumbasses." I frown, wrapping my towel around my waist. "Unless you want to get kicked off the team and go back to your parents' houses, where you can watch porn in your bedroom and whack off to hopes and dreams you'll never reach."

They both stare at me for a moment before looking at each other.

Brody scowls. "What a fucking buzzkill you are."

I shrug. "Coach is a fucking stickler on weed. You both know this."

"Coach is a stickler on all things fun," Link murmurs.

"Well, this blows," Brody whines. "I'd give anything to smoke a blunt and go to McDonald's."

"Same," Link agrees. "How about we pretend we just burned one, and we'll hit McDick's anyway?"

"Yeah ... I guess." Brody sulks. "You coming with us, Cam?"

I pull my shirt on. "Nah, you two go. Have your romantic date. Perhaps buy a milkshake and share a fucking straw." I laugh. "I'm going to sleep."

Looking at each other, they both start to crack up.

"Yeah, right. You might be going to your bed, but you sure as hell ain't going to sleep. And definitely not alone," Link says, shaking his head.

"Why would you say that?" I pull my sneakers on.

"We just won. You love finding a little lady to celebrate with after a victory." Brody winks. "No shame in that, brother."

"Whatever," I mutter, grabbing my bag. "Bring me back an apple pie."

I see Coach in his office, giving an interview, but when his eyes catch me walking by, I swear he almost smiles. Holding my hand up to wave, I head out into the hallway.

Pulling my phone out, I check my notifications, reading through texts from my parents and Mila, congratulating me. They wanted to come tonight, but weren't able to. So, they streamed it online.

"Papa looks grumpy in this picture, Mommy," a small voice says, and when I follow it to see where it's coming from, I see Addison holding Isla as they stand in front of the team picture. "Wook at all the handsome men."

Her little voice makes me struggle to hold in a laugh. She's the spitting image of her mama. She's definitely going to be a heartbreaker one day with those same heartbreaking eyes.

"Again, baby, it's just his face. Papa loves his job," Addison says back to her before yawning. "Hopefully, Papa hurries along. It's past our bedtime, girlfriend."

"Mommy, mommy, you is a grown-up. Why do you need a bedtime?"

"Because if not, I'm as bad as I am without coffee." She touches her nose to her daughter's. "Let's go, babe, and see if we can find Papa."

I wonder how she is without coffee. Hell, I even wonder what she looks like in the morning. That hair couldn't possibly be any wilder than it is right now.

Why the fuck am I wondering what she'd look like in the morning?

Before I can stop myself, I reach into my duffel bag, feeling around until my hand finds the plush wolf that the school store gave to all the hockey players. I have no idea why they thought we'd want a damn stuffed animal of the Brooks mascot, but now, I'm kind of glad they did it.

"You must have missed my face when you said *handsome men*, huh?" I grin as I walk toward them. "Otherwise, that's the best dang compliment I've gotten all week." Looking at Addison, I nod. "Just out here, admiring your dad's beautiful smile?" I look at the picture and fight a laugh. "That sure looks like a man who loves his job."

She widens her eyes at me. As if trying to send me a silent message, asking what the hell I'm doing right now.

"Mommy, is this boy your friend?" She gazes from her mother to me like a bobblehead.

"This is one of Papa's hockey players, I." She slowly sets her daughter down in front of her, swinging her gaze back to me. "He was one of the guys you watched play tonight."

Isla looks thoughtfully and nods. "Okay, Mommy. But is he your friend?"

When Addison's facial expression looks strained, I crouch in front of Isla. "Yes, I am one of your mommy's friends. Do you like wolves, Isla?"

Her eyebrows pull together as she sighs. "The last school Papa coached, they were Wildcats. I like wildcats better than wolves."

"Why's that? Do you like dogs better than cats?"

"No, I'm 'llergic to cats." She takes a breath in and sighs. "So, I'm not a fan."

"Well, that's good news then. Because a wildcat is just a big ol' cat. So, you'd be allergic to it anyway. But the wolf is the OG of the dog family. Basically, a big puppy with sharp teeth." I shrug, taking the stuffed animal from behind my back and giving it to her. "You probably don't have time to take care of this guy, do you? Someone gave him to me, and I just don't have the time."

I expect her to smile. To jump up and down and squeal.

Instead, she looks at me as serious as a damn heart attack. "I'm busy too, ya know."

I try to keep my face somber, but when I hear Addison laugh, it's hard. "Oh, I'm sure you are. But you'd really be doing me a favor. I'd really, really, *really* appreciate it."

She narrows her eyes at me, thinking before she finally grins the smallest grin. "Okay, I'll do it. I'll be his owner." She looks down at it. "What should we name him?"

"Oh, wow," I say. I look up at Addison, who watches me with a surprised look on her face. "I'm not all that good at picking out names. I had a goldfish once, and I named him Goldfish. So, I think you'd better take the reins on this one."

"Bwooks," she says proudly. "Like this school."

Brooks. I chuckle inwardly. "Strong. Sturdy. Cool. I like it. I like it a lot."

As I push myself to stand, Addison watches me like a hawk.

"What?" I whisper once I know Isla is a few feet away, playing with the dog at a tiny table.

"Why are you doing this?" She shakes her head. Seemingly mad. "Why are you trying to get in good with my daughter? She isn't a pawn, you know. She's a person. She's *my* person."

"I'm a nice guy, Addison. And I want to be nice to you too." I hold my arms out. "That so hard to believe?"

"Yes, actually," she answers sharply. "It is. Did you not listen to anything the other day at our … quick hangout? I told you, rules. There will be rules."

"The rules never stated I have to ignore you or be a dick to you and your kid when I see you in a public setting," I toss back. "Sorry, I guess? For assuming you don't like assholes."

She grunts before walking past me and heading toward Isla. "I, let's go see if Papa is finished yet."

She sulks. "I don't wanna go, Mommy. I wanna play with my new friend—" She stops, looking at me. "What's your name, friend?"

"Cam." I grin.

"Isla, *now*," Addison's voice says lowly.

"Fine." She mopes behind her mom but turns. "Can you come over sometime and check on Bwooks? You know, to make sure he is okay?"

Addison's face is steaming as she shoots me a warning glare.

PUCK BOY

"Maybe sometime. But until then, I know you'll take good care of him."

"Addy, there you are," a woman says, barely getting the words from her mouth before Isla barrels toward her and leaps into her arms. "Sorry. I got tied up, talking to random people." She groans. "I felt like a jerk, walking away."

"It's okay, Mom. Is Dad ready?" Addison glances back at me nervously.

"Afraid not," she says. "He'll be at least another hour."

"Nena, did you meet Mommy's friend? His name is Cam." She holds her dog up. "He's gots no time to care for Bwooks, so now, I'm gonna be his mom."

"Is that so?" her mother, who is most certainly a MILF by all standards, says, her eyes on me.

After setting Isla down, she walks over to me. "Cam Hardy, I have a feeling you know what's wrong with this picture." She keeps her voice low. "You do realize this is your coach's daughter, correct?"

"Yes, ma'am." I glance at Addison. "I saw these two ladies waiting around for Coach and figured the least I could do was give the stuffed animal to someone who might like it."

"Boy, please. I saw you on our Blink cameras Halloween night." She raises an eyebrow at my surprised look. "No, before you ask, Addy doesn't know that I did. Up until that morning, they hadn't even been working properly. Just be thankful my husband can't run anything newer than a late 2000s flip phone and hasn't figured out how to check the cameras himself."

Addison watches us, narrowing her eyes as we whisper back and forth.

"I'm not trying to hurt her, Mrs. LaConte. Just want to be her friend." I breathe out a laugh. "And if I'm being honest, she might damn well break me first. She's …"

"Tough as nails," she says proudly.

"Yeah," I answer blankly. "She is."

"Yes, well, there's someone else in the equation, you see. Someone who gets attached very easily." She tilts her head to the side. "Boys like you play a good game on the ice. But life isn't a hockey game, you know."

"Understood, ma'am. I'm not playing any games. You have my word on that."

"Good," she mumbles. "Keep it that way."

Turning around, she holds her hands out to her granddaughter before Isla runs into her arms. "Ready, my girls? Let's go try to convince Papa to get out of there. I'm ready for bed."

"Same." Addison yawns before gazing back at me.

I've always been good at reading girls. And yet I don't have a fucking clue what's going on inside Addison LaConte's pretty head.

There was a minute or two during our last hookup when she melted into me. She'd already chased down her orgasm. The high was fading, and reality

73

was creeping back in. And yet, even if only for a few minutes, she rested against me. It felt good. It felt right.

But just like it always does, it ended.

ADDISON

My mom and I walk toward Dad's office, both hopeful we can whisk him out of here and go the heck home. After having the most awkward run-in with Cam, where he gave my child an adorable plush wolf, my mother spotted him near me. And judging by the silent trek to Dad's office, she's suspicious.

"What were you saying to Cam Hardy?" I break the silence, knowing she's going to ask me something about him anyway. "And why the hushed voices?"

"Well, I thought about asking him for his autograph. You know, since his picture has been popping up on my phone." She pulls her phone from her purse and turns it toward me. "But figured, better not."

On the Blink app, I see a video of Cam walking toward our house on Halloween night.

My heart sinks. "Did Dad see this?"

She laughs lightly. "Girlfriend, you know he can't use anything past the dinosaur ages in technology. Besides, Cam is still alive, isn't he? So, what do you think?"

Isla holds each of our hands as we swing her forward. My heart beats a zillion miles an hour from the revelation that my mom might know something is going on between Cam and me.

"When did this all start?" She keeps her words subtle. "And what is actually going on? Is it a fling? A friendship? What?"

"Whatever it is or isn't, you can blame yourself, lady. I wouldn't have even met him if you hadn't insisted I go out with Tess that night a while back," I say, keeping it vague because I can't exactly tell my own mother I'm using a gorgeous man strictly for orgasms. "But it's not going anywhere. Don't worry."

"Why would I be worried, Addy?"

I sigh. I've put my parents through enough during my time on this earth. I really don't want to cause them any more stress. And although I knew Isla's dad was a vile human being, he still broke my heart when he left me alone and pregnant. He was my first love. He was my first everything.

"Because I've gone down this road before. You know, with Nick. But I promise, this isn't like that. Cam's well aware that this isn't going to be some fairy tale, where life is cupcakes and rainbows and glittery shit. We're just friends." I cringe, knowing I'm lying.

We aren't friends. What we have is more of a business arrangement. Only instead of money, it's sex. But I can't tell her any of this.

"Mommy said a bad word." Isla giggles. "Mommy said shi—"

"Isla Rose. Finish that sentence, and you'll have a time-out when we get home."

"Sowwy, Mommy." She looks up at me. "I'm sowwy."

Widening my eyes at my mom, I nod toward Isla. "We'll talk about this later. *Alone.*"

"Oh, you know we will." My mother gives me a look, letting me know we aren't finished discussing this. As if I had any question about that.

I blow out a breath as we reach my dad's office door. Cam gave Isla a freaking stuffed animal. No man—besides my dad—has ever done anything like that for her before. And even though I want to remain cold inside, focusing solely on the sex … he just made that a hell of a lot harder by being sweet.

Why can't Cam Hardy make my life easier and be a jerk? The last thing I expected from him was a good guy.

CAM

"What a little bitch Beau is." I shake my head, looking at my sister. "Did he actually just blow you a kiss? Hell has frozen over. Shit, I might even see a pig fly. Beau Bishop is acting like a pansy."

My childhood best friend and my sister's boyfriend, Beau, is tattooed from head to toe. Most people that meet him are intimidated as shit by the dude. I mean, I'm not. Never have been. But I also never thought I'd see him blowing kisses from the football field—that's for sure.

Here my sister stands, decked out in Florida East attire, Beau Bishop's name and number on the back of her shirt. "Hell yes, he did. He loves me."

I made the trip to Florida after practice today. I don't go to many of Beau's games because of my hockey schedule. But when I can, I try to show up. He does the same for me now that we've finally buried the hatchet. For a long time, we didn't exactly see eye to eye.

"He could probably take his cup off now. You know, since he's got a vagina between his legs instead of a pecker these days."

"I can promise you, there is no vagina between those le—"

"Okay, okay," I growl. "Jesus Christ, don't finish your sentence."

"You asked for it, making fun of my man." She smacks her palm against me. "You're just jealous because you're going to die alone. Probably with, like, five dogs living with you in a dirty house, filled with beer bottles and empty pizza boxes." She raises her eyebrows. "You'll probably have weekly prostitutes come over."

"Prostitutes? I'm not paying anyone to ride on this train." I shrug. "Even at eighty, I'll have bitches begging for it."

"Ew, you're so gross. I literally just vomited a little," she grunts. "Someday, you're going to meet a girl who will knock you on your ass. You won't be able to eat, sleep, or breathe without thinking of her." She points a finger at me. "Just wait and see, big bro. And I, for one, can't wait to see it happen. The day Cam Hardy is bewitched."

"Doubtful," is all I say back.

"Whatever you say," she drawls slowly, waving at Beau as he looks up at her for what could be the hundredth time. "Whatever ... you ... say."

"Y'all are gross with this touchy-feely shit." I shake my head, sitting forward. "What happened to big, bad Beau Bishop, the man everyone feared?"

"He's still big, bad Beau Bishop," she mutters. "He's just ... better. Just like you will be when you find your other half." My sister pats my knee. "You'll see."

I say nothing back because I've had a certain girl on my mind for weeks now. And after the game this past weekend, it's only been getting more intense. The most fucked up part is the fact that it got worse after I saw her with her daughter again. This time, I saw them without the initial shock I'd felt at Halloween. I respect Addison in a way I've never felt before. I'm selfish. I have been my whole life. She's the opposite, selflessly putting herself last every day.

Addison is a cool girl, and even though she insists we're nothing, I'm not going to sleep around while she and I are hooking up. It just doesn't seem right. Besides, she more than satisfies what I need.

But I'm also painfully aware that I've never *ever* stopped sleeping with other chicks because of one girl. Especially one who acts like she hates me most of the time. But in this situation, the thought of being with anyone else just doesn't sound appealing. At all.

I'm being used for my ability to fuck a woman senseless. And right now, I think I'm okay with that.

Most times, I'm the one doing the hurting. This time ... Addison might be the one bringing me to my knees.

ADDISON

I push the swing, sending Isla higher for likely the hundredth time.

"Push me higher, Mommy," she squeals, her blonde curls blowing in the breeze. "Like Papa does!"

"Papa gives me a heart attack when he pushes you on the swing." I frown. "This is high enough. Dear Lord, child. You're three. Why must you already be a thrill seeker?"

"Mommy, is my special fwiend coming to check on this guy?" She snuggles the plush wolf against her as I slow her swing to a stop. "Doesn't he want to see him and make sure I'm a good mommy?"

This is what Cam didn't understand when he gave her that damn wolf. She's a child. She believes in magic and fairy tales and the overall good in people. He's not going to actually spend time with Isla or step in as a dad figure, and that was my problem with him being so friendly that night.

"We will see, baby. He's just a friend I see at school, you know? So, it would be sort of weird for him to just show up." I pat Brooks the wolf on the head. "But I know you've been a good mommy to this guy. Good job." Taking her out of the swing, I set her on her feet. "Slides next?"

She looks at the slides before glancing up at me. "Last one is a wotten egg!" she shouts before taking off running, her little legs carrying her just as fast as they can.

As I run after her, fully taking in her giggles as she barrels toward the stairs, I smile. This is my life, and I love it. But it isn't for everyone. Especially college kids. They don't want to be at a playground in the afternoon, and that's why it's easier to keep my circle small. It's Isla and me against the world. Just like it has been since she was born.

The day after Mom saw Cam talking to Isla and me after the game the other night, she pushed for more information when Isla was in the other room. I told her the truth—not in so many words. I couldn't exactly tell her it was only about the sex, but I told her we were strictly casual, nothing heavy now, nor would it ever be.

She told me to be careful and that Dad would be very angry if he knew there was any connection at all, which I'd already known. But she also told me that not every guy I meet is bad. And that sometimes, real men come along at the right time.

I told her that was a load of crap.

Because it is.

When Nick ghosted me after I carried his child for nine months and birthed her without him being next to me, holding my hand or telling me it was all going to be okay, I was crushed. I'd never felt rejection or abandonment that deeply in my life. When I had been younger, I'd always had this vision in my brain. It never involved the father of my child treating me like I didn't matter. Like *we* didn't matter. And even though my father has proven time and time again that good men are out there and my parents have shown me love can be a fairy tale … I believe they are the exception and that most people aren't so lucky to find what they have.

And even if all guys aren't bad, I'm not about to sign myself up to find out.

Hours later, we sit at the table, passing around enough food to feed a small army. My mother loves to cook, and I've been blessed enough to learn from her. Well, maybe not blessed, but more like forced. When I was a kid, my parents made me choose one night a week to make dinner for the family. It wasn't always pretty. And sometimes, it meant my parents choked down something barely edible. But it taught me a little bit of independence, and I'll be passing that tradition down to my daughter for sure.

"Isla girl, did you visit the gift shop at campus?" Dad asks, nodding toward the stuffed wolf sitting in the chair next to her. "Is that where you got the team mascot?"

"No. Mommy's handsome fwiend Cam gave him to me." Isla stuffs a forkful of mashed potatoes into her mouth, not bothering to finish swallowing them before she continues to talk. "Him is going to come over sometime and visit too. To make sure I am a good mommy to this fella."

"Cam?" My father's voice is low as his gaze swings to mine. "Cam, as in Cam Hardy?"

I swallow a mouthful of stuffing and grab my water, washing it down. "Um, yeah … so, funny story—"

"Isla and Addy were in the hallway, waiting for you after the game. Isla was getting restless, and Cam noticed and gave her the toy when he was walking out from the locker room," Mom says quickly, pushing out the words as fast as she can. "Quite a nice guy you have on that team of yours, Barren."

"That true?" Dad mutters, his eyes still on mine. "Why did Isla just say you were friends?"

"She's three. She probably thinks we actually like it when Aunt Gladys visits us, and that sure as hell isn't true."

"Mommy said a bad word." Isla points at me. "Put a quarter in my jar, Mommy."

"Sh—yes, yes, I will in a bit." I smile.

"Wait." Isla's eyes grow wide. "You don't like it when Aunt Gladys comes and stays the night? But, Mommy, she smells good." Her little button nose scrunches up. "Well, sort of. And she gives me cookies."

"I was just kidding. We love it. It's great. Really, really great."

I nod quickly before changing the subject to her ballet class so that she'll forget what I said about my aunt Gladys. She likes to repeat things she isn't supposed to. Aunt Gladys would have a field day with that one.

Once Isla tells us all about her dance class and her new tutu, she asks if she can be excused to the playroom.

"So, you and Cam Hardy aren't friends then, right?" my dad asks once Isla is gone. "Because, Addy, he's no good. He really isn't."

"Relax, Dad." I stand, gathering the dirty plates. "It's a damn cheap plush animal. He didn't offer to be her dad or something. He's not trying to be my boyfriend. He was passing by and wanted to be nice. To *your* granddaughter."

"I'd let him offer to be my daddy." My mom whistles, her cheeks turning red as soon as the words leave her mouth. "Sorry ... I'm kidding." She blushes. "That was inappropriate."

"You're damn right it was, Jennie," Dad grunts. "Boys like that have no morals. His only care in the world is making it to the pros. That's all. Oh, and adding more notches to his belt."

"Just to play devil's advocate here, while I'm sure all of that is true, isn't that the goal with a lot of your players, Dad? To make it to the pros?" I shrug. "Wasn't that your goal at one time?"

I swear one of his eyes twitches with anger.

"It's a bad thing when it comes to dating my daughter, damn it." He points at me. "He isn't any better than Nick was. Haven't you learned your lesson with these ... these ... morons?!"

"What are you even talking about, Dad?! We aren't dating!" I hold my arms out at my sides. "My God, what are you so scared of? Isla simply mentioned a damn stuffed animal the man gave her. That's it!"

"I'm worried you'll end up in the same situation as before!" He hits his fist on the table before standing abruptly. "Do you want another baby with another selfish prick of a hockey player? Do you, Addison?"

"What has gotten into you, Barren?" my mother hisses. "She isn't dating, or seeing, or sleeping with that boy! You're acting like a maniac, and frankly, you're out of line."

"He didn't walk up to her and Isla out of the kindness of his heart, Jennie. He isn't that good of a guy, trust me," he says, stopping at the doorway. "He saw Addison and noticed a pretty face. Giving Isla that stupid toy was just to act like he gave two shits so that he had a better chance of taking advantage. That's all."

"It was *one* time," my mom argues. "And it made your grandgirl happy, for fuck's sake."

My mother rarely swears. And hardly ever drops an F-bomb.

She must be really mad.

"It's never one time with people like him." My father seethes. "He noticed her; he'll be back." His eyes narrow to slits as he nods toward me. "I won't allow it. I've been through this before. I'm not doing it again. Stay away from that boy. That isn't a request either."

"Wow. This is insane, but okay, yes, whatever," I mutter, looking away.

"It's not insane if it saves you from another—"

I point, cutting my father off. "I know what you're going to say, and don't finish your sentence. *My daughter* could walk out here any second. Do you think she needs to hear her grandfather talking like she's a burden? Like she's the worst thing that ever happened to me? To us?" I whisper angrily. "That's the last thing that kid needs to hear. She's going to have enough thoughts in her head about that as she grows. I won't allow her to hear it now."

He looks pained. "I wasn't … I don't feel that wa—"

My mother puts her hand on my shoulder. "She's right, Barren. I know that isn't how you feel, but you're speaking out of anger right now. And Isla girl doesn't need to hear it."

He looks down, ashamed. "Isla is the best thing that's ever happened to us. That isn't what I meant," he says softly. "But none of what happened with Nick was easy on any of us. I don't want to see you getting wrapped up in the same bullshit of a person. That's all." His eyes lift to mine. "Isla is the furthest thing from a burden, Addy."

"I know," I say, nodding. "You just have to trust me when I tell you that I'm not going down the same road."

Reluctantly, he blows out a breath. "All right."

I wring my hands together with guilt. I'm being honest when I tell my dad I'm not going down the same road again. No way will I end up pregnant and brokenhearted. But I'm having relations with Cam even if it is just physical. And I lied. And my mom lied.

We're both big, fat liars.

And the thing is, I *have* put my father through this before. I put him through it, and now, he's forced to help raise a toddler because the guy I chose to have unprotected sex with was a piece of shit—just like my father had said.

I don't want anything from Cam aside from a quick escape from reality. Something to take my mind off the constant pressure life throws my way. That's it though.

But that's over now. My father was very vocal about not wanting me near Cam Hardy. Dad's done enough for me; I can do this for him.

It's not like Cam and I were anything anyway.

CAM

I walk into the campus coffee shop, sweeping my eyes around the clusterfuck of students all looking for their caffeine fix. Until Layla, I hated coffee. Then, she got me addicted to the shit, and now, here I am, like every other pathetic loser in this line, itching for an iced coffee.

A girl orders, and even though I can't see her face, I know her voice. When she turns around, I recognize Tessa, Addison's friend.

Keeping her lips in a tight line, she starts to walk toward the exit.

"Tessa," I say when she's almost by me, "wait."

Slowly, she stops. "Yes, the oh-so-famous Cam Hardy. What can I do to make your day better?" she says sarcastically.

"It's been over a week. I haven't seen Addison anywhere. Thought about driving by her house—"

"Don't," she hisses in warning. "Seriously. If you want to keep the dick that you are so fond of shoving in every female you see ... don't. Barren forbids her to date hockey players. And he isn't one to be messed with, especially when it comes to his family. They've been through enough without you coming between them."

I cringe at the thought of losing my penis. *That wouldn't be much fun.* Then, the one thing Addison actually likes about me would no longer be. Can't have that.

"I mean, he doesn't have to know." I try to grin. "I could sneak over when he isn't home."

"I talked to her yesterday, and he already does know," she whispers. "Or at least, he's onto you. After your little stunt with the stuffed animal, he wasn't happy. He lost his shit at the dinner table when he found out the other night."

It all clicks. For a few practices, he had let up a little. But the past few days, he's been worse than ever.

"So, that's why he's been extra dickish at practice," I mutter, looking down. "I thought maybe he had a stick shoved up his asshole, turned sideways." I look at her as the line moves up. "Talk to her, would you? Put in a good word."

"For what, Cam? What could you possibly want with her? Be real." She gives me a sympathetic smile. "Let it go. It's never going to happen. You can't be what she needs." She pauses. "What *they* need. It was fun while it lasted … but she doesn't need drama in her life."

I don't answer or try to argue because guess what.

She's right.

I'm nobody's dad. I'm not the guy who knows what to do or say to the chick with a kid. Not to mention the fact that the game is where my sole attention needs to be. I don't have time to be worried about what Addison is doing.

The smartest thing I can do is forget about the coach's daughter. But I know that'll be easier said than done.

CAM

"I don't think I've ever seen Coach this on edge, and that's saying something because that fucker is never relaxed," Link says, stopping in front of me on the ice and nodding toward Coach. "I heard he hates the coach on the other team."

"Nah, that ain't it," Hunter says, coming from behind us. "Cade heard some rumors that Coach's daughter has bad blood with Nick Pelletier on the other team. They say he did some fucked up shit to her."

"Like what?" Brody frowns. "How would she even know him?"'

Hunter shrugs. "Hell if I know. But whatever it is, it can't be good. Just look at Coach right now."

We all shift our eyes to him, watching him scowl down at the notepad in front of him. Even from here, he visibly looks angry.

I look up in the seats that Addison, her mom, and Isla usually sit in, only to find them empty. Ever since I saw her best friend in the coffee shop over a week ago, I haven't tried to see her again. I'm not dumb enough to sabotage my place on this team by continuing to hook up with the coach's daughter. Besides, Addison has never attempted to find me either, I'm sure. And what was I really hoping to get out of us? I'm not boyfriend material, let alone *stepfather* material. Hell, I can hardly take care of myself, never mind a kid.

As I look at the opposing team, my eyes find Nick Pelletier as he and his teammates warm up. I played against him last year. He's good, but he plays really dirty. He's also a bit of a whiny ass, if my memory serves me right, because when they played us last year and lost, he basically pouted on the ice like we were back in peewees and not college athletes. Even so, in the game tape I've studied, he's their leading scorer in almost every single game. And like me, he's also a center.

Fuck, what if he's Isla's dad?

Maybe that's why Addison didn't show up tonight. The thought pisses me off, picturing him with her. I can't imagine he'd see his daughter much if that were the case. After all, he plays for North Carolina. That's a long-ass way from Georgia. But then I remember that Coach moved here from New Hampshire, which is where Nick Pelletier is from. Before coaching Brooks, Coach was a high school coach. So, in reality, it's possible that Nick is the father of Addison's kid.

Shit.

"Hardy," Coach says, calling me over.

Skating toward him, I stop, tipping my chin up. "Yeah, Coach?"

"I don't call in personal favors much. But I really, really need this win. You're this team's captain; they listen to you. We can't fuck this one up."

"Yes, sir." I nod.

As he dismisses me, I shake my head in disbelief. Because that motherfucker was actually just decent to me. And that right there is cause for a celebration.

ADDISON

After she begged me to paint her nails for twenty minutes straight, I paint Isla's last fingernail, warning her not to move until they dry. Which shouldn't be too hard, seeing as I knew that with a squirmy three-year-old, instant-dry nail polish was the only way to go.

"It's weird, isn't it? Not being there tonight." My mom sighs, flipping through the channels on the television, fully avoiding any televised footage of tonight's hockey game at Brooks. "But I'm glad we aren't. I feel bad your dad has to be though."

"Yep. And just think, they have to do it all over again tomorrow night. Gotta love those college hockey schedules." Blowing on Isla's tiny pink nails, I tap one to make sure it's dry.

"Can I go play, Mommy?" she asks, sticking her bottom lip out. "This took one thousand, million years."

"Girl, it's only been, like, three minutes," I deadpan. "But, yes … go on."

As she trots away, headed toward the playroom, I pat Mom's knee. "I feel bad too, leaving Dad to go through it all alone. But the thought of seeing *him*—or worse, *her* seeing him …" I drop my voice lower. "I know she wouldn't realize that's her D-A-D, but still. It hurts my heart to even think about it for some strange reason. Plus, he's ignorant enough to start something."

Mom looks pained. "It hurts my heart too."

Isla's sperm donor, Nick, is on the opposing team tonight. Up until I had Isla and he pretended she didn't exist, my father was actually his coach. Luckily, he played his senior year somewhere else, and my dad didn't have to look at his face. The thing with Nick, he's a good hockey player. A human being though? He plain sucks ass at that.

Mom and I talked and made the decision not to attend tonight's game. Nick had seen Isla before in public places before we moved to Georgia, but she was younger. He'd walk by, a smug smile on his stupid face, not feeling the least bit ashamed of his actions. No matter how much I tried to not let it affect me, it did. I became bitter. A town I loved no longer looked the same through my eyes. The trees somehow looked deader. The grass dryer. The pavement more worn and cracked. Since coming to Georgia, I'm happier and lighter. So, tonight, staying home, eating Chinese food, and hanging out with my mom and Isla was a no-brainer.

It isn't lost on me that the only two guys I've physically been with will be facing off tonight. Of course, neither of them knows about the other—I hope.

"So, to change the subject, have you seen that forbidden, gorgeous, muscled hockey player again?" My mom raises an eyebrow. "And don't even try to lie."

"Nope," I say slowly. "After Dad voiced his opinions that night, I decided it was for the best that I didn't see him anymore. Besides, he hasn't tracked me down on campus either. So, he must have come to the same conclusion—that it was a bad idea and needed to stop."

"Maybe he's been busy," my mom suggests.

I laugh. "Cam Hardy doesn't strike me as the sort of guy who lets anything stop him from what he wants. If he wanted to see me, trust me, he'd see me. That's something I realized quickly about him. He's insistent."

"Are you disappointed he hasn't sought you out at school?" She tilts her head to the side. "In all honesty."

I pick at my nails, realizing mine need to be done way more than my three-year-old daughter's. "I don't have time for a boyfriend. Or really any sort of fling."

"That's not what I asked."

"He was fun to be around the few times we hung out. He has this charismatic personality that's refreshing. So many people I'm around at school sweat the small stuff. He seems like the type of guy who sweats nothing." I relax further back on the couch. "I never wanted it to go anywhere. That would be too complicated, given my life. But I'll admit, I enjoyed our short time together." I blow out a breath. "But, no, I'm not disappointed. I didn't want him getting the wrong idea and expecting more from me than I could give. I don't have to worry about that now at least."

I can always speak candidly with my mother. I know that she'll never cast judgment or make me feel bad about any of my decisions. She's also much more reasonable than my father is when it comes to my dating life, which I appreciate greatly.

"You know, your daddy would kill me for saying this, but, damn it, someone's got to." She rests her head on the back of the couch, giving me a sad smile. "You know, Addy, not every hockey player is like Nick. Not every man is either."

"I know," I admit. "But I don't want to take the chance either." Tears threaten to spill from my eyes as I swallow back a lump of emotion. "I wouldn't change being a mom for anything even if I probably wasn't ready when she came into this world." I swing my eyes to the playroom, making sure Isla is still in there and not close enough to hear me. "But being reckless enough to have a baby with someone who dropped me and never looked back? That ruined me, Mom. It ruined me for anybody else. The day I told him I was pregnant and he told me to leave and never come back … I've never felt so alone in my life. I can't do that again." My eyes remain on Isla, playing through the open door. "And even if I could, I can't take that chance with her. She'll have enough pain when she's older without me making it worse. And I clearly am a shitty judge of character because never in my life did I foresee Nick doing what he did."

The truth is, I worry about the future every second of every day. She's little now. She doesn't understand what it feels to be abandoned. One day, she'll question why she wasn't good enough for her dad to stick around. She'll carry the burden with her for her entire life, and there's nothing I can do besides try to love her enough for the both of us. But still, I'm petrified that it won't be enough and she'll blame herself.

"I understand your concerns. I do." Mom touches my hand, her eyes soft. "But it's an awfully long life to be alone. And such a waste to hide such a beautiful heart from the world." She smiles. "One day though … one day, I know you'll be ready to show it again. I know it."

"Maybe I will. We will see," I say, not believing my own words.

CAM

My head is soaked with sweat. I gaze up at the clock. Twenty-eight seconds.
This game is almost over.

It doesn't sound like a long time to hold them down, but a lot can happen in just twenty-eight seconds. And we're only up by one goal. If they tie the game up before that final buzzer sounds, we'll be forced into overtime. My teammates have played their hearts out tonight. They know it's an important game for Coach, making them want the win more. But in overtime, anything can happen. No, we don't want that. We want to finish this now. Though if I'm being honest, I wish this were tomorrow night's game and that we had already whooped their asses once and were about to finish the weekend strong. But I guess, win or lose right now, tomorrow night, when we play them again, we'll lace up our skates and give 'em hell.

I'm thankful as hell right now for our goalie, Watson Gentry. Last year, he was a freshman, and even though he was better than the starting goalie, our previous coach refused to play Gentry much. This year, he's taken the starting role, and he's killing it. I wouldn't feel comfortable with anyone else besides him defending our goal right now.

Cade Huff, a defenseman, skates by me just before the face-off. "Let's go, Hardy. Let's end this night, so we can get the fuck out of here and celebrate."

Tapping my stick to his, I smirk. "Sounds like a plan, Stan."

I face off against none other than Nick Pelletier. Giving Coach a final nod, I let him know I've got this. Whatever this asshole did to hurt Addison, he'll pay for it now when I embarrass the fuck out of him and his team. He's been on my ass all night, and just like I noticed in the game tape, he plays a dirty game.

"Better be ready, Hardy," he sneers.

"You know what's damn funny?" I say, grinning. "Your mama said that same thing to me last night."

"Fuck you."

"Oh, don't you worry, baby boy. She did." I wink. "What a wild fucking ride that was."

His nostrils flare, and even through his shield, I can tell he wants to murder me. His mouth opens to say something back just as it's go time.

One thing I've learned about playing this game, it never hurts to get inside your opponent's head. Especially during crucial times like right now.

Before he can recover, my stick reaches out, taking control of the puck. He's quick to slam into me, desperate to get it out of my possession, but it's no use, as I move away from him, sending it right over to Hunter. With Link on the other side of the ice, skating alongside him, Hunter glides the puck to him, and Link takes the shot. One thing about Link: he has a really, *really* good shot.

And with just seven seconds left on the clock, we just pulled ahead by another goal. They know it's over. And I can't help but look at Nick Pelletier, giving him a smug look as I skate backward toward my team to celebrate. Happy as hell to put the man who hurt Addison in his place. Even if it doesn't really fix whatever their deal is.

Coach should be beaming, but instead, when I look at him, he's staring over at Nick Pelletier as he makes his way across the ice to me. Coach glares, and even though he's clearly pissed, there's also another emotion all over his face, one I never thought I'd see.

Sadness.

And to think, we have to do this all over again tomorrow night.

"You might have gotten this one, Hardy," Pelletier chants next to me, his eyes narrowed to slits. "Tomorrow night, you won't be so lucky."

"Oh, we'll walk away with another W tomorrow. Just as long as your mom doesn't keep me up too late tonight." I tip my chin up and skate away, a content look on my face, seeing his scowl.

Now, we just have to win again.

ADDISON

Class passes at a snail's pace, and frankly, it's obnoxious. I want to be home, snuggling my baby. She'll likely be asleep by the time I get home, but there's always that small chance that she's a turd for her nena at bedtime, and I'll get to swoop in and save the day. Those nights when she is difficult at bedtime are the nights I let her fall asleep with me in my bed. And on long days like today, nothing sounds better.

This past weekend, the Wolves won both of their games against North Carolina. Dad was happy to advance over Nick's team, obviously. But seeing Nick again always puts my dad in a weird funk for a few days after.

The morning after the first game, I overheard my father talking to my mom. He was claiming Cam Hardy proved himself to be the better hockey player over Nick at the game, which is saying something because, as much as I hate to admit it, Nick Pelletier is stupid talented on the ice.

The professor *finally* tells us we're free to go, but not before giving us a huge-ass reading assignment to do. Closing my books, I stuff everything into my bag and hightail it for the door.

I break into the hallway, beelining it for the exit, when a deep voice stops me. "It's Addison, isn't it?"

I sigh inwardly. I don't have time for small talk, and whoever this might be, I honestly don't care.

Turning slowly, I'm taken aback by the attractive man standing before me. He looks vaguely familiar, though I'm not sure why.

"Yes?" I tilt my head slowly. "Can I help you?"

A soft grin breaks across his face, and he shakes his head. "Nah. I've just been telling myself for weeks that one of these days, I'd say hi to the pretty girl who sits at the front of the classroom. I guess tonight's the night I finally blurted it out."

His dark hair is kept short on his head. And even though he's put together, he doesn't seem like the pretty-boy type who gels his hair and wears a pound of cologne before leaving the house. He seems … normal. He also seems nervous to talk to me, which I find somehow comforting that maybe he isn't a complete fuckboy who flirts with girls all day long.

Tucking my hair behind my ear, I shift on my feet. "Oh, well, hi, I guess?" I hold my hand out. "Nice to meet you …"

"Hunter," he says, taking my hand in his. "Hunter Thompson."

I can't fight the grin from spreading across my lips as the light bulb goes off. "Hockey player?"

"I'd try to lie, but I feel like it's no use." He shrugs. "For what it's worth, I wanted to say hi to you before I knew your dad was my coach."

"That's not worth a whole lot. You *have* met him, right? I mean, he is your coach," I joke as he releases my hand.

My phone vibrates, and as I hold my watch up, I see my mom texted me, saying that Isla is out cold for the night and asking if I can pick up some milk on my way home. She sends another message behind it, telling me I don't have to rush home, that I can meet up with "Tessa" if I want to. I fight back a smile, knowing she's using Tessa as code for Cam even though I told her we weren't hanging out anymore.

He laughs. "Oh, yeah, I've met him. That's why I knew it was probably a bad idea to say hi. But, fuck it, I did it anyway." He pauses. "You wouldn't want to go get something to eat, would you?"

In my mind, it's late. After all, on nights I don't have class, I'm in bed with Isla at her usual bedtime of seven o'clock. I don't sleep. I do homework or read. But still, I'm in my pajamas and sure as hell not out to dinner.

"I don't date hockey players. Actually … I don't date anyone. But *especially* hockey players." I give him a sympathetic smile. "Sorry. Have a nice night."

As I turn away from him and head toward the door, he catches up with me.

"What if it isn't a date at all? Hell, you don't even have to talk to me. We can just sit and grab a quick bite."

I start to open my mouth, telling him I can't, but he stops me.

"Look, I got dumped this summer by a girl I'd been dating since high school. I'm not looking for a relationship. Just would be nice to go out to dinner with someone. You're not like the other girls who are overkill and bat their eyelashes and shit."

"So, now, you're using me?" I narrow my eyes. "To get over your ex?"

"What? No!" He waves his hands around. "No, that's not what I me—"

"Relax," I say. "I'm kidding. As long as you understand that this isn't a date. We aren't going to have sex. *Ever.*"

"Understood." He nods quickly. "I won't even take you anywhere nice. We'll go to Club 83, and I'll treat you to some crappy fried food. Deal?"

"Club 83 has food?" I ask, surprised.

"Fuck yeah, they do."

"I love crappy fried food." I shrug. "Deal."

In all honesty, I don't know why I just agreed to dinner with this man. Maybe part of me knows my mom is right; it's okay for me to occasionally act like a normal college kid.

Even though that isn't really what I am.

Once we're in his truck, I buckle my seat belt. "So, it appears we share the lovely Pathology class. Are you here for a nursing degree too?"

"Nah, sports medicine," he answers pleasantly, but he doesn't exactly sound excited.

"Oh," I say, nodding awkwardly. "So … you're hoping to become a …"

"Not a doctor." He laughs, but it's forced. "That's my parents' dream, not mine. I'm just biding my time, doing the college classes they expect me to until the phone rings, giving me my way out. Then, I'll be holding my middle fingers in the air to everyone and chasing my own dream."

"NHL?" I guess, turning toward him.

"Yep. That's the dream, anyway"

"How will you tell them?" I ask curiously. "You know, when the day comes."

He's quiet for a moment before he shrugs. "I suppose I'll have to let you know when it happens. Because honestly, I haven't got a clue right now."

And as we pull into the parking lot, he grins. "You're in for a real treat. Looks like the entire hockey team is here. Just ignore them."

I sink into the seat when we park right next to a familiar truck.

Cam Hardy's truck.

CAM

What the fuck?

What. The. Fuck?

What in the motherfucking fuckity fuck?

I grind my back teeth together, trying my best not to lose my cool as I watch Hunter fucking Thompson sit in a booth across from Addison. My friend and fucking teammate. Sharing a table. With *my* Addison.

I don't even understand how this happened. She doesn't date. At least, that's what she told me. Yet here she is, on a date with Thompson.

When they walked in, she froze when her eyes found mine. The last time I had seen her was the day I gave her daughter that damn stuffed animal wolf, which apparently pissed her old man off. Luckily, after we beat Pelletier's team, I've been on his good side, it seems.

I talk to some of my teammates, trying to keep my eyes away from their table as their meals get delivered. But a little while later, once they're done, I see Hunter get up and walk to the restroom, and I decide I have to take my shot now. I can't take it anymore.

Pushing myself up, I head straight to his seat and slide on in.

"Cam, what are you doing?" she gasps, her eyes widening at the sight of me. "Why are you in his seat?"

"*His*, as in your date?" I jerk my chin up. "Funny, Addy. I thought you didn't date." I lean in closer, dropping my voice. "Hell, I'm surprised you didn't duct tape his mouth shut so that he couldn't speak during your meal. You know, since you hate talking and all."

"You're annoying," she murmurs. "And this isn't a date."

"Don't piss in my ear and tell me it's rainin'," I drawl. "I mean, hell, y'all look awfully cozy, sittin' here." I smirk, tilting my head to the side. "But tell me, Addy. Are you going to let him bury his face between your thighs the way I got to?" I watch her squirm, unable to answer. "Yeah, I didn't think so. But just in case you need a reminder of how good it felt, I can take you to the ladies' room, and we can lock that motherfucking door. I'm looking for something sweet after dinner anyway."

"Cam," she hisses, "what are you doing?"

"Tell me you aren't thinking about it right now." I hold my eyes with hers. "Tell me you don't want me to fuck you against the supply closet door right now, making you cry out again. Go on. Tell me."

Her cheeks turn a deep shade of red as she drags in a breath. But when her mouth opens to answer, Hunter appears next to the table.

"Hardy … the fuck you doing in my seat?"

"Just sayin' hi to my friend." I slide out of the booth, and Hunter sits back down. "Been a minute since I'd seen Addy. Wanted to say hi."

"You know her?" he says, sounding surprised. "How's that?"

"Oh, we go way back. Ain't that right, Addy?"

"Hardly," she mutters. "I have to go." She looks at Hunter as she stands, giving him a sweet smile. "Thank you for dinner. I appreciate it."

His face falls, and he looks like someone killed his damn puppy. "Let me give you a ride back to your car. It's dark out."

"I'm good. I don't mind walking. Besides, it's only a five-minute walk from here. Fresh air will do me good," she assures him. "Really, I'm alright. Thanks again for dinner. I'll see you in class. We'll hang out again, I promise."

Reluctantly, he nods. "Sounds good, Addison." Swinging his eyes toward me, he looks annoyed. "Hardy," he mumbles before walking over toward the pool table, where some other teammates are gathered.

As she shuffles past me and out the door, I don't try to hide it from Hunter or anyone else that I follow her.

"Come on, Addy. Get in my truck. I'll take you to your car."

She continues to walk away from me, not so much as a damn one-worded answer muttered from her lips.

"Addison," I say into the darkness, "it's late. Contrary to what you might believe, there're still bad people lurking around this campus. I can't let you walk this late. I'm not Thompson. Which, by the way, so sorry to interrupt y'all's date."

When she doesn't slow, I walk behind her. "You're leaving me no choice by not answering me, babe."

As she continues to speed-walk away from me, I grip her by the waist and toss her over my shoulder.

"Cam!" she screeches, hitting my back with her tiny fists. "Goddamn you, asshole!"

"Woman, hit me all you want, but you ain't walking at night. Over my dead body." I give her ass a small pat. "Don't make me spank you for being a bad girl. Oh, wait, you'd probably enjoy that too much."

"I am a grown-ass person. I have a child. I am capable of walking a few minutes in the damn dark!" she roars. "Put. Me. Down!"

"If you're so hell-bent on walking, fine. But I'm walking with you," I say, stopping in my tracks and gripping her legs, wishing I could inch my hand further up her thigh. I've craved her since I had my first taste. "Deal?"

She's quiet for a moment, aside from her angry, labored breathing. "Fine," she finally says. "Whatever."

Gradually, I set her down, letting her body slide down my own as I put her on her feet.

"You look pretty tonight." I look down at her. "You always do."

"Shut up," she grumbles before turning away from me. "My toddler doesn't act like as much of a baby as you just did. And that's saying something because she's three."

Stuffing my hands in my pockets, I walk right behind her. "Keep walking angry, babe. Your ass is doing a hot little sway thing as you move. I'm not mad at it."

Holding her hand up above her shoulder, she sticks her middle finger up.

"We can do that right now, if you want," I call to her. "You know you want it. *Need* it."

She ignores me, continuing to walk.

"Tell me, Addison. Why couldn't I take you to dinner? I don't get it." Not that I asked her, but she always made it clear that we were strictly only having sex. Nothing else.

She doesn't answer, so I'm forced to annoy her even further. "Are you into Thompson?"

Whipping around, she marches the few steps toward me, poking a finger into my chest.

"Shut up! Shut up! Shut the hell up! No, I'm not *into* Hunter Thompson. Are we in eighth freaking grade?" She scowls. "He asked me, and I had nothing else to do. Isla is home asleep, and I guess I figured I should just go try to be around other college kids." She looks me up and down. "That was clearly a mistake. But even if I *were* into him, it'd be none of your damn business!"

As she starts to turn away from me, I grab her wrist, pulling her into my chest.

"What makes you madder, gorgeous? That you think I'm just like your useless ex or the fact that you can't stop thinking about me?"

"Fuck you. You don't know the first thing about my ex. And I sure as hell don't think about you," she says through gritted teeth.

"Oh, but you do. You think about riding my cock, how good it felt. You think about opening that pretty mouth and letting me shove my dick in it, and you think about sitting on my face while I drive my tongue inside of you." I grip her chin, brushing my thumb across her bottom lip. "Don't even try to lie, baby. We both know the truth."

"No," she says, barely whispering the word as she drags in a long, shaky breath, trying to seem unfazed. Like she isn't really, really turned on right now.

She's a horrible actress.

"Why can't you just leave me alone?" she whispers.

"Because I'm thinking about all those same things too, babe," I say, a cocky smirk resting on my face. "All the motherfucking time."

I lean closer, giving her the idea that I might kiss her. But when her eyes flutter shut and she starts to give in to me the smallest bit, I release her chin.

Stepping around her, I stuff my hands in my pockets. It's the only way I won't touch her. "Come on now. We've still got a little walking to do."

I'm not used to girls playing hard to get. I've also been reading girls since I was eight years old. And normally, I'm what they want. Only not with Addison LaConte. Fuck no. Aside from using my penis, she wants me to leave her alone.

Too bad for Addy ... I've never been one to do as I'm told.

ADDISON

Damn you, heart, for beating that fast when he touched your face.

Damn you, knees, for shaking when he gripped your chin.

Damn you, brain, for becoming fuzzy when he leaned in closer.

Damn you, vagina, for doing that tingly thing you do whenever he's close enough to smell.

That accent. *Wowzer.* His delicious, sexy scent. *Yummy.* His playful smirk. *Lord have mercy.* His arrogant eyes. *Okay, I'm pathetic.*

We walk along quietly. Truthfully, I just wanted to tear his clothes off when he mentioned all the filthy things we had done. A hot recap, reminding me of how nice it was to have my body feel desired the way it did when we hooked up. As a female who has birthed a child ... that emotion isn't something I typically feel when I look in the mirror. But the times I was with Cam, it was never a question that I got him hot and bothered. And that in itself was empowering. The fact that I could bring a man to his knees. And not just any man. One like Cam Hardy. Who looks like sex and smells like heaven. With lickable abs and fuck-me eyes.

"Thought you said a five-minute walk," he says slowly. "It's been over fifteen, and we ain't even there yet." He looks at me, grinning. "Oh, I get it. You were trying to convince your date back there that it was fine to let you walk back alone since you said it was a short walk."

"He drove us there. He knew how long it was, dipshit." I shake my head. "Honestly, I thought it was five minutes." I can't stop the giggle that bubbles from my chest. "This is much longer than I thought."

"Real winner he is. Letting his date walk at dark." He scoffs. "Unreal."

He says the words, but I know he and Hunter Thompson are friends. I could tell by the way they interacted at Club 83.

"First of all, you sound like an egotistical maniac. No man lets a woman do anything. She does whatever the hell she pleases. And second, I thought you and Hunter were teammates?"

"We are," he says quickly. "And friends."

"So then, why are you talking shit about him?" Our walking slows as we glance at each other. "Isn't there a bro code about that?"

"Fuck bro code." His eyes connect with mine. "And I get it. You're an independent woman. I like that. I find it hot as fuck. But he took you to dinner. He should have made damn sure you made it back to your car safely." He grins, his eyes playful. "Don't get me wrong; I'm glad he didn't because, now, I get to. But still, it's fucked up."

"It wasn't a date, Cam. So, it really didn't matter."

He stops, grabbing my hand. "Then, why go?"

"What do you mean?"

"Why did you let Hunter take you to dinner, Addison? Hell, you barely wanted me to speak. I couldn't even ask you questions. You're telling me you sat there, across the booth from him, and didn't speak? I don't think so. So, why him? Why agree to go at all?" His forehead creases. "I just don't get it."

"I have no answer for you, Cam. I guess tonight just seemed like an okay night to go out for a bit. He asked. He swore it wasn't a date. I agreed. End of story."

"Are you into him?" He frowns.

"No," I say, watching him visibly sigh in relief. "But would it have mattered if I had said yes?"

As the question rolls from my lips, I hold my breath while I wait for him to answer. And truthfully, I have no idea why.

"Yeah." He gazes down at me. "To me, it would have."

"Why?"

"Because if you're going to take the time to be into someone, it'd better be me. And if you're going to go on dinner dates, I want to be the guy taking you on them." He reaches out, cupping my cheek. "Your friend might be right. Maybe I can't give you whatever it is you need. But, fuck, you never even gave me a chance to try."

"My friend?" I ask, confused. "I don't have a lot of them here. Tessa?"

"Ran into her at the coffee shop. She's feisty, that chick." He smiles the smallest bit. "She said your daddy wasn't happy about the stuffed animal."

I could be mad that Tess pushed him away. But I'm not. She's protective of me. And even though she helped convince me to hook up with Cam, she never anticipated he'd want a repeat. She knows what I went through with Nick. She knows my heart can't handle being strung along again.

"Is that why you've been avoiding me?" I guess. "Because of whatever Tessa said?"

"I mean, sort of. There are a few reasons though. Number one … your dad is my coach. And honestly, he's fucking scary. He's already not my biggest fan, and a lot of my future is in the palm of his hand. And two, she's right. You've got a kid. You have the kind of responsibilities I can't even imagine at our age. Three, all you've ever done in the short time we've known each other is tell me what we were doing was strictly physical." His other hand grazes my waist. "Trust me, I *love* doing physical shit with you. But I would have loved to take you on a date too, Addison. Instead, you let Thompson take you. And I don't get that shit because he's not an angel either."

"I went to dinner with Hunter because there was no chance I'd fall for him," I blurt out before I can stop myself. "He's not my type. I mean, he's sweet. He's clearly attractive. But he doesn't do it for me. I don't have to be scared because there's nothing to protect myself from when it comes to him. Nothing to protect Isla from."

"And with me?" He swallows, and his other hand leaves my cheek and grips the side of my waist. "You scared with me?"

"I act like a coldhearted bitch because, frankly, hanging out with you terrifies the hell out of me." I look down. "I had a lot of fun during our hookups. And trust me, it was all very much needed." I peek up at him. "But now, please … leave me be. I don't want to be the next victim whose life you leave in shambles. I'm still picking up the pieces from the last time I let someone like you in. I can't do that again." I blow out a breath. "It's not just me I have to think about."

He stares at me for a moment, and I truthfully have no idea what's about to come out of his mouth. I'm learning with a guy like Cam Hardy, it's hard to guess.

"I understand," is all he mutters. "I wish I could stand here and say nobody would get their feelings hurt. But I'm not the type of guy who makes promises he can't keep. I know I'm not what you need. I'm not good enough. But, hell, Addison, when I saw you with Thompson, it made me crazy. I saw red."

"Lust will do that," I whisper, feeling his fingertips dig into my side. "Don't worry, puck boy," I say, completely joking with him about his nickname. "Give it a few more weeks, and you'll be right back to the old Cam, charming the pants off all the women."

"Maybe," he mutters.

Leaning down, he presses a kiss to my forehead, and my heart pounds like a thousand wild horses.

"Let's get you to your car."

As he releases me, my body feels instantly chilled, and I feel my heart sink in my chest.

What if, deep down, he's one of the good ones?

And I pushed him away.

CAM

I lace up my skates and lean forward on my thighs as I sit on the bench, preparing for another grueling practice. I didn't get much sleep last night; I was up all night, remembering how Addison peeked up at me. It's obvious she's so scared to let another man in after whatever her ex pulled. I can't be the man she lets in. I'm not that good of a guy.

"Yo, Hardy," Hunter's voice calls. "What the hell was that with Addison last night?"

My eyes swing toward him, and I glare. "Why don't you say her name a little louder, dumbass. You want Coach to come kick us off the team or what?"

He looks around nervously. "Oh shit. I forgot about that."

Widening my eyes, I give him a douchey, sarcastic look. "Ya think?"

Making his way closer to me, he leans against the lockers. "But, really, are you two, like ... a thing?"

"If I say yes, you gonna stop hitting on her?"

His mouth snaps shut for a moment. "I will, yeah. You're my boy. And my captain."

That's the thing with Thompson; he is a good guy. And even though he's no angel, he isn't a complete dog either.

I sigh. "She's complicated as hell, man."

He's quiet before finally answering, "I just did it to make Paige jealous." He sounds ashamed.

"Why Addison though?" I mumble.

He shrugs. "She's gorgeous. And she seems nice and normal. Any other chick would be a stage five clinger. No way could I have simply gone on a date and then moved on with my life. The way she keeps to herself or acts like she doesn't have time for the world? I don't know. I guess I thought she'd be a good choice. Besides, she seemed like she'd make a good friend. She's a cool chick. I just figured she'd be fun to chill with."

"She is," I say softly, looking down.

Reaching forward, he pats my shoulder. "See you out there, brother." And then he heads out to the arena.

And I suddenly feel like a dick for interrupting their completely fake date.

ADDISON

"Boy, she's hungry," Tessa says, watching Isla shovel her mac and cheese in her mouth. "You sure you're feeding this kid, Ad?"

"Parenting. Some days, your kid eats like a rhino, the next like a damn insect. I swear, it's different every day." Picking at my soup and sandwich, I wiggle my eyebrows at Tessa. "So, what's new in the outside world, friend? We've both been so busy that we've barely seen each other."

"Not a lot, honestly." She sighs. "I'm sad you aren't on the team with me."

"I haven't been on the team since junior year," I point out. "You've been killing it without me."

In high school, both my and Tessa's lives revolved solely around cross-country and track. That's still true for Tess, but I haven't competitively run in years. And in all honesty, I like running to just run now. Even if that means pushing a stroller and stopping every ten minutes to pick up something Isla dropped or to open a package of crackers or refill a sippy cup.

"Doesn't mean I can't still miss my running buddy," Tessa says, pouting.

"Mommy is … is … my running buddy now, Auntie T," Isla says in between bites of macaroni and cheese. "We go fast. Right, Mommy?"

"Right, girlfriend." I run my hand through her curls. "Well, next to Auntie T, we probably look like turtles, but we have fun."

"I've seen you on the treadmill the few times we've hit the gym. You sure as shit aren't slow."

"Auntie T said a bad word! Put a quarter in my jar!" Isla says, looking up from her food.

Jar? Tessa mouths to me with a confused look on her face. "What is this jar she speaks of?"

"A bad-word jar," Isla answers with enough attitude to fill the entire room we're sitting in. "Pay up, missy."

Digging through her crossbody, she slides two quarters across the table. "I figured I'd pay for my next one in advance," she deadpans. "You run a tight ship, Miss Isla."

"Someone's got to," she answers, sounding so much older than three years old before she tightens her hold on the plush wolf under her arm. "Might as well be me."

Tess and I try to keep our faces straight, but it's hard. I swear, I never know what will come out of my kid's mouth.

We're limited to what we can talk about right now, as I don't like to say anything in front of Isla that would confuse her in any way. And even though I can tell Tessa is dying to ask me if I've heard from Cam, she knows now isn't the time. So, instead, we spend the rest of our lunch coloring with Isla before ordering a massive brownie sundae to share.

And I only thought of Cam twenty times throughout the entire meal.

ADDISON

As I focus on my studies and try to take as many classes as I can to graduate a little early, the fall semester flies by. And before I know it, it's Christmastime. If I thought I loved Christmas as a child, nothing compares to now being a parent during the holidays. Drinking hot chocolate and watching Christmas movies, pretending it's snowy outside, like it is back in New Hampshire. Isla, my mom, and I make so many cute crafts, and I package them up to send to my grandparents. It is magical, and I wish I could freeze these moments to hold on to. Because before I know it, they'll be gone.

I rock her in the chair even though she's been out for at least twenty minutes. The older she gets, the less she falls asleep in my arms. When she does, I just want to soak it in.

My mom sits down on the couch, pulling a blanket over her legs before looking at me. "Addy?"

Confused, I glance at her. "Uh … yeah?"

"Your dad and I want to run something by you. Okay?"

My dad is completely zoned out on the TV, sitting in his recliner.

"Right, Barren? We had something to ask her." When he doesn't answer, her tone changes. "Barren!" she snaps.

"Wh—yes? What is it, hon?"

"I was telling Addy that we had something to ask her. You know, the thing we talked about."

His eyes narrow, like he's trying to remember what the heck she's talking about. He stares blankly at her for a few moments before, finally, the light bulb goes on.

"Oh, yes. The thing. I remember now."

"What is this thing you keep tossing back and forth without just telling me? Are you getting divorced? Having a baby? What is it?"

Mom clears her throat. "January 7 to the night of the 10, we'd like to take Isla to New Hampshire for Aunt Kathy's surprise fiftieth."

My smile fades. "Classes start back up on the ninth. We can't go. I'd miss the first day."

"No, darling. *You* can't go," my dad says softly. "Isla could … if you let her."

"That's *three* nights. We've never spent one away from each other. Let alone three."

My mom gives me a sympathetic look. "Baby, what are you so scared of? She'll be with us. And if you're scared the Pelletiers will see her, don't be. We aren't going to Trescott, only to Cannon to stay in a nice motel right near Kathy's. There's a small children's museum across the street, and there's a kiddie pool made just for little ones." She tilts her head, giving me a small smile. "She'd have a blast, honey. I promise."

I know she'd have fun. She's three and a half years old, so of course she'd love it. But she's never even been to a museum. I should be the one to do these things with her. If I'm not, she'll notice and think I don't care about making memories.

As if reading my mind, my mom reaches for my hand. "Addy, since you've given birth to that beautiful baby, you've barely even taken time for yourself. Aside from going to school, you're here. With her. This could be a good break for you too. I know you have class for a bit of it, but during the other times, you could hang out with Tessa. Or go shopping or on a run. Heck, maybe even go to a party—"

"Nope. She's not doing that," my dad grumbles from his recliner. "No, ma'am."

Mom rolls her eyes. "Sweet Lord, Barren. She's a junior in college, for Pete's sake."

"Doesn't mean she needs to go to parties. They aren't safe," he mutters back before looking at me. "But aside from this party bullshit, I do think you deserve a break. And we deserve to take our grandgirl on a mini vacation without you hovering over us."

"Rude," I mumble. "And what if she doesn't want to go?" I look down at her sleeping face, combing my hand through her hair. "What if she wants to stay with me?"

"I guess we'll find out when you talk to her about it, right?" Mom says, looking down at my angel baby. "If you're really uncomfortable with it, we won't bring her. She's your child, and I don't want to be pushy or overbearing."

"What about practice, Dad?" I ask, confused. "You're right in the middle of the season."

"I talked to the other coaches, and they agreed to cover those practices for me," he says, and I honestly can't believe what I'm hearing. My dad has never been one to miss hockey. "It means something to your mom to go, so it means something to me too."

That's my mom. She's thoughtful and sweet, and she always gives much more than she ever takes. She's the epitome of a saint.

My dad gets up from his chair and pats us both on our heads. "Night, ladies." He leans down, kissing Mom's hair. "Love ya."

"Night, Dad. Love you." I smile as I watch my mom look up at him and say good night.

They are so in love that it's almost annoying. Only it's also really cute.

Once he's gone, we sit in the quiet living room for a few minutes. The Christmas tree shines on Isla's face, lighting her in the most stunning way as she snores softly against my chest.

"Mom?" I whisper, stroking my daughter's cheek. Feeling myself cringe that I'm about to get into my feelings.

"Yeah, babe?"

"The reason I never want to leave her or for you to take her without me is … I'm scared she'll feel like both her parents have dropped the ball. Like neither of us cares to be around." My eyes water. "I never want her to feel like she's not enough in this life. Because she is. She's so much more. That's all." I sniffle. "I know it's weird. And I worry she'll need me. She'll need me, and I won't be right there."

She's quiet for a moment before she sighs. "You know, when you were a baby, it was rough." A small laugh escapes her lips. "You didn't like to sleep—at all. I didn't know what the heck I was doing or how to soothe you when you were colicky. But even so, I refused help for months. I wanted to do everything myself." She pauses. "Well, aside from your daddy. I let him help. But your Mimi and Nana? Pfft … I pushed them away."

"Really?" I ask, surprised.

"Yep," she says, nodding. "Until one night, you had an ear infection. You had been so sick for days. You weren't able to sleep, so neither were we. And Nana LaConte? Well, after talking to your dad on the phone and hearing you wailing in the background, she showed up at our door. I tried to tell her I was fine, that she should go home. But instead, she sat down with me in the kitchen and asked if I would please let her help. She explained that not only did I deserve a break, but that I was robbing her of precious time with you as well." She smiles, sighing. "I went to bed, and I slept for six hours straight. And guess what. When I came out of my bedroom … you were fine. And your nana? She was the happiest I'd ever seen her as she sang to you while rocking. And I realized right then, momming is hard. Parenting is hard. And it's okay to let go sometimes. And that's why your dad and I made it a point to take breaks every now and then from that day forward. Because taking a break doesn't make you a bad parent. It makes you human."

"You watch her while I'm in class." A tear rolls down my cheek. "You help a lot."

Granted, I've done half of my schooling online. That is one thing I love about Brooks. It is flexible for my crazy mom schedule. But during the two classes I have to take on campus, my parents are Isla's caregivers. Never batting an eyelash at the job.

"And I love every second of it," she says, and I don't doubt her words for an instant. "If you don't want her to go to New Hampshire because you're nervous to be apart from her or you'd rather her go when you can go, that's fine. But if you don't want her to go because you think it makes you a bad mother, well, girlfriend, then I'll have a problem with it. Because, Addy, you're the best mom I know."

"I learned from the best." I smile through the tears. "Okay, you can take her. But you have to FaceTime me, like, three or four times a day. And if she misses me—"

"Then, we will head home early. Promise." She pulls me against her for a hug. "I'd never ever make her stay when she wasn't comfortable."

She holds on to me for a few minutes before pulling back. "Who knows? Maybe, in your spare time, you might just see that handsome devil who gave Isla that dang stuffed animal."

I shake my head but force out a laugh. "Not happening."

Even when I say the words, I can't help but wonder …

Why does my heart hurt when I say them?

CAM

"Hey, loser. Why are you being so quiet?" my sister, Mila, says, tossing a pillow at me.

I catch it, chucking it back at her as hard as I can, hitting her in the stomach.

"Dick," she murmurs just as Beau walks in the room, handing her a water.

"Thanks, babe," she says, grinning as he takes the seat next to her, resting his hand on her thigh protectively.

When it comes to my sister, he'd kill for her. That's how much she means to him. Then again, she'd do the same for him.

"Gross," I groan.

"Back to you, asswipe. Why are you being so quiet? It's Christmas night. A magical day has been had. Why do you have your pissy pants on?"

"I don't," is all I mutter back. "Just tired, and I have to wake up at the asscrack of dawn to head back to Georgia."

"Big whoop. We have to drive to Florida. Don't be a pansy." Mila glares. "That isn't it, and I know it. So, what is it? Problems with the team? Your coach still being a horse's ass?" Her eyes widen as she leans forward. "It's a girl, isn't it? You're all mopey and stuff over a girl."

"Now, that would be funny." Beau chuckles. "Please say that's it. Tell me Cam Hardy has finally met his match. Someone to be a pain in his ass all the time."

"Oh, yeah, that's comical right there." Mila socks him on the arm. "The only pain in the ass in our relationship, my love, is you and your grumpy ass. Now, shut up. We're talking about Cam, not you."

My sister fixates on me and only me as she tilts her head to the side. "Okay, big bro, spill the deets. Who is she? Where is she? And most importantly ... what did you do?"

I open my mouth to speak, but honestly, I have nothing to say. I've thought about Addison a lot, and yet I still know that I have no business thinking about her. Even if she ever did want to give me a chance, it wouldn't be fair to her if I strung her along, pretending to be something I'm not. I'm not the guy who saves the single mother from raising a kid herself. And I'm not the guy who gives up his future in hockey by doing something as reckless as dating the coach's daughter. I know my place. And next to her isn't it.

"Nah, it's not like that," I say, plastering on my fake carefree grin just as my dad walks into the living room. "Whatcha say, old man? Want to take the Challenger out for a Christmas cruise?"

His face lights up. I didn't follow in his footsteps when it came to racing, like Mila did, but I still appreciate a sick muscle car the way he does. And his Challenger is no exception. The time I have shown up at the racetrack in the past, he's been nice enough to let me drive it.

I don't get home to see my parents nearly as much as I'd like to. Between classes and hockey, it's hard. So, times like this, when I'm back home, even if it is only for two days, I try to spend as much time with them as I can. My sister and Beau too. I missed that fucker when he took his little hiatus from our family. I'm happy to have him back. Really happy.

As I stand and follow him to the door, he hollers over his shoulder to my mom as she continues to wash dishes in the kitchen, "Be back in a bit, hon. Gotta make Cam piss himself."

"You wish," I say, smacking him on the shoulder. "I've ridden with Mila before. Nothing can scare me."

"True that," Beau mutters under his breath, earning him a harsh glare from my sister.

"Let's go, old man." I point at Beau and my sister. "Y'all get all that touchy-feely shit out now. When I get back, I don't want to see it." I pat my stomach. "The turkey and mashed potatoes I ate are still settling; don't make me puke it up."

"I'll take care of that," my dad says with a laugh as we walk out the door.

And I have no doubt he means it.

About forty-five minutes later, after we take turns driving way too fast, trying to scare each other, I pull the car into a parking lot in town and shift it into park.

"So, bud, you gonna tell me who she is? Or am I going to have to keep on waitin' till I'm old as fuck?"

My gaze swings over to find him grinning.

"I know my boy. And you've only had this look one other time. It was when you were ten and injured your hand. Couldn't play hockey the rest of the season." His eyes stay on mine, leaving me no way to hide from telling him the truth. "Who is she? Hockey has always been your love, but I'm beginning to think you might have finally pulled your head out of your ass and found your *real* love."

I know there's no sense in lying. He'll know that I'm keeping something from him. *Love* is a strong word; I wouldn't toss that around right now. But I'm definitely thinking about her much more than I should be.

"Addison," I say, turning my gaze forward. "Trouble is, she's the coach's daughter."

"Shit," Dad mumbles. "I take it, he isn't a fan of the two of you?"

"He'd probably cut my nutsack off if he knew." I cringe. "And … she's sort of got a kid."

"What the hell you mean, sort of? I've got two of you little fuckers. Let me tell ya, there ain't nothin' *sort of* about it. She either does or she don't."

"She does. A daughter. Think she's three." My head falls back on the headrest. "The kid looks just like her mama."

"Pretty? This Addison?"

"Gorgeous," I say, thinking about just how beautiful she is before snapping back to reality. "But like I said, coach's daughter. Has a kid. Never gonna work, Pops."

"Now, don't be so sure of that." He nudges me. "Do y'all like each other?"

"I wouldn't go that far." I chuckle, looking at him. "I mean, I like her. I don't know what she likes. She's difficult."

"The good ones always are." He grins. "What are you more scared of, boy? The coach being mad or dating someone who has a child?"

I think about it, not sure how to answer his question. On one hand, hell yes, I'm scared Coach would single-handedly fuck my future up simply because I hooked up with his daughter. But, on the other hand, to hell with him. I might mess up sometimes, but I'm a good man. I was raised by great parents. Who is he to decide that I'm not good enough for Addison?

Even though I'm probably not.

Then, there's the other side of it. The side where there's a kid involved. That would make this dating thing so much harder. If it didn't work out, there'd be more than just my and Addison's feelings involved.

And then there's the third side. The side where she pushes me away like I'm the damn plague.

"Both, I guess." I drag a hand over my face. "I've never even had a girlfriend. I doubt my first one ought to be a mature chick with a kid."

"You know the funny thing about love, Cam? It doesn't really care about the obstacles that might make things tough. After all, nothing in this life that's worthwhile is ever gonna come easy."

"I *don't* love her, you crazy old bastard. Hell, I barely know her."

"All right then," he says coolly. "Then, what the hell you so wound up for? Move on with your life, boy."

I know he's testing me. Or calling my bluff. I don't love Addison, not yet anyway. But if I kept going around her, that might be a different story. Chasing her would be like playing with fire. And I'm not really looking to be burned.

"Let's head back home before Mom has our asses for missing dessert." I put the car in drive and pull out of the parking spot. "I know you've had your eye on that apple pie all afternoon."

"Damn straight." He rubs his hands together.

And as we start to drive home, he pats my shoulder. "Just follow your heart, Cam. You do that, and you'll never fail."

I don't answer. Just give him a nod.

Because even if I do follow my heart, how do I know she won't rip it from my chest and stomp all over it?

14

CAM

"Run that last play again, boys," Coach McIntire calls to us, tucking his clipboard under his arm. "If you do it perfectly, I'll let you get on out of here." He smirks. "Mess it up, and I'll make y'all do it till you get it right."

We run it, and as I suspected, it's not perfect.

Coach McIntire shakes his head and points to the center of the ice again. "Do it again."

We go through this three more times until we finally get it right.

Clapping, he smiles. "About time. Get on out of here."

I wipe the sweat from my forehead, making my way off the ice behind the rest of the team. It wasn't a terrible practice by any standards, but we still worked, and I'm fucking smelly and ready for a shower.

"I'm just going to say it. Practice was much more peaceful without LaConte screaming at us, telling us we suck," Brody mutters, walking behind me. "How long is that grump ass gone for anyway?"

"Not long enough," Link deadpans. "I heard he'll be back in a few days. Went back to New Hampshire to visit family."

I wonder if Addison is with them or if she and her daughter stayed back here. The boys can talk shit about Coach all they want, but I think we all know our team has been playing better than we ever have, and it's all thanks to him. Asshole or not … dude cares about one thing. Winning.

I grab a towel and head for the shower. Turning it on to a level of heat that basically burns my skin off. I'm happy as hell that we have the weekend off from games. Although, during a game is the only time I get to see Addison's pretty face, sitting in her usual seat. After the one she skipped because of Nick Pelletier, it was nice to see her at the one last weekend. Her and her mini Addison.

When I traveled home for Christmas, my dad told me to follow my heart. The trouble with that is, I don't even know what the hell that entails. So, I've just been doing shit how I've always done it. Hockey. Party. Sleep. Repeat.

"A bunch of us want to go to that sick indoor go-kart track tomorrow," Brody hollers from the other shower. "You in, Hardy?"

I squirt some body wash into my hand, rubbing it over my sweat-soaked skin. "No can do. Sorry, brother. I'm headed to Florida tonight. Beau's team is playing in the championship tomorrow. Told Mila I'd go watch."

"Whatevs," Brody calls back. "You always race dirty anyway. You got that Jaxon Hardy blood advantage."

"Fuck that. I'd say Mila Hardy blood." Link chuckles. "Either way, without Cam there, I'll have a better chance of winning this time."

They aren't wrong. Growing up around drag racing with my dad, I'm no stranger to driving the wheels off anything—even a simple go-kart.

Turning the water off, I grab my towel and dry off. "Y'all have fun with that. Don't hurt yourselves."

"No chance." Brody laughs. "I'm putting Link right into the wall."

"Fuck off," Link grumbles.

Wrapping my towel around my waist, I head to my locker. I have my bag packed in my truck, and time's a-wasting. I don't want to be on the road in the middle of the night.

"I'll see you boys when I get back. Don't have any parties and ruin the apartment while I'm gone."

"No promises!" they both yell to me as I head out the door.

And with those two, I'm sure they aren't kidding.

ADDISON

I pull into the convenience store and unbuckle my seat belt. The last thing I wanted to do was cook a dinner for just myself, so I ordered a crappy gas-station pizza.

Pulling my phone out, I shoot my mom a message.

Me: How's it going? How's Isla?

I wait impatiently for a few minutes, considering calling instead. My parents can call and text, but they aren't exactly tech-savvy.

Finally, my phone dings.

Mom: Same as an hour ago. Perfect. Busy playing.

Me: Sorry.

Mom: Don't be. I know you're missing her. But I promise, she's doing great. We're keeping her busy so that she won't miss her mama.

Mom: Are you enjoying your quiet time?

Me: No. Just grabbing a pizza. Check back in an hour.

Mom: I don't doubt it.

I set my phone in my cupholder and head inside.

They left early yesterday morning, and just a few hours ago, I received an email that, due to the professor's illness, my class tomorrow is canceled. So, that means I could have gone on the trip. After reading the email, I immediately looked up flights to New Hampshire. Unfortunately for me, there were no reasonably priced flights till the day they are due to fly back.

Pushing the door open to the store, I head to the deli counter, where they make the pizzas.

"Hi," I say, smiling my best to look friendly. The cook here is known to be grouchy. "I called in a pizza. Under Addison."

"Yep, right here." He grabs the box from the warmer and drops it down onto the counter.

"Thank you." I wave, picking it up.

"Uh-huh," he grumbles before going back to what he was doing.

My eyes widen before I head toward the coolers. Normally, I'm not a drinker, but a few beers with my pizza doesn't sound bad at all tonight.

"Crazy Sunday night, huh?" a deep voice drawls next to me.

Craning my neck, I see Cam grabbing a Sprite.

Looking down at my pizza in one hand and a six-pack of Coors Light in the other, I cringe. "About as crazy as mine get."

He looks around. "Where's Isla?"

The way he says it, he's not judging me for being here without her. He's simply curious.

I sigh, remembering I'm going home to an empty, quiet house.

"With my parents in New Hampshire, unfortunately. Trust me, I'm not a bad mom. I would have loved for her to stay home with me. But when they mentioned a pool and a children's museum to her … yeah, suddenly, staying home with mom didn't seem too cool."

He eyes me over, the wheels in his head turning. "Why didn't you go too?"

"Because classes start tomorrow, and I didn't want to miss it." I look down. "Sort of regretting my choice, truthfully. Especially since I just found out my class was canceled."

Tessa is out of town with her team. And honestly, I have no other friends at Brooks yet. So, essentially, I am on my own.

"Come to Florida with me tonight," he says, letting the words roll off his tongue so carelessly. Like he isn't asking me to drive across a state line. "My buddy Beau's team, Florida East, is playing their championship game tomorrow. I don't have practice tomorrow and no class till Wednesday, so I told my sister I'd go."

He must see the confusion in my eyes about why his sister would want him to go to his friend's game because he grins.

"Beau is my childhood best friend and also my sister's boyfriend."

"Ahh," I say, nodding, "I see."

I fight an internal battle in my head, not knowing what the heck to say. I haven't spoken to this man in weeks. Besides, if we stay somewhere together tonight, we'll end up naked. It's inevitable.

"What do you say? Bring that pizza of yours, grab some candy, ditch those beers for sodas, and we'll be on our way."

"When are you coming home?" I ask.

"I'll be heading back early Tuesday morning," he answers. "Gotta get back for practice."

I'm picking my parents and Isla up from the airport Tuesday night. So, technically … I could go.

"Come on, babe. What's the worst that could happen?" He smirks, leaning lazily against the cooler.

"We could get naked *again* and hook up," I deadpan.

"That'd be the best-case scenario, gorgeous." He tilts his head. "You're alone. I'm alone. Let's go be loners together."

116

I seriously consider his offer. It sounds fun. *A hell of a lot better than sitting at home alone, remembering my best friend is a toddler.*

"What about your friend? And your sister? Won't they ask who I am?"

"I'll tell them the truth," he says, his eyes piercing into mine. "That you're a friend."

I chew my lip before finally opening the cooler and tucking the beer back inside. Walking around Cam, I grab a Diet Coke. "Okay ... you're on. But we can't have sex."

"Why the hell not?"

"Because sex makes things messy. We've already had sex a handful of times. No more. It'll only complicate things."

"Sweetheart, I don't know if you're forgetting our hookups, but there was nothin' complicated about it." He reaches for my stuff, piling the pizza and soda up in his hand. "Let's go find some snacks before we hit the road."

As he saunters toward the candy aisle, my legs nervously carry me behind him.

I'm going on a trip with Cam Hardy.
A trip where we will spend multiple nights together.
What could possibly go wrong?

CAM

I wait in the truck outside of her house. After I convinced her to ride to Florida with me tonight, she informed me, before we left town, we needed to stop at her house so she could drop her car off and grab an overnight bag.

After talking to my dad at Christmas, I told myself to just leave her be. And that even though she was the one pushing me away, one day, she'd be asking me to stay, and I wouldn't be able to. Because there will come a day when the pros call me. And when they do, I won't have time for girlfriends.

But then I saw her tonight, her curly hair pulled into a messy ponytail, and something inside of me snapped. I needed to be around her. I wouldn't take no for an answer.

She shuts the door, locking it behind her, and heads toward my truck, a small duffel bag in her hand. Pushing my own door open, I jump down from the truck and jog around to the passenger side.

"I got ya," I say, reaching for the bag before pulling the door open for her to get in.

As she climbs up in the seat, she looks at me with a shy smile on her face. Resting her head against the leather seat, she sighs. "What the heck am I doing?"

Running my thumb along her chin, I lean in and kiss her cheek. "Keeping my ass company and saving both of us from a night of boredom."

She smells so sweet. And I love the way her hair kinks up around her face. She's a natural beauty—that's for sure.

"Well, I suppose we should get going then, shouldn't we?" She looks at me.

"Yes, ma'am," I say softly. "Buckle up."

Closing the door, I wonder how in the world I'm supposed to keep my hands off this beautiful creature.

Especially when we'll be sharing a damn hotel room tonight.

Fuck.

ADDISON

The ride starts off sort of quiet. Both of us not really knowing what to say or where to begin. But about twenty-five minutes in, I find myself immersed in a conversation that shows no signs of stopping.

"You must be sooo sad that my dad's gone for a few days, huh?" I giggle.

"Fuck n—" He catches himself. "Uh ... yeah, obviously. I'm basically his biggest fan."

"Ha," I blurt out. "Right."

He glances over at me. His brown hair always seems to fall perfectly even though I know he doesn't try. "Honestly, he isn't too bad sometimes. And other times, he fucking hates my guts."

I know my dad's a hard-ass on all players. But I also know he isn't Cam's biggest fan simply because of his stunt, giving Isla the wolf, harmless as it might have been.

"Did any of those times when he was harsh happen to fall around that one time you decided to give his granddaughter that damn wolf?" I look at him, a knowing look on my face when his jaw tightens. "Yeah ... I figured."

"He never said anything about it ... but, hell, I knew he was pissed." He cringes. "He'd have a heart attack if he knew you were with me right now."

"Probably," I say quietly. "But even you said there're times he isn't too bad. So, maybe, just maybe, he doesn't hate you as much as we both think."

"Yeah, right." He laughs. "Only times he's been halfway nice was, one, when we did that damn trunk-or-treat shit and, two, when I helped us win that game against North Carolina."

I stiffen at his words, knowing he means the game against Nick. Of course Dad was happy with Cam if he helped the team get that win. That game meant everything to Dad.

"The last thing I'd ever want to do is make you uncomfortable, but if it isn't too personal … would you mind sharing the history there? Between him and Pelletier." He looks over at me for a moment. "Noticed you guys weren't at that game."

"You noticed?" I can't hide the shock in my voice.

"I always notice you, Addison. I always see when you're there."

I shift my attention out the window. I suppose now is as good of a time as any to dive into my history with my ex. It isn't something I like to talk about often, but I can understand why he's curious about who Nick is and why we weren't at that game.

"Nick is Isla's dad." I blow out a breath, the words tasting like vinegar, coming from my mouth. "And a former player of my dad's. Let's just say … he wasn't the man we'd thought he was. And Dad isn't exactly fond of him."

"He see her?" he says quietly in the dark cab of the truck. "Isla, I mean. Does he see her?"

"He does not," I say, wringing my hands together.

"Has he, uh … ever?"

"Not that she's aware of." I swallow. "When we still lived back home, we'd see him and his family in town from time to time. They never acknowledged her, and I didn't push." A sad, small laugh, mixed with bitterness, escapes my lips. "After I told him I was pregnant, he told me it was either I get an abortion or we were done. It was the easiest, best decision I've ever made."

I feel that familiar ache form in my gut. The guilt, wishing I could change Isla's story to make it less painful for her later in life.

"I'm sorry. That couldn't have been easy." He reaches for me, taking one of my hands in his. "Having a baby on your own …"

"It wasn't. And to be honest, I tried calling him right after she was born, but he had blocked my number." I look down, shaking my head. "And if that doesn't make me pathetic enough, I showed up at his house after too. I just wanted to make sure that he was one thousand percent positive that he didn't want to know his daughter, you know?"

"And?"

"He and his family basically wanted to toss some money at me and my family to make us leave town. His dad is the mayor. They didn't want anyone to know that their perfect boy had gotten a girl pregnant in high school." I swallow back the lump forming in my throat. "I'd never seen people be so cold. And she's *their* blood. He created her too." I sigh. "I'll never be able to make sense of it."

"That's fucked up," he practically whispers, giving my hand a gentle squeeze. "I'm so, so sorry, Addison. But that girl is so lucky to have you as a mom." He pauses. "You'll always protect her. Even at your own expense."

"That's what being a parent is," I say. "Or what it should be at least. Take right now, for instance. I miss the crap out of her. And it's barely been a couple of days."

Talking this openly about the situation with my ex is something I've only done with Tessa and my mom. I've never said much to Dad because, frankly, he gets angry, and it only causes him pain to rehash the past.

"You know what? I think we've got time for one stop. And this stop just happens to be one where it needs to be dark," he says playfully. "What do you say?"

"I say, what the hell? YOLO, right?"

"YO-fucking-LO," he singsongs, quickly turning down a side road. "I have a surprise for you then. Because I heard about this place on Facebook, and we just so happen to be driving right by. No time like the present, right?"

I have a feeling he is trying to lighten the mood. Or cheer me up. Either way, I'm both nervous and excited for wherever he's about to bring me. And even though I'm having fun right now, in the back of my head, I'm thinking I need to be careful. Any woman could fall in love with that grin.

Cam is the kind of guy who's easy to lose yourself in. And I can't do that. After all, I still need to find myself.

CAM

I don't understand this feeling in my chest whenever she looks at me. Or the way my skin prickles when my hand touches her skin. Or why the fuck I melt into a puddle at her feet when she gushes about her daughter.

Get. It. Together. Asshole.

I've never given a fuck about anyone else's happiness besides my family's. But with her? I'd do anything just to make her smile.

"The Botanical Gardens?" She whirls around. "I've always wanted to come to them. I figured the lights were taken down since Christmas is over."

"They keep it going till the end of January, apparently."

I admire her taking in the lights. They are beautiful, no doubt. But not nearly as beautiful as her seeing them for the first time.

Thousands of twinkly lights span over the entire park. Over trees and on the bushes.

"I almost feel like I'm home," she whispers. "Besides that we're walking in light sweatshirts, and at home, I'd have full snow gear."

The way she says *home*, I sense she misses New Hampshire. I guess I don't blame her. Georgia and New England are two entirely different places. I'm sure it's been a big adjustment.

As she walks ahead of me, she stops and looks up at the huge archway that's covered with lights.

I reach for her, holding her waist as I put my chin on her shoulder. "Thanks for coming on this trip, gorgeous."

Craning her neck slightly, she peers at me. "Thanks for asking. I'd probably be three or four cookies deep and FaceTiming my mother for the tenth time today to see Isla."

"Sweetheart, I know you said no hookups, but I really, *really* need to kiss you."

"Cam," she says, barely whispering, "you shouldn't kiss me. We shouldn't complicate things."

Stepping back, I turn her to face me. Slowly backing her up into the darkness behind the archway, I press her chin up with my thumb. "Yeah, I've told myself that for weeks. But you know what? I'm done with that now." Resting my other hand on the tree behind her, I dip my head closer to hers. "What's the point in trying to stay away when all I want is you?"

She blinks. "Cam, you don't mean that—"

"I do though. I really do."

"How can you be so sure?" she says, challenging me. "How do you know that, in a week or two, this won't fizzle out? That you won't lose interest?"

"Because I've never given a fuck about anyone until you." I move my hand to her cheek. "Ever since you rocked my world our first night together, you haven't left my mind."

Her eyes fill with tears. "You don't understand. I can't take chances. My dad. Isla—"

"Your dad will get over it. And as for Isla, it doesn't scare me that you're a mother. Not at all. Which actually scares the shit out of me."

She stares up at me, the light hitting her tear-soaked cheeks. "If this is a game, I don't want to play."

"Not a game. I'll prove it to you."

I waste no time before kissing her hard. Her lips tangle with mine, and her hands find my back.

A small moan comes from her mouth, and I swallow it up.

Pulling back, I rest my forehead against hers. "We need to go before I fuck you against this tree and someone sees." I step back, pulling her with me. "I don't think either one of us feels like going to jail tonight for public indecency." Feeling my dick swell up against my zipper, I cringe, adjusting myself. "Though it sure would be worth it to feel you wrapped around my co—"

She presses a finger to my lips, widening her eyes. "Shut up! There're people around us, you know!"

"Good. Hope they enjoyed listening to you get all hot and bothered." I wiggle my eyebrows. "I sure did. Though I'd prefer you save those sounds just for me."

She smacks me lightly, but I throw my arm around her shoulders as we walk toward the rest of the lights. This feels unbelievably right. So, how on earth could it be wrong? So what if I don't know the first thing about kids and her daddy is going to kill me? We'll figure it out.

I hope.

"This is truly magical," she whispers. "I wish Isla could see it. She'd freak out."

"She will one day. We'll bring her," I say, dragging her in closer to me, tucking her small frame under my arm. "I promise."

And the scariest part of that promise I just made?

I meant every word.

15

ADDISON

Tonight honestly feels like a fairy tale. The dark night was lit by the most beautiful display of lights at the botanical gardens. Christmas music played lightly through the air as we walked around in absolutely no rush at all. And as Cam promised that, one day, we'd bring Isla back here ... I believed him. Which was crazy because this was still so new.

I think back to when he said he'd be right back and he came back with a hot chocolate for me and a popcorn, grinning from ear to ear when he saw my excitement. Cam Hardy is nothing like who I pegged him to be. Which would be awesome, if I wasn't scared to death of falling for him.

We drive toward the hotel he called earlier. He said it sounded like a nice place, but honestly, as special as the botanical gardens was ... it could be a dive, and I'd be content.

Luke Combs plays over the speakers as Cam sings quietly along with him. With his Southern accent, he can actually carry a tune, and it makes my heart squeeze in my chest as I listen to him sing the words to "Going, Going, Gone."

During the ride, I've learned more about his family and where he grew up. But what was refreshing was, he asked more about me. In fact, I kept having to point the conversation toward him to get the attention off of my life. But it showed he cared, and that was different than my past relationship. Cam wanted to know what my life goals were after college and what it was like, being pregnant in high school. He even asked about Isla.

"So, can you do me a favor?" I say once the song ends. I didn't want to ask him in the middle of it, in fear he'd stop singing. "With Beau and your sister, could we just stick to the story that we're just friends?" I feel my palms start to sweat. "I mean, I know we are just friends. But, like … you know."

He must hear the nerves in my voice because he glances over and smiles. "We aren't just friends, and you know it. Not sure we were ever just friends. But, sure, I'll play along with that … for now."

I laugh. "Well, back when this first started, I definitely wouldn't say we were friends."

"Only because you were a jerk," he says, pretending to pout. "Basically stapled my lips shut during sex and didn't let me speak."

"You talk a lot!" I giggle, clutching my stomach. "*Chatty Cathy.*"

"Still don't know who this Cathy is and why she's chatting, but oh well." He shrugs before his body language changes. "So … your dad. How do you want to go about handling that whole deal?"

I suck in a breath. My dad isn't going to like this. At all. It needs to be managed delicately.

"We'll figure it out when we get back to Georgia. Deal?"

"I suppose that's fine," he says before turning into a parking lot.

As we gaze at the hotel, he shrugs. "Oh, good. Doesn't look like a place we'll get shot tonight. That's a plus."

I shake my head, reaching for my bag in the back as he parks. "Thank God for that."

And as I push my door open, I feel those familiar butterflies growing in my stomach that he always seems to give me. Because, in a few minutes … we're going to be alone.

For an entire night.

CAM

"I don't really understand. It's showing up on my online banking that you charged my card. How do I not have a room reserved?" I show the guy behind the counter the charge that went through not long ago. "So … yeah, we'll leave and stay somewhere else, but you're going to have to give me my money back."

"There really is no need to have an attitude, Mr. Hardy," he says, rolling his eyes.

The dude is a dick. He looks like a dick. Sounds like a dick. *Is* a dick. And it's no surprise when I glance at his name tag that it says Richard.

"Hey, Dick—can I call you Dick? Good. So, here's what's up. If you continue to be a prick, I'll gladly show you just what sort of attitude I can have." I glance over my shoulder at Addison waiting on a bench, tossing her a smile.

Directing my attention back to Dick, I lean over the counter. "So, either figure it out with a fucking smile or shit's going to hit the fan. Okay?"

"I'll get my manager," he mutters, acting annoyed.

Shortly after, a man in his mid-sixties with white hair walks around the corner, Dick right on his heels.

"Hi, sir. I'm Jansen, the manager here. What seems to be the problem?" he asks once he reaches me. His eyes narrow slightly before widening. "Cam Hardy? Brooks University center Cam Hardy?"

"Uh … yep," I say, looking around. "Look, I booked a room here. Y'all charged my card, but this nice fella, Dick—"

"Richard," Dick corrects me.

"Dick," I say, continuing my story, "seems to think I don't have a room."

Jansen's eyes swing to good ol' Dick, and he shoots him a glare. "The star player of my favorite hockey team sure as hell has a room here," he grumbles at his coworker. "In fact, he'll have the *finest* room here simply for this inconvenience."

"Oh, sir, that's not necessary. Really—" I start to say, but he holds his hand up.

"Nonsense."

Typing a few things on the computer in front of him, he hands me a key. "Finest suite in the entire resort. Enjoy your stay, Mr. Hardy. And I hope you'll forgive Richard here."

"Of course," I say, grinning at the pair of them. "I sure appreciate it. Y'all have a good night."

As I make my way toward Addison, she narrows her eyes questionably. Probably wondering what in the hell took so long.

"Looks like we have ourselves a suite," I say as she stands. Dipping my mouth closer to her ear, I smirk. "Can't wait to check out all the different places I can fuck you." I feel her shiver against me, so I push it further. "Where, oh where, will we start?"

As I step back, I pick her bag up and jerk my chin toward the elevator. "Come on, sweet thing. That clock's ticking, and I need my hands on your body right now."

As I press the button to the elevator and impatiently wait for those doors to open, I glance over at the beauty next to me, thankful she's here. I didn't come here tonight, looking for an upgraded room. But I'm going to enjoy every square foot of it with Addison.

A beeping noise, followed by doors opening, has never sounded better. I look at her, tilting my head toward the opening, and slowly, she makes her way inside with me right on her ass.

"Floor twelve, babe," I say and watch as her finger presses the button.

Setting our bags down, I pull her back against my chest. Her ass teases my cock, and I bury my face in her neck.

"Fucking hell, I'm dying to feel you wrapped around my cock, Addison. It's been way too long."

She shivers, grinding her ass against me harder.

"I'm going to make you realize just how much you missed me too." I slide my hands down her sides and grip her waist. "We can watch the sunrise together, baby, because I plan to still be balls deep inside you when it comes up."

Just as the elevator reaches floor twelve, I give her ass a slap and grab our bags. I haven't been inside of her since that day in my truck. I'm not wasting another second.

ADDISON

Whirls of emotion run through my entire body as I watch Cam slide the key over the door sensor. But mostly ... between my legs tingles with need. When I told him at that gas station that we wouldn't be having sex, did I actually believe it? I don't think so. And if I did, I was dumb. Obviously, when you put Cam and me together, in a room alone, our clothes are magically going to fall off. It's practically basic science, the two of us.

Since becoming a mother, I've tried to always do the responsible thing. I look at things from all angles. Study them. Maybe make a pros and cons list. And then, after careful thought and deliberation, I make a decision. I did it with my first car, when I chose what career I hoped to pursue, and when it came to moving to Georgia. Hell, I even do it when I'm ordering a coffee. Everything is so. Thought. Out. Not tonight. Not when Cam kissed me at the botanical gardens and told me he wanted me. I didn't push him away even though the list of cons sure as hell would be long. I didn't push him away because ... it felt right. It felt good.

I'll probably regret letting him in one day, but right now ... I'm diving in headfirst.

I texted my mom on the way here. They were busy at my aunt's birthday party, and when I asked to call just before we got to this hotel, she told me Isla was passed out cold.

The door makes a small clicking noise, and Cam pushes it open, whistling when he sees the inside.

Holding it open for me, he nods for me to walk in. The door barely shuts behind him before his hands wrap around me, spinning me around to face him. He cups my cheeks, dragging my mouth to his.

As his lips attack mine, he backs me up until my ass hits what feels like a table. Tearing my shirt over my head, he tosses it to the side, leaving me in my bra. And when he peels my jeans and panties down slowly, I somehow feel more naked than ever even though we've been together multiple times now.

Maybe it's because, now, it isn't so cut and dry as just sex. Something has shifted, and I find us looking at each other differently. More in depth.

Kissing his way down my neck and to my stomach, he doesn't stop until he reaches my thigh. And when he does, he stretches his hand across my belly and pushes me backward so that I'm lying back on the table. His tongue hits between my legs, and I can't help but grasp at his hair, tangling it in my fingers.

I lean forward just as his tongue glides inside of me, making me whimper with pleasure. And when he hears me, he looks up, his eyes hooded as he continues working me with his mouth. I feel my orgasm building as my lower stomach begins to tingle. A feeling that washes its way down my body, stopping at the center and making me cry out.

Knowing I'm at my release, he slips a finger inside and then another. Pumping in and out, bringing me to a whole other universe.

I'm barely down from my high when he climbs out from under me and pulls his pants and briefs down. His cock springs free, and when he palms himself and begins to pump, I moan with need.

"Cam," I say, sounding completely desperate and probably pathetic.

He reaches for my bra, unclipping it before he rears back to study me, and I find myself painfully aware of the fact that my boobs probably don't look like the other girls he's hooked up with. I'm a mom. Things stretch. And change.

He must sense my discomfort. "What's wrong, babe? If you want me to stop, I'll stop."

I shake my head. "I'm just … could we maybe dim the lights a bit more?"

Looking around, he scowls. "Fuck no. I want to see every inch of this body. And when you sit on my cock, I need to watch your face." He runs his hands up my sides. "What do I have to say to make you believe how gorgeous you are?"

"I have stretch marks. On my breasts. Stomach. Thighs. Probably vagina for all I know." I sigh. "My body isn't as new and shiny as the other girls you've been with. I'm sure you haven't been with many people who have been pregnant. Pregnancy changes everything."

"Trust me, there're no stretch marks on your vagina, babe. Just pure magic." He tilts his chin up. "And guess how many girls I've been with who I cared about seeing again or who I even remember jack shit about, whether the actual sex *or* their bodies. Zero." He kisses me, hard, but not aggressive. "With you, I remember every fucking inch of this body that was made for me. And it's perfect." His eyes suddenly look sad. "I just wish you could see yourself through my eyes, Addison. Because to tell you the truth, you practically give me a damn heart attack every time we get close."

When I just stare at him, still holding my chest, he grabs one of my hands and puts it over his heart. "Feel that?" he whispers. "That's what you do to me. And that's what happens every single time we do this."

His heart beats fast and hard against the palm of my hand, and I smile.

Who would have ever thought the campus puck boy actually had this big of a heart? And the craziest part? He's showing it to me.

"I love every part of your body, Addison," he says. "But if you don't want to do this, it's okay."

"I want to," I say quickly. "Please."

His hand returns to his length, and his breath hitches. "Good. Because truthfully, I don't know how much longer I can go."

Bending over, he pulls a foil packet from his jeans and rolls it over himself. Starting at my ankles, he glides his hands up both of my legs, pushing them apart. "Goddamn it," he hisses. "Fucking perfect."

He pulls me upward, and I wrap my legs around his waist as he keeps my ass on the table. Nudging his hard length inside of me little by little, he groans.

"You have no idea how many times I've thought about this the past few weeks. How many times I've fucked my hand, remembering what you felt like, wrapped around my cock."

"Cam. Oh … God," I whimper.

The combination of him slowly filling me to the max and his filthy mouth pushes me over the edge of need.

"That's right; say my name while I drive my dick so far inside of you that you scream," he growls, moving faster in and out of me.

My breasts are on full display, and I no longer care. He looks at me with nothing but desire, making me feel beautiful.

His hands grip my thighs as he spreads my legs further apart, driving himself impossibly deep inside of me. It hurts. But it also feels too damn good to pay attention to the pain.

This gorgeous man is anything but gentle with me. And somehow, I wouldn't want it any other way. The way he possesses my body, claiming it as his, is incredibly erotic.

Without warning, he pulls out and tugs me off the table. Dragging me to the window, he turns the light off and bends me over. My hands find the glass, and I gaze down at a river, realizing someone could see us and yet I don't want to stop.

All at once, he fills me, and I cry out from the sheer fullness. My forehead presses against the glass as he slaps my asscheek hard.

"This angle—Christ, Addy. You're so goddamn beautiful."

His thighs slap against the backs of my legs as he works in and out of me.

Grabbing a fistful of my hair, he pulls my head back slightly. "Tell me how much you missed me, baby."

"So much," I say, trying to force the words out while my brain is spinning into complete oblivion. "So, so much."

He leans forward, kissing between my shoulder blades before moving to my shoulder and giving my skin a bite. "Tell me you're mine, Addison."

"Cam," I whine out as he somehow seems to bury himself deeper.

"Fucking say it," he grunts, tightening his hold on my hair and biting down harder.

I try to form words, but nothing comes to mind. Pulling out, he turns me to face him before lifting me up and pressing me against the wall next to us. His erection drives inside of me, and I yelp.

"I've never wanted anything so bad in my whole fucking life, Addy." He kisses me, one hand tangling in my hair and the other holding the weight of me up. "Put me out of my misery and just say you're mine."

Gazing at him, I breathe out, "I'm yours." I feel a tear, followed by another, roll down my cheek before I can even comprehend that I'm crying. "I'm all yours."

He stills. "What's wrong?" His forehead creases. "Don't cry. I don't want to make you cry."

"Don't stop," I say, sounding breathy and desperate. "Please."

He looks nervous, but slowly, that look fades away, and he pounds into me, pushing me harder against the wall. We don't speak as he continues to fuck me. And when his head drops down against my shoulder and he breathes heavier, it's clear he's close.

"Addy," he whispers, "come with me?"

"Yes," I say, trembling as a wave washes over my body.

And for however long this orgasm lasts, there's nothing else in the world besides me and Cam. And in this moment, I admit to myself something that I've tried to avoid …

I'm falling for the guy who was supposed to be a simple hookup.

A while later, once we've finally peeled ourselves off each other and showered, we look around the extremely nice room we are lucky enough to stay in tonight.

"Holy fuck, I guess it's good they messed up on their end, huh? This place is sick," he mutters, walking behind me.

One entire wall is nothing but windows, giving us a view of a river below. A view I got well acquainted with when Cam had me bent over a little while ago. A fireplace, couch, and love seat make a small yet cozy living room. And the kitchen has a full-sized refrigerator, microwave, and every other appliance a normal kitchen would in a dang house.

The bedroom is bigger than mine is at my mom and dad's house. With a dark wooden sleigh bed and the fluffiest pillows and softest comforter. And that isn't even the best part. The best part is the huge-ass Jacuzzi tub in the bathroom.

After our shower, I changed into my pajamas. Something about showering and changing with him made this thing between us seem so much more … real. And now that the high from the sex has worn off, I find this knot in my stomach growing with worry.

I'm suddenly nervous. Like something has shifted between us and I am afraid to mess it up.

Slowly, I collapse on the bed, lying on my side.

Coming next to me, he flips onto his side and strokes my cheek with his thumb. "What's going on inside that pretty head of yours, girl?"

I don't know how to answer that. I'm not even sure what's going on inside of my brain or how to dissect all the thoughts pumping through it. I know that I'm here … hours away from home with a dude my dad has forbidden me to see. My daughter is in New Hampshire, having the time of her life, yet somehow, I feel guilty for being on this little trip. And on top of it all, I'm scared. I can feel my guard melt away when I'm with Cam. In a perfect world, that would be a good thing. Only, in my world, there's a whole lot more than just a story about a girl and a boy who like each other. There's my daughter and my dad. And also the fact that I've sworn off falling in love again for a long, long time. I want to only depend on me and Isla for my happiness. Now, it suddenly seems like I'm just giving all of that away and diving in, throwing caution to the wind, even though I know it's a bad idea.

Everything feels jumbled. And honestly, I don't like it. I don't feel safe.

"Oh, nothing really." I continue to stare at the ceiling. "Well, I should say … everything."

"Isla?" he asks softly.

"Sort of. Just not used to being away from her—that's all." I blow out a breath. "And being here with you. My mind has a thousand thoughts filtering through all at once. Truthfully? I'm a mess."

"Dirty thoughts, I hope?" He winks before pulling me toward him and rolling onto his back.

As he holds me to his chest, he rubs my back. "We don't have to have it all figured out tonight, Addy. Just the basics."

I peek up at him. "And what do the basics entail?"

"That I love being around you. That I miss the hell out of you when you're gone." He glides his hand down to my ass. "That when you were with Hunter, I saw red. And that when you're near me, I can't keep my fucking hands off of you. You drive me crazy, Addison."

I bury my face against his skin. "I feel all those things too. Even when I tried to fight it, you made it so damn hard."

He chuckles. "I'm pretty irresistible really. I know."

I swat his chest and roll my eyes. "Shut up."

He tickles me for a second, and I flail around in his hold. A mix of a squeal, giggle, and scream erupts from my lips.

"Stop!"

After at least ten pleas, he obliges and stops tickling me. Thank God, too, because my stomach literally hurts now.

We snuggle under the blankets, and I tuck myself against his warm body. His fingertips drag slowly up and down my back, and the calm I feel is something I've never felt before.

"What is all of this going to mean when we get back home tomorrow, Cam?" I force the words out. "I'm not trying to be pushy. I just—"

"Be pushy, Addison. Be really fucking pushy with me. I want you to. I'm going to admit to you right now that I'd give you whatever you wanted." His hand pushes me against him even closer. "I want to try. Like, really *try.*"

"Try what?" I whisper.

"Being with you. Like fully and completely together." He glances down at me. "I can't promise I'll be any good at it. I've never had a girlfriend, and I probably don't know jack shit about romance. But I'm in this." He pauses. "If you'll have me, I'm in it. All the way." He brushes his thumb across my cheek. "Even with Isla. I know it'll take time for me to prove myself. But, Addy, I want to meet her. If that's okay."

I blink a few times, taking in his words. What do I even say to that? He wants to give me the world. The truth is though ... I already have my own. One where my daughter and I get by just fine without a man in our lives. Well, other than Dad.

But I'll admit to myself that I'd love to have Cam be a part of that world. *If I knew he would stay.*

131

"And when something new comes along?" I croak out, barely hearing my own words. "Where will that leave Isla and me? She's getting older every day. She understands more and more." I swallow the lump of emotion that's formed in my throat, feeling like burning lava. "She'll get attached easy. I know she will."

"I'm not going to hurt you, Addison. Or Isla. Y'all have already been through enough from that fuckstick Nick." His fingers move to my hair, playing with it softly. "For the first time in my life, I want something that doesn't involve hockey. And that something is you."

Without answering, I crawl up his naked body. My breasts fall against his chest as I feel his erection harden beneath me. We don't have long with just the two of us, and I want to savor every second.

"Sit on my cock, baby," he mutters. "Show me you want me too."

I don't hesitate. Truth is, I've missed him too. And now that we're alone, I'm sure as hell not missing an opportunity to feel his body on mine.

CAM

The sun casts its rays through the windows, and a part of me curses myself for not closing the curtains last night. The other part is thankful I didn't. Because watching Addison sleep on her stomach, her head turned to the side, with the covers pooled down by her lower back, exposing her sun-kissed skin … she's something from another world. And I can't believe I convinced her to stay here with me last night.

Since the moment I met her, she drew me in, making me want more. I'd never met anyone like her, and because of that, she made an impact. I don't have all the answers, but I know we can't be apart.

Last night, after we lay here, talking, she climbed on top of me and rode me like she'd been waiting to do so for forever. She didn't try to hide her body from me like she sometimes does. She let me take in every perfect inch of her skin and feel her curves with my fingertips. And then, hours later, I woke up, needing her again. I had no idea my dick was capable of having so much sex in a short amount of time, but I'm not mad about it. Fuck no. Last night was the best night of my entire life.

I've never been more than the dumb hockey player who partied on the weekends and slept with the hottest chicks. But I don't want to be that guy anymore. I want to be better. And that's scary as hell.

I'm aware her daddy is going to be pissed. Even so, he needs to hear it directly from us. I'm hoping he doesn't punish me by ruining my season. For all I know, he could bench me or somehow take my position on the team. But I hope he does neither.

My whole life, all I've wanted to do is play professional hockey. Now, I'm risking it all for a girl.

And the funny thing about that? My dad would be fucking thrilled. He'd say, *About time, son. I knew you'd come around one day.*

Slowly, she starts to stir. Rubbing her eyes in her sleepy slumber, she smacks her lips a few times before her eyes finally pop open.

"Hi," she whispers, looking at me, doe-like.

"Hi," I say back, grinning. "How'd you sleep?"

"Good." She slowly sits up, grabbing her phone from the nightstand. "I call Isla every morning."

Giving her some space, I climb out of bed to head toward the shower. But first, I kiss the top of her head.

And as I walk toward the bathroom, I figure out I haven't felt this light in … well, ever.

I'll admit I've never felt this happy either.

16

ADDISON

“**D**on’t be nervous,” Cam says, glancing over at me as he gives my hand a squeeze. “They’ll love ya, babe.”

I swallow in an attempt to push down the sick feeling brewing in my gut. Cam’s parents are here. His sister. His friend Beau. All of them … here. And shortly, I’ll meet each and every one.

I’m terrified.

My experience with Nick’s parents was so awful that it’s spoiled the excitement. Instead of looking forward to walking into this stadium and shaking their hands, I’m convinced they’ll probably hate me from the get-go. Just like the Pelletiers did.

“I’ve heard that before.” I sigh. “But thanks for the, uh, words of encouragement?”

Cam’s body visibly stiffens, and he frowns. “My family is *nothing* like your ex’s. I can promise you that.”

“You know them?” I don’t try to hide the look of confusion on my face.

“Nope. But they pushed their own blood away. And they didn’t make their bitch son man up for Isla.” His eyes narrow. “I’m *nothing* like them, and neither is my family.”

"I didn't mean it like that." My shoulders sag. "I just meant ... maybe your parents won't think I'm good enough." I shrug. "Something like that. Plus ... I have a daughter. That is enough to scare away any parents of a college boy."

"My old man already knows," he says coolly. "Told him when I was home for Christmas."

"You did?" The wheels turn in my head. "We weren't even talking at Christmas though."

He stops, pulling me toward him, and he wraps his arms around my upper body. "Guess I'm a pathetic ol' bastard because I even told my daddy about you."

My heart pounds in my chest. "And ... what did he say?"

Kissing one cheek, then the other before moving to the corner of my lips, he pulls back. "He told me to follow my heart." He grins. "Just took me seeing you with a six-pack and a pizza box to get my head out of my ass." He kisses me again. "My dad loves kids. That ain't gonna scare him, trust me. And my mother? She'll be tickled to death."

When he steps back, his thumb tilts my chin up, and he winks. "Just relax, babe. My parents are some of the nicest people you'll ever meet."

"And your sister?" I chew my lip nervously. "Is she nice too?"

He begins walking, tugging me along with him. "Sweet as pie. Just don't get on her bad side."

My eyes widen.

Great.

CAM

I watch my sister barrel down the steps, darting straight for Beau. Confetti rains down on the field, and I'm thankful as hell I could be here today. This will be a memory Beau will always remember, and despite the differences we had in the past, I couldn't be happier for him.

"Look at that boy's smile," Dad says, nodding toward his future son-in-law on the field. "Man, what I wouldn't give for Dusty to be here for this." His eyes grow misty as he watches Mila leap into Beau's arms. "He'd be so damn proud."

I know times like this are when the guilt consumes my father. Dusty's death might not have been Dad's fault, but since his car crashed into Dusty's, making him hit a wall, Dad'll always think it was.

136

I lost my dad for a long time after Dusty's death. He was drinking too much and a downright mess. It's nice to have him back to normal. Or as normal as it can get. Dusty was his best friend. I know we will all carry that day with us forever, like a heavy burden.

Especially Beau. Nobody should lose their dad that young. Or have to watch it happen.

"Yeah, he sure would, old man. Beau's done damn good for himself." I lean forward, gripping the railing as I watch the celebration below. "Always knew he was goin' places."

"Just like we've always known you are too." He elbows my side lightly. "Won't be long, and I'll be watching my big-shot pro hockey player son on the TV."

"I know it's not what you wanted for me though. But thanks for always getting me into all the hockey camps and allowing me to work with the best of the best coaches." I nod at him. "Couldn't have done it without ya."

He scowls. "Whatchu talkin' about, boy? What I want for you is to be happy, and that's exactly what hockey makes you. Lucky for your mama, driving too damn fast down a drag strip didn't." He chuckles. "I don't think she could have dealt with two kids being in race cars." He looks around me. I don't have to turn around to see he's looking at Addison, who's talking to my mom. "And that pretty thing, she seems to make you some happy too."

I glance over. Addison appears to be in the middle of telling a story— likely about Isla, I can tell, just by the way her face lights up with every word.

"I followed my heart." I turn toward him again, grinning. "But I'm new to this stuff. I've never even dated someone. I'll probably fuck it up."

"No doubt you will," he says quickly. "But that's what it's all about. Ain't nothin' ever going to be perfect. That's life. Just tell her she's pretty when she doesn't feel it. Give her chocolate when she's sad. Oh, and when she says the words *it's fine*, she don't actually mean it."

I chuckle. "Good to know. Guess that's how you got Mom to stay all these years, huh?" I nudge him. "Must be some good chocolate for her to put up with your shit."

"Or it's just that good lovin' I gi—" he starts to say, but I hold my hand up.

"Don't even finish that sentence. For the love of fuck, just don't."

"You asked," he says, shrugging as he grins like a fool.

And when Addison comes next to me, resting her head against my shoulder … I realize just how gone I am when it comes to this girl.

Dating the coach's daughter is just like playing with fire, and I must be one dumb motherfucker … because I'm okay with being burned.

I stand at the bar as the bartender slides me my drink. I had a feeling, with a celebration like tonight's, the bartenders would forget to card some of us. Beau's mom and sister, his teammates, and my family are all scattered around the room, talking before we eat dinner.

"Look at this dude who made the trip down just to watch his brother-in-law play ball," Beau says, throwing a huge, tattooed arm around my shoulders.

"Was there a wedding I didn't get invited to?" I smirk. "Last I checked, you had to marry my sister to be my brother-in-law."

"One day, brother. One day." He releases me. "Who's the chick? Seems nice."

I glance over at Addison as she talks to my sister and a few other people.

"She's a friend from Brooks," is all I give him.

If that's what she wants to tell everyone tonight, I'm going to respect her wishes. Even though we sure as hell aren't just friends.

Looking back at Beau, I shrug. "That's all."

"Yeah, I bet," he drawls slowly. "I know all about them *friends*. Never works out that way." He nods toward her. "Especially with girls who look like that. Good luck, man. You're gonna need it."

I shake my head. "Whatever you say."

Luckily, before he says anything else, everyone starts to take their seats at the table.

Strutting toward Addison, I plant my hand on her hip. "Time to eat, babe."

"Oh, good. I'm starving." She sighs. "Everything the kitchen is making smells so good."

I lean down, kissing her cheek. "I'm starving too. Just not for anything that's going to be at that table."

She bites her lip, looking up at me shyly before I lead us to our seats. She fits in so easily here with this crew. Beau is practically a brother to me. And the fact that Mila and my mother seem to like her means we're off to a good start. Of course, they also think we're just friends. But if they are anything like my dad, which they are, they see right through this "friends" bullshit.

After looking at the menu, we all place our orders, and I have to hand it to the waitress; she handles this crazy-ass group with ease. We're loud. And the energy is on about one thousand after the Florida East boys just won the football championship. It's a lot.

She deserves a huge-ass tip.

Addison's sweet scent keeps drifting its way to my nostrils. And when she laughs at something someone says, she leans against me, teasing her skin against mine. Having her so close is torture. I have to touch her.

Under the table, I stroke her thigh softly. Feeling the goose bumps erupt as I glide my hand higher and higher under her skirt. Her eyes swing toward mine, and I hold her gaze. I know she's sending me a silent warning. A plea to stop, but I can't.

Finally, my fingertips tease the cotton thong. Swiping my finger against the fabric, I feel how turned on she is on my skin.

Putting my lips to her ear, like I'm telling her something, I feel her shiver. "Wet for me, Addison?" I murmur.

She shoots me a glare and then widens her eyes. *Stop,* she mouths, her cheeks on fire.

I pretend to listen in on a conversation next to me to look like I'm paying attention, but instead, I tease her more by continuing to graze my fingers over her skin. Finally, I sneak my fingers inside of her.

At first, she tenses. Trying to fight the fact that she wants this as badly as I do. But finally, she wiggles against me the smallest bit, greedy for more.

Suddenly, she pushes the chair back, causing it to scrape against the tiled floor.

Standing, she smiles nervously as everyone looks up at her, but once their heads turn and they return back to their conversations, she leans down. "Restroom. Two minutes," she hisses.

Grinning, I watch her as she makes her way out of the dining room, noticeably hot and bothered. And before it's been two minutes, I'm up after her.

When I catch Beau watching me, I pull my phone out. "Have to call her daddy. He's wondering when I'm bringing her home," I lie through my teeth to my best friend. Really not giving a fuck either because I'm about to be balls deep in the hottest chick on the planet.

His eyes show he doesn't believe it, but I continue to walk off, not wanting to keep my hot date waiting. Knowing damn well she could chicken out, and I really, *really* don't want that happening. I need her.

I reach the restroom, and it's locked. I knock a few times, and she cracks it open before pulling me inside and quickly locking it behind her.

"You cannot do that in public, Cam! Jesus Christ, what is the matter with you? Your mom and dad are here, for crying out loud!"

As she stands against the sink, I make my way toward her. "Is that right?"

"Y-yes," she stutters.

Reaching her, I put my hands on her waist and press her further against the sink. "So, when I slipped my fingers inside of you, you didn't like it, baby?"

"Not here," she whispers.

Dropping my hand down, I glide it up her skirt, cupping between her legs. "For someone who didn't like my fingers inside of her, you're awfully wet. In fact … you're downright soaked. All for me too, isn't it?" I kiss her neck. "You didn't bring me in here to lecture me about what an inappropriate time it was to finger-fuck you. No … you wanted me to come in and fuck you right in this restroom." I waste no time in unbuttoning my jeans, letting them pool at my ankles as I take my painfully hard cock into my hand. "You don't even have to lie, babe. I'll give it to you. I'll always give you what you want."

Her lips part when her eyes see my hardness, and I hoist her up, sitting her on the sink.

"See what you do to me?" I murmur against her lips. "I have no control when it comes to you. Turns out, you're my undoing."

"Cam," she whines, wrapping her legs around my waist and pulling me between her legs. "We shouldn't." She moans as I graze my tongue along her jawline. "God ... we *really* shouldn't."

"Want me to stop?" I murmur, already knowing the answer.

"No!" she growls. "Don't you dare."

"Thought so." I smirk. "I have no condom," I say, my dick pressing against her, begging to be inside.

She pushes me to the point of insanity. And I don't care because, for once in my life, I'm feeling something.

"It's okay," she says, looking up at me. "I have an IUD. Just as long as you're—"

"I'm clean," I say, finishing her sentence.

She swallows thickly. "Are you sure?"

"I promise." I dip my forehead to hers, running my hand up her smooth thigh. "I'd never do anything to put you at risk, I swear." I kiss her again, teasing her tongue with mine. "But I'm going to fucking die if I'm not inside of you soon. This skirt? Christ. What are you trying to do, kill me?"

She reclines, letting the back of her head rest against the mirror as she stares at me. Her eyes show how turned on she is and how much she wants this. "I trust you," she barely whispers, and that's all the go-ahead I need.

But something about those three words means so much more than just a simple sentence. She said she trusts me ...

I hike her skirt up higher and pull her thong to the side. I slowly nudge the head of my cock inside of her, and she bites her lips and sucks in a breath.

"Ahh." The sound comes from her pretty lips as a whimper, but when I don't push any further, she tightens her hold on my waist with her thighs, dragging me deeper. "Don't stop," she breathes out. "Don't stop."

I push deeper as she squeezes around me so tightly that I damn near lose it. But when I finally get it together, I pound into her, never being gentle as her nails claw their way up and down my back.

Every time I thrust inside of her, her eyes glaze over a little more as she stares up at me. A sheer layer of sweat gathering on both of our bodies.

"Cam ... oh ..." Her eyes flutter shut.

I feel her gripping my cock, and it pushes me over the edge that last bit that I was trying to hang on to. Once I know she's done, I grip her thigh tighter.

"Lift your shirt up. Let me come all over these perfect fucking tits."

Reaching for the hem of her shirt, she pulls it up over her head, bringing her bra along with it and leaving her completely bare. Leaning my head down, I take her nipple into my mouth.

"All mine," I say before pulling out of her and pushing her down to her knees.

Grabbing her hand, I wrap it around my cock and place my hand over hers. And just a few short pumps later, I lose myself all over her full, naked chest. A sight that will forever be etched in my brain.

I drag in a few gulps of air, trying to steady my breathing. I've slept with many women. All beautiful and striking. But no one compares to her. Not a one.

Handing her a wet paper towel, I kiss the top of her head. "My little sex monster."

"Am not!" she gasps, her mouth hanging open. "Okay, maybe I am. But it's your fault!"

I wink, pulling my jeans up over my hips. "What can I say, babe? I'm *that* good."

And as I watch her fix herself in the mirror, her cheeks flushed and her hair messy, I realize I'll never get bored of that look right there. And then something even bigger hits me.

I've fallen in love with Coach LaConte's daughter. And I don't even think I can deny it.

ADDISON

I wonder if his mother suspects what we just did in the restroom. God, I hope not. I'd die.

I like exhibiting the image of being the smart girl. The good girl. The girl … who doesn't have sex on a dirty restroom counter. Even though that's apparently what I am these days. Practically a sex fiend. Always needing more.

"So, your daughter is three, huh?" Cam's mother, Kimberly, says sweetly. "Gosh, I miss that age. Don't blink, girlfriend. Goes by too dang fast."

I sigh. "I get that. I mean, I feel like I was just bringing her home from the hospital, and now, she's three and a half and a whole actual human being."

I smile, thinking about how much I can't wait to hug her. "She's hilarious. And dramatic. And extra. And ... perfect," I gush. "Sorry, I'm rambling. I haven't seen her in a few days. My parents took her on a trip with them to visit family."

"I can't wait to meet her." She says the words so genuinely. Like ... like ... she actually means them. "When will y'all bring her down to Alabama?"

I've just opened my mouth to answer when Mila comes next to me. "Mama, you'd best not be interrogating this kind girl. Play it cool, remember?"

Mrs. Hardy frowns before she lets out a long sigh. "I know; I know. It's just hard! You know this *never* happens."

Mila pats her mom on the shoulder. "Yeah, well, it won't happen for even longer if you don't cool your jets." She turns toward me. "It's unprecedented for my brother to bring a girl to family get-togethers. We're intrigued."

"No, we're thrilled!" Mrs. Hardy corrects her. "But my Mila girl is right. I shall not push this. Besides, if I do, Cam will have my ass."

Someone calls to Mila, but before she leaves, she smiles. "I really hope we get to see you again, Addison." She lets out a small laugh. "My brother is a lot by anyone's standards. He's loud. He jokes at the wrong times. He's stubborn as a bull and stupidly particular. He's way too hard on himself, and he never thinks he's done good enough ... in anything. *Even* if he pretends nothing bothers him, it does. He's deeper than anyone thinks and sort of a pain in the ass. But I promise, he's a good man. Don't let him fool you into thinking differently." She tilts her pretty face to the side. "Besides, y'all look awfully cute together." She winks before turning around and walking away.

Mila Hardy might just be the coolest girl I've ever met. She races cars. She has the most beautiful jet-black hair and most badass style. And she seems to like me. I call that a victory.

"Are you two spending the night?" Cam's mom asks sweetly. "We could meet for breakfast or lunch tomorrow if you are."

"We are, but unfortunately, we're hitting the road first thing in the morning." I give her an apologetic smile. "Cam has practice in the afternoon, and my parents and daughter get back tomorrow night. I am actually picking them up from the airport."

"You must be so excited to see her."

"You have no idea," I say, feeling my eyes fill up. "But I truly am happy that I got to come here and meet everyone in Cam's family. I really had a great time."

"Not to sound like a big ol' mama bear," she drawls. "But please don't go breaking his heart. He's much more fragile than he looks." She blows out a long breath. "And he loves you. So, please, try not to hurt him. He's never had a broken heart, and I don't know if he could handle it."

I stand, dumbfounded. "He doesn't love me, Mrs. Hardy," I whisper, shaking my head softly. "We're still figuring out what we're even doing."

She opens her mouth to answer when, suddenly, I feel a hand on my shoulder.

"Ready to head out? Gonna be an early morning," Cam says, pulling me against him. "Ma, it's been good seeing ya. Keep the old man out of trouble."

His mom laughs, rolling her eyes. "As if." She pulls us both in for a hug before releasing us. "Safe travels back to Brooks tomorrow," she says to him before her eyes connect with mine. "Good luck figuring it out."

As she walks away, Cam looks confused. "Figure what out? What did she mean by that? Is that some weird fucking code for something?"

I know she was talking about what I said … that we were still figuring out what we're doing. But I don't want to tell him I said that. So, instead, I just pat his back. "A class I'm going to be taking. She was saying I hopefully figure it out since, you know, I heard it's hard."

"Ah, gotcha." He nods, keeping his arm around me. "Let's go say good-bye to everyone and head to the hotel." His mouth goes to my ear. "We have an early morning and need our rest. So, tonight, we'll have to have one of our famous quickies."

"Famous, huh?" I smirk, lifting an eyebrow. "News to me. Guess you'll have to remind me sometime."

"Oh, I plan to."

ADDISON

Isla snores against me as I finish my homework. I find myself distracted every few minutes, looking down at her perfect little face. Finally, once I'm done, I shut my laptop and lift her off of me, tucking her in on the other side of my bed.

I turn the monitor on and head toward the kitchen, where I know my mom is. The teapot screeching gave it away.

"Hiya," I say, stretching my arms over my head. "Geesh, I could have fallen asleep with her, I swear. If I didn't have class tonight, I would have."

"You should have." She shrugs, pouring the hot water into her mug before fixing me one and sliding it across the counter. "I feel like I've barely talked to you since we got home a few days ago. How was your time alone? Do anything fun?"

Just as she asks that last question, I'm mid-sip. Tea sprays from my mouth and nose, and I cough. "S-sorry." I grab a paper towel and wipe the counter. "Wow, I'm a mess."

"Perhaps," she says, sounding unaffected. "Or maybe you're hiding something and you don't want to be asked about what you were up to while we were away."

My heart stops beating inside of my chest. I know I need to tell her what really went down while she was away, but I'm scared. I promised Cam I'd tell my family. He doesn't want to sneak around; he thinks it will make my dad hate him more than if we were honest. He's probably right, but it doesn't make telling the guy any easier.

Cam wanted to be with me when I told him. But I know my father, and he's going to need a minute … or a million. He'll do better if I tell him alone. If Cam and I do it at the same time, he'll feel bombarded. So, my plan is to tell him and Mom … today.

"Talk to me, babe," she says, setting her cup down and grabbing a wet rag. "You can tell me anything. Anything at all."

I look down at the light-brown water in my cup, scared as hell to blurt the words out but knowing I need to.

Just as she starts to wipe the counter down, I open my mouth to tell her the truth. "I went to Florida with Cam Hardy. We stayed together in a room."

She drops the rag, her mouth hanging open.

"I like him, Mom. I, like, really, *really* like him."

She's speechless.

I, on the other hand, can't stop blabbering words out. "But I'm scared too. He's got this larger-than-life personality that the entire campus eats up. They adore him. Not to mention, how attractive he is. Girls are always going to be coming for him, and ultimately, he'll find someone better, and I'll be—"

Holding her hand up, she silences me.

"Please don't tell me you're already trying to self-sabotage this, Addison. Because, girlfriend, you're a catch by anyone's standards. You're beautiful, smart, funny, independent … stubborn as hell," she says, muttering the last part. "I won't say I'm not shocked that you didn't tell me before you took off to Florida, but either way, I'm happy you made a choice for you." She washes her hands off. "Don't get so consumed with what could happen that you miss out on things that bring you joy."

I sigh. "I know. I *know!* I am my own worst enemy." My eyes widen. "And then there's the whole Dad part of it. I don't want him derailing Cam's career because of this. But, Mom, you know how Dad is. He's ruthless when it comes to his family. Especially after the whole Nick situation."

She reaches across the counter, putting her hand on mine. "First off, he would never destroy Cam's future in hockey just because of this." She looks nervous. "Though I'll admit, your dad isn't going to make Cam's life easy. But first, babe, you've got to tell your dad. He loves you; he'd hate to have this secret kept from him. No matter how he might initially react, you can always tell Daddy anything. So, when he gets home from the store, talk to him."

"Talk to me about what?" my dad says, strolling into the kitchen and pecking my mom's cheek. "What's going on, Addy?"

I give my mom a look that says, *When the hell did he walk through the door?*

My stomach does flips, making me feel nauseous. There's no time like the present; I guess that's true. I'm petrified he'll forbid me to see Cam anymore. And if I'm being honest, even if my father forbids it, I can't walk away from Cam right now. Even the thought kills me.

"I'll give you two a minute," my mom says nervously, her eyes shifting to mine.

"Please stay," I plead. She's always been a good moderator to have around. She can talk my dad down like no one else can. "It'll be helpful to have you here."

Slowly, she nods and takes a seat on the stool, motioning for my dad to do the same. And as I take one last deep breath, I look into my dad's eyes, preparing for the worst.

"I, uh … I'm sort of seeing Cam Hardy. Or at least, I'd really like to." I pause, swallowing back what might be vomit. "I know you're going to be angry, but, Dad, he is a good man—"

"Bullshit," he says, his face reddening. "Bull-fucking-shit he is."

"Barren," my mother hisses. "There's no need for foul language."

"I don't give a fuck, Jennie. You know what there's no need for?" He glares. "Her seeing Cam Hardy—that's what. No *fucking* need for it."

"You don't even know him, Dad!" My voice rises. "Aside from that arena, you know nothing about him!" I challenge him, leaning forward slightly on the counter. "Tell me I'm wrong."

"I hear things, damn it!" he roars. "He fucks his way through the campus, gets drunk on the weekends, and has no respect for women!" He gets a look on his face, and I know he's about to say something harsh. "I would think you'd want better for your daughter. I would *hope* you would have learned your lesson in high school."

"Barren! That's—" my mother starts to hiss, but I cut her off.

"You know what? I don't need this." I shake my head. "I'm a damn good mother. I put her first—always. I get good grades. I double up on classes so I can graduate early to give her the best life I possibly can. And you know what else? I'm a good daughter. I hardly ever drink. I don't do drugs. I'm responsible—for the most part. So, I don't need this lecture. I care about him. I'm going to keep seeing him. That's that."

I push myself off the stool.

"I forbid it," he says, keeping his voice low but just as intense. "You will *not* see that boy."

"I'm twenty-one years old, Dad. With all due respect, that isn't your call to make."

"You're living under my roof, Addison. So, unfortunately, it is."

"Guess I'll go looking for an apartment." I feel anger pumping through my veins, consuming every fiber of my being.

"Over a guy?" He shakes his head. "I'm disappointed in you, Addison. So disappointed."

Something inside of me snaps, and I pound my fist against the counter. "It has nothing to do with Cam, Dad! This is about the fact that ever since I got knocked up in high school, you don't let me make any decisions for myself! I'm like a damn prisoner!"

"That is not true." He laughs bitterly. "How the hell do you figure?"

"You try to control everything in my life to keep me from making mistakes." I hold my arms out. "It's just life, Dad. We're supposed to make mistakes. We're supposed to fall down and get back up."

"Don't you dare bring Isla around him," he says through gritted teeth. "She doesn't need to be exposed to your dating."

"She came out of my vagina, Dad. I'm her mother. So, that's my call to make." I lean against the doorframe, wrapping my arms around myself, trying to keep myself from breaking down. "You can either trust me or you can drive a wedge in our family. The choice is yours." And with that, I leave, walking back to my room and quietly closing the door.

I lie down next to Isla, staring down at her. I don't want to lose my family over a guy who's inevitably going to get bored of me one day and leave. But for whatever reason, I can't say good-bye to him yet either.

When I was least expecting it, Cam Hardy hit me like a freight train. And for some crazy reason … I'm not sure I'll ever be the same.

Even when he's gone.

CAM

I lace up my skates, my back teeth grinding together from these fucking nerves that are taking over my body. No dad would be thrilled his daughter was dating me, especially not Coach fucking LaConte. So, when the message came through from Addison a few hours ago, letting me know she told him about us … well, I've been dreading this practice since.

Trying my best to be an optimistic ray of sunshine, I messaged her back, asking how it went. She sent a thumbs-down and said that it wasn't good, but that we'd talk later because Isla was waking up from her nap. So, she dropped a major shitty bomb and then expected me to skate into practice, grinning, like I normally do.

Yeah, that ain't happening.

I'm only scared or intimidated by a few people. And that dude, he's one of them.

"You're awfully quiet, big dawg." Brody pats my shoulder as he walks by. "Need to talk about it?"

"What the fuck are you, his shrink?" Link says, closing his locker. "He needs a beer. Or ten."

"Nah, this is more of a shots problem. Lotta shots." I stand. "Whatever happens in the next few hours, just don't let Coach murder me. Or cut my dick off. I *really* don't want my dick cut off."

"So, if it comes to death or dick, what do we do?" Brody says, smirking like a damn idiot.

"Well, jeez, dumbass. I don't know." I shake my head. "If I'm dead, I suppose I wouldn't have much use for a penis, now would I?"

"You gonna tell us what this is about?" Link asks, leaning on his hockey stick. "I don't get it."

I throw my head back, blowing out a breath. I don't want to blurt out the truth. Even if Addy told her parents, I still feel like it's not my story to talk about.

"Let's go, fellas," Hunter calls out, nodding toward the door. "Coach is probably waiting, and I'm not all about doing suicides just because you want to have a powwow in the locker room when our asses are supposed to be on the ice."

Link and Brody both nod, heading toward the door.

Once they are gone, I tip my chin up at Hunter. "Thanks, I guess."

"I'm guessing chasing after Coach's daughter finally caught up to you, ol' boy." He grins. "I'll do my best to not let you die or become dickless."

I follow him out the door, confused as hell. Not that long ago, I ended his date with Addison early. Today, he's distracting my friends to get me out of answering questions about my relationship with her. I suppose he's a better man than I thought he was. I'd feel bad for what I did, except I can't. As long as I'm breathing, that girl will never be on a date with anyone who isn't me.

"Heads-up, he's looking right at you," Hunter mutters when we get inside the arena.

"I wouldn't call that lookin', brother. I'd call that glaring with intent to murder me." I look away from him, feeling awkward as hell. "Fuck, I'm about to piss myself."

"I'd give you words of encouragement, but honestly, I don't have any. I'm scared for you actually."

"Really fucking nice, dick," I grumble just as Coach heads toward us. "Fuck. This ain't good."

"Hardy, a word," Coach says, sending me another glare. "Now."

149

"Good luck," Hunter whispers as my other teammates watch in confusion.

I follow him to the other side of the rink, preparing myself for the worst. Knowing that, no matter what, I won't cower. He can bench me. I'm not going anywhere.

"You might have my daughter fooled, but not me. I see right through the bullshit, Hardy."

He's fuming red as he runs his hand up the back of his head, nostrils flaring.

"Sir, with all due respect, I'm not trying to fool your daughter. She knows me. It's you who doesn't."

"My daughter has a knack for seeing what she wants to see in people and not what's actually there," he spews. "It's why she's in the position she's in."

Something in me snaps. I know he loves his daughter. I know he's angry and scared. But that doesn't mean he can shit all over her and the life choices she's made.

"Addison sees the best in people. That isn't a bad thing, *sir*. And that *situation* she's in? Well, I'd say she's handling it all just fine."

"Are you going to stay away from her or not?" he growls low.

"No," I say quickly, "I'm not."

The veins at his temples bulge. "Stay away from her or get off my ice."

I stare at him in disbelief, yet without thinking twice, I turn away and head off the ice and back toward the locker room.

For the first time in my life, I'm choosing something that isn't hockey. Something named Addison.

And I don't have any fucking regrets.

Yet.

I pull my truck into Addison's driveway. I know Coach won't get here for another few hours, so now, I just have to hope her mother doesn't hate me the way he does.

I quickly throw the truck in park, wasting no time in climbing down and walking right to her door. I hold my fist up to the door, but before I can knock, it swings open, and out comes Addison's mom.

"Mr. Hardy," she says, frowning. "I take it, practice didn't go well."

I shake my head. "Nah. Figured it wouldn't though."

"So, you just left?" Her eyebrows pull together. "As in ... left one of Barren's practices early?"

"Didn't even begin." I run my hand over my head nervously. "He told me to stay away from her or get off the ice." I attempt to grin, holding my arm out at my side. "So, here I am."

"That stubborn ass," she mutters before her face grows serious. "So, you're saying you left practice … instead of losing my girl?"

"That's pretty much it, yeah." I chuckle. "I mean, I'm hoping like hell he lets me keep playing. I could probably get a career as a stripper or some shit, but hockey sounds a little better." I attempt to joke, but she rolls her eyes. "I'm kidding. But, yes, I'm not going to stop seeing Addison just because he thinks I'm a piece of shit."

"Well, are you?" She raises an eyebrow. "A piece of shit?"

"I mean, I don't think so." I shrug. "I don't run a meth lab in my basement, or kill kittens, or steal from old people … so I'd say I'm good."

She fights a laugh but eventually smiles. "And what about the fact that she has a daughter? How are you going to be with that?"

"To be honest, Mrs. LaConte—"

"Jennie. Mrs. LaConte makes me sound ancient."

"Okay, Jennie. Look, I don't know shit about kids. Especially girls. But I want to get to know Isla. She means the world to her mom—that's clear. And watching Addison with her just makes me like Addy more. She's a good one." I look down. "Far too good for my hillbilly ass, but I promise, I'm not going to hurt her. For once in my life, I can swear that."

Her chin tilts up the smallest bit as she takes in a breath. "And hockey? What do you plan to do about Coach?"

I exhale. "Hockey is my past, present, and, God willing, future. So, I'm hoping that once your husband sees I'm not a bad guy, he'll come around to the idea of us being together." I frown. "I can't picture my life without the game. But as insane as it sounds—and I'm aware it does—I can't imagine walking away from her either."

She offers a small smile. "I'll talk to Barren. As for Addy, she took Isla for a walk not long before you pulled in." She points down the road. "Go that way, and you'll catch them when they loop around the neighborhood."

Wasting no time, I start taking steps backward as I wave. "Thanks! Good-bye, Mrs. La—" When she shoots me a hard glare, I hold my hands up. "Jennie. Thanks a lot, Jennie!"

ADDISON

"And that's how come I love strawberry ice cream the mostest," Isla says, holding my hand as she finishes her painfully long story on ice cream. It's a regular topic for us.

"But yesterday, you said chocolate was the best." I look down at her, swinging her little arm as we walk. "And I sort of agree with yesterday's choice more, to be honest."

"But chocolate ice cream sometimes wooks like poop. And strawberry ice cream wooks like … well, beautifulness."

I scrunch my nose. "Thank you for bringing that to my attention. Gross."

"You're welcome," she says sweetly and begins humming a song.

After the blowup with my dad, I needed to get out of that house. He isn't home—luckily. But being in the four walls gave me way too much time to think.

Think about how disappointed my father is about my life choices. Think about how he basically said I am not capable of making a smart decision. And think about the possibility that Cam will get over me in a week and I'll look like a moron. Not to mention how bad it will hurt.

The thing is, I know I'm being a little reckless with my heart, but I want to do it anyway. I want to laugh and smile with someone. I miss that feeling, like you can't wait to see the person even if it's only been a day or two. I know I'm taking a huge chance. One that likely won't pay off. I guess if I'm going to get my heart broken, who better to do it than a guy like Cam Hardy?

He has this way of making me feel like I'm the only girl in the room. His eyes drink me in, and his hands consume my entire body. I'm falling—hard and fast. The only thing I can hope for is that I don't hit the ground headfirst.

"It's the handsome man, Cam!" Isla suddenly squeals. "Bwooks's dad!"

I look up and find that my daughter is right. Cam struts toward us in gray sweatpants and a Brooks U hockey hoodie. His hair curls under his cap the slightest bit. He mentioned the other day that he needed a haircut, but to be honest, I kind of love it the way it is.

"Yes. Yes, it is." I look at him, confused.

Practice isn't due to be over for at least another hour, so why is he here?

"Well, look at that. You're even taking him for a walk, huh, little lady?" He reaches us and kneels before Isla, pointing to Brooks the wolf.

"Oh, yes," I say, giggling. "Where she goes, he goes."

"I'm a good mom," Isla says in a very serious tone. "Moms don't leave their babies home while they go for walks."

"I'd hope not anyway," Cam says, grinning at her. "He'd best be behaving for you. I'd hate if I gave y'all a naughty pup."

"Sometimes, he gets pwetty wound up and chews stuff," Isla says, looking down at the wolf. "But I don't mind."

I shake my head, knowing that when she claims he is wound up, it's only because *she* is wound up. Ever since the night Cam gave her that damn thing, she's lugged it everywhere. It's quickly become her favorite stuffed animal or toy she has.

"Cam, can you come to the park with us?" she says in her cutest voice, pushing her little lip out just enough so that he won't be able to say no.

Cam stands and looks at me. "If it's okay with your mom, I'd love to."

Tilting my head to the side, I give him a questioning look before blinking. "Sure. He can come to the park with us."

"Yippee!" she screams, tucking Brooks under her arm and taking Cam's hand. "This is the best day of my life!"

I try to remind myself that she says things like that all the time and that it has nothing to do with Cam joining us. I also tried to ignore the way he looked down at their hands when she grabbed for his. Or the way he's looking down at her now, smiling like a fool.

Slowly peeling his eyes from her, he looks at me and winks. "Thanks."

"For what?"

"Letting me be here."

Oh ...

After a ten-minute walk, we arrive at the park, and Isla goes crazy, running to all the little slides. At first, Cam goes down every slide with her. But after a while, she makes a new friend who won't stop following her and plays with her. Which is fine by me because I need to talk to Cam without her little ears eavesdropping.

We sit on a bench, and he puts his hand on my knee.

"You look beautiful today, Addy. No surprise there though."

"What happened at practice?" I ignore his compliment and cut right to the chase. "How bad was it?"

I watch him frown when Isla disappears for a brief moment. I know she's behind the slide stairs, and she'll pop out in a second because I've brought her here countless times. And when she runs out and he can see her again, he sighs in clear relief. It's weird ... I think he was nervous over my daughter.

"Not great," is all he gives me, and I smack his knee.

"Tell me what happened!"

"It's a short story. He called me over, and I asked for his blessing for marriage. He said yes, and then we smoked cigars and slapped each other's ass."

I tilt my head down and groan. "Be serious. For five seconds of your life, just. Be. Serious."

He adjusts his ball cap and leans back. Doing his best impression of my dad, he acts tough. "He said, 'Stay away from her or get off my ice.' Now, I'm here."

"Cam!" I smack him harder this time. "What the hell?!"

"What?" He shrugs.

"You shouldn't have left practice! He'll remember this shit forever. What were you thinking?"

Snapping his eyes to mine, he narrows them. "I was thinking that I'm crazy about his daughter. That I think about her every morning the second my eyes open. And that it'll be a cold day in hell before he tells me who I can hang out with. Even if you are his daughter. I don't give a fuck. I'm not a bad guy. I don't have a basement full of dead people or any shit like that. He's being ridiculous, Addy."

"Cam, hockey is your entire life. You can't risk messing your future up for me. We need to end this. Trust me, it won't pay off. He might not be able to kick you directly off the team, but it will cause enough drama to mess up your season. I can't let that happen."

The words make my heart squeeze, and my throat grows sore as a lump begins to form. I don't want to say good-bye to him, but if it means him being able to play hockey, I will.

He runs his thumb along my bottom lip and dips his forehead to mine. "No chance in hell. Like you said, he can't actually kick me off the team for dating his daughter—that's not even legal. Just give it a few days. It'll get better." He smirks. "The grouchy fucker will come around. I know it."

"He's such a stubborn dick sometimes," I whisper. "But I know it's all out of love."

He pulls me into his side, and we both watch Isla as she continues to make more friends on the playground. They all chase her around, and her blonde curls bounce as she runs and giggles.

"Gotta admit, I'm happy as hell that the parents of those random kids haven't come to sit with us. I am not all about those awkward encounters." He looks around the playground. "So far, the playground isn't all that bad. Not compared to what I figured anyway."

I poke his side. "Jeez, jerk, what did you expect it to be, hell?"

"Kids picking their boogers and rubbing them all over the bench I'm sitting on. Awkward parents who don't get to be around other adults, dying for conversation. A big bully shoving her down on the playground, and I'd have to kick their dad's ass." He shrugs. "Like I told your mom, I know nothing about kids."

"Well, all of that is insanely accurate most days." I burst out laughing until it dies in my throat. "You spoke too soon," I say, watching two ladies from the corner of my eye inch closer and closer to us. "Because here they come. And let me tell you, the playground mamas are gonna eat you up. You're the hottest piece of ass that's been on this park bench probably ever," I tease him. "Prepare to be flirted with."

"Fuck," he groans, but he still watches Isla with nothing but fondness.

I could get used to having him here for everyday things. Just like this.

CAM

I walk into the apartment to find Link in the recliner, watching game tape.

Not looking away from the TV, he keeps his voice low. "What the fuck was that about at practice, man? You left. Do you have any idea how mad Coach was?"

I fall back onto the couch, pulling my hood up. "Wouldn't have mattered if I'd stayed, Link. He would have been the same amount of pissed."

Lifting the remote, he pauses the TV. "What'd you do, Cam? The fuck you gotten yourself into?"

"His daughter." I cringe.

His eyes fly to mine. "Are you fucking serious right now? Are you dumb? Do you have a brain?"

"I mean, it's debatable, but my mama says I'm smart," I drawl slowly. "But in my defense, I hooked up with her before I knew she was Coach's daughter."

"Is it really worth it, Hardy? Fucking your season up for a piece of ass?"

"I'll give you a pass for right now, Link. But next time you refer to Addy as a piece of ass, I'll lay your ass out, I promise." I tip my chin down. "And, yes, *she's* worth it. For the first time in my fucking life, it isn't just about hockey, or parties, or—"

"Getting laid? Sleeping around?" He finishes my sentence. "You'll want to go back to that, and you know it. And when you do, you will have made Coach hate you so much that he'll make your life hell," he groans, tossing his head back. "Jesus fucking Christ, did you even think about the team? Or just with your dick?"

"It might have started with thinking with my dick, but it ain't like that now. And as for the team?" I say, standing. "Y'all are gonna have to get the fuck over it. She's going to be in my life whether any of you agree or not. So, you can get on board or don't. Either way, I don't give a shit."

Walking away, I slam my door shut. It seems like not one person is rooting for our relationship. Everyone believes it's meant to fail.

CAM

During a time-out called by our team, Coach talks to me while not talking directly *to* me. The game is all tied up, and since I'm the captain, he knows deep down that I'm the one who's going to rally my team.

Last week, I willingly left the ice when given the ultimatum to leave Addy alone or get out of his arena. But when I went to see Addison after, Coach LaConte's wife told me she was going to talk some sense into him. Whatever she said or did must have worked because when I showed up the next day at practice, he didn't say a word to me. He hasn't really spoken straight to me at all since either, but I know which parts of his speech are made for me.

He's been avoiding Addison, too, but I know he'll come around ... someday. Aside from his hatred of our relationship, the past week has been the best days of my life. I've taken Addy and Isla to the movies, for dinner and ice cream. I never thought I'd be the guy who would date a girl with a kid. Yet here I am. And the most insane part of it all is, I actually love hanging around Isla. She's the coolest three-year-old I've ever met.

Link apologized the next day for everything he'd said. And just as I'd suspected, Brody wasn't mad when I told him the truth. He laughed and told me I had a death wish and then said good for me. Word got around to the rest of the team, but none of them were nearly as annoyed as I'd thought they'd be when Coach made practices extra shitty, strictly because of my own doing.

"One, two, three … WOLVES!" we all yell, skating back out to the middle of the ice.

My eyes shift upward to those same damn seats I have been checking on this entire game, and there they are, both smiling like fools—Isla and her MILF.

"It's all over for you, Hardy," the other team's best player, Ben Comstock, chants.

He's also the most annoying dude I've ever faced on the ice. He almost never shuts up, always trying to get in our heads and cause us to fuck up.

"Whatever you say, Cum-stocking." I grin. "Whatever you say."

"Fuck off, Hard D," he drawls out, mocking my last name. "You get a hard D for your teammates, do you?"

"Nah, man. Your mom makes me hard enough. Don't need anyone else. Just ask her about it." I wink. "Man, she's wild. And those tits? Wow."

I'll never outgrow mom jokes, no matter how old I am. They always work, too, because dudes go from being cool as a cucumber to mad as hell.

Seconds later, the game starts back up, and he smashes me into the glass. I knew he'd be all over me, which is why the last twenty seconds of this game is likely going to depend on Hunter and Link.

I see Link skating toward the zone, struggling to get there because defensemen are headed right for him. Breaking away from Comstock before the ref can call anything, I head toward the other team's goal.

"Thompson," I call out just before he gets into dangerous territory.

We can't afford for the other team to get the puck this close to the end. I'd also hate to go into overtime because I'm exhausted as hell and I'm ready to see my girls.

Distracting the two defensemen near him just long enough for him to get a clean shot, he sends the puck to me. Without looking at him, I send it back to him, and he wrist-shots it right toward the goal. And no matter how fast those last few seconds are winding down … I swear, time stands still as it glides toward the goalie.

The goalie attempts to stop it and force it out of there, but somehow, by the grace of fucking God, it goes in, and the light goes off.

And we win another game.

ADDISON

"For as many times as that boy was looking up here, I can't believe how well he played." My mom does a low whistle. "No wonder your daddy didn't kick him off the ice again. He's too damn good to lose."

I roll my eyes. "We both know Cam's talent had nothing to do with it. I think it was the fact that his wife, whom he is a tad scared of, told him to cut the shit."

"Eh ... maybe." She shrugs. "I'm taking your dad for pizza."

"I want pizza, Nena! I want pizza!" Isla holds up Brooks the wolf. "So does he!"

Mom scoops her up, twirling her around. "I was hoping you'd say that."

"This should be fun. Dinner where my dad doesn't speak to me, just shoots me an occasional glare. Who wouldn't sign up for that?" I mutter so that Isla can't hear me.

My dad has basically avoided me like the plague since last week, when I broke the news to him about Cam and me. It's awkward at the house, so Isla and I have spent a lot of time outside of there. We've even spent a lot of that time with Cam.

Dad walks toward us just as Mom sets Isla down.

Barreling toward him, she leaps into his arms, wrapping her little hands around his neck. "You won, Papa! You won!"

"We did!" He chuckles. "We sure did."

Her eyes widen, and she wiggles to get down from my father's hold. As he sets her down, she runs toward Cam as he walks from the locker room. His hair still wet from his shower and his duffel strung over his shoulder.

"Cam!" Isla squeals, and he drops his bag down, anticipating she's going to dive into his arms headfirst. "You won! You won! That guy was a bully, and him was being mean to you, beating you up."

Picking her up, he throws her into the air and catches her, holding her up over his head. "I promise, Isla girl, nobody's gonna beat me up." He throws her up again, and she laughs hysterically. "What'd you eat for snacks? Save me any?"

"We eated popcorn and Skittles. I even got to have a slushy. And guess what, Cam! Guess what!" She puts her hands on his cheeks.

"What, girlfriend?"

"Mom let me mix red and blue!" she squeaks, her eyes as wide as pizzas.

"What? No way!" He pretends to be astonished. "Best mom ever!"

As he sets her down slowly, she throws her arms around his neck and squeezes him, and I swear I see him grow emotional.

As she lets go, running back to me, I'm aware that my dad watched the entire thing.

"Well, we'd better get going if we're going to get to dinner before they close." My mom holds her hand up at Cam. "Great game, Cam."

"Thanks," he says, his eyes finding mine. "Talk to you later?"

I nod awkwardly. "Yep."

As I start to turn, my dad clears his throat. "Cam … we're, uh … going to get dinner. If, uh, you'd like to join?"

Cam stares at him, as if waiting for him to change his mind or say he was just kidding. But he finally nods. "I'd love to. Thanks."

And even if it seems like a small step to most people, I know it's a freaking ginormous one for my father.

We finish eating, and I sort of don't want this night to end. The entire meal went smoothly. At first, my father was quieter than he normally is, but after a while, he came out of his shell. He and Cam actually talked. *Unbelievable.* All seems right in the world.

Not to mention, Isla has been smiling so hard that her cheeks probably hurt. I should know because mine hurt too. I should be scared. I should probably be running away. But if, in the end, I wind up with a broken heart, this feeling right here might make it worth it.

Part of me thinks I'm falling in love with Cam. The other part knows I fell in love with him weeks ago.

We file out of the booth and head to the parking lot. On the way here, my parents took my dad's truck, and Isla, Cam, and I took my car. And now, I have to drive Cam back to the arena to get his truck. Part of me doesn't want this night to end, but I know it's time for Isla to go home and go to bed. Actually, it's way past her bedtime. Though she disagrees.

"Addy, why don't you drive your mom and Isla home, and I'll give Cam a lift?" my dad says, and I feel my body tense.

Is he going to leave Cam on the side of the road to walk? Is he going to tell embarrassing stories about me to get Cam to not want to hang out with me anymore? Dear God, this isn't a good idea.

"Uh … okay," I say, swallowing hard. "That okay with you, Cam?"

Even though Cam is a good actor, always plastering on his carefree smirk that the entire world is used to seeing, I can sense he's nervous.

"Sounds good." He turns to my dad. "As long as you don't murder me or anything." He grins.

My dad shakes his head but chuckles. And I widen my eyes at my mom, who simply shrugs.

Dear Lord, please just let Cam get home safely tonight.

CAM

I climb into Coach's truck, thinking that this perfect day has a high probability of not ending that way.

"Nervous, Hardy?" he asks, fumbling with the radio.

"I mean, I don't know if you watch much real-life crime shit, Coach, but a lot of the time, the killer takes the victim to dinner or somewhere nice to gain their trust and then—*bam*—murders them, and they end up hanging in their basement."

A small laugh comes from him, and he shakes his head. "I don't want to go to prison. That just doesn't sound like much fun."

"Thank fuck," I mutter.

"Addison has been through more in her twenty-one years than a lot of fifty-year-olds have, Cam. She got pregnant in high school and was basically shunned from our town because of the Pelletiers. She had to birth a baby without the dad next to her, supporting her and rubbing her back. And now, she has to carry the weight on her shoulders that, one day, Isla might feel less than, just because the boy who fathered her was an idiot." He sighs. "Since the day Nick walked away, she's trusted nobody but me, her mother, and Tessa." He pauses. "Until you."

Unsure of what to say, I take a breath. "She's been through so much, sir. She's the strongest person I know."

"Please don't be another thing she's got to recover from, Cam. Please don't make her … or me lose faith in the human race altogether." He stops. "Isla loves you, son. She really, really does."

"With all due respect, Coach … *I* might be the one who has to recover from your daughter. The only person who will ever potentially walk away from *us* is her." I feel my stomach turn. "And that would fucking kill me." I look at him. "I know Addison and Isla are a two-for-one package. And as for Isla, I love her right back."

As we turn into the parking lot of the stadium, he sighs in relief. "Good."

We pull next to my truck, and he hits the unlock button to let me out. "Have a good night, Hardy. Good game tonight."

Pushing the door open, I give him a head nod. "Thanks, Coach. See you at practice tomorrow."

As he drives away, I grin like a fucking moron. Because now that her dad is on board, nothing can go wrong.

Right?

19

CAM

I sit in the coffee shop, sipping whatever concoction Layla ordered for me this time. I trust her to order my iced coffee. After all, she's basically a professional at this shit.

"What is this anyway?" I take another sip. "I like it, but it's a bit much."

She rolls her eyes. "For your information, it's a brown sugar cookie iced latte with cold foam. It's my new fave, and it's the bomb diggity."

I shrug, taking another sip. Every sip, it grows on me a little more, but it isn't my favorite coffee she's ever gotten for me.

"So, in other news, besides you being a coffee snob these days, you're officially dating this Addison chick." She widens her eyes, clearly happy. "This is huge, Cam! Before her, you were like me ... only worse. Because I wasn't using men's dicks to fill a void, the way you were using vaginas."

I scowl at her. I hate when she or anyone else says shit like that.

"I was getting used just as much as I used others," I say, defending myself. "And you know it."

"Geesh, someone is touchy." She leans back in her chair, smirking. "Calm down, baby boy. You know I love ya."

"Sorry," I say, trying to relax. "I'm trying to prove to Addison and her daddy that I'm worthy. I don't need a reminder of all the fucked up shit I've done in my life to know I'll never be enough. But I'm trying, Lay. Like, I'm really, *really* trying. Hell, I don't even smile back at the chicks in my classes when they try to get my attention. And it's not even hard because she's all I see."

Her eyes widen before she bursts out laughing. "Whoa … I don't remember ordering a side of cheese with my coffee."

"Fuck you," I say, reaching across and shoving her. "You and Dane are as cheesy as they come."

"Well, that's because he's adorable. Okay, so anyway, you're serious with this girl. And what about being a stepdaddy? How's that going?" She snorts. "Big daddy Cam."

I throw my head back. I'm far from a stepdad to Isla. But if things keep getting more serious between Addy and me, like I anticipate and hope like hell they do, someday, that is something I'm going to have to step into the role of. It won't be hard either. Hell, I love that kid already.

"I'm just figuring it as I go, Layla." I raise my eyebrows at her. "*Just* like you and Dane."

"Fair enough," she mutters, hitting her coffee against mine. "I'm proud of you, Cam. Even when you were being a pervy dick, I knew, inside here," she says, jabbing her finger into my chest, "you were just a giant marshmallow."

I laugh, but I know she's right. Back when Henley Hayes thought I was a piece of shit, Layla, even being her best friend, believed in me. And she became one of my best friends.

Eventually, I want Layla and Addison to meet.

ADDISON

On my way to class, I stop at the coffee shop. Walking with a slight skip, I hum an annoying Miley Cyrus song I can't seem to get out of my head, thanks to Isla.

I place my order, a coffee way bigger than I normally get because momming ain't easy. But when I turn my body and grab a straw, someone catches my attention.

Cam is sitting at a small table across from a gorgeous redhead. She laughs, touching his chest as he says something funny. Just like he always does. Charming Cam … not only for me, it seems.

My stomach turns. *Why did I let my guard down? I'm so dumb.*

164

His eyes find mine, and he does something even more shocking. He holds his hand up and fucking waves! Like I didn't just catch him dogging on another person.

The barista shoves a coffee across the counter, and I grab it before turning and heading straight for the door as quickly as I can.

"Addison," I hear Cam call from behind me, sounding panicked. "Addison!"

I push out through the door, willing the tears not to fall as I suck in a breath. My heart breaks inside of my chest as I fumble for my car keys to unlock the doors.

"Addy, wait!" he yells. "Fucking wait."

"No," I hiss, wiping the wetness from my cheeks. "Go back inside."

"What you think you saw is nothing. Layla is a friend. One of my best friends."

"If that were the case, surely, you would have mentioned her before," I snap, whirling around. "Go inside."

He grabs my wrist before I can open my door. "Don't run off. Let me explain."

"Explain what?!" I bark. "You're out, getting coffee, tee-heeing with that hot piece of ass. That's all there is to it. I get it. It was all a game to you. You win. Congratu-fucking-lations. Leave me alone."

I turn and try to open my door, but he slams it shut, spinning me around.

"Cam, stop," I cry. "Why couldn't you just leave me be?"

"Addison, listen to me. I need you to quit acting crazy and listen to me, damn it! She's my fucking friend."

"Now, I'm crazy? I don't need this. This isn't what I signed up for."

"Neither did I," he growls, releasing me before dragging his hand up his neck. "You're being unreasonable."

"Crazy and unreasonable in one conversation?" I shoot him a hard glare. "Fuck off."

I pull my door open and quickly climb inside, locking the door behind me.

And he stands there … letting me go.

CAM

"You just gonna let her leave, Romeo?" Layla says from behind me.

"She's acting insane," I growl. "Like certifiably crazy. You're my friend. What the fuck is the issue?"

Spinning me around, Layla takes my hand. "Cam, I love you, but, God, you're so thickheaded sometimes. Let's do something, okay? Let's change the scenario, yeah?"

"What?" I mutter.

"Let's say you're driving by the café, and you're like, *Wow, I'd like a muffin. I think I'll stop.* And when you stop and walk in, Addison is sitting across from some hot dude." She stops, winking. "Because, you know, I'm clearly hot."

When I don't smile back, she sighs. "Anyway, they are laughing, touching, having a great time ... and you knew nothing about the fact that she was meeting him. How would you feel?"

I look down. "I'd be pissed."

"Exactly. So, what are you going to do about it?" She smiles, patting my shoulder.

Pulling her in for a quick hug, I release her and jog to my truck.

Because apparently, I fucked up and didn't realize it.

ADDISON

I make it into class just before the professor closes the door. Here is the last place I want to be. I feel like dog poop, and tears just won't stop coming from my eyes.

"Psst, you all right?" Hunter says, looking concerned.

Brooks is a pretty big campus. So, when I walked into a brand-new class at the start of this semester, I couldn't believe it when I spotted Hunter sitting behind a desk, once again sharing a class with me. I suppose, given the fact that we're both studying for health degrees, it makes sense. It was nice to see a familiar face again.

Wiping my eyes with my sleeve, I attempt a half-assed smile. "I'm fine. Allergies."

Looking at the front of the room, he sees the professor is still at his desk, and he stands, coming to the seat next to mine.

Reaching in his bag, he pulls out a packet of tissues and sets them on my desk. "I've gotten those *allergy* things before too. Right around the time my ex told me we should see other people." He pats my shoulder. "Allergies fucking suck."

A half laugh, part cry escapes me, and I look at him just as class begins.

Thank you, I mouth, tearing open the package and wiping my nose.

With a curt nod, he takes his laptop out and relaxes in his chair, preparing for this long and boring class.

The lecture is only about ten minutes in when the classroom phone rings. The teacher rolls his eyes but reluctantly walks over and answers.

"Hello?" he mutters, looking around at the hundreds of eyes on him. "Mmhmm. Yep. Fine."

Quickly hanging the phone back on the wall, he walks back to his podium.

"Addison LaConte, you're needed outside. Grab your things. It appears you won't be back tonight."

I frown, trying to figure out what the heck just happened. And then it hits me. It could be Isla. She might be hurt.

Scurrying around, I gather my things up and bolt toward the door.

Only, when I get outside into the darkness, I'm not greeted by my dad or mom. And it isn't a police officer.

It's Cam standing under the streetlight.

And he's holding two dozen pink roses, a gloomy look on his face.

"Cam, why are you here?" I put a hand on my hip. "I thought I made it very clear that I didn't want to see you."

"Well, tough shit, LaConte."

"*Excuse* me?" I attempt to level him with a glare.

When he struts toward me, I back up until my back hits the brick wall. Tossing the flowers on the grass beside me, he cages me in, planting both hands on the building.

"Tough ... fucking ... shit," he growls. "I should have explained that I had a best friend who has tits and a vagina, so that's on me. I'm new to this, Addy. I'm going to fuck up." He drops his lips closer to mine, and, damn it, he smells so good. "That doesn't mean you can run off every time I do. Otherwise, we'll be doing this cat-and-mouse game far too often."

"Cam," I whisper, looking up at him, "I can't handle being hurt by you."

"And I can't handle watching your car drive away every time I do something to piss you off," he says, his hand moving to my hip, his fingertips digging into my skin. "You have the ability to fucking wreck me, Addison. How do you not see it?"

I stare at him, unable to form words. I acted like a lunatic. I know that. But disappointment and jealousy took over my entire body, mind, and soul. Making it so I couldn't see or hear anything other than my thoughts telling me what I'd always been scared of. That I'm not enough. That he needs other women around.

He cups my cheek with his other hand. "I am sorry I didn't tell you about Layla, but I swear on everything, today wasn't a planned-out thing. I was headed for a coffee, and she just happened to call me and be nearby. She moved to be closer to her boyfriend a few weeks ago, so I hadn't seen her in a while. Plus, I had been so preoccupied with you, I guess I sort of forgot to bring her up." His eyes shift between mine. "If this is ever going to work, we've got to trust each other. I know my reputation sucks, and I know you've been burned in the past, but, damn it, Addy, I'm not Nick Pelletier, I promise." He takes a breath. "I'd cut my legs off and never skate again before I ever hurt you."

Slowly, I nod. "I'm sorry. I'm just—" My voice cracks. "I'm so scared. Of being hurt. Of Isla getting hurt too." I sniffle.

"Don't you see it yet, Addison?" He dips his forehead closer. "Can't you feel it?"

"Feel what?" I ask, confused. "What are you talking about, Cam?"

"Do you see that there are guys out there who want to stick around? Do you feel it when I tell you I care about you? Or what about when I tell you that I love you? Because I do, Addison. I fucking love you more than I've ever loved anything in my life. And as crazy as it might sound, I love Isla too. I love both of you, as a pair. You're my future. My present. Hell, somehow, it feels like my past too." His lips connect with mine before he pulls away the slightest bit. "I'll spend the rest of my life making sure you feel it. Making sure *she* feels it. I'm not going anywhere. This thing? It's forever. I'm yours. Both of yours now."

"You're insane." I cry harder, melting into him. "I love you too though. I really do."

His hand slides from my cheek and pushes my hair back, gripping it slightly. He kisses me like he hasn't been able to kiss me in a thousand years and is starved for my lips.

Hoisting me up, he throws me over his shoulder.

"Where are you taking me?"

"To my place. To my bed," he growls, slapping my ass. "Because if I'm not buried inside of you soon, I'm going to fucking lose it."

Minutes later, he's speeding toward his place.

"Nobody's home," he says, lifting my hand up and pressing his lips to my flesh. "You'll be able to scream as loud as you want, baby."

I shake my head at him as I blush, but it's all I can do not to clench my thighs together with pure need. And when we pull up in front of his place shortly after, I'm eagerly pushing my door open.

Running to the front of the truck, he lifts me up as he walks us toward his stairs. His lips are on mine, even as he fumbles to open the door.

I moan into his mouth as he walks into his room, shutting the door behind him.

Tossing me onto the bed, he wastes no time in pulling his own jeans and briefs down. "I love you," he says, palming himself and giving his length a few pumps.

Slowly pulling my leggings and panties down, he parts my legs and climbs between them. And when he kisses my inner thigh before dipping his tongue inside of me, I cry out, unable to control myself at his touch.

His hands snake under my shirt, and he cups my breast as he works some sort of magic with his tongue, making my head spin. As good as it feels though ... I just need him inside of me. This afternoon was emotionally draining, and I need him close.

"Cam, please ... I need you." I'm embarrassed by the amount of emotion in my voice.

I have no idea how I could love someone so much, this soon. But I do. My heart thumps to a different beat when he's around.

Slowly moving his head from between my legs, he positions himself above me. "Sorry, you just taste so good that I can't control myself."

He nudges the tip inside of me, slowly pushing deeper and deeper. I feel full and complete. And ... whole.

I wrap my legs around his body and drag my fingernails down his back as he pounds into me. Something about this time feels different. Maybe it's because we just had our first real fight, making this more intense. Or perhaps it's because we just admitted out loud what we'd known for weeks ... that we love each other. Either way, I know I'm not going to last long. Especially with the way he's looking at me.

I drag my heels down the backs of his legs, pushing him even deeper. So deep that I cry out from the most delicious pain I've ever felt in my life.

"Cam," I moan against his shoulder as everything gets dizzy and my belly tingles. "Oh ... God."

"I love you, beautiful girl. Come with me. Every orgasm, every bit of pleasure of yours, is mine. Let me fucking feel it. Drip down my cock like a good girl."

His filthy words always push me over the edge. I love the way he talks dirty, his mouth spewing things that some might view as disrespectful. Not me. I eat it up, wanting more.

He pours himself inside of me, gripping my hip with one hand and my thigh with the other. His body trembles just before he kisses my forehead.

"So, yeah ... I totally knew that would happen when I kidnapped you from class," he says sarcastically.

I roll my eyes, running my fingers through his hair. "Sure ya did."

"Nah. I figured you would probably pull a knife out and stab me in the balls." He kisses my nose. "This was much, much better."

I swat at him. "I'm not that crazy, dick."

"I sort of beg to differ." He holds me against him, like he doesn't want to let go. "Christ almighty, Addison. What was life before I found you?"

I simply smile and shrug, unable to knock this cheesy smile off my face.

Because honestly ... I'm not sure.

Brooks's very own puck boy is finally in love with someone. And I'm the lucky girl.

20

ADDISON

I take Isla's temperature as she sleeps. She shivers slightly, but her body is on fire.

"One hundred and one," I whisper to my mom, trying to quiet my own cough. "It's gone down a little since the Motrin."

"You try to get some rest. I'll take the first shift." My mom tightens the blanket on herself. "Gonna be another long night, I'm sure."

Influenza hit our household, bringing Isla down first, followed by me and my mother yesterday. We're praying Dad doesn't catch it. He's the worst sick person on the planet, I swear.

It happened just five days after the whole Cam and Layla ordeal, where I acted crazy. I keep thinking maybe it's my karma for acting so insecure.

"It's okay. I can't sleep anyway when I know she has a fever." I yawn. "You go to bed. I'll stay awake."

Too tired to disagree, she nods. "You come and get me if she worsens. Or if you do. You hear me, baby girl?"

"I will," I say, coughing a few times. "Love you."

These are the times I think of as being in the trenches when having a little one. It's tiring. And even when they seem okay during the day, night falls, the fever spikes, and—bam—you're in for the longest night of your life.

But despite how tired you get, you push through. Because that little human depends on you.

My mom made my father go get a motel room. He was angry. He didn't want to leave his family, but Mom wasn't taking no for an answer. Her argument was pretty good too. That if Dad got sick, it'd only leave her with another human to worry about. So, he gave up and went to the motel. It also happened to be right after she said she booked a nonrefundable room.

My phone buzzes with Cam's name on the screen, and despite how crappy I feel, I smile.

"Hello?" I say, sounding like a mix of a ninety-year-old chain-smoker and a kid wearing homely nose plugs.

"Whoa. Lay off the ciggy butts." He laughs. "Seriously, my baby doesn't sound good."

I toss my head back. "I know! Trust me, I feel even worse."

"I've got something to make you feel better."

"A sex joke right now? Really?" I groan.

"Hey, you miss one hundred percent of the shots you don't take," he says, and I can hear the smirk in his voice. "Come to the door."

"Wh-what?" I panic, realizing how shitty I look. "You're here? Like, *here*, here?"

"Yep," he says smoothly. "And if you're worried about how you look, don't. No matter what, you're still the hottest mom anyone's ever seen."

Fastening my robe around myself, I head toward the door and slowly pull it open.

"Don't laugh," my voice rasps as my throat screams for me to stop talking.

Eyeing me over, he shrugs. "I'd still do ya."

I start to laugh, but it just turns into a bark, making Cam frown.

"Christ, Addison," he says, pushing past me and into the house with an armload of stuff. "I should take you to the doctor."

"No way," I say, following him into the kitchen. "I'm fine. I'm more worried about Isla."

His eyes move to mine, his expression anxious. "She that bad?" He looks around. "Where is she?"

"My room." I see the two large iced coffees he's putting in the refrigerator, and I smile. "Coffee?"

"For you and your mom." He sets the brown paper bag in his arm down and heads toward my room.

Pawing through the stuff, I can't help but swoon. Cough drops, cold and flu medicine, saltines, Popsicles, soup, Gatorade, and I almost die when I see a Disney princess coloring book with new crayons for Isla.

After I put the stuff away, I head down the hall to find Cam on his side with Isla curled against him. He holds the thermometer over her head, waiting for it to beep.

"One hundred and two," he whispers. "Isn't that high?"

"Crap, it's going up again." I wipe my eyes.

No mom ever wants to see their kid sick even if it is just the flu. No matter how many times she gets this crap, it scares me.

"Should we take her to the doctor?" he asks, staring at her as he strokes her hair. "I know nothing about this shit, but I can tell you, I hate it already."

"There's nothing they can do really." I lie on the other side of her. "It really, really sucks. I feel helpless."

Isla's cheeks are blotchy red as she breathes faster than normal. She begins coughing and hacking in her sleep, and I already know what's going to happen next.

When I scoop her up, she vomits down the front of me.

"Shh, it's okay. Get it all out, baby." I rub her back as she cries.

"When she gets coughing in her sleep, she coughs so hard that this happens," I explain to Cam. "I feel so bad. Her little body needs rest, and she can't get it."

He pales as he looks at her. "I'm not trying to be pushy, Addy, but are you sure we shouldn't take her somewhere?"

"If her temperature gets worse, I will," I tell him. "She's back asleep now. I'm going to get her clothes changed. She's sweated through them and now puked on herself." I look down at myself, frowning. "And on me."

Taking my robe off and putting it in the hamper, I'm thankful I had it on. It shielded the rest of me from the nasty vomit.

Going into Isla's room, I grab her a fresh pair of PJs and head back to change her.

Luckily, she doesn't wake while I pull off her dirty clothes. Just shivers more when the air hits her skin. And once I've finished dressing her, I tuck her back in and continue to monitor her temp.

"So, don't get me wrong," Cam says, grinning at me, "but I'd totally still do ya and all. But, babe … your hair. You've got puke in it." His nose scrunches up. "I could overlook it, but, yeah …"

I know he's only kidding, that he isn't expecting or wanting sex right now. That's just his personality. He jokes to make things lighter. And in times like this, I appreciate it.

He stands and walks into the bathroom in my room, and I hear the shower turn on.

"Take a shower, Addy. I've got her."

I stare at him in disbelief as a huge yawn rips through me. "How are you even real?" I ask, barely able to keep my eyes open from sheer exhaustion.

He chuckles before taking my hand and walking me into the bathroom. Peeling my shirt over my head, he tosses it in the dirty laundry before kneeling down and taking my sweats, panties, and socks off.

I step into the shower and let the hot water spray down my hair and onto my body. It feels so nice. And I sort of never want to get out.

He walks out for a minute before coming back in. "She's sound asleep," he says before grabbing a bottle of shampoo and squirting some into his hands. He reaches inside the shower and massages the suds through my hair.

The feeling of a man actually caring from me is so foreign, and at his touch, I grow even sleepier.

"You shouldn't be in this germ-infested house," I say, yawning again. "The team can't afford for you to get sick."

"I'm not going anywhere." He rinses my hair out before moving on to conditioner. "Besides, I've got a bulletproof immune system." He pauses. "And I might have eaten a shit ton of those Emergen-C Gummies before coming over here."

I giggle. "Hate to break it to you, but I ate them, too, and look how that turned out."

The water washes through my hair, rinsing the conditioner out before the shower turns off.

The second the hot water is gone, my body starts to shake, and my lips quiver.

"C-cold," I whisper just as he wraps a towel around me and pulls me against him.

He wastes no time in bringing us back into my room, and I know it's because he doesn't want to leave Isla alone for long. And I appreciate that so, so much.

"I'm so tired." I barely get the words out before sitting on the edge of the bed. Up until now, I was exhausted yet restless. Right now, I can barely stay awake.

Rifling through my drawers, he pulls out some matching fleece pajamas with a cat on the chest. I reach for them, but he shakes his head.

"Let me," he mutters.

Slowly, he dresses me. And I feel like a loser, but honestly, I don't have the energy to do it myself.

"Thank you, Cam," I say, shivering as I climb under the covers. "You should go. Really. I don't want you to catch this crap. *Bulletproof* as your immune system might be … it fucking sucks, to be blunt."

As he brushes my hair gently, I swear his eyes look into my soul, and I know I actually need him right now.

"I'm not going anywhere. So, rest, babe. Plenty of more fights you'll be able to take part in. But right now, you need sleep." Kissing my head, he tucks the blankets around me tighter. "I'll be right here if Isla needs me. Sleep."

"I love you," I mumble before my eyes close, and I sink into the mattress, falling into a deep sleep for the first time in days.

I don't know the reasoning behind it, but I trust him to keep my baby safe.

CAM

Addison goes from shivering to sweating and back to shivering as she sleeps. Her cough makes it damn hard for her body to actually rest, and I can't believe I'm willingly here, in this germ-infested house, just days before our big game in North Carolina, against her dick of an ex-boyfriend. But there's no way I am leaving her.

Isla has coughed off and on, and I've checked her fever at least twenty times in the past three hours. Luckily, it hasn't gone up. I've found myself watching her chest to make sure she is breathing. She has the flu. She isn't dying. And yet I'm fucking scared. No, I'm terrified.

And feeling this way only makes me hate Nick Pelletier even more than I already did. He shares the same blood as Isla, and he can't be bothered to be in her life. I'm just some dumbass who is dating her mama, and it makes me sick, thinking that, in another hour, I'll need to leave her and Addison to go to practice.

I hear the floor creak and glance over to find Jennie. She looks like hell, just like the other two, and I can tell she doesn't feel well either. Still, she smiles.

"You voluntarily stepped into this flu-infected household?" She sounds surprised. "Barren is at a motel."

I chuckle. Addison told me that her mom made Coach stay in a motel. Apparently, he's a pansy when he gets sick.

"After I leave here, probably going to shower in sanitizer and drink a gallon of Airborne or Emergen-C." I look down at Addison as she coughs. "Y'all are having yourselves a rough week, huh?"

"Not the greatest." Her forehead creases with worry. "So … bound for North Carolina tomorrow. Cut Coach some slack if he's extra douchey. There're a few people who can get under his skin, and anyone with the last name Pelletier is one of them."

Coach was on edge more than I'd ever seen him the last time we played North Carolina. He's not usually a cheerful dude, but add his baby girl's ex, who left her after knocking her up, into the mix, and, yeah, no good.

"After the last time, seeing Coach that worked up, I think the guys and I understand how crucial it is to whoop their ass," I say with a grin. "He'll be fine. The team is like a family, and we've got each other's back. Coach's too. *Even* if he did go days without speaking to me."

"Yes, well … keep proving him wrong," she says with a raise of her eyebrows before tapping the screen on her watch. "You'd better get going to practice soon."

Isla rolls against me, snuggling into my side.

"I'll be back right after. With food too. She needs to eat." I nod toward Addison.

She turns to leave.

"Oh, Jennie, there's an iced coffee in the refrigerator. Figured y'all would need all the energy you could get."

She points to me. "Now, you're talking. Thank you."

Once she's gone, I kiss Isla on the forehead, followed by her hot-as-hell mama.

Addison's eyes flutter open, and she stretches. "Hi."

I kiss her again. "Gotta go to practice. But I'll be back right after. What do you want for dinner?"

Reaching up, she touches my face. "Are you real, Cam Hardy?"

"You know it, babe." I wink. "You need to eat, so what do you want? Pizza, Chinese, pasta?"

She thinks about it for a moment. "I'm not sure what sounds good. I feel like I can hardly taste anything."

"I'll give you something to taste," I groan against her neck, and she giggles.

"How about Chinese? Isla loves that, and so does Mom."

"Orange chicken and spring rolls for you, chicken fingers with sweet and sour for Isla," I say, remembering what they ordered the time we ate at the Chinese restaurant last week. "What about your mom?"

"She likes vegetable lo mein. And I'll steal some of it." She runs her fingers through my hair. "God, I love you."

"I love you too, even when you're all snotty and germ-infested." I stand up. "See you in a bit."

ADDISON

I shuffle into the kitchen, still clearly sick but feeling a thousand times better after getting some sleep.

My mother sits at the counter with the iced coffee Cam dropped off in front of her and a magazine. She looks up at me, pulling her glasses down. "How ya doing, love?"

"A little better, I think." I take my own coffee from the fridge and sit next to her. "Whatcha reading? Anything good?"

"I don't know why I buy these things anymore. It's all ads, except maybe ten pages. And those ten pages are nothing interesting." She slides it away from her. "So, Cam was here, playing nurse." She wiggles her eyebrows. "A *hot* nurse at that."

I almost spit out my coffee, wiping my mouth when a little bit comes out. "Mom!" I laugh. "You can't call my boyfriend hot. It's weird."

"Girlfriend, he is hot. I might be getting old, but I'm not senile." She pats my back. "And boyfriend, huh? It's official then?"

I blush. "Well, not really, I guess. He hasn't come out and asked, but what else would I call him?"

"I'm happy for you," she says sweetly. "He's a good one. And you know what?"

"What?"

"He's crazy about *both* of you." She leans her head against my shoulder. "He's not pretending to love her for your benefit. He really does. And it's beautiful to watch, my love."

She stands, patting her hair down. "Now, if you'll excuse me, I need to shower. I'm probably beginning to smell how I feel."

"Good call." I grin.

I never thought I'd find anyone who treated my daughter the way she deserved to be treated. And I certainly never thought Cam would be that guy. He's full of surprises. But nothing shocks me more than just how much I'm beginning to trust him with not only my heart, but Isla's too.

As corny as it sounds, I feel like the luckiest girl on the planet.

For now.

CAM

The ride to North Carolina seems like it's taking forever. I've tried to fall asleep, but it's no use. Now that Addison's starting to feel better, I even thought about sending her a few dirty text messages because it's been days since I've sunk inside of her. But seeing's I'm sitting with a busload of dudes and I'd likely have to hide my boner, I decide against any sex messaging.

Addison told me that Isla finally seemed to be feeling a bit better this morning. What a relief that was. Knowing I was going to have to travel hours away today, I would have been a wreck if she was still really sick. Last night, when I took Chinese back to them, Coach ended up saying fuck the motel room and came back to the house. We sat around the table, talking and eating, and everything seemed like it was supposed to. And even if, deep down, he might think I'm putting on an act to sell him on the fact that I love her, I'm actually just treating her exactly how I would even if he wasn't watching me under a microscope. I want to see her smile. I want to hear Isla giggle. Hell, even I don't recognize myself these days.

"Hardy," Coach says from the front of the bus. "Get up here."

"Yes, sir," I answer and slide out of my seat.

"Someone's in trouble," Link taunts me, his hat pulled down as he pops his earbuds in.

I give him the middle finger and shake my head. Something tells me this chat is going to have nothing to do with his daughter and everything to do with Nick Pelletier.

"What's up?" I say, sitting in the seat behind him.

He holds his iPad in his hands, tapping the screen gently.

"Pelletier is going to have his protectors all over you. You know that, right?" He tenses. "You won't be able to breathe without someone taking a cheap shot. And if we somehow walk away with the W tonight, tomorrow, they'll come swinging ten times harder."

I nod once. "Yeah, I figured as much."

He taps his screen again, looking at the different play options. "We've got to figure out something else. Something to hold our position in the season."

Every center has a giant or two behind him, waiting to strike. Guardians of the ice, people call them. They take matters into their own hands and act almost like mercenaries. Nick Pelletier might have a few monsters backing him up, but I have something he doesn't have.

I have Brody O'Brien. He waits; he watches. And when he sees a cheap shot, he's there, making the player regret ever taking it.

Wayne Gretzky was one of the greatest players to ever grace the ice. But without the protection of Dave Semenko and Marty McSorley, he would have taken many, many more hits. Hockey is a team sport for a reason—we need each other.

"I promise, Coach, O'Brien is ready. And there ain't a college hockey player out there who isn't scared of that motherfucker." I grin. "But we've got all the time in the world, and I've got a few ideas. Let's go over some plays."

He looks over his shoulder at me and gives me a curt nod. "Let's do it."

ADDISON

My mom and I sit in the living room, watching the hockey game. Normally, we don't watch when it's a game Nick is a part of, but Isla is in bed, and I think both of us felt the need to support our men. Even if it is from states away.

Everything in Cam's body language screams he's on edge. Whatever Nick is saying to him is getting under his skin. Not to mention the fact that it's a bloodbath out there. I might be watching it through a screen, but I can feel the tension in my bones.

"Jesus," I hiss under my breath, watching what could be the most contact I've ever seen at a college hockey game. "There won't be one player who isn't going to feel this game tomorrow."

"And the next day," my mom murmurs back. "At least the Wolves are holding them. Gosh, I hope they can walk away with the win."

Cam still skates with ease, making hockey look like an art. But there's something about the way his shoulders sit on his body. He isn't himself. And when the camera cuts to my father, he chomps his gum so fiercely that my jaw hurts a little as I watch him.

When I was in high school and before I had baby Isla growing in my belly, there was a time when Nick and I talked about the day we would go to college in North Carolina … together. We had big plans. He was charming. His family tolerated me just enough that I thought it could all work out. Now, I look back, and I think of how dumb I must have been. How could I have ever seen him in a romantic way? He's a douche.

"Whatcha thinking about over there?" my mom asks when the TV cuts to a commercial. "You look like you just traveled far away."

I give her a half smile. "Honestly? Just trying to figure out what I ever saw in that toolbag. And how I ever thought Cam and Nick were the same, I have no idea. Cam is a million times the man Nick will ever be. I wish—" I stop, embarrassed to finish my sentence.

"Go on," she says quietly.

"I know it's crazy because we haven't been together nearly long enough to say this. And I suppose Cam could also be someone he isn't … but I wish he could have been Isla's dad. Even if it didn't work out between us, I get the feeling he'd still stick around. If he were her father, you know?" I shake my head. "I know; it sounds insane and weird."

She sets her mug down. "It doesn't sound insane or weird. But we can't change the past. What's done is done. I promise that girl will be okay, no matter what, because she has you." She tilts her head. "It's good to see you with Cam. I've never seen you so happy—I mean, with Isla, you obviously are happy. But this is different. Anyway, it's nice. Being in love looks good on you." She winks.

"How do you know it's love?" I eye her over. She doesn't know we've been using the *love* word.

Rolling her eyes, she tosses a stuffed animal at me. "Lady, I know my only daughter."

The game comes on, and I tense back up as I watch Cam come back on the screen. The tension in his shoulders is still there.

If I could do anything, it would be to fast-forward time and just have him back at Brooks.

CAM

I never could have anticipated the way I'd feel out on this ice tonight. Or the amount of spite I feel when I look at Pelletier's smug fucking face. He must keep pretty good tabs on Addison because he knows I'm with her. Even had the audacity to bring up Isla too.

He's trying to get in my head, and unlike most games I've played since I was a kid, it's working. I can't shake the words, and I can't get rid of this sick feeling in my stomach.

He's never cared enough about his daughter to reach out, yet he knows who Addison is dating.

"You good?" I say as Brody skates by just before the game starts back up.

He's had my back all night, just like he always does.

"Oh, you know I love a reason to fuck up someone's life." He smirks even though I know he's exhausted.

This game has been one of the most brutal and physical games I've ever played, and it isn't over yet.

"Let's finish it out." I bump my fist to his just as Link skates toward us.

"Let's do it," Link chants. "Finish this shit, get out of here alive, and come back tomorrow, ready to do it again."

Brody nods and taps his stick to Link's. "Let's fucking go, baby."

Once they skate away, Nick is right on my ass, just as I knew he would be.

"You like my leftovers, Hardy?" He gets in my face. "Fuck, that girl knew how to suck my dick just the way I liked it. Nothing I loved more than gagging her with my co—"

I shove him backward, gripping his jersey and smashing my helmet to his. "I'll murder you on this ice, Pelletier. Fucking try me."

He knows what he's doing. He wants to get me wound up so that I do something to fuck this game up. There's still four minutes left on the clock, and we're only up by one.

"Too bad that tight, perfect pussy of hers is ruined now that she's pushed out that bastard child. I guess I got out at the right time, huh?"

Ripping his helmet off, I start raining down punch after punch. He grabs my shirt, and we spin around on the ice, both trying to get our footing enough to land another blow.

Blood pours down his face, and still, he doesn't shut up. "I had her first. Next time you're with her, remember that my dick has already been in there, bitch. And when you're tasting her, you're tasting my cum. Enjoy."

He's on the ice on his back with me on top of him, and the only thing that saves his miserable fucking life is the referee who tears me off of him.

Pushing me off the ice, I skate by Coach. "Sorry, sir. But no man is ever going to disrespect my girls like that. They can suspend me for the season. I don't fucking regret it. Hell, if I had my way, he'd be in a hospital bed right now."

He closes his eyes and drags his hand down his face.

The ref directs me to the sin bin, and I look down at the ground so that I don't look at Nick's smug face.

"You're lucky we all have daughters or wives and heard all the terrible things he said," the ref with the orange sleeves mutters before shutting the door. "You're out for the rest of the game, but I think that'll be the extent of your punishment."

I don't answer, just blow out a breath and pray to fucking God that my boys can pull this win off without me.

Coach walks into the locker room, and I hold my breath, waiting for the worst. We might have won the game, but chances are, he isn't too happy with my actions.

"The fuck got into you?" Link whispers.

"I liked it." Brody grins. "Feels good to beat the fuck out of someone who deserves it. Doesn't it, Cam?"

"Fuck if I know," I mutter, still feeling unsettled throughout my whole body. This must be what Nick Pelletier's presence does to Coach. Now, I see why he gets so worked up over these games.

"I know you guys are expecting me to come in here and yell. To tell you the way certain players acted is unacceptable and that I won't stand for it." His eyes find mine, and he jerks his chin down. "I can't say any of it to you right now. Truth is, that punk has had it coming for a long time."

He sits down in the center of us on a bench. "It's no secret that Hardy going out early wasn't what was best for the team. It's true that you had to work harder just to fill the void of him not being there with you. There are going to be a lot of times in this game when you've got to separate your personal life from the ice. But there's also going to be those times when that line gets blurred. When you need to stay true to you and do what's right. So, I can't sit here and tell you that I wouldn't have done the same thing Hardy did tonight because if I had heard the shit coming from Pelletier's mouth, I'd probably be in jail right now."

He looks up, swinging his gaze to each and every one of us. "I'm hard on you because I know you are champions. I'm tough because I want to take you as far as I can. Congratulations on the win tonight, fellas. Despite the low blows and cheap shots, you played your hearts out and left it all in the arena. I'm proud of all of you."

Adjusting his hat, he claps Thompson and a few others on the shoulders before walking out of the room. And even though we'd normally be cheering, his words seemed to sober us up.

And I'm leaving this arena with a hate in my soul I've never experienced before. A hate for Addison's ex.

And that hate is only going to grow at tomorrow's game.

ADDISON

"**G**oddamn it, I've missed these perfect tits," Cam growls against my breasts, working his way to my lips.

I moan at his touch, needing him so incredibly bad. It's been weeks since we've had sex. Between being sick, him traveling to North Carolina, me living with my parents and being a mom, and his crazy hockey schedule, it's hard to find the time. So, here we are in his bed, in between my classes, like a couple of sex-crazed teenagers.

Topless and turned on, I sink to my knees and unbutton his jeans. My mouth watering already in anticipation.

As his length springs free, I gaze up at him as he runs his thumb down my cheek.

"Tell me what you want," I whisper, loving when he says exactly what he wants. "What you want me to do."

His eyes narrow slightly as he palms himself in his hand and pumps. "I want you to open your mouth and swallow me whole." He moves his hand to the back of my head. "I want to feel my cock hit the back of your throat. Need to know this mouth was only made for my pleasure."

"Only you," I say lowly as he pushes my face closer to his hardness.

"Stick your tongue out and lap me like a good girl."

Eagerly doing what I was told, I run my tongue up the underside of his length, drag it back down, and pull it between my lips.

"Fuck," he hisses. "You look so beautiful with my dick in your mouth."

I work harder and faster, taking him in as deep as I can and keeping him there. Reaching around to his ass, I pull him toward me, making myself lose control and gag as he begins to rock into me.

"Goddamn it, that's hot." He looks down at me with hooded eyes. "You always take me so good, Addy."

I hum against his shaft, making his hips jerk. Between my legs throbs with need, and he must sense my desperation because he yanks me up and lies back on the bed, pulling me on top of him.

"Ride my cock like you've been dying to, Addison. Make us both come undone."

I sink down onto him, slowly adjusting to the fullness. "Oh," I moan. "God … Cam."

It feels too good, and when his hands cup my breasts, pushing my upper body upward, I gasp.

My hips start to work as his hands glide to my waist, and his mouth moves from one nipple to another, biting and sucking, driving me wild as I pant against him like an animal of some sort.

My orgasm isn't a gradual build, but instead hits me like a freight train, making me dig my nails into Cam's shoulders and cry out.

Tangling his hand in my hair, he pushes my mouth to his. "Fuck," he groans against my lips as he pours himself inside of me. "You feel so good when you squeeze around me, milking every fucking ounce."

I breathe against his lips as a final shiver runs down my body, and I collapse on him.

"No, not fucking done with you yet. We still have a few more minutes," he growls against my hair. "I need you once more. Been way too long."

I slide my hand to his length again, finding him still hard. Quickly, he flips me onto my stomach and climbs over me. Pulling my belly up, he cups me at my waist as he pushes my chest into the mattress. Parting my thighs further, he nudges his hardness between my legs, working himself inside until he moves in a rhythm. His grip on my waist tightens with one hand while the other fists my hair, giving it a tug as he fucks me from behind.

"Cam," I whimper, "you feel so good. You're so deep."

Releasing my waist, his hand comes down hard on my ass, again and again. I wince, but it also sends a shock of excitement coursing through my body, and I bite my lip in pleasure.

"Seeing your ass this way? I'm not going to last long."

Arching my back, he hits deeper, and we both moan. His hand snakes around to my mouth, and he slips his finger inside.

"Suck my finger like you just sucked my cock, baby," he grunts.

And not long after his finger slips into my mouth, he loses it, as do I.

"Jesus, Addy," he breathes out. "Goddamn, girl."

As he rocks slowly into me, I muffle a scream in the pillow as I come undone on him. And once we're finally done, I flop in the bed, exhausted as hell but with a big-ass smile on my face.

That is, until I realize I'm going to be late for class.

"Damn you," I say, shoving his chest lightly. "Distracting me from my studies with your penis."

He rests his hands on the back of his head. "My beautiful penis." He winks. "My perfect, *giant* penis."

"Whatever you say." I roll my eyes and stand, grabbing my clothes.

"That's right. You're getting it now," he tosses back. "You jealous that you don't get to hang out with the cool kids, me and Isla, tonight?" He raises his eyebrows. "I might even become her favorite. I have quite the night planned."

I can't help the stupid grin on my face. He asked me earlier if he could watch Isla tonight while I was in class, and she talked about it the entire day. I know whatever they do, he'll make sure she has fun.

I start dressing quickly, pulling my brain from swooning over my boyfriend, when Cam's phone rings.

He looks at it for a moment, almost like he isn't sure if he's going to answer or not, but eventually, he puts it to his ear. And for some reason, I feel like the call might be something important. Something … big.

CAM

"Hello?" I say, bringing the phone to my ear.

"Hi there. I'm trying to reach Cam Hardy," a deep voice answers.

"Well, you've got me." I watch Addison as she eyes me cautiously, tugging her shirt over her head. "How can I help ya?"

"This is Coach Jim Montgomery of the Boston Bruins. I've also got Assistant Coach John Gruden here as well. How's it going?" he replies, and I almost drop the phone.

"Hello, Mr. Hardy," another voice says.

"Hello." I blink a few times, suddenly feeling light-headed. "Uh … good. Can I—is there something I can help you with?"

He chuckles. "Well, I sure hope so. We've been watching you, Mr. Hardy. Along with the other coaches here in Boston. Helluva player you are. And a few weekends ago in North Carolina? You were playing on a whole other level. Must have felt good to win both of those games." He pauses. "I'd like to have you join us next season. If you're interested. Of course, there'll be some terms and conditions, as I'm sure you can imagine."

"Holy shit, are you serious?" The air leaves my lungs. "Are y'all fucking with me right now?"

Addison takes a seat at the end of the bed, looking concerned.

They both laugh.

"No. No, we aren't," Coach Montgomery says. "We want you. Isn't that right, Coach Gruden?"

"It sure is," he answers quickly. "Like Coach said, there will be some terms and conditions. We'll go over all of that with you when we can meet sometime. But we're really hoping you're still a free agent. We think you'd be a great addition to our team."

I open my mouth to say hell yes, but then it hits me when her eyes pierce into mine. Even though Addison is from New England, she's never mentioned wanting to move back. Her parents are here. It isn't like she can just pick Isla up and move her away from her grandparents.

"When do you need an answer by?"

There's silence before Coach Montgomery answers, "Whoa, kid, I figured you'd leap at this. But I understand. There're things to consider and family to talk to. I know Massachusetts isn't exactly a hop, skip, and jump to your hometown in Alabama." He pauses. "How about one week? Is that enough time?"

I nod even though they can't see me. "Yes. Yeah, sir. A week is perfect. Thank you."

"We'll talk to you soon, Cam," Montgomery says.

"Congratulations, son," Gruden says. "Talk to you in a week."

They end the call, and I flop back on my bed, letting all the air out of my lungs.

"That was Coach Montgomery and Coach Gruden of the Bruins." I tilt my head forward to look at her. "They want me to play for them."

Her eyes grow big as she jumps on top of me, her hair blanketing my head. "Are you serious, Cam?!" she squeals. "Holy shit! That's amazing!" Leaning forward, she kisses me. "Congratulations! This is incredible!"

My hands hold her against me, but suddenly, we both grow serious.

"Addison," I murmur, "I want to make this work too. I'd love it if you went with me. If you both went with me."

She presses her lips to my cheek before she stands. "I'm so proud of you, Cam. All of your dreams are coming true."

I can't hide the frown on my face. "So, I'll head over for Isla in a bit?"

Toeing her shoes on, she looks up at me and gives me a single nod. "Yep. She's looking forward to it."

And even when she comes closer, giving me one last hug … she feels a thousand miles away.

"This is a big day for you. I couldn't be prouder," she whispers with a small smile.

It should be the biggest day of my life. Yet here I lie, conflicted as fuck. Before I met Addison, I wouldn't have thought twice. I love my parents, but they've always known this was my dream. The Boston Bruins is as good as it gets. I never imagined they'd be the ones calling me. Yet here I am.

Life was easier when I only had to think about myself. But I don't want to live that life anymore.

At least, I don't think I do.

ADDISON

I pull my car into a parking spot and grab my bag. Looking at the clock, I sigh in relief because there's still five minutes to spare.

I can't push down the sick feeling in the pit of my stomach. I've felt it ever since Cam looked at me and said the Bruins called. I shouldn't have been surprised. He'd worked his entire life for that very moment. But I guess a part of me thought we had more time.

Looks like I was wrong.

One week. That's how long he has to make this decision. A decision that's going to shape the rest of his life. I'm not stupid. I know I probably played a factor into his reasoning for asking for a week to decide. He doesn't need a week to know that this is something he's been dreaming of. But the truth is, I can't move to Boston with him, not when we've only just begun really, actually dating. Isla was just uprooted this fall to be here at Brooks. I can't do that to her again. Not to mention, my parents—my support system. But I'm scared if I tell him no, he'd either try to do long distance or, worse … he'd tell the Bruins no. I can't imagine him throwing his future away for me, but I don't want to take the chance either.

I love him. So very much. But the last thing I'd ever do is compromise his future. He's going to be in the NHL. And I'll be here, at Brooks, with my daughter.

It's his time to soar.

I need to cut him free. Even though it's going to hurt like hell.

Even if he hates me for it right now … one day, he'll thank me.

CAM

I look at Isla in the backseat of my truck as she stares out the window. That damn wolf I gave her is tucked safely under her arm.

"Cam, are you gonna marry my mom?" she blurts out, never looking away from the window. "I hope so."

My head rears back. That wasn't at all what I was expecting her to say. "Maybe one day, Isla girl."

"You make her happy. She sings in the shower now." She widens her eyes. "She's awful, but the effort is there."

I swear, I never know what is going to come out of this kid's mouth. She's got to be the smartest three-year-old there ever was. I mean, I guess. I don't have much experience with many ... well, any three-year-olds. But, dang, she's smart as a whip.

"Did you have a good night?" I ask her, changing the subject. "I know I sure did."

"Mmhmm," she says slowly. "Mommy is going to be jealous. She wuvs going to the trampoline park. And she really likes ice cream. How did you jump so high, Cam?"

I laugh as we pull into Addison's driveway. "Honestly, I have no idea."

"Well, it was really cool," she says, nodding her head.

A year ago, I wouldn't have even known such a thing as a trampoline park existed. And I sure as hell wouldn't have taken a random kid to it. But she's not random. She's awesome. And I can't wait to go on more adventures with her.

I point to Addison's car. "Look, Mama's home from school."

"Um ... okay. But can you stay longer? Can we watch *Frozen?*"

"Maybe. Let's see what your mom says. If she says it's too late, then I promise we will this weekend."

"With popcorn?"

"Obviously."

"And candy?"

"Well, yeah."

"And ice cream?"

I shake my head, pushing my door open. "Now, you're just getting cray-cray."

Walking around to her side, I unbuckle her and lug her to the door. I knock a few times, and Addison pulls the door open, but when I see her face, I instantly know something isn't right.

"Mommy, can Cam pweeeease watch *Frozen* with me? He can be Anna, and I'll be Elsa."

"I feel like I'm more of an Elsa." I shrug, keeping my face serious. "Whatevs."

"Not tonight, baby." She peels Isla from me. "Nena is going to tuck you in, okay?"

"What? Why?" Isla pouts. "I'm not even tired!"

I raise my eyebrows at her. "I don't know about all that. You jumped for, like, two hours nonstop. I'm tired just from chasing you, and my legs are a lot longer."

"You took her to the trampoline park?" Addison whispers, looking at me like I killed her puppy.

"And ice cream! Cam even got me extra sprinkles," Isla cheers. "It. Was. Awesome!"

"I'll be right back," Addison says, never looking at me.

She disappears for a few minutes before returning.

"Can we go outside?" She nods toward the driveway.

I know something's wrong; it isn't hard to sense it. But I have no clue as to what it could possibly be. Four hours ago, she was naked in my bed.

What the hell could have happened from then to now?

"Thank you for taking her," she mutters, emotion thick in her voice.

"Thanks for letting me." I lean against my truck. "What's going on, Addy? You're freaking me out."

She wraps her cardigan around herself tighter. "Cam … I can't do this with you anymore."

And that's when my heart stops beating in my chest.

I stare at her, not comprehending anything coming from her pretty mouth.

ADDISON

"Come again?" He looks like I slapped him. In a lot of ways, it feels like I did. "What the fuck are you talking about?"

I look away from him because if I don't, I'll never be able to do this. One more look in his eyes, and I'll melt.

"This whole thing is just confusing for Isla. And with you leaving, it's only going to get worse. I'm sorry, Cam." I suck in a breath, begging my eyes to hold the tears in for a measly few more minutes. "I, uh … I don't want to see you anymore. Please, respect my wishes and walk away."

"No, fuck that," he growls. "I don't know where this shit is coming from, and honestly, I don't care. I know you don't mean it."

"I do," my voice barely squeaks out. "I really do. I'm sorry." My head hangs in shame. "I'm really, really sorry. You are going to go chase your dreams—just like you should. But I can't wait around while you do."

"Then, I won't go," he says quickly. "I'll tell Montgomery no."

The way he says it, I know he means it. And this is exactly what I was scared of. His future is so bright. The last thing I would ever do is dim it.

"Go be great in Boston, Cam," I whisper, tears flowing down my face. "Please."

When he doesn't respond, I turn to walk away, but he grabs my wrist, pulling my body to his. His hand slides up the back of my neck, and I whimper from his touch.

"This is fucking bullshit, and you know it, Addy."

"Let me go, Cam." I break down. "I'm begging you."

"You don't want me to let you go, Addison. And we both know it." His nostrils flare. "Don't do this. Don't leave me. You'll regret it if you do. I promise." His eyes float to my lips. "You love me. I know you fucking do."

My heart breaks inside of my own chest as I tell the biggest lie of my entire life, but it's the only way he'll let me go. "No. I don't."

He flinches. "What the fuck have we been doing then? Huh? Why the hell did you waste my time? And what about earlier today, when I fucked you in my bed? And all the times you told me you loved me? Was that all just fake? Sure as hell didn't seem like it to me."

I swallow, wiping my nose. "It was physical for me, Cam. I'm s-sorry." I start to back away. "If you care about me at all, you'll leave and not look back."

"Fuck you, Addison," he snarls, looking at me like I'm a stranger. "Since day one, I was painted like a villain. Turns out, you're the real monster, Addison. Not me."

I wrap my arms around my body as my shoulders begin to shake. "I know I am."

His eyebrows pull together, and he flinches, like I physically hit him. But what was pain is quickly replaced with anger. Not the quiet, slow-moving kind either. No … this kind of anger will ruin everything in its path.

Getting closer to me, he crowds my space, giving me no choice but to press my back against the truck. "What was the fucking point, Addison?" he growls, pointing in my face. "Why the fuck did you come into my life at all? Why did you bring *her* into my life if you were only going to tear it all apart?"

His chest heaves with raw, real emotion. I want nothing more than to comfort him. To tell him I love him. That I need him. Only I can't because it won't make a difference in the long haul. The quicker I cut this thing off between us, the better.

My heart shatters into a million tiny pieces. Miniscule shards of it, broken to smithereens with no hope of ever being repaired. You see, he owns a part of my beating heart. Without him, it'll never be whole again.

"Wreck me then, Addison. Do your worst. Walk away and ruin my entire fucking life," he says through gritted teeth. "Want to know my biggest regret?" He laughs bitterly. "Asking you to ride to Florida with me when I saw you at the store. If I hadn't done that, we wouldn't be in this position." He takes his keys out of his pocket. "I hope I never have to see your fucking face again, Addison LaConte. Because I hate you."

And then he leaves.

And my entire world feels like it's coming down on me, and I can't breathe. I hate myself for being scared.

And there's not a thing I can do about it besides watch him leave, knowing I told him to.

He'll never forgive me. And I don't blame him.

23

ADDISON

I push the stroller, thankful the sun is out for Isla's sake, but for myself, I just wish it would storm. I wish it would rain so hard that the hurt and pain would melt from my body into a puddle. I wish the wind could blow so hard that it turned me numb. Numb would be better than feeling this pain in my chest. If I thought I knew heartbreak before Cam Hardy, I was wrong. This isn't just heartbreak; this is unbearable.

What haunts me the most is the way he looked at me, like all I had said and done during the time leading up to that was a lie. Like I never cared about him, and that was clear. Through Cam's eyes, I'm the villain. And that kills me. The last thing I ever wanted was to hurt someone who made me feel more myself than I ever had.

"Mommy, is Cam coming over tonight?" Isla asks, just like she has for two weeks since the day he dropped her off and I told him not to come back.

I don't know what to tell her. This is the thing Nick and his family don't care about—my baby girl's emotions. She has grown to love Cam. Knowing he had taken her to the trampoline park and for ice cream the day I had to end it only made it worse. Cam Hardy is the type of man you read about in romance novels, but never believe actually exists. Only he does. And he loved me.

Had Cam not had to bring Isla home that night, I would have waited until the following day to end things. But I couldn't sit through one more movie or snuggle up to him, knowing that when the sun rose the next day, it would never come back up. I needed to get it done with, like squeezing your eyes shut and pulling a Band-Aid off.

"No, I don't think so, babe." I force the words out, too exhausted for anything else.

That's how I feel all the time, no matter what. I feel really fucking exhausted.

"Why not, Mommy?" she whines. "Why can't he come over? I miss him."

She doesn't understand. She doesn't realize I'm only trying to protect her from getting further hurt from this in the future. Once he's in the NHL, he isn't going to have time for us. She doesn't deserve that either.

I push the stroller faster. My lungs feel like they might explode. Not from the exercise, but from keeping emotions buried inside. I know I can't stuff them down forever. I'm like a balloon, ready to explode.

"He's just really busy with hockey," I say back. "Want to go to the playground?"

"I want Cam," she whispers, and when I peek over the stroller, I see her bottom lip trembling. "That's all I want."

And if I ever thought I felt like a failure as a mom before … nothing could have prepared me for this.

CAM

I finish showering and step out, still feeling nothing.

Pulling my clothes on, I reach for my shoes. I haven't told a soul about my call from the Bruins. Not even my parents, mostly because I don't want to talk to them. What I did do was call Coach Montgomery back the day after Addison dumped my ass and I told him I was in. And if I didn't love my team so much, wanting to finish this season out with them, I'd move to Boston right now. But I know I need to talk to Coach LaConte. And at some point, my teammates too.

"We're thinking of going to get some steaks after this, you game?" Link says from his locker. "There's a new place downtown. Supposed to be good."

"They serve liquor there?" I say, never looking his way. "That's the only way I'm goin'."

Out of the corner of my eye, I see him hang his head.

"I mean, bring your fake ID and see what happens. Fuck if I know. It's a weeknight, dude. Do you have to get hammered tonight too? Last night and the night before weren't enough for you?"

Slamming my palm on my locker, I snap, "No, they fucking weren't." I grab my bag. "You know what? I'm all fucking set. You and O'Brien can go jerk each other off."

"What the fuck, Cam?" Brody roars, marching toward me. "I've had about enough of your bitch-ass attitude. You keep it up, and you can protect yourself on the ice." He gets in my face, narrowing his eyes. "See where you are without me, dick."

"I'd be fine, O'Brien," I growl. "And you know it."

I'm not mad at him. I just can't scream at the person I'm really angry with. And the truth is, I know I need him on the ice. But I'm hurting too fucking bad to say it. All I can do is hurt him and anyone else who lands in my path.

"You're lucky I want to keep my spot on this team, you little bitch," he mutters. "I'd fucking ruin you right here, right now."

My arm reaches back, but before I can make contact, someone pulls me back.

"Cool it," Hunter's voice booms in my ear. "I'm not playing."

He pulls me out of the locker room and into the hallway.

"Hardy, whatever the fuck you've got going on, you've got to figure that shit out. Before you ruin this entire team."

"Y'all won't get the fuck off my case!" I tear from his hold. "I can't do everything right! I can't fucking fix everything!"

My chest heaves, and he sighs.

"Hardy, man to man … this isn't the way to go about things. Trust me, I know. I've been there before. Hell, some days, I'm still there." His eyes soften. "But this is your team. Your brothers. Don't turn on them. Not when they've been rocking with you since day one."

I look down, my nostrils flaring with anger, but the guilt starts to creep up my spine.

Patting my shoulder, he turns. "See you tomorrow, brother. Sleep on it."

"Hardy," Coach's voice rumbles from the end of the hall. "My office. *Now.*"

Just fucking great. As if this day could get shittier.

Dragging my feet, I head to his office.

"Close the door and sit your ass down," he orders.

And even though I don't want to, I listen.

"For weeks, I've done what Addison has asked me, and I've stayed out of it. She told me it wasn't working, so she ended things, but she's miserable. You skate around practice like a zombie, ready to fight your best fucking friends." He slams his fist down on the table. "This is exactly what I didn't want to happen. This shit right here. My star player is distracted. My daughter is in agony. It's all bullshit."

I suck in a breath and narrow my eyes. "Your daughter is in agony?" I laugh resentfully. "Your daughter, who dumped me after I took Isla to the jump park, is in agony?" I shake my head. "Wow, that's just fucking amazing, Coach. That's really somethin'." I give him a hard look. "If you think she's the one in pain, y'all really should talk more. You kicked me off your ice, afraid I'd hurt your princess, and she walked all over me like I was a fucking rug."

He stares at me, confused. "I don't know what happened. She won't talk to me."

I stand. "Well, Coach, that makes two of us."

As I start toward the door, his voice stops me. "If you're trying to get her back, acting like this isn't the way."

Keeping my back to him, I ball my fists. "Who said I'm trying to get her back?"

"Well, are you?"

"No." I look at him. I guess now is just as good of a time as ever. "Coach Montgomery called me. They want me next season. I'm leaving Brooks." I feel my chest tighten. "There's nothing left for me here. Not anymore."

He watches me for a moment before he stands, holding his hand out. "You made it, Hardy. Congratulations."

"Are you mad?" I shake his hand. "You know, since this will be my last year?"

His eyes crinkle at the sides. "That was the goal, wasn't it? You worked for it, son. And if I'm being honest … I suspected you were going to get that call." He exhales. "They've reached out for game tapes several times as well as asked some general questions. I told them they'd be lucky to have you on their team." He pauses. "But I'm sorry about Addison. I really am. But I guess that *when one door shuts, another opens* bullshit is true, isn't it?" He slowly sits back down. "You're gonna do great, Hardy."

I nod before heading out. My hand taps the doorframe. "Thanks, Coach. For making me a better player."

My dreams are all coming true. But she's gone. And now, this dream … well, it just doesn't feel like a dream at all without her standing next to me.

ADDISON

I pull Isla's hood up and stuff my hands in my pockets. It's cold out tonight, only thirty degrees, and it's a shock to my system. When I was living in New England, this wasn't even considered all that cold in the winter months. But now that I've gotten used to Georgia's mild winter, this is torture.

"You sure about this?" my mom says quietly. "No shame in not going. Your daddy will understand."

"We missed the last two, Mom." I pull in a deep breath and slowly let it out. "Besides, Isla wants to go watch Papa's team."

"And Cam. I want to see Cam play." She cranes her neck to look at my mom. "Him has been too busy with hockey to visit. I can visit him."

"I see," my mom answers, patting her on the head.

I don't have to look at my mother to know she's giving me a concerned look. But life can't just stop because of the shitty situation I've put myself in. The show must go on. And Barren LaConte's girls must show up to support him and his team.

Even if it's going to gut me inside.

The second I open the large glass door and walk inside, the hot air of the overhead heater blows in my face briefly before the chill of the air coming from the arena hits my nose. I feel my heart start to race, and my legs grow wobbly.

I'm going to see Cam for the first time in weeks. And it's going to suck not to be able to touch him.

CAM

We warm up, and even though the crowd around me is loud, it's all muffled, and all their faces are blurry.

Everything is numb. My body. My brain. My emotions. Pretty much my entire life.

I'll drown myself in oceans of liquor and piles of weed and pick the biggest fights to stay this way if I have to. Numbness beats the hell out of thinking about her.

I've been going through the motions. I go to class. I go to practice. I show up on game day. But as soon as I'm done, I drown myself in whatever I can find. I don't know what this feeling is in my stomach, but it sure as fuck can't be normal.

The trouble is when I stumble back home, landing in my bed, the spins start, and I almost feel her next to me. I hear her voice, her breaths. Her touch fucking haunts me like a ghost. And when I close my eyes, she's right there. But when I wake up in the morning, I'm hit with the cold, harsh reality that she's gone.

Having her brought me to life. And without her, I feel like a dead man walking.

The game begins, and even though he shouldn't be, Brody is still protecting my ass the best he can. As fucked up as it sounds, I wish he weren't. I wish he'd let me fight my own battles right now.

Seconds after the game starts, I get control of the puck and head toward the other goal when I'm slammed hard into the Plexiglas. The motherfucker smirks, like he's the man or some shit.

"I'll break your fucking leg off so that you can't skate again," I chant, needing to fight this dude more than I can explain.

He might have thought he was tough with that shit he pulled, but I'm a grenade, ready to explode at any second. And I'm not stopping at anything.

He shoves me again before he skates by, and that's all I need. Heading toward him full force, I bash my shoulder into his body, sending him flying before he lands in a heap on the ice. He scurries to get up, but it doesn't matter. Two of his teammates are headed for me, just like I knew they would.

One grabs my jersey, but I nail him right in the nose a few times before he falls back. When the next one comes at me, I land a blow to his face, and he backs away, not wanting any more.

By now, a handful of my teammates are fighting with the other team's guys, and it's becoming a full-on bloodbath. I feel the pain creep back in, but for a moment, when I was beating those fuckers, it dulled.

I feel her eyes on me, and I swing my gaze to that same box where Isla and Addison used to always sit—until a few weeks ago.

Addison's hands are over Isla's eyes, shielding her from what's going on. Her eyebrows pull together as she shakes her head subtly, and I see the disappointment on her face.

As I turn away, the shame sets in. Not because Addison had to see me make an ass out of myself. No, I don't give a fuck about that. She's the reason I feel this way.

But because that sweet girl next to her did. And I never wanted Isla to see me as a monster.

ADDISON

Once they finally get the game under control and it resumes, a bunch of players sit in the sin bin, Cam included.

It's more than clear that Cam is in pain. He's acting out because of that. Well, guess what. So am I. I'm not going around, trying to fight everyone.

He doesn't know that though. He doesn't realize my heart physically hurts. He doesn't understand that I have to drag myself out of bed every day, reminding myself I have a daughter who needs me to be happy, even when I feel like I'm dying a slow, painful death. Cam knows none of that. How could he? It's my own doing.

What choice did I have? Cam's future in hockey and the custody of my daughter are two black-and-white areas. There is no gray in the equation. When it comes to that, it's a clear choice. I'd never risk Cam's dreams coming true, just like I'd never let it be a possibility that I could lose my daughter.

This whole thing has left me understanding one hard truth. There are people who come into your life to physically stay forever, and then there are the ones who come in and make a forever impact on your life before leaving. Cam might be the latter, but I'll never forget him. I'd never want to. With him, I was loved with no terms. He wanted me just the way I was. I wasn't expected to mold to his liking. To him … I was perfect.

I met Tessa for lunch yesterday. I want to say it was nice to get out of the house, but it wasn't. And as much as I love her, she doesn't understand what I'm going through. Mostly because I can't tell her the truth. To her, she just assumes I'm making the wrong choice. She doesn't get that there is no choice. If there were, I wouldn't be apart from him.

I feel myself pulling away from everything, except for Isla. Even a conversation with anyone else just seems to be too much work. I'm falling into a dark place … and he can't pull me out of it. But I also don't have a choice but to endure the pain and face the darkness. I can't let it take over. Isla needs me. I need to get my shit together and get over it.

If only there were medicine for a broken heart.

I do my best to sneak out of the game right after it ends in hopes of avoiding Cam. I know if Isla spots him, she'll run over and ask when he's coming to see her again, and I know him well enough by now to know that would break his heart.

Unfortunately for me, a few of my dad and mom's old friends happened to be at the game, and now that the game has ended, they decide they want to chat my ear off.

I give my mom a look, widening my eyes. "I really should get Isla home to bed. I'll see you and Dad at home."

At first, she looks at me like I'm crazy, but then it clicks, and she nods frantically. "Yes. Oh, yes. Definitely. Waaaay past your bedtime, girl."

"That's not—" Isla starts to blow our cover, but I cut her off.

"It was wonderful to see you all. Have a great night!" And then I quickly pick Isla up and dart toward the entrance.

The players still have interviews after, so I should be safe.

"Mommy! I want to wait for Cam!" Isla kicks her feet—something she's never done in my hold. "Put me down!"

"Isla Rose, what has gotten into you?" I lecture her as quietly as I can so as not to make a scene. "That is not how you speak to me. We are going home. Cam is very busy with post-game things. I'm sorry, baby. Not tonight."

Her head hangs, and she rests it on my shoulder. "Sorry," she says, her voice heartbreakingly low.

I start to answer, but suddenly, she scurries down my body. "There he is! Mommy, he's right there!"

I try to grab her, but she slips away, darting through the few people in the lobby.

"Isla," I yell angrily. "Isla! Get back here. There're strangers!"

Just as I lose sight of her blonde curls, I watch as Cam scoops her up. Her arms wrap around his neck, and she tucks her face into his shoulder. His eyes glass over, and I feel my heart get stabbed again. Everything I could ever want is in front of me, yet I can't have it.

Putting my shoulders back, I exhale and walk toward them.

"Isla, you cannot just run away from me. There are people we don't know here," I say, pinching the bridge of my nose. "You know better."

"Your mom's right, Isla girl." He speaks softly. "You need to always stay with Mommy or someone you know, okay?"

She nods before peeking at me. Resting her head on his chest as he holds her in his arms. "Sorry, Mommy. I just saw Cam, and I got excited." She looks up at him, touching her hand to his face. "Where have you been? I thought … I thought you forgot about me."

Slowly, he sets her down and kneels down with her. "I could never forget you, Isla. Ever." He hugs her, pulling her tiny frame into his huge arms. "I'm sorry I haven't seen you. I've missed you too."

The lump in my throat makes it hard to talk, but I try my best. "Come on, sweetie. We should get going. It's getting late."

Her shoulders sag, but she hugs Cam one last time before walking toward me and taking my hand.

"Bye, Cam," she whispers. "I love you."

I can tell he's trying not to cry. She's never said that to him. At least, not to my knowledge.

"Bye, Isla. I love you too." His eyes stay on hers, not so much as glancing my way.

And if you've ever wondered what a broken heart looks like, you should look at mine, lying in a thousand pieces on the floor.

25

CAM

The sun beams through my window, and I flip over, pulling my pillow over my head, not ready to take on the day. No practice today, and I'm not feeling like going to class much either.

"Ain't you a ray of fucking sunshine?" an accent matching my own drawls. "Get the hell up. It's almost noon."

Shooting up, I find Beau sitting at my desk.

"What are you doing here?" I groan. Last night's hangover hits me like a Mack truck. "And how the fuck did you get in here?"

"Snuck through the window," he deadpans.

"Really?"

"No, you dumbass. I opened the front door, walked inside your shitty apartment, then went room to room till I found your pathetic self." He widens his eyes. "I did walk in on your friend as he was balls deep in some blonde. Awkward as fuck, but he didn't seem to care."

"If he didn't care, it was probably Brody." I run my hand down my face. "Why are you here?"

He grins. "Remember when your sister decided to ruin my life and broke up with my ass?"

"Yep, that moment when she used her brain cells for a few days?"

He holds up his middle finger. "Piss off. As I was saying, I was a mess. I wanted to be left alone. And then you showed up like the big pussy that you are and made me talk about feelings. Besides, Mi told me you made it to the NHL. She had to find out through your parents. Why the fuck didn't you call to tell us?"

After ignoring my parents' calls for weeks, I finally answered. I told them the news about the Bruins and pretended to be as thrilled about it as they were. Guess they decided to spread the word. I told my team too. As happy as they were for me, I could tell they were also a little bummed that this would be our last season together.

"I guess it slipped my mind." I shrug. "And I ain't talking about my feelings, B. I'm over it."

"So, that's why your buddies called Mi and told her you were a mess? You're lucky. She wanted to come down here herself, but I took one for the team, and here I am." He stands up. "So, get the hell up. I'm hungry."

"You're always hungry," I groan.

He pats his stomach. "Yeah, I'm a growing boy. So, get showered because you smell and look like ass and meet me in the truck. Turn that frown upside down."

"Who are you, and what have you done with my grumpy best friend?" I say, staring at him.

"It's like we've traded places. Now, I'm happy and shit, and you're sulky and self-destructing."

"Am not."

"Are too. Hurry the fuck up."

I finish my beer, signaling to the bartender for another one while Beau finishes his fries.

"Starting early, huh?" He nods toward the fresh beer that slides toward me. "You ain't gonna solve your problems with that shit, you know."

"Whatever," I grumble, bringing the icy-cold glass to my lips.

"Your parents are worried. Mila is worried." Beau rests his palms on the sides of his plate. "You don't answer their messages or calls, and when your buddy Brody called Mi, well, that just solidified the fact that you're all kinds of fucked up."

After the shit I pulled with Brody, he still cares.

"Talk to me, Cam. I can't read fucking minds." He breathes out a laugh. "If I could, dating your sister would be a helluva lot easier."

"Talking won't fix anything, B."

I finish my beer, but when I start to signal for another, Beau shoves my hand down.

"You're all done for the day," his voice drawls, monotone. "You've had enough."

"The fuck I have," I say, smacking my hand down on the wooden bar top. "Some nerve you have, showing up here, trying to tell me how to live my life. Do you remember a few years ago? When you ghosted my entire fucking family?" I glare at him as the booze kicks in, making me feel invincible. "Do you remember when you went through two years of cutting everyone out, acting like a little bitch?"

"My dad *died*," he roars, lifting a finger to my face. "I'll give you one pass, Cam. One. Fucking. Pass. And the only reason why is because I promised Mi I wouldn't beat your ass. But mention that shit again, and I'll beat your ass senseless."

Suddenly, he stands. Grabbing the back of my shirt, he hauls me off the stool.

"You know what? I can't take this shit. Let's go for a walk," he barks. "And, no, I'm not fucking asking."

I fight back for a second, but quickly realize he won't give up and leave me be. Might as well get this shit over with now.

Once we're outside, he releases his hold, shoving me slightly.

"It's that girl who was at the championship game, ain't it?" He walks beside me. "Abigail or whatever."

"*Addison*," I say, correcting him. "And I'm not fucking talking about her to you."

"Mi said she has a kid. A daughter, right?" He softens his voice.

I know Beau Bishop enough to know that it's taking every ounce of his patience to not lose his shit on me right now. Beau has always had a temper. And when he's mad, he's one scary motherfucker. But honestly, I don't care. I've never been one to have much of a temper. Until now.

I keep walking, pulling my hood up.

"Can't be easy, getting attached to her and her kid." He looks over at me. "You talk to her at all lately?"

"No," I snap. "Besides at the last game when Isla ran away from her mother to come to me." I feel a shooting pain in my chest. "Then, they left."

"Isla," he echoes. "How old is she?"

"Three. Gonna be four in the spring."

Every time I mention her or Addison's name, every time I have to talk about them, the numbness I've worked hard to keep wears off, and I'm forced to feel everything.

"She probably misses you too, man—"

"Damn it, B!" I hiss, shoving him against a building. "I can't fucking talk about them! Why can't you just leave me the hell alone?!" I release him. "My whole life, I've been the dude who doesn't give a fuck about anything but hockey. A simple life of random women, the game I love, and parties is what I should have stuck with. If I had, I wouldn't feel like I'm dying right now." I close my eyes. "She ruined my entire fucking life. I hate that bitch."

I don't mean it. Even as mad as I am at Addison, I'll never really think she's a bitch. I fucking love her. I thought I'd finally figured out where I was meant to be. Now, I know I'm just meant to be the fuckboy everyone makes me out to be. That's all I'll ever be.

"I promise, it'll get better." He puts his hand on my shoulder, dropping his head closer to mine. "But not this way. This isn't how you go about things, and you know it. And you don't know; she might come back. They sometimes do."

"She's not coming back," I mutter.

"Don't be so sure. And if you want her, if you're sure she's the one ... you can't just give up. You don't know what's going on inside her head, Cam. But acting this way, calling her a bitch and getting hammered every second you aren't on the ice, isn't how you get her back." His hand clasps my shoulder tighter. "It's gonna be all right, brother. I promise. But you've got to get it together."

"Thanks," I say, not believing a word of it. "Let's go before people think we're a couple, having a domestic fight."

He shakes his head, his lips turning up. "We both know I'd win."

"Yeah, in your dreams." I start walking, stuffing my hands in my pockets.

He's probably right. If I were Addison and I had a front row seat to my demise, I wouldn't want me back either. I need to get my shit together. Even if she never comes back, my parents didn't raise the loser I've been acting like.

I tip my chin up. "I'll make you a deal. You and I do something stupid tonight, for old times' sake. And then tomorrow, I'll get my shit together."

He looks over at me, narrowing his eyes like he's about to argue why that's a dumb idea.

"I'll be good after tonight. Come on. Let's get drunk and do something stupid." I slap his back. "You know you want to."

"Man ... I don't know."

"What happened to you? You used to be the craziest motherfucker I knew." I poke his chest. "All soft and gooey now or what?" I nod toward his arms. "Probably ought to get them tats removed now that you're no longer a badass."

"Make no mistake, I'm still a badass." He runs his hand up the back of his neck. "What happened is, I got with your sister."

"The fuck does that have to do with anything? Mi doesn't want a vagina of a man."

"Well, you see, I'm pretty sure there can only be so much crazy per relationship. And seeing's I'm with a woman who straps herself in a car and goes one hundred fifty miles per hour down a track without batting an eyelash ... I feel like our crazy meter is already skyrocketing. Like that thing's probably 'bout to bust."

"Come on, B. One night, big dawg. One night, and then tomorrow, I'll be a better man, and you can go back to tucking your dick between your legs and being a bitch."

He looks up at the sky, groaning for a moment. "Fine. But if Mi asks, this was your idea."

"Brother, I've been pissing her off since the day she was born. Why would I stop now?"

He shakes his head but grins. "All right, let's do it."

ADDISON

The fluorescent lights of the glass room are bright, making my headache worse than it already is. Every now and then, I get these migraines, typically stress-induced, so it only makes sense one would hit one of these days.

I open my laptop, pulling up my notes from last night's homework assignment, and pull my reading glasses from my bag, sliding them onto my face.

Hunter struts in the door, his bag slung lazily over his shoulder, and all the girls in the room instantly lock their eyes on him. Cheeks turn red, and a few "accidentally" drop something on the floor, needing to bend down to pick it up. He's completely oblivious to any of it though. His facial expression remains somber as he heads my way.

Sliding into the seat beside me, he hands me a doughnut. "Grabbed an extra."

I don't miss the daggers coming my way. I even catch the busty brunette seated in front of me grumble something about *that bitch gets all the guys*.

Shrinking into my seat, I peek at the doughnut. Strawberry frosted. Not my favorite, but I've never met a doughnut I didn't like.

"Thanks." I smile. "You've got quite the fan club in here."

"They don't even know me." He relaxes in his chair. "They just think they like me."

His words remind me of conversations I've had with Cam. He always felt like the entire campus acted like he belonged to them. He wasn't allowed privacy, and he was always expected to be the guy who was grinning.

I bet they aren't thinking that now.

After that last game … it's clear he has another side to him. A monstrous side I helped to bring out.

"So, I hope I'm not overstepping, but Cam's been pretty upset. He's … well, Addison, he's a damn mess. Not that you probably don't already know that."

"It's not my job to know how Cam is, Hunter. It's over. Everyone needs to let it go," I snap.

"So, if it's over, you won't care if he leaves to play for the Bruins after this year then, huh?"

My heart sinks at the thought of him being there, in Boston. Women likely throwing themselves at him daily. He'll have any chick he wants.

The professor walks in, and I swallow the lump in my throat.

"No, I don't care. Good for him. That's what he wanted, isn't it?" I sigh. "Now, if you'll excuse me, I actually want to pass this class. I don't get the star athlete treatment."

He flinches beside me, and I sigh.

"Sorry," I say. "I have a lot going on. Puts me in a bitchy mood—that's all."

He pats my hand. "It's fine."

I try to give him a smile to prove that it is fine.

But it's fake. Because *nothing* is fine. And I sit through the rest of the class, remembering that.

Class finally ends, and I can't wait to go home, take a long bubble bath, and climb into bed. My migraine has dulled, but it isn't completely gone. So, a scorching hot bath sounds perfect. I've been trying to sell my parents on the *I'm over Cam, and this is for the best* lie that I've been telling. So, for now, I'll shove my feelings down deep and just keep pretending it's all good and that I didn't just make the worst decision of my life.

I'm gathering my things up when my phone vibrates, and I see it's a video from Tessa. Pressing play, I turn the volume up just enough for me to hear it, but not so loud that the entire class, including the professor, will.

Cam and Beau Bishop stand on the stage at Club 83, both looking drunk, singing the words to "Cold As You" by Luke Combs. Cam wears his hat on backward, shouting into the microphone like he's actually performing at a concert.

If I wasn't so heartbroken still, I'd think it was funny.

A message follows it.

> *Tess: Yeah … I'm going to go ahead and guess that he isn't over you.*

> *Tess: Also, why does he have a good singing voice? Dude really should be bad at some things when he looks that good.*

> *Me: He doesn't sound that good. Or look that good.*

I'm lying with every word.

> *Tess: Yeah … okay. Anyway, you should come down here. It's a big party. Besides, I know you miss him too.*

> *Me: I can't. Sorry. Leaving class to head home.*

> *Tess: Fine. Call you tomorrow.*

Another video comes through, but before I can open it, she writes again.

> *Tess: Just one more for the road.*

I open the video and watch as he finishes the song and reaches down to slap people's hands like he's a damn rock star.

"Thank you, thank you," he says, bowing. "I'll be here all night!"

Beau Bishop laughs, slinging his arm around Cam's shoulders. Making it clear that he, too, is also drunk. I only met Beau that one time, but he didn't seem like the type of dude to be touchy-feely with his friends.

"Wow, looks like Cam's partying without me," Hunter's voice says next to me, and I click out of the video, feeling my cheeks heat.

"Yeah, well, my friend sent me it." I stand, hiking my bag up on my shoulder. "That's Cam for you. Always looking for the next party or the next place to show off."

He shrugs. "At least he's smiling in those videos. What did you want him to do, Addy? Sulk around and self-destruct forever?"

I hold my phone up. "This *is* self-destructing. It's all he's ever done his whole life."

I stop myself from saying more. When I broke things off with Cam, I lost the right to care about what he does. When I see the videos, I see a man who just wants to make everyone laugh to make himself feel better. I see a person who everyone always expects to be fine, even when he isn't.

But what hurts the most? I see a man who's getting over me.

211

And I don't want him to. That probably makes me sound selfish, but it's the truth.

26

CAM

Pulling my jersey over my head, I see Brody lacing his skates up.

"O'Brien," I call.

"Go ahead," he says, keeping his head down, never taking his eyes off his skates.

I walk toward him. "I'm sorry for being a dick lately. You're a brother to me, and you always have my back on the ice." I clasp his shoulder. "I promise that guy's gone now."

He looks up, nodding once. "Good. Because that guy was a dickhead."

I chuckle. "I know," I agree. "They say we take our shit out on the ones closest to us, right? Guess that shit is true."

Standing, he throws an arm out, patting my back. "All good, Captain. Women make us do the unthinkable. I'm just glad you're finding your way back."

"Slowly," I mutter. "Let's get our asses out there and get to work."

Turning, I start to leave the locker room when Hunter slaps my back. "I'm surprised you made it in today. Figured you were out on tour now." He laughs. "There're videos going around of you, giving Luke Combs a run for his money." Walking in front of me, he looks back. "But I'd say you'd better stick to hockey, Cap."

"Fucking cell phones and social media," I say, giving the middle finger.

I step onto the ice, cursing the lights for being too damn bright in the arena. The pounding in my head at practice makes me realize I probably should have listened to Beau and not insisted we get hammered and sing karaoke last night. But, damn it, I needed some fun in my life before I try my best to turn this new leaf, making Addison realize I can be the man she needs. I'm aware she might never take me back. I'm just not ready to accept that yet.

I didn't fall for her overnight. But it wasn't slow either. Looking back now, I realize I fell in love with her during all the moments and memories. Each time, I lost myself to her a little bit more. What started as off-the-charts chemistry in hookups ended up with me needing her all the time. I was knocked right on my ass. Just like my dad had told me I would be one day. I'd never been the guy to look for love. Hell, I didn't even have crushes, growing up. All that ever mattered was the game. Then, Addison came along. And suddenly, hockey wasn't the most important thing anymore.

"Coach, can I get a word?" I skate toward him before stopping. "Won't take long."

"Go on, Hardy. What's on your mind, boy?" He leans against the Plexiglas.

"I just wanted to say, I'm sorry for fucking off the past few weeks. I've been hurting, but that doesn't mean I can ruin the rest of the season for you and the guys." I nod. "I'm better now. She'll see it too. I hope so anyway."

His eyes study me for a moment. "As miserable as she's been, I hope the hell she does." He pats me on the shoulder. "Get back to work, Hardy. Glad to have you back."

"Yes, sir." I skate off, ready to work my ass off to prove to my team how sorry I am.

ADDISON

On my way to Isla's ballet class, I stop at the gas station.

"Mommy, can I get a snack?" Isla says sweetly. "I'm weeeally hungry."

"Of course. I can't let my little dancing star starve."

After filling my tank, I pull my car into a parking spot.

"Do you want anything, Mom? Or are you coming in?" I ask my mom as she sits in the front seat, playing some word game on her phone.

"I'm all set." She smiles. "Oh, wait, you know what? I'll take a water. Lord knows I haven't had enough to drink today. Need some money?"

"No, ma'am," I answer quickly.

I push my door open and get Isla from her car seat. When I set her down, her little legs skip along in her hot-pink tights.

She looks too dang cute with her bun and leotard. I could just squeeze her, I swear.

Once we're inside, we search the aisles. My hands find some salt and vinegar chips. Even though I shouldn't have them, I want them. And seeing as I skipped lunch today, I think I deserve some carbs. I grab my mom a bag, too, and her water. She'll complain that she doesn't need the chips, but she'll eat them and love them.

Isla holds her Rice Krispies Treat in one hand and her juice in the other.

"Ready to go?" I smile down at her. "You can't be late for ballet."

"Ready!" She beams. "I can't wait to see Miss Molly! I think I'm her favorite."

I start toward the cash register when I get an unsettling feeling in my gut. The hair on the back of my neck shoots up, sending a tingle down my entire spine. But before I actually see what's going on, I hear the click of a gun's safety, followed by a deep, terrifying voice. Stopping my whole world.

Today was a normal day. Just like the rest. And now, it's my worst nightmare.

"Get on the floor. Now," the man's voice yells. "Don't make me ask twice!"

My eyes find the monster as I take in the man who looks high, holding a gun with one hand and scratching his flesh with the other, and my stomach turns.

Isla's eyes widen as she looks at me. Even as a toddler, she knows we're in trouble.

"Shh," I say before she can scream. I help her onto the ground, and she starts to cry. "Please, baby. Just be very quiet and hold on to me. I promise, it will all be okay," I lie to her. Because for the first time in my life … I don't know if it's all going to be okay.

We're stuck in here with a maniac who has a gun. Who the hell is going to save us now?

Once we're on the dirty, cold ground, I do something I haven't done in a long time.

I pray to God.

And I hold my baby closer.

215

CAM

At practice, I feel lighter than I have in weeks. I dread practice ending because I know the second I leave this ice, it's back to reality.

"All right, boys, bring it in," Coach calls. "I suppose I've beat your asses up enough for one day."

We head toward him, all pulling our helmets off and wiping the sweat from our heads.

"We smell like ass," Brody groans. "I think I pulled a muscle in my ballbag. Hurts."

"That's what happens when you play like your body can't break." Link nudges him.

"We're getting closer and closer to the Frozen Four, and I'd be lying if I said I didn't really, *really* want to make it there. But either way, I'm damn proud of this team." Coach messes with the bill of his hat.

"You see, you might not know it, but I watched a lot of last year's games before I accepted this job. You were good; don't get me wrong. But you weren't playing like a true team." He looks at all of his players. "That's changed. Because when I look around now, I see a team." He chuckles, smacking me in the arm. "Aside from Hardy and O'Brien last week, that is. But they've kissed and made up. Isn't that right, boys?"

"You know it, Coach." Brody grins. "Cam-Cam can't stay mad at me."

I shake my head but laugh, knowing it's true.

Coach opens his mouth again, but before he can talk, Coach McIntire rushes over to him.

"LaConte." He sounds out of breath.

Bringing his mouth to Coach's ear, he mutters something, and I watch the color drain from Coach's face as he starts to shuffle backward. His eyes fill with fear, and he looks like he's going to pass out.

"Fuck!" he shouts as he heads off the ice as fast as he can.

"What's going on?" I get closer to Coach McIntire. "What the fuck did you just tell him?"

He doesn't look at me as he stares off into the distance, tears in his eyes. "Mrs. LaConte had been trying to reach Coach and couldn't. She called me." His face pales. "It's Addison," he whispers, and my heart drops. "She and Isla are being held at gunpoint at the gas station in town."

As soon as the words leave his lips, I'm skating to the exit and pulling my skates off. I fight back the emotions, needing to sprint as fast as I can to a vehicle and get to them.

"Coach!" I scream as he gets into his truck and starts to drive away.

The truck roars toward me, and I rip the door open and jump in. My door isn't even shut yet before he floors it, pulling out of the stadium parking lot, heading toward town.

His face sweats, and he's white as a sheet. My hands shake, and I can't seem to steady my breathing, no matter how much I try. I feel like I'm having a heart attack, but I have to get it together for my girls. I feel my stomach turn, and I roll the window down, puking onto the road.

You read about these things happening on the internet. You hear it on the radio and see it on the news. But never did I think the person I loved most would be the one who needed saving.

Coach drives with his emergency lights on, both of us knowing that if a cop tries to pull us over, they'd have to high-speed chase us to the store.

We don't speak. I don't think either of us can stomach saying any words out loud, much less form an actual thought that would make any sense.

And minutes later, we're pulling in on two wheels next to the gas station, where police cruisers block every entrance off.

We throw our doors open, not bothering to take the time to close them behind us. Both of us sprint toward the commotion, but two police officers step in front of us.

"Stay back," they bark. "We have a situation."

"No fucking shit, moron! My daughter and granddaughter are in there!" Coach drives his finger into the officer's chest. "Are you going to get them out, or am I?"

The police officer's face softens, but he stands firm. "Sir, I'm extremely sorry that you have loved ones in there. But I can't let you go any farther. We have strict protocols that we have to follow in circumstances like this."

"What the fuck is going on in there?" I roar, dragging my hands through my hair, looking at the dozens of officers outside. "What the hell are you guys doing out here?! Get the fuck inside that store and save them!"

Another police officer steps forward. "The offender has locked himself and the hostages inside. But I promise, we are doing everything we can. Like Officer Hicks just said, we have protocols we must follow in situations like this."

"Fuck your protocols." I get in his face. "Fuck every fucking protocol and save the hostages in there!"

"Oh, Barren!" I hear Jennie cry before she pushes through the officers and hugs her husband. "I should be in there with them." Sobs break from her throat. "I should have put my damn phone down and gone in with them. They must be so, so scared."

"It's okay," Coach whispers, pulling his wife closer against him as he stares at the building. "They are going to be okay."

I look around, not really grasping the situation fully. *How can this be happening? How can I live in a world where this shit goes on? And if Isla and Addy survive this, how will they be okay? How will they ever go into a store again? How will I ever let them leave my sight?*

We wait for what seems like forever, though I know, in reality, it's only minutes. The police deter anyone from getting closer and follow instructions from their superiors. Every second that goes by, I lose my mind a little more. The cops' time is running out. I'm not going to let my girls wait much longer. Even if they aren't really my girls, I'm sure as hell not letting them get hurt.

ADDISON

My cheeks are soaked, and my nose runs continuously as I rock Isla against me. After God knows how long, he has instructed us to sit against the wall. I shiver, feeling colder than I have in my entire life, even though it isn't cold in the building.

I glance around at the other people next to me. Seven of us total. Three workers. Four customers, only one of them an innocent child.

My daughter.

She'll carry this day with her forever. She'll never go a day without this fear. This man has given her that burden, and I'd kill him for that if I could. None of this is fair.

"Do I look stupid? I know there's more money than that somewhere!" He kicks the male employee's leg. "Where the fuck is it?!"

The man cries. He looks to be in his sixties with his white hair and glasses. "I-I'm sorry. There is no more money here. It was all in the register, I swear."

He's already taken all of our wallets and jewelry. Now, we're stuck here, wondering which breath could be our last. I look down at Isla as she buries her face into my shirt. Her small shoulders shake as she cries.

I want to promise her it'll be okay.

I wish I could pick her up and run her out of here.

I wish I could erase this day from her memory. And my own.

Tightening the hold on his gun, he points it upward before firing multiple rounds into the ceiling. Isla's cries turn to screams, and I cover her ears to shield the noise. I can't breathe, but I know I can't check out mentally right now. Not if I'm going to somehow save her.

As soon as the gunshots stop, a huge crash happens. The glass window breaks into a thousand pieces as someone leaps through it. The gunman turns, holding his gun toward the commotion, and pulls the trigger. And even though I'm certain he hits his target, the brave soul launches toward him. Punching him countless times until he gets the gun out of his hands and throws it through the broken window.

The punches slow, and the hero's head starts to fall forward along with the rest of his body as his hand goes to his chest.

And that's when I see it.

The Brooks University jersey with the number nineteen on the back. And in large letters ... is the name Hardy.

Cam ...

The hero is Cam.

I never thought anyone would ever love me enough to jump in front of a bullet. To be honest, I never even thought that sort of love existed. Then came Cam, proving me wrong.

CAM

I try to open my eyes, but I can't. My body feels weightless as an ear-piercing ringing invades my brain.

"Addison." I try to say her name, but my throat doesn't let me. "Isla." Again … nothing.

My mouth curses me for trying to talk, but I need to know where they are. I need to know they are all right. I start to panic. Attempting to sit up, I fall back. It's hopeless. I'm useless.

"He's agitated! Give him something to relax him!" the muffled voice of a lady screams.

My head feels like I'm underwater, but I know I'm not.

"Let them know we have a male, early twenties, with a GSW to the chest. We're about three minutes out, and they need to have an OR ready!" the same voice yells before I feel someone squeeze my hand. "Hang in there. You're a hero. Just keep fighting."

I feel hands on me, but everything feels prickly.

"Damn it," the voice hisses. "Pneumothorax. We need to hurry!"

"Trust me, I'm working on it!" a second voice calls back. "You think I want the Wolves star player dying on my watch? Hell no! This dude is going to be a legend."

I feel myself start to fade. It's weird … whatever this feeling is. There's a white light that starts to fill my entire brain. It's so warm and comforting. I'm so tired. If I could just relax in that light for a moment, I'd feel better. If I could just let my mind rest …

My mind drifts to my favorite place. A place where I feel complete and everything is right in the world.

A place with my two girls.

My idea of heaven.

"He's flatlining!" I barely hear the voice scream.

But it's too late. I have no fight left in me.

ADDISON

This is the day I stop believing that anything good can come of this world. The day I realize that evil always wins. The day I question why the fuck I've tried so hard to paint a perfect picture of this place when it's a barefaced lie.

I've sat here for hours, wedged between my mom and dad. Both refusing to be more than an arm's length away. Isla clings to me, just like she has since we ran out of that gas station. She hasn't spoken to anyone. She's just … shook.

Cam's parents rush into the emergency room waiting room, all looking a mess, like the rest of us here, waiting. I stand, keeping Isla attached, and rush over to hug them. As do Mila and Beau, who got here not long ago.

"He's still in surgery," Beau says to Mr. and Mrs. Hardy while protectively holding Mila. "They said they'd come out just as soon as there's an update."

They already know the hardest parts because they were informed over the phone. That Cam had taken a bullet to the chest. That he had lost a significant amount of blood and flatlined, but—thank God—was resuscitated. And that he was in emergency surgery to remove the bullet and stop the bleeding.

So many horrible things, all of which were told to them while they drove here.

Mrs. Hardy clings to me, burying her face into my shoulder. "God … let my boy be okay. Please."

I cry with her, feeling my chest cave in.

This is my fault. He ran into that building for me and Isla.

"I'm sorry," I say, my voice barely squeaking. "I'm so, so sorry."

"For what, baby?" She pulls back, cupping my cheeks. "This is not your fault. My son did the right thing. Stupid probably. But he did what he knew in his heart he had to." She gives me the saddest smile. "My son finally knows what it's like to love someone with his whole heart. I can thank the two of you for that." She peeks at Isla. "Cam thinks the world of you, little lady."

Isla hugs me closer, not saying anything. So not like her usual self. She's been through more this afternoon than anyone should go through in their entire life.

"Sorry," I whisper. "Rough day."

She pats Isla on the back and clings to her husband. And for the next three hours ... we wait. Hoping and praying that Cam pulls through. The thought of losing him is unimaginable. So, right now, I'm going to pretend that it isn't a possibility. Because truthfully, I don't think I'd survive that.

I sip the coffee Tessa brought me, or try to, but when she hands me the bagel, my stomach aches.

I shake my head. "I can't."

My eyes stay on Isla as she plays with some of the toys Tessa grabbed from my house. Mila and Beau sit on the floor with her, pretending to make the toys talk to each other.

Finally, after being held hostage and barely speaking for hours and hours, she started to come back to herself this morning. Though her smile isn't as big and bright as it normally is, I'm just thankful Tess was able to get her to eat a part of a doughnut and drink some water.

"I can take Isla back to your house so she can rest," Tessa says, putting her hand on mine. "Might do her good to get out of here."

Panic rises in my gut. "I can't," I whisper. "I'd be too afraid if I wasn't with her. Too many bad things could happen." I feel shaky as my eyes fill with tears, blurring my vision. "I ... I can't."

Pulling me against her, she puts her forehead to mine. "Addy, she's safe. You're safe. I promise." She squeezes me tighter. "It's okay. Isla is safe."

We stay like that for a while until I can pull myself together.

Releasing me slowly, she wipes her own eyes. "Whatever you need, I'm here. Okay?"

"I know. I love you," I whisper, looking at the clock. "It's been over twenty-four hours since surgery. I need him to wake up."

The hospital has limited visitation to his room to only his immediate family. They tried to get the hospital to give me access, but they said, right now, the fewer people in and out, the better. He still has a breathing tube in.

223

And until he regains consciousness and proves he can breathe without it, he's staying intubated. When he does wake up, the doctors have warned he's going to fight the intubation. They also said seeing that will be a bit traumatizing.

"He will." She pulls my head to her shoulder, resting her head on mine. "I know it."

When he wakes up, I'm going to tell him I'm sorry and I'm going to beg for his forgiveness.

Sometimes, it takes almost losing someone—like ... really losing them— to realize you'd walk through fire to keep them with you.

I'm ready to walk through fire for Cam.

CAM

Fuck, my throat is sore. And what the hell is in my mouth?

I gag, making the pain worse. And when I finally get my eyes open, I fucking panic. My parents stand from their chairs, running toward me. I can't make out exactly what they're saying, but I think they are telling me to calm down. Only I can't.

The gagging continues as I figure out I have an actual tube down my throat. My body flails around even though I know that's the worst thing I could possibly do. Somehow, I just can't stop it.

"We need help in here!" my dad screams down the hall. "I SAID, WE NEED SOME FUCKING HELP IN HERE!" he yells louder as my mom attempts to calm me down.

People in scrubs run into my room, and even though I want to know what they're saying to me, I can't hear them. All I hear is that damn ringing noise and a bunch of muffled voices.

My mom disappears, running out of the room as I grab to pull the tube out myself. My heart pounds in my ears, and I feel like I'm about to have a heart attack.

"Cam, stop ... please stop," Addison says, coming beside me and grabbing my hand.

My mom walks next to her.

So, that's where she went.

My nostrils flare as I gag again, but I try to focus on Addison's eyes.

"Please, calm down," she repeats. "They are going to take it out. I need you to just relax. I know it's hard, baby. I know it is. But please." Her eyes fill with tears as my chest heaves. "Please … for me and Isla, let them take it out. Otherwise, they are going to sedate you."

I relax for a moment before the panic starts to creep back in. Her hand squeezes mine as the doctor and nurse come beside me.

"I promise, son, the worst is about to be over. Just let us get this out, okay?"

I nod the best I can, though my head probably doesn't actually move.

It's not a sensation I ever want to feel again. It seems to take forever, but eventually, the tube leaves my throat, and I can fucking breathe normally.

I cough a few times, wincing at the pain that comes with it. Not only in my throat, but also in my chest and abdomen. Basically my entire fucking body.

"My boy." My mom walks around the doctor, running her hand over my head. "I've never been so happy to see those beautiful eyes of yours in my life." She kisses my forehead. "Don't you ever scare me like that again. You just took ten years off of my life."

"Ten? Christ, I was thinking at least twenty," my dad drawls, coming beside her. "Once you're healed, I'm gonna kick your ass for that, son."

Mom kisses my forehead again, and my dad clasps my shoulder gently.

"We're going to give y'all a minute." She nods toward Addison before she walks out, Dad right behind her.

I laugh the smallest bit, but the pain that shoots through my chest brings tears to my eyes.

I look at Addison. "Maybe you aren't mine, but kiss me anyway, would ya?"

She smiles as the tears stream down her cheeks. "I will always be yours." She presses her lips to mine. "I love you so much."

She cries harder, pulling back to look at me. "Thank you for not dying."

"Hey, what can I say? I aim to please." I try to wink but fail miserably from all the pain medicine I'm jacked up on.

"I was yours, even when you thought I'd left you." She cups my face. "I'll make it up to you, I promise. I just got scared, and I did what I thought was best for you and Isla both." Her eyebrows pull together as she sobs. "But even when you thought we were over, you jumped through a window to save our lives." She looks at the cuts on my arms, hands, and face. "Thank you. Thank you for being you."

"You are my girls. I promise to keep you both safe. Always." I bring her hand to my lips. "I'm sorry I failed. Never again."

"Are you kidding? You didn't fail. You're a hero." She kisses me again. "You're my hero."

"And you're gonna be my wife one day," I slur slightly, suddenly feeling the meds kicking in more. "And Isla will be my daughter."

She smiles, shaking her head. "They've got you on the good stuff, huh?" Kissing my cheek, she runs her hand through my hair. "Someone once told me to rest. They said there would be plenty more fights I'd be able to take part in later. But right now, you need sleep. So, rest, handsome. I promise, I'll be close by when you wake."

Even though I'm afraid to fall asleep—in fear when I wake up, this will have been a dream, and I'll be alone in a hospital bed, probably intubated and shit all over again—I can't stop my eyes from closing.

"Love you and Isla so much," I barely get out before it all goes dark.

And I pray that when I wake up, I'm still in my happy place.

Addison
Two Weeks Later

I look around the guest bedroom one last time, just to make sure it's perfect. After he's spent two weeks in a smelly hospital, I know Cam is more than happy to be leaving today. Especially since he thought he'd be out a week ago, but a nasty infection in his wound, followed by a few other complications, bought him an extra week. But we got word this morning that he is one hundred percent getting discharged today, and I'd be lying if I said I wasn't happy that he'd be staying with me. Even if the next month or so will be challenging for him as he heals, I'll be content with just lying next to him without the sound of beeping machines and nurses constantly poking their heads in.

Surprisingly, it was actually my father's idea to have him stay with us while he recovers. With the stipulation that he stays in his room ... on the other end of the house. It made the most sense because his apartment with Link and Brody is on the second story and our house is one level. His mom and dad really wanted him to come home for a while, but he wanted to stay at Brooks. Even though his hockey season is done physically, he wants to be there mentally and emotionally for his team. From the sidelines, of course.

I tried to make the room as homey as I could. With his posters and pictures from his room at his apartment and some new pictures of him, Isla, and me that we took before I made the biggest mistake of my life.

It's been odd, seeing him in the state he's in. The man who usually lifts me with his strong arms and skates down the ice, damn near melting it as he goes, is wheelchair-bound for a few more weeks. I know he's discouraged, but he's handled it so well.

The man who held us hostage is dead. With the window broken, the police had a clear view of him. After he fired shots at Cam, they made the call to pull the trigger before he could harm anyone else. Part of me is thankful. If he were alive and in jail, I'd have known that, one day, he'd be out. And the fear of that would have only made everything worse.

I hear a knock on my door and find my mom in my doorframe.

"Ready to go? He should be set anytime now." She smiles. "I know he'll want his girls next to him when he leaves that place."

I take one more look around and nod. "I've never been more ready for anything in my life. Let's go."

"Jeez, guess I ought to jump through gas-station windows and get myself shot more often." Cam grins, looking at the line of nurses and doctors who clap as his dad pushes him toward the exit. "I feel like a goddamn celebrity or some shit."

"I'm still waiting on you to heal so I can beat your ass and land you right back here for taking so many years off my life, you dink," his dad jokes. "You made your point, Cam. You're brave. Now, cut it out."

"Yeah, no kidding," I agree, shooting him a look. "Or else *I'll* kick your ass myself."

"That sounds fun." Cam winks. "Wanna try right now?"

"Right here," Jaxon mutters. "And, boy, you'd best not be doing any of that business for a long while. You heard the doc."

Cam's expression turns grumpy, though he tries to hide it as he waves to the last few nurses. "Don't remind me," he grumbles.

When we reach the large exit, the doors open to show Isla, my parents, Mila and Beau, Mrs. Hardy, the entire Brooks hockey and football teams, and the redhead named Layla, who accidentally caused my and Cam's first fight. I met her and her boyfriend last week when they came to see Cam. I'm a little embarrassed for the way I acted, seeing her with my man, but honestly … she looks like a supermodel. Any bitch would be a little jealous of her.

Brody, Link, and Hunter are the first to come forward.

"Nice to see the sun, isn't it?" Hunter grins. "You know, if you didn't want to deal with Coach's practices anymore, there were other ways to get out of it than getting yourself shot."

Cam holds his hands out. "Hey, I was desperate. I was one suicide drill away from quitin'," he jokes.

I think, in this type of situation, you've got to be able to joke even though it's absolutely horrible and traumatizing.

I should know. I've had PTSD since it happened. So has Isla. But we're both getting the help we need to cope and handling it the best that we can. When I look at Cam, it hits me that not only is his entire season over, but he might also never be the same player he was before that day, and guilt consumes me. Hockey is his world. I can't imagine what would happen if he couldn't continue to play it.

But I'm trying to stay positive. And days like today, seeing how many turned out to watch him leave the hospital, sure help.

"Look at you, bringing out the entire university and all." I lean down, pressing a kiss to his cheek. "You are loved by many, Cam Hardy."

He looks around, holding his hand up to wave to everyone. "Don't let the football team fool ya. A few of them motherfuckers hate me."

"Oh, and I wonder why that is," Brody says, folding his arms over his chest. "When you fuck with dudes' old ladies, they don't for—"

"O'Brien. Do you not see Addison standing there?" Link elbows him before smiling at me. "Cam wouldn't dream of doing such a thing. He's a perfect gentleman, always has been."

"That's what I'm saying," Cam chimes in. "I'm a good boy."

I dip my head down, narrowing my eyes. "You're so full of shit that your eyes are turning brown." I look at Link and tap Cam on the shoulder. "You think I used to call him puck boy for nothing?" I laugh. "I'm aware he used to be a little shit, trust me."

"You can say that again." One of the football players steps closer, and I realize he's got to be twins with Layla's boyfriend. "Hardy here and I have had a few runarounds. Isn't that right?" He nods, his eyes smiling. "Glad to see you alive, ol' boy."

"Weston Wade. Bet you never thought you'd be cheering for my ass in my wheelchair, huh?"

"Fuck no." Weston chuckles. "But here we are."

I recognize Cole Storms, the captain of the football team, as he comes forward. "Get well, brother. You'll be back out on the ice soon." He points to the hockey team. "We're lucky, you and me. We both have damn good guys who have our backs. Pain in the ass as they sometimes might be."

"Hey, I take offense to that." Knox Carter punches Cole in the arm before slapping Cam's hand. "You still look good, my man. Wheelchair and all. Still fucking got it."

Cam laughs. "Damn right I do."

"Cam! Cam!" Isla squeals, running toward him.

"Be gentle, Isla girl," my mom says. "He's still healing."

"It's okay, sweetie. You won't hurt me," he says, holding his arms out and pulling her into a hug. "You ready to have me as a roommate?"

"Yes! We can finally watch *Frozen!*" She beams. "And then *Frozen II!*"

"Damn straight we will." He releases her, but not before kissing her forehead. "Thanks for taking care of your mama while I've been in here."

"You're welcome," she says sweetly. "But now, I'm ready for a vacation."

Everyone laughs at her response, making her giggle harder. The bond they have built in such a short time is wild. But it's beautiful. And for some crazy reason, I don't think it can ever be broken.

Person after person greets him until, finally, it's time for us to take him home. And seeing the crowd here just proves to me more that nobody is more loved than Cam Hardy. He's truly one of a kind.

And he's all mine. Well, mine and Isla's.

CAM

While Addison gives Isla a bath, I lie in the bed in their guest room, mindlessly flipping through the channels. Finally, I stop when it lands on *Step Brothers*.

"Knock, knock," Coach says as he pushes the door further open. "How are you settling in, Hardy?"

I turn the volume down and stretch. "Not bad. Thanks again for letting me stay here." I laugh. "Or should I say, for saying yes to Addy when she asked?"

"No way was my girl letting you go back to your apartment." He sits down in the accent chair in the corner. "She worries about you. Feels real bad too."

"Nothing to feel bad for, Coach. I did what I had to do."

His face looks pained. "It should have been me. I should have jumped through that window before you got the chance. I'm sorry, son. I was paralyzed with fear, and now, you're paying for it. She's my daughter; it's my job to keep her safe."

I look down for a moment, taking a breath. "Sir, believe me when I say, even if you had jumped through the window first, I would have been right behind you. So, please, don't feel guilty for how things went down." I smirk, tipping my chin up. "Besides, you been on Facebook lately? I'm being called a hero and shit."

I say the words to lighten the mood, but really, I know I'm not a hero. I should have been in there sooner than I was. Addison is the real hero for keeping Isla safe while they were in that gas station.

"Well, I have to give credit where it's due. You are a hero, Hardy. And I'm grateful for you." He clears his throat. "But I also have something else I need to talk to you about. Something I wish I could wait to say, but I feel like you need to know."

I eye him over, knowing whatever he's going to say might not be exactly what I want to hear. "Boston call you?"

Slowly, he nods. "Yep ... I talked to Coach Montgomery of the Bruins a few days ago." He gives me an apologetic look. "They aren't pulling back, but they want to make sure you're going to make a full recovery before they fully commit to you coming down there for the season."

"Why do I suspect you're holding back?" I ask. "What else is there, Coach?"

"Unselfishly, Cam ... I think you should hold off—just until after next season here at Brooks. Sure, I'd love to have you as a player for another year, and obviously, it would be best for my girls, but more importantly, I think your body needs that extra time to get back. You know, before you go to the big leagues." He sighs. "Because it's a whole other animal, playing in the NHL."

"Do you think I'm going to get it back? Hockey? The game?"

His eyes narrow. "I don't have a single doubt about it, Hardy. But do it on your own terms. Trust me, you've got what it takes to get there. I just don't want you to jump before you're fully ready." He waves at my body. "You were shot two weeks ago. Let yourself heal."

As he stands, he looks around the room his daughter decorated for me and smiles. "Whatever you decide, it'll all be okay."

And then he walks out of the room. Leaving me with far too many thoughts to sort out.

CAM

I sit in the white room with the lights that are way too fucking bright, completely paralyzed with fear that he's going to tell me something didn't heal right. But the fear I feel today is still nothing like what I felt twelve weeks ago. On the worst day of my life.

I squeeze my eyes shut, feeling my palms start to sweat. The vision of Isla and Addison being held at gunpoint invades every cell in my body. I've traveled to this dark place more times than I care to admit since it happened. But after all Addy has been through, the last thing she needs is to think I'm too weak to be there for her and Isla. So, I hide it as best I can, plaster on that carefree grin I've been mastering for most of my life, and call it a day.

Not only did my team not make it to the Frozen Four, but I'm also not headed to the NHL. Not yet anyway. The Bruins didn't retract their offer, but wanted to wait it out to see if I made a full recovery. And given the fact that nobody, including myself, knows if I'll ever be the same on the ice, I expected that much. But when Coach suggested I play another year for Brooks to get myself completely healed, I decided he was right. It doesn't hurt that I'll be here for Addison's senior year too. And as long as I can get back to the player that I was, more offers will come through. I hope so anyway.

The important thing is that I am alive. And that Addison and Isla are too. Without the people we love, our careers don't mean jack shit. So, I know, in another year, I'll have to make a plan to ensure that Addy and I are going to make it, living states apart, but we will figure it out. We always do.

The door swings open, saving me from my own thoughts as the doctor strolls in.

"What's crackin', Doc?" I nod toward the clipboard in his hand. "You'd better have some good news written on that thing for me."

He sits down, rolling the chair closer to me. "As a matter of fact, Mr. Hardy, I do. You passed all the tests we'd put you through with flying colors." He pauses, setting the clipboard down. "We never can say for sure what the body is going to do after something as traumatic as what yours endured. A gunshot wound to the chest with multiple complications, yet you've fought every step of the way to heal. So, I guess what I'm saying is … if I was a betting man, I'd bet on you getting right back on the ice, as good as new, by next season." He adjusts his glasses. "It won't be easy—"

"It never is," I say, interrupting him. "Never would want it to be either."

His lips turn up slightly. "I'm happy to hear that because it won't be a cakewalk. You're used to constantly conditioning your body. And even though you've still been doing PT, we both know that's not the same. So, couple that with the fact that you had major surgery, you've got a long road ahead of you. But I can tell you want it. So, I have no doubt on my mind that you'll take it."

"You saying I've been a lazy fucker the past twelve weeks, Doc?" I joke.

"Not at all. PT is hard work. I should know. I had a crap ton of it when I had spinal surgery years back. But I talked to Dr. Palmer at the PT office, and he was impressed with your dedication. He also said there was never a dull moment when you were in the office."

"Ha! Good to know." I scratch my chin. "I always thought he seemed like a grumpy old bastard. Glad to hear it's just his face."

"He's my younger brother," the doctor says in a serious tone, and my eyes immediately widen.

"Oh … fuck. I'm sorry." I cough, trying to think of what the hell I'm going to say to make this better. "For what it's worth, you look fresh as a daisy, if I do say so myself."

He bursts out laughing. "I'm joking, Mr. Hardy. Dr. Palmer is old and grouchy." Standing, he shakes my hand. "It was truly my pleasure to work with you. One day, when you're in the NHL, I can't wait to brag that I helped heal the player who jumped through a glass window and saved seven people's lives. But for now, instead of saving lives, maybe try a cooking class or golf. Something less … dangerous." He backs away, his hand resting on the doorknob. "If you need anything, anything at all, call me. Now, go home and celebrate."

"Yes, sir." I nod. "I sure will."

30

ADDISON

I guide Cam across the stadium parking lot, tugging him by the hands. After I found out he was cleared to go back to normal life, this is the first place I wanted to bring him.

"Where are we?" He tries to tilt his head back to peek, but I smack him lightly.

"No peeking, jerk!"

"If I peek, will you punish me?" He wiggles his eyebrows above the blindfold. "If so ... I can be a bad, bad boy."

"Shut up, you idiot." I laugh. "I find you annoying right now, and I'm regretting my decision to do something nice."

"Hey, as long as you find me, that's all I care about."

I lead him through the hallway, taking the elevator down because blindfolds and stairs don't mesh well. Plus, I'm not ready for him to be injured again.

We stop in front of the door leading out to the ice, and I push it open.

"Wherever we are, it's cold." He smirks. "Not cold enough for shrinkage, so no worries there, babe. We can still have *plenty* of fun."

I sit on the bench, switching my shoes to skates before I untie the blindfold, letting it drop to the ground. Holding his skates in my hand, I tilt my head. "Skate with me, Cam. Because I've got to tell you, this arena has missed you as much as you've missed it."

He looks nervously at the skates. "Hell … I don't know, Addy. I haven't, you know … in a long time."

"Skated?" I say, and he nods, taking a seat on the bench.

Stepping between his legs, I cup his face. "I know you carry the weight of that day around every day. I feel it when you drift off somewhere far, far away, where we all aren't safe. Where maybe … someone didn't make it out of there." My vision clouds with tears. "My mind takes me to that same place way more often than I care to admit. And I know you don't think I can handle your pain and my own. But I promise, I can. You saved my life. You saved Isla's life. The three of us? We went through something unimaginable—"

"I wasn't there," he whispers, looking down. "For way too long, I wasn't in there with you, and now, she's going to live in fear every day because I didn't come in time." He looks up again, his eyes misty. "When you go to the grocery store, or the school, or hell, even when we take her to the movies … I'm fucking terrified, Addy. I'm so scared all the time." He wipes his eyes. "If you guys had died that day … I can't. I just can't—"

"We didn't die, Cam. We're alive. And all because of you." I kiss him. "I see the fear in your eyes when it comes to Isla and me. And I love you so much for it. Really, I do. But life is scary. And wild. And beautiful, all wrapped up in one. We just need to take the days as they come. And I know, deep down, you're afraid you won't get hockey back to where you had it before. But, Cam, you were born to be on this ice. And I know you. If you want something bad enough, you'll never fail." I press my forehead to his. "I know, next year, you'll be a Bruin."

"No matter what happens in the next few years, Addy, promise me you'll be there. Because NHL or not … if we aren't all together, it's no dream of mine." He keeps his voice low. "I know you don't want to uproot Isla, and I'd never ask you to. So, I need you to promise me, no matter how far away we are from each other, we'll make it work."

"We will," I say. "But the fact that we'll be in Boston with you will make it easier."

He pulls back, looking confused before his eyes widen. "What are you saying?"

"I'm saying, I'm coming with you. Isla too."

"Your parents? What about them? She'd miss them so much."

"Yes, she will," I agree with him. "But I know my mom. She'll travel as much as she can. And when you're on the road, I'll come back here and visit them."

His eyes fill with tears as his hands hold me at the waist. "We're going to Boston?" he whispers.

"We're going to Boston!" I pull his face toward mine and kiss him. "We're family. You, Isla, and me. I can't wait to see what our future holds."

Kissing him again before I step into the arena, I wave my hand. "Now, skate with me. Because even back when I was trying to convince myself I hated you, you had me mesmerized when you were on the ice."

He winks before pulling his own skates on. "You could never hate me, and you know it."

"Well, back when it was just about the sex, I was sure trying my best to."

Coming onto the ice with me, he puts his hands around my waist. "It was *never* just about the sex. We both know that." He bends down, kissing my neck. "But if it were, I can't blame you. I'm sort of a magician in the sheets ... I know."

Even though I roll my eyes, I feel a tingle in my stomach. We've fooled around a little since he was shot, but we haven't had sex. Between him healing, us living with my parents, and me having a toddler running around, it hasn't exactly been easy to find the time for romance. I miss him. I miss his hands on me and the way he can consume every cell of my being with one touch.

I skate away from him, racing toward the other end of the rink. My dad was a hockey player, a good one at that. Of course he made sure his daughter could skate. Heck, even Isla can too. Not great, but she'll get there.

He chases after me, slowly getting his rhythm back after so much time away. His face always lights up in this place. So does everyone who gets the privilege to watch him on the ice.

We both laugh as I attempt to do a few tricks and fancy footwork, failing miserably. We chase after each other like a couple of lovesick teenagers.

Holding hands, we stop in the middle of the rink.

"When was the moment you knew that hockey was it?" I ask. "That big aha moment."

"When I was a kid, we took a trip to Boston. My dad was having his race car engine rebuilt by a shop out there, so we made a whole trip out of it." He laughs. "Mila was interested in the engine shop, of course. I bet those poor bastards thought she'd never leave. She was only just a little thing, but her eyes were like saucers while we were there." He smiles as he thinks about his sister.

"But Dad got us tickets to a Bruins game. We'd been to NFL games when traveling for Dad's races, even went to a few NBA ones too." He grins, looking down. "But the minute their skates hit the ice, I couldn't tear my eyes from them. I'd never even watched hockey on TV before. In Alabama, it isn't really a big sport, you know?

"Besides, I was supposed to be like Mila. I was supposed to want grease on my hands and a hunger to tear things apart and build them back to make them go faster. I was supposed to have fuel running through my veins." He shrugs. "Only I didn't. And when I saw Patrice Bergeron on the ice, leading his team so flawlessly, like they all trusted him or something ... I knew right then that I wanted that. Even as just a kid, sitting up in the stands, I could see he was a team player. I could tell he made his entire team better because he wasn't focused just on his own game, but also every man with a Bruins jersey on." He tilts his head slightly. "Might make me sound like the world's biggest pansy, but I wanted a purpose like that. I wanted to be a leader. I wanted my team to trust me."

"And look at you now. One of Brooks University's greatest players to date, a team captain, and a center." I lay my hand on his abdomen. "It looks like all is right in the world. Cam Hardy is back on the ice." I smile, taking his hand as he holds it out to me.

"You always know what will make me feel better." He hugs me, burying his face in my neck. "God, I love you."

He smells so good. It's a calming scent, one that makes me feel at home as he holds me close. There hasn't been anything easy about his recovery, but if anything, it's tested us, bringing us closer than ever. But physically, I need him. Sex might not be the key to a perfect relationship, but when Cam makes love to me, there isn't a single part of my body or mind that doesn't feel how much he cares about me. I need him. And given that my parents are at the park with Isla for the afternoon ... we have some free time.

His lips kiss my neck. It's slow and unintentional at first, but the closer his mouth works toward mine, it becomes apparent that he's just as desperate as I am.

He kisses my jawline, and I feel the stubble of his facial hair brush against my flesh.

"Cam," I whisper.

His mouth is on mine, showering me with kisses. They are slow and sensual at first, but before long, his touch becomes more heated as he kisses me faster, possessing my lips with his.

"I want you so bad," he rasps before lifting me up.

My legs wrap around his waist, but I panic. "Is this too much? I don't want you to get hurt."

He nips my bottom lip, looking at me with hooded eyes. "Trust me, I can handle it. What I'm about to do to this body will be much more strenuous than this right here." He cups my ass as his hardness presses against me. "I've missed you so fucking much. But I'm back now. And I can't wait to savor every inch of you."

He skates toward the exit, taking us into the small room that's used for exams on the players. As he walks us inside, his lips never break from mine, and I hear the door click as he locks it behind us.

He sets my ass on the exam table. "You might not be injured, but I'm sure as hell gonna do a thorough check anyway," he growls, pulling my skates off.

Tugging my shirt over my head, he dips his head down between my breasts. When he runs his tongue up my chest, a loud moan escapes my throat, and I'm thankful that the arena is closed today to everyone besides us.

Slowly, he pulls my jeans and underwear off before settling between my legs.

Fumbling with desperation, I finally get his jeans unbuttoned, pulling them and his briefs down just enough for his hardness to spring free. I reach for him, but he pushes my hand away.

"Let me touch you first. Because it's been a while, and I can't last with you, Addy. You're too fucking hot." He begs before desperately tearing the shirt and bra from my body.

Starting at my knees, his hands run up my thighs before he takes one hand and cups between my legs.

He dips one and then another finger inside of me as his eyes darken. "Soaked for me." His breathing deepens. "Fuck, that's hot. Makes my dick harder than it already is."

His thumb drags circles over my most sensitive spot as his fingers work in and out of me. Both things driving me completely mad.

To make him feel some of my agony, I tease him by cupping my own breasts. Slowly, I pinch my nipples and watch him draw in a shaky, long breath.

"Goddamn, Addison," he groans. "You haven't even touched me yet, and I'm close to blowing my load."

I continue to caress myself, knowing, little by little, he's losing control.

Lifting my feet up, I drag him closer with my legs, squeezing him between my thighs.

"Don't make me wait a second more," I breathe out. "I need you inside of me. Right now."

One hand grips my thigh while the other fists my hair as he plunges inside. I cry out, biting my bottom lip so hard that I expect to taste blood.

"Mine forever," he whispers. "Promise me, Addy. Tell me you aren't going anywhere."

It's so much deeper than just asking me to spend my life with him. It's his thoughts out loud. He's scared something's going to happen to me, just like I'm petrified the world will try to rip him away from me. Having the experience that we had will do that. When I close my eyes to sleep, I see him in his practice jersey as he crashes through the window like he's a damn superhero. I still imagine him on that stretcher, getting loaded into the ambulance. Shattered glass everywhere and people crying, hugging their loved ones who were outside, waiting.

"I promise. You're stuck with me forever." I lean up to kiss him as he dives into me again. "I love you." I wince.

I pull his mouth back to mine as he thrusts in and out of me, my feet pushing him deeper.

"Come all over me, Addy. Let me feel you on my cock," he growls against my lips, picking up the pace.

My nipples harden unbearably so, and my head falls back as I drift into oblivion. Kissing my neck, he shudders as he loses himself inside of me. His rocking slows, and he buries his face into my shoulder, gently biting down on my skin.

Once we catch our breath, he grins down at me. "Thanks for today. It was fun." He kisses me again, and his smile grows bigger. "But now, let's go get our girl and go get ice cream."

I nod against him. "Sounds perfect."

CAM
SIX MONTHS LATER

"You have to keep the blindfold on," I tell Addison, watching her in the rearview mirror as she sits in my backseat. "Surprises are fun, right, Addy?"

She smiles, but under the cloth, I bet she's rolling her eyes. She's done this same thing to me before, when she got me back on the ice months ago. Now, it's my turn.

Isla is asleep in her car seat next to her, which is good because I know Isla would peek if she had a blindfold on.

This night means everything to me. I have to get it right. They deserve it. After the year they've had, all I want to do is make them happy.

I still hate when they go somewhere without me. And when I travel out of town for a game, I wish they could just stay inside the house with the door locked. But Addison isn't a kept woman. She's strong and independent. The last thing she'd ever want is a man who told her what to do. So, instead, I just check in with them every five seconds.

As the doctor expected, I made a full recovery both on and off the ice. And while I won't say it was like I never left, I got back to where I was. It took a lot of hard work, determination, and sore fucking muscles. But I did it. And now, I'm headed to begin my training for the Bruins after I finish my junior year.

Addison, Isla, and I moved into a small house just off campus this past summer. As much as I enjoyed living with my coach, I was happy not to have his hawk eyes on me every waking second of my life. And surprisingly, he was okay with Addison and me sharing a house so soon.

I got to be there to celebrate Isla's fourth birthday. Which, after changing her mind at least fifteen times, she ended up having a *Frozen* birthday party, where I had to dress up as Kristoff. I've seen the movie at least one hundred times now, and I can sadly recite every word. Link, Brody, and the guys got a good laugh out of that. But not nearly as much of a laugh as they did when Halloween rolled around and I had to be Ken because Isla insisted her Barbie costume needed a Ken to go with it. So, there I was, floral shirt, six-pack out, matching shorts, and some pretty-boy boat shoes. Honestly, there's not much I wouldn't do if that little girl asked me.

"You're awfully quiet up there," Addison says. "Just because I'm blindfolded doesn't mean we can't talk."

"Sorry, babe. Just thinking what a year it's been. Good and bad."

The corner of her lips turns up. "I'd say the good's outweighed the bad ... somehow."

A while back, I wouldn't have thought that was possible. But the worst day somehow brought us closer.

I put my blinker on, pulling into a familiar parking lot.

"Remember, no peeking," I warn her.

Holding her hands up, she raises her eyebrows. "I'm not!"

ADDISON

Cam carries a sleeping Isla while somehow also holding my hand, guiding me on this obstacle course of a walk. I shiver slightly from the nip in the air. Even though it's nothing like December in New England, it's cooler than it normally is here in Georgia. But with Christmas just a few weeks away, I sort of like the cold air.

"Finally, sleepyhead is waking up," Cam says softly before releasing my hand and moving his fingers upward to untie the cloth around my head.

"Wow, where are we?" I hear Isla's sleepy voice just as my blindfold falls.

Looking around, I feel a rush of emotions. "The botanical gardens. You brought me back."

He holds her as he pulls me against them. "I promised you that we'd bring her here. I never break a promise when it comes to my Isla girl."

"Mommy, look." She whirls her head around. "This is so magical. Are we in the North Pole?"

"Not quite." I smile, patting her head. "But it sure is beautiful."

Setting Isla down on her feet, he stands before us. "Isla, I brought Mommy here last winter. It was the first real date we went on … even if she still didn't want to consider it one." He holds my hand, keeping her between us. "That was the night I fell in love with her. It was a good night. But you know what was missing?"

"What?" Isla whispers.

"You." He kneels down. "It was almost perfect, but I didn't have both my girls here. But now, I do."

He looks up at me. "I've always wondered what it would feel like to have a happy place. The kind everyone talks about. It's usually at their home, with their family. But for me, I just figured mine was on the ice. Because for as long as I can remember, that's when I felt the most at peace. But it turns out, I was wrong. My happy place isn't a place at all. It's a person. Or … people. It can't be found on a map, and there's no directions to it. It's constantly changing, and given my career choice, it probably always will. Because my happy place is wherever the three of us are.

"So, here it goes. My happy place is you. That's never gonna change. So, marry me. Let me give you and Isla my last name. A name that probably doesn't sound like much, but it's who I am. Marry me because I want to be your happy place too. I want to coach Isla's T-ball team and take her to the daddy-daughter dance and embarrass the hell out of her in front of her friends. I want to teach her how to drive a car and scare the piss out of her first boyfriend."

He reaches out, touching Isla's cheek. "I want to marry your mommy so that she can be my wife, but I also want to marry her so that you can be my daughter. Because trust me, I've never wanted anything more than that in my entire life."

Reaching into his pocket, he takes out a box. But when he opens it, it isn't just one ring. It's two. One is tiny, but both are white gold and have a solitaire diamond in the middle.

Tears stream down my cheeks as I hold Cam's hand with one of mine and rest the other on my daughter's shoulder. "What do you think, Isla girl?" I say, sniffling. "I know my answer."

She stands for a moment before leaping into Cam's arms. "Yes! Yes, Cam. I would love for my mommy to marry you."

He puts the small ring on her finger. "I was hoping you'd say that."

"Can I tell you a secret?" she whispers, looking at him. "I was already pretending you were my daddy."

His eyes glaze over. "Can I tell you a secret? So was I."

Giving his neck a big squeeze, she steps back, looking at both of us. "Go on, Mommy. Answer his question."

"My answer is yes." I sob as he slides the ring onto my finger. "Yes, yes … one thousand times … yes!"

Lifting me up, he twirls me around as our lips collide. Isla skips around us, cheering loudly as her blonde curls bounce.

Once he sets me down, she grabs both of our hands. "Now, let's go see the rest of the magical, twinkly lights!" Yanking our arms, she heads toward the pathway. "This is the best day of my whole life."

I glance over at Cam, seeing the joy and contentment on his face.

"Mine too," I whisper.

And I truly mean it.

ADDISON
FOUR MONTHS LATER

"They did it!" I lift Isla up and twirl her around. "They really, really did it!"

"Papa and Daddy won!" she cheers, squeezing my cheeks. "They should get an ice cream party!"

"Sounds like a good plan to me!" Jaxon, Cam's dad, says, taking her from me and putting her on his shoulders so that she can wave to Cam.

He spots her instantly, his entire face lighting up as he waves.

"That's my boy." Cam's mom wipes her eyes, pulling me against her. "I'm so proud of him. You and Isla are truly the best things that have ever happened in his life. My son has always been a good boy with a heart of gold, but he sees the world differently now. In the best way."

"Thank you," I weep, hugging her back. "He's the best thing to happen to us too. You did good." I look from her to Jaxon. "Both of you."

"Mommy, can we go see Daddy? Please!" Isla shouts, holding on to Jaxon. "I just have to squeeze him! I have to!"

"Soon, babe. Soon," I promise her.

The first few times she called him Daddy, it seemed so crazy to me. Actually, the first month or so, it did. Now, it's second nature. He is her dad. He shows up for her like her biological father never has. And it isn't hard for him. In fact, he makes it look easy.

Last year, Cam lost his chance to lead his team to the Frozen Four when he was recovering. And despite my father's and the other guys' best efforts, they fell short. But one good thing about that is, this year, they all earned it together. Cam included.

We ended up getting married one month after he proposed. In the same exact spot too. The ceremony was small but magical. Brody, Hunter, Link, Tessa, and a few others threw together a huge reception for us, and we had the time of our lives. Isla danced the night away, stealing the show. I'm close to becoming a registered nurse. Everything seems to be falling into place.

This summer, we'll move to Boston so that Cam can start his training as a Bruin. I'd be lying if I said I wasn't a little nervous. But above nerves is excitement. Excitement to start our lives together. And excitement to watch my husband soar in the NHL.

I see him skate toward the Plexiglas, and I grab Isla from Jaxon and rush down the stairs to where he stands.

When he puts his hand against the plastic, Isla lifts hers to meet his. "Good job, Daddy." She smiles.

"Thanks, my Isla girl. I think you were my good-luck charm." His eyes move to mine. "Hey, mama. You were lookin' pretty damn good up in those stands. I could see you getting all worked up over me." He winks.

"Was not." I roll my eyes. "Is this the greatest day of your life or what?"

"Nah. I've already had that. But it's a good day—a *damn* good day."

Some teammates holler to him, chanting his last name, and he grins, shaking his head.

"Go on," I say, nodding toward them as they act like a bunch of fools.

"Love you both." He moves backward. "See you soon."

As he turns, I cup my hand next to my mouth. "Hey, nineteen, nice ass!"

He looks at me, a smirk on his face as he skates farther away.

"Mommy, you said a bad word. Put a quarter in my jar!" Isla scolds me.

"My bad." I shrug and head up the stairs and back to the group of family and friends who are here just for Cam tonight.

I thank God every day that I took a chance on Cam. Or perhaps that he took a chance on me. I trusted the boy who I thought was just a pretty face and a hot set of abs. Only to be loved unconditionally by the man who puts his family and his team first and shows my daughter what it is like to have a dad.

When I peed on that stick all those years ago, I felt like life as I knew it was over. And I guess, to a point, that was true. I never expected to get a fairy tale, and what I never saw coming was the fact that I'd find a partner who could love my child as much as I did. Just because my family isn't traditional doesn't make us any less perfect. Cam might not be related to Isla by blood, but he is her father, and he loves her with his whole heart. And that's pretty special.

It's hard to risk your heart for something that isn't promised. But in those rare times when it all works out and when you find that person who sets your soul on fire, awakening every part of you that was asleep, it's pretty damn beautiful.

THE END

Curious about Link? You should be! Preorder *Broken Boy* to read his story.

Already obsessing over Brody? Me too! Preorder *Filthy Boy* now!

OTHER BOOKS BY HANNAH GRAY

NE UNIVERSITY SERIES

Chasing Sunshine
Seeing Red
Losing Memphis

BROOKS UNIVERSITY SERIES

Love, Ally
Forget Me, Sloane
Hate You, Henley

FLORIDA EAST UNIVERSITY

Playing Dane
Stealing Bama
Catching Kye

THE PUCK BOYS OF BROOKS UNIVERSITY

Puck Boy
Broken Boy
Filthy Boy

acknowledgments

Wow, book ten! I can't believe I'm even saying that right now. And the best part? This book was hands down one of my favorites to write. I loved having a heroine who had a daughter. So much of Addison as a mother was a reflection of how I oftentimes feel, as I'm sure many moms do. Maybe we all have that same guilt when taking time for ourselves even though we shouldn't. And Addison's mother, Jennie, was actually named after my own mom. And called Nena, just like mine is.

Cam Hardy has been my favorite character I've written thus far in my writing career. But one of the coolest parts about Cam for me was his journey to get to this book. In *Hate You, Henley*, he was a jerk! And in *Playing Dane*, he wasn't much better. But slowly, through each Florida East University book, we watched him grow into a better person. And in *Puck Boy*, I truly think he's a gem. Though I'll admit, I might be partial since he's a product of my own imagination. Either way, I hope every person finds their Cam Hardy, someone to love them unconditionally and make them laugh through the hard times.

I'm eager for this entire series, and I cannot wait for all the books to be out in the wild! But none of that would even be possible if not for my team and the ones supporting me.

First off, my three babies, who are each so special yet so different. You are strong. You are worthy. You are going to change the world. I love you to infinity and back. Thanks for making my world turn.

My husband. It's no secret that being an author can be emotionally draining. Thank you for always keeping me balanced. I love you forever.

My mom. I just had to include you in this book because in this story, Jennie is patient. She is kind. And she is everything a daughter and granddaughter need. Just like you. The girls and I love you so very much.

My father. Thank you for showing me what a strong work ethic can do. And that the best things in life won't come easy. I love you lots.

My sister-in-law, Tara. I don't think anyone hypes me up the way you do. And when you finish my books, I can guarantee I'll wake up to a text—usually in the middle of the night once you've gotten the babies to sleep—telling me how proud you are of me. You came into our family, becoming a Gray with some grace, and have loved my brother unconditionally ever since. I love you, sister. So very much.

My brother, Isiah. Thanks for being so proud of me and always spreading the word about my books—even when they do have half-naked men on the cover. I love you, and I am so proud of the dad and husband that you are.

My niece and nephew, Georgia and Jeremy. I can't wait to see what you grow up to be because I can already tell that it's going to be something magnificent. Auntie loves you both so much.

Tatum Hanscom, who isn't just my beta reader, but also one of my best friends. You're always one of the first eyes to see my words on a new book. And no matter how incredibly busy you are, you drop everything to give me that extra push I need to release that book into the world. You love Cam, and I hope everyone else does too.

My beta readers, Jaimie Davidson and Anna Zetterberg. Thank you for taking time out of your busy lives to read through my work and make sure I didn't miss anything. I appreciate you both so much! And thank you for always pumping me up with kind messages when I need them the most. It's readers like you who go the extra mile to make us authors feel seen and heard.

My editor, Jovana Shirley at Unforeseen Editing. Working with such a badass girl boss is always an honor. No matter what life throws at you, you come through, amazing me with your work each time. (Though I have no idea when you sleep!) But either way … You. Are. Amazing. This is the tenth book we've worked on together, and I can't wait for many, many more!

Autumn Gantz. Gahhh … I love you so damn much! I know you don't believe it, but you truly changed my life the moment you brought me into the

Wordsmith family. I became your "baby bird." And while I know it isn't always easy, keeping me on track, you do it with grace and patience while also giving me tough love when I need it, just like a mama does. Things I never imagined I could do, I've accomplished with you by my side. And the goals on my checklist, you've helped me check them off time and time again. Thanks for always believing in me and pushing me to my full potential. Lifers.

Amy Queau with Q Designs. As always, it's been a pleasure working with you. I am obsessing over the covers you created for this series. They are everything I wanted and more!

Sarah Grim Sentz at Enchanting Romance Designs. I have absolutely loved working with you on stickers and bookmarks, but working with you on these alternative covers was a dream! You somehow did exactly what my brain was picturing—only better! I can't wait to work together on future projects!

Mark Mendez at mcmpix. Thank you for giving me my perfect Cam photo! From the moment I saw this model on my Instagram feed, I knew he was the one. Thanks for capturing the most beautiful shot.

Collin J. Thank you for sharing your beauty with the world and for being Cam. I couldn't love the picture or the cover more.

To my readers. From the bottom of my heart, thank you for taking the chance on my book. I hope you loved Cam and Addison as much as I do.

about the author

Hannah Gray spends her days in vacationland, living in a small, quaint town on the coast of Maine. She is an avid reader of contemporary romance and is always in competition with herself to read more books every year.

During the day, she loves on her three perfect-to-her daughters and tries to be the best mom she can be. But once she tucks them in at night—okay, scratch that. Once they fall asleep next to her in her bed—because their bedrooms apparently have monsters in them—she dives into her own fantasy world, staying awake well into the late-night hours, typing away stories about her characters. As much as she loves being a wife and mom—and she certainly does love it—reading and writing are her outlet, giving her a place to travel far away while still physically being with her family.

She married her better half in 2013, and he's been putting up with her craziness every day since. As her anchor, he's her one constant in this insane, forever-changing world.